OFF IN A BOAT

Off in a Boat

by

Neil M. Gunn

Front cover: colour photograph of Tobermory,
Sue Anderson, Argyll and Islands Photography,
Taynuilt 01866 822291
Cover design by Jimmie Murray

British Cataloguing in Publication Data
A catalogue record for this book is available
from the British Library

ISBN 1 899863 25 7

First published 1938
This edition by House of Lochar 1998

Text © 1938, 1998 Neil Gunn
Foreword © 1998 Dairmid Gunn

The publishers acknowledge subsidy from the Scottish
Arts Council towards the publication of this volume.

THE SCOTTISH ARTS COUNCIL

Printed in Great Britain by SRP, Exeter
for House of Lochar, Isle of Colonsay, Argyll PA61 7YR

Foreword

In 1937 Neil Gunn, then a Civil Servant in the Customs and Excise Service, and already a novelist of considerable distinction, decided to make the break with his former life of writing within a service that offered him financial security at a time of mass unemployment. The break took the form of giving up his post, selling his house and buying a boat. It was a bold and courageous step and brings to mind other authors' ideas of changes of direction.

In Kipling's poem *Sestina of the Tramp Royal* the wanderer writes, ...

> 'But presently you feel that you will die
> Unless you get the page you're reading done,
> An' turn another – likely not so good;
> but what you're after is to turn them all.'

The wanderer's philosophy, although laudable, portrays a sort of restlessness, a desire for change for change's sake.

Joseph Conrad in his story *The Shadow Line* writes about that farewell to youth, even youth abounding with success and useful experience, to cross the barrier into another world – possibly a world less certain in terms of hope and the realisation of youthful dreams.

For Neil Gunn the break with his past pattern of life and his crossing that invisible barrier into a new form of existence were done for different reasons and were not simply part of the natural process of moving from late youth into early middle age or, in his case, more remarkably, a movement within the vast bracket of middle age itself. A remark made in the early part of the book explains much; it concerns the buying of the 'Boat'. 'I had been thinking of it for some time. To be passing out there, where no craft was visible, would be a sailing out of time. To cast our warps, not for escape, but for adventure – into that which all our moorings have kept from us.' The remark is positive and hints at the author's need to stand back and reflect on the human situation in a world that was becoming increasingly torn apart by political strife and the clash of ideologies (1937). In the book it becomes clear at an early stage that the tools for this detached survey include a profound knowledge of Celtic mythology and tradition, a love of Celtic culture and a deep interest in his own ancestry. For him, ancestry meant both the Celtic and Nordic influences – sometimes at variance, sometimes in concord. This interest had been translated into imaginative history in an early book *Sun Circle* (1933), which could be called the Genesis of Caithness, Neil Gunn's native county. It was no accident that Gunn decided to make the West his area of exploration. That 'never ending' direction that fascinated Celtic minds with the idea of Tir nan Og, the land of the ever young, the Gaelic paradise, and enticed the Vikings to go further and further afield to satisfy their land lust and their penchant for destruction and plundering. The place names in the West, both Celtic and Nordic, thrilled Gunn and provided the compost needed to sustain his thinking.

But back to the 'Boat' – no Viking longship, but simply a 27-foot motor cruiser, appropriately named 'The Thistle'. The noun odyssey has often been used in connection with this book. Strangely enough, a great admirer of the English Tennyson, Neil Gunn was fully familiar with the Victorian poet's poem, *Ulysses*. In that comparatively short poem Tennyson delicately dipping into Greek mythology mentions the 'Happy Isles' where the great Achilles found his final resting place. In *Off In A Boat* Gunn can match these allusions with his many references to the heroes and heroines of Gaelic mythology. This is an easy balance as both classical and Celtic mythologies, although dealing with the remote past, have an immediacy about them that appeals to the imaginative mind. A knowledge of Homer or Virgil adds much to the delight of the seaman viewing such islands as Malta, Gozo, Sicily and those off mainland Greece. Celtic and Nordic mythologies are equally important ingredients for the complete enjoyment of the Hebrides. Although these similarities are worth noting, there is a big difference between the *Odyssey* and *Off In A Boat*. Ulysses is returning to his beloved Ithaca to perform an act of retribution; Gunn is completing his voyage to enhance his creative life through the memories of a voyage round the Inner Hebrides and his reflections and thoughts gleaned from his love affair with the West.

There is another great difference between Neil Gunn's *Off In A Boat* and the works of Joseph Conrad and the great Homer. There is in *Off In A Boat* a thread of humour that winds its way throughout all the episodes and anecdotes that form the core of this curious sea voyage – at once concrete, spiritual and timeless. In this context Neil Munro's inimitable *Para Handy* comes to mind as 'The Thistle' at times resembles her sister ship 'The Vital Spark'. A description of the Clyde puffer is as humorous and vivid as that of Neil Gunn's 'Thistle'. 'She wass chust sublime. A gold bead oot of my own pocket, four men and a derrick, a watter-but and a pan loaf in the fo'c'sle. My bonnie wee *Fital Spark*.'

Compare this to the advice given to Neil Gunn when on his quest for a boat. 'Man', he said turning to me with his dark smile, 'I know the very thing for you. I saw her last week in Skye. She's mahogany from the keel up and she has the lines of a girl. You could dance in her cabin and she has a wash-basin you tip up and a lavatory that cost over twenty pounds.' The description is of a 'real' boat that will initiate Gunn into the practicalities and mystique of life at sea.

Like Neil Gunn, Joseph Conrad can be extremely lyrical about the sea and ships. Yet, behind the lyricism there is the presence of the matter of fact in the form of good seamanship, pilotage and navigation. In his novel *Heart of Darkness* a man who is in danger of losing his spiritual bearings in the upper reaches of a jungle river finds consolation and assurance at the sight of an Admiralty publication that contains concrete advice on tides, currents, topography, local politics and place names. Neil Gunn derived much pleasure and comfort from publications of this type. In fact, they intrigued him and reminded him of the good common sense so necessary for the safety and enjoyment of life at sea. They kept him fully aware of the 'here and now' and the age old rhythm of life in the Western Isles, a rhythm that reached back in time and introduced a feeling of timelessness. He writes, 'What really prompted the buying of this monstrous boat? Was it that I wanted to outdo the folk of the West in their disregard of time, to have some sort of revenge on the monstrousness of time itself?' He certainly outdid Ulysses in terms of his crew. No band of seasoned warriors to aid him, but only his wife Daisy and occasionally his brother John, my father. Daisy's culinary attributes and skill with the camera added much to the pleasure of the voyage and the value of this book.

As a former naval officer, I cannot but be amazed by this book, which contains something for everyone. It is a book for the amateur yachtsman, the philosopher, the geographer, the historian and those who avidly adhere to Kenneth Grahame's famous dictum – 'There is nothing – absolutely nothing – half so much worth doing as simply messing about in boats.' The book is complex, and yet has the freshness and beauty of an early June morning at sea off the Hebrides. I leave the final word to the author who in his dedication to the crew writes, 'For the Crew – This simple record of a holiday in a boat, bought in ignorance and navigated by faith and a defective engine, knowing she will be happy if it inspires others to find themselves further at sea.'

Dairmid Gunn
1997

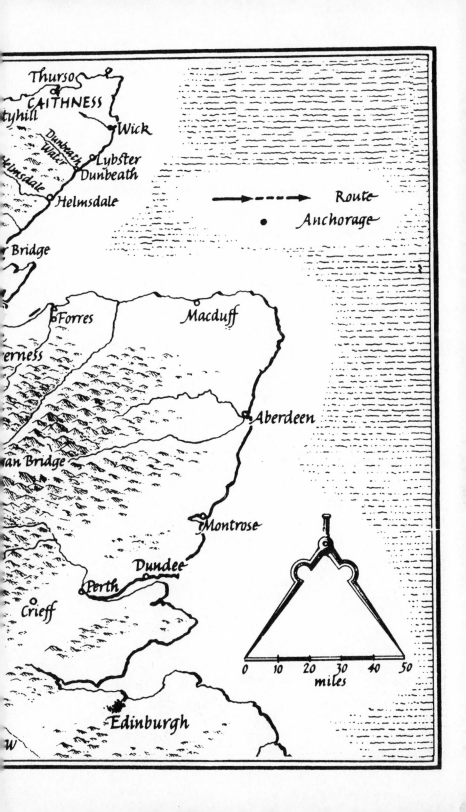

★   *For the Crew*   ★

This simple record of a holiday in a boat, bought in ignorance and navigated by faith and a defective engine, knowing she will be happy if it inspires others to find themselves further at sea

Contents

I

How not to Buy a Boat

Eoin is the sort of friend who can always do 'the very thing' for you. If you have a vague idea of buying a motor-car or a house or any other little luxury beyond your means, it is unwise to mention it to him. One night as he was going out the door I said, 'By the way, Eoin, you don't know of a smart little craft, something about thirty feet, with cabin to sleep two, a sound engine—sort of boat a man and his wife could work around the West Coast and the Islands?'

'Man,' he said, turning with his dark smile, 'I know the very thing for you. I saw her last week in Skye. She's mahogany from the keel up and she has the lines of a girl. You could dance in her cabin and she has a wash-basin you tip up and a lavatory that cost over twenty pounds.'

'Sit down,' I said, and I got hold of his glass again.

We left Inverness at six in the morning and were at Dornie Ferry before half-past eight. It was a lovely cool April morning and the Kyle was a grey shimmer. The ferry-boat was on the other side, and Eoin, stretching himself after the keen run, filled his breast with all the West. This was his own land, and, having reached it, he left haste where it belonged.

'I want to introduce you', he said, 'to a friend of mine.'

So I followed him until he found his friend, who from the

13

byre took us into his parlour, where he was very hospitable, early though it was. Through the window I presently saw the ferry-boat coming across for us. When it could wait no longer it went away with the postman. But later on it came back, and, after a last round of words, we went with it.

In Kyle of Lochalsh the fishing boats—smart Loch Fyne craft—were coming in, and we arranged to buy two cod of next day's catch to take home with us.

The business air of hurry and responsibility is difficult to maintain in the West; and when Kyle was behind us, and Broadford, and the small new bungalow with the boarded windows that no one will inhabit because it is haunted by a woman out of the stream behind, we decided that the day was opening up very well. Then the hill beyond Loch Ainort, with its striped tawny skin, and beyond that the round summit of Ben Glamaig, white with snow.

I have so many happy memories of Skye that its bareness has an intimate attraction. Peat smoke was ascending from the small hamlets by the sea. Folk were stirring here and there. The Island of Raasay, with its sugar-loaf hill, lay ahead of us, small Paby far behind, and Scalpay over from us on our right. The seaways between were quiet glimmering channels.

'Think', said Eoin in the drowsy voice of legend, 'of sailing down them.'

I had been thinking of it for some time. To be passing out there, where no craft was visible, would be a sailing out of time. To cast our warps, not for escape, but for adventure— into that which all our moorings have kept from us.

'That is the life I would like,' he told me confidentially. Behind his tone was the echo of what may never be won— but for the hope that comes again on such a morning in the West.

How not to Buy a Boat

The business he had in Portree was probably in his mind as well, for it was of an intricate nature—nothing less than attempting to get a drinking licence for an hotel which he had rented in the north end of the island.

But if he knew little about hotel-keeping, he certainly knew most of what any one man may know of the complex Gaelic mind. And here was occasion for exercise of the astutest in all the devious ways of its courteous diplomacies.

For the motives that move the licensing authorities of an island like Skye may appear on the surface bland as Ah Sin's face but in reality are deeper far than Shakespeare's well. This is no simple affair of a popular vote; no question of elected representatives carrying out the will or desire of their constituents. At one point I was called into an office, charged around with black deed boxes like children's coffins, and asked to vouch for Eoin's character (to a man who knew of him and his antecedents far better than I), so that he might be deemed a fit and proper person to hold a licence. This was a thing I could do, with my bonnet off, for if there is one matter that should be sifted out beyond all others it is the character of the man in whose company a drink would retain all its friendliest, most refreshing, and inspiring properties.

'But wouldn't the folk in his hotel area like him to get the licence?' I asked innocently.

'No doubt.'

Whereat I all but blushed.

Landowners, female teetotallers also landed, ministers of the Gospel, bankers, retired gentry—from such as these are the company of licensing authorities gathered together. And each in the light of his or her peculiar beliefs decides what is good for the commonalty.

When Eoin said he was not going to ask any favour from anyone, I saw the matter was getting too complicated for me, so I left him and went down to the harbour, and there saw a converted ship's lifeboat about thirty feet long.

I had a prejudice against conversions and the sight of this one deepened it, for all her new paint. She looked top-heavy and swung to the fitful airs in a way that made it easy to visualise her flat bottom. Bravely tricked out, too, with her high cabin, brass portholes brightly polished, and small windlass forward. But the game of pitch and toss in a western sea needs more qualities than a stout stomach. So I left her and climbed the hill behind the harbour.

Portree is finely situated overlooking a noble anchorage. The town itself is not very interesting architecturally, and the new bungalows on the heights behind could hardly be said to have improved the scene. But perhaps it is all too easy to vision what might have been, for here surely is the very situation for the queen of the whole north-west. Certainly nature did her best. And man with his limited resources, harried by barbarians out of the south, doubtless did his best too—just as he did with the lifeboat conversion in the harbour, though that was a neat job.

But what I was looking for was the black reef—and when I saw it, out beyond the harbour to the left, I got a touch of the old thrill. I had gone across to Raasay with a girl in a rowboat, leaving another couple on shore, and on the way back a growing wind very nearly beat us. Feeling gone from wrists and arms and pulling with the dead weight of the body, I was lucky at last to beach on Skye, where all four of us managed to heave the small boat beyond high-water mark near An Tom Point.

Presently we saw a fishing boat leave Portree. It was now blowing half a gale and getting dark, so she could never be going to sea. At last, three of us got on board her in the shelter of a headland, and I went back along shore to launch our boat to be taken in tow. In the midst of this manœuvre, the fishing boat's engine broke down. Mast had to be stepped and canvas rigged. And then right in the teeth of it, we tacked back into Portree harbour.

The exhilaration of a sea-storm turns dull men vivid, dumb men into a shout, and slow men into the leap of a sword. There is no intoxicant to be compared with it.

As the skipper went for the black spit of rock, his two sons stood ready. At his quiet word, they leapt. She came up towards the eye of the wind, hesitated for one long desperate moment, then fell away again, defeated. The yawing swing of her head was a strange living gesture, like the movement of the head and neck of a horse I once saw drowning. Quietly, without word or movement, the skipper gave her defeated head its way, the canvas all the wind it could carry, and made straight for the root of the reef. When the last moment seemed long past, he spoke again. Bravely she came up from her steering way, strained through the desperate moment, then fell away on the new tack and passed the reef's point with a plunging forefoot.

So naturally I should like to praise Portree, its people, and their kindness.

But the country folk feel that the inhabitants of their capital look down upon them as provincials and barbarians, and in heated argument they will damn the town as 'a drunken hole'. But then Portree basks in the sun of the licensing authorities and city men do have their superior ways.

Eoin was certainly lost in labyrinthine ways, when I got hold of him hours later. I could see the dark entanglement in his eyes. While we sped northwards, he unburdened himself, and something bigger than an Admiralty chart would be needed to record all the soundings on that rock-infested sea of island diplomacy. There had been, moreover, a sensational crop of applications for new licences—no less than the staggering total of five. For tourism is increasing in Skye, and soon the ancient Gael of the Misty Isle may be living by selling beer, if he is lucky, or ginger-beer if he is not, and taking in washings in any case. Furthermore, these applications were for no low pubs or public bars. Each applicant would be fully satisfied with a refined 'table licence' for the use of tourists who know how to behave themselves and, coming from the south, would expect the usual civilised amenities.

But there was a snag that even the licensing authorities could not overcome, for the law had made no provision for the granting of an exclusive table licence. A licence must be a licence to retail strong drink, and accordingly the native, brutally indifferent to civilised refinements, might walk in the front door and in his quiet way demand his dram. A very difficult and complicated situation for landlords, female teetotallers, etc.

Sympathetically Eoin and I discussed their difficulties, as, heading northward, we passed croft houses and cattle and hens, living in the inoffensive quietude that seemed to have come down from the dawn of time. I could remember, too, from my recent reading of ancient statutes, that once in the Isles, hundreds of years ago, each man had his own still for making his own whisky, and then there was neither licence duty nor drunkenness. Legislation against drunkenness came in with foreign wines, which were forbidden except to the landlords, etc., and so the folk had to remain perpetually sober on whisky.

However, one thing was clear to us: the court, due to sit in a few days, would have to grant all five licences or none at all. Democratic logic acting on sets of similar circumstances made that sure. It was the general opinion even in Portree, said Eoin.

When the court did sit it granted two and refused three. Eoin was one of the rejected. Doubtless the bench could give reason for its wisdom. Equally doubtless it never did.

But while all this was going on, at the back of my mind was a boat sailing the seas. Skye is called in Gaelic the Isle of Mist. But its name is also traced to another word meaning The Winged Isle; and that surely is the perfect description. For one is always coming on the sea, on inlets like heron wings, on mountain tops about to take off or already above the clouds. Always I seem to have been rushing through the island. Though that is not true, for I have spent autumn weeks of perfect laziness on the west side of the Cuillin, when speed or haste in mind or body seemed an odd sort of treachery to the strange fact of being. There is one stretch of moorland, when Talisker distillery is left behind and the moor begins to roll down again towards Glen Brittle, that has an autumn tint of such austere loveliness that an ex-president of the Alpine Club once assured me he had never met anything like it in all his travels, and he had climbed in the Himalayas, the Andes, and the Rockies. It occurs when the early autumn sun has turned the bent not to gold but to a wine that in colour is somewhere between golden brown and amontillado. No trace here of the flamboyant, of the vivid primitive. An ancient mood, but still as honey in the comb. Heats and humours evaporate before it, and the stillness invites the mind away. Let the colour deepen into the dusk of evening—into that hour when the wings of the Cuillin fold on dark breasts and eagle heads sleep unbowed.

'We go down here,' said Eoin, pulling up at last. 'They may be at her.'

How not to Buy a Boat

It was not without some excitement that I followed him down the path to the beach. And there I saw her. She was high and dry, lying over against a grassy sea-bank, like a stranded sea-animal, and there was no one about her.

I became aware of Eoin's voice drawing attention to her lines. He made me stand in front of her bows, drew me aft to the cockpit. Half the engine—a 14 h.p. Kelvin—lay about the grass, together with worn linoleum, floor boards, small bricks of pig iron ballast, oars, mast, rusty anchor, rusty chain, while the folding top of a teak table helped to support her side.

'You are seeing her at her worst,' he said, and stepped in over the stern seat. From this open cockpit aft we entered through a double door into the cabin. This door looked like mahogany but, as I learned later, was actually teak. She was built throughout of teak and pitch pine, except for the transom of the square stern, which was oak. The engine was on the threshold. A simple wooden seat ran down each side of the cabin full length, about fourteen feet, and the beds were two simple cots, opposite each other as one entered, that folded back against her unlined walls. Forward against the fo'castle bulkhead on the port side was a cupboard with little doors and drawers. Otherwise there was no locker accommodation. In the fo'castle the expensive lavatory faced the entrant, with chain locker to left and washbasin to right. There was some shallow but useful shelving right in the bows. As far as accommodation went, her slimness was evident, but that did not worry me at the moment, for you cannot fill a given space with lockers and mattress beds and still have it to move about in. Moreover, I had never yet struck a small boxed-in cabin that wasn't smelly; and with a thick smell about, it doesn't require much of a sea to upset a delicate stomach. The two skylights were large and healthy looking.

How not to Buy a Boat

I took out my pen-knife and pricked her joints and planking all the way aft, and then performed the same friendly rite to her outside skin. She was hard and sound and the water-line rang to the knuckles. With his steel tape, Eoin measured her over all. From stem to stern she was twenty-seven feet. In beam, seven. And she would probably take a good three feet in draught. I must have wondered if she was a bit narrow, for I heard Eoin's voice, 'That's where she'll get her ten knots.'

But what I was really thinking was something quite other, if it could be called thinking at all, for it came over me, moving about her helpless condition, that she might become my boat.

Had I seriously thought of buying a boat? Had the jaunt to Skye been undertaken with any such real intention? Had it been anything more than one of those vague desires that torment us intermittently through life? Had I expected to find a boat that I would buy?

But there was something deeper than that, too—a feeling, almost uncomfortable in its excitement, that not only should I buy this boat but that it might completely alter my whole way of life.

Eoin may have thought me not very enthusiastic about his find. Possibly I looked more than a trifle vague.

We failed to see the owner, and as our appointment, by telegram, was for the following morning, I did not mind. Nor do I remember much of the journey that followed, except for two clear pictures: the first, of Uig Bay, for as you come in over its southern horn the white cottages on the green slopes opposite look like toy cottages set down between thumb and forefinger by one of those giants who stalk through the ancient legends; the second, of Waternish headland running far into the western sea and bathed in fiery mist. There was a distinct feeling of relief in the involuntary thought that at least one should never have to attempt to describe the marvel of that headland at that hour.

Not that surprise was done with, for as at last we stepped from the car we saw the full red ball of the sinking sun caught amid the ruins of Duntulm Castle. But that was an effect over-dramatic, and a sensible mind refuses the incredible symbol.

While we stood there looking to the west, we saw the Hebrides, low down on the horizon, like a band of purple cloud. Despite ourselves, we were held.

In that evening light, dimming through fire and purple to the illimitable grey wings of the sea, that autumn of the day with April in its breath, was all the West of legend—disturbing, inviting, leaving one very still, hearkening for one knew not what. Those who have never known the West like this may find it easy to jeer at phrases like 'the Celtic Twilight'. But I have the uneasy feeling that that does not end the matter.

Eoin took me through his unfurnished hotel, and then in the gloomy loft of an outside building we started up the small engine that was to provide electricity. Engines are fascinating things to those who know something about them. This was a compact unit that would be set in motion at any time by the simple process of switching on a light, any light, in the hotel.

A rare game for children in the dead of night!

Still smiling, we stood outside again, drawn by the last edge of the sun as it disappeared. A shadow came in over the waters; there was a soft wash on the shore; the shrilling of two sea birds. The world was very quiet. 'Who would want to go back?' said Eoin.

So back we went, through Kilmuir, where Flora Macdonald's grave is and the monument on a hill. All over Skye and the outer Isles you come on the shadowy track of the Prince. Bonnie Prince Charlie. The guide books are full of him. And of Flora, the heroine, who guided him through the meshes of the military net—cast by the authorities in London and dragged so relentlessly through the old Gaelic sea. Over there was her home, Kingsburgh. The Prince slept there—and, in the same bed, some thirty years later, so did Dr. Samuel Johnson. ('I have had no ambitious thoughts in it.')

But before Johnson came, Flora was writing to the Duke of Atholl: 'My husband by various losses and the education of our children . . . fell through the little means we had, so as not to be able to keep this possession, especially as the rents are so prodigiously augmented; therefore of course must, contrary to our inclination, follow the rest of our friends who have gone this three years passed to America. . . .'

Prodigiously increased rents and America. It is the true Highland story: the tragedy, without the fine legendary air, of the folk themselves.

She is begging His Grace's help for her son Alexander, who 'is bordering on nineteen years of age . . . your Grace's doing something for him would be the giving of real relief to my perplexed mind before I leave (with reluctance) my native land, and a real piece of charity. . . .'

It does not appear, however, that His Grace provided the charity, for a few months after the learned Doctor's visit, Flora with her husband Allan and some of her family were on the high seas, and within three years Allan was writing, 'I am here with one (Alexander) of my Sons, seventeen months a Prisoner. My wife is in North Carolina seven hundred miles from me in a very sickly under state of health, with a younger Son, a Daughter and four Grand Children.' Allan Macdonald had helped to raise a Highland force in the

American War, and after the defeat at Widow Moore's Creek was taken prisoner with his two sons.

'Always the same old story,' said Eoin. We were heading in the Dunvegan direction. 'Take Borreraig over there, the home of the MacCrimmons, the greatest pipers the world has ever known or ever will know. And not only the greatest pipers—but the greatest composers of pipe music. Creators. Think of their *piobaireachd*. My God!' said he reverently. 'And to think of the Macleod chief coming in the end to MacCrimmon and demanding a rent! He must not only retain him as his piper but he must at last have a rent, even if it was to be only half a rent. Nicely calculated, what! That finished Borreraig. They put up a fine commemorative tablet to the MacCrimmons there, short ago, in great style, pipes blowing an' all.'

I laughed at the change in tone.

'And what happened,' I asked, 'to Mary Macleod, your greatest Skye poet, and a great lyric poet anywhere? Didn't she write a poem or something that the reigning chief thought was hardly respectful enough to him, and didn't he banish her from his realm?'

'He did,' said Eoin.

'You took that turn a bit sharp,' I suggested.

'Never mind,' said Eoin. 'Did you ever find the chiefs doing anything else?'

I had once heard him give a talk on the rising of the Glendale crofters, and as the car sped along, we spoke of our kinsfolk and of the way the chiefs or lairds had dealt with them.

It is a strange story, almost incredible at times in its vanity and greed and treachery and savagery. Wherever we went in the West we encountered it, until at last we hated the burden of thinking about it.

How not to Buy a Boat

The key to its understanding turns in the lock of landlord-ism, particularly the money-landlordism that came in after the '45 and culminated over half a century later in the un-forgivable brutalities of the land evictions or Clearances. Many think that the ruthless driving or burning of the folk from their immemorial homes was peculiar to one or two regions of the Highlands, like Kildonan in Sutherland. This is not so. For over two generations these Clearances went on all over the Highlands.

I once talked to a man from Tiree who, as a boy, had seen his bed-ridden grandmother carried out from his burning home and placed under an upturned boat, while the land-lord's men stood by until the house was consumed. That man should have succeeded his father in the large comfort-able croft on Tiree, but now after most of an adventurous lifetime at sea, he had the job of looking after the discharging and loading of boats at a West Coast pier. He could neither read nor write and had such fine character that he was simple and kindly. I remember the day he came across to the har-bourmaster's office, his face white with wrath. An order had come down from The Office up at The Works to stow a miscellaneous cargo in such a way that time might be saved at different ports of unloading. If 'the Serang' (as we called him) had obeyed this order the cargo might, in his estima-tion, have shifted in a heavy sea and so endangered the vessel and her crew. Not only was the fulfilling of such an order un-thinkable to the Serang, but I truly believe he would have sacrificed his life rather than have carried it out. When his foreman appeared and publicly reprimanded him, he stood outraged and speechless. Then he found his tongue, gave it to the foreman for a raking minute, and walked off the pier. He came straight over to the harbourmaster and myself who were his friends. His English at such a moment was naturally uncertain. But I remember the culminating sentence: 'I could have broken the pugger in three halves.'

He lost his job, and what finally became of that great man I do not know.

But somehow he stands in my mind as representative of his race, the race that was outraged and beaten and driven forth by the money-changers of a new age of greed and fear. The civilisation of the Celtic folk. Tenure of the land was the Gael's by immemorial custom. Decency and character, kindliness to children and to strangers, love of heroic deeds and heroic men, came out in his oral literature and in his music. The chief in ancient times had been his heroic leader, his heroic neighbour, and so it was in his blood to trust and respect him.

A child of the mist? Everything but that—except to the nostalgic or cynical modern, or to the chief who cunningly provided himself with a charter—and acted on its imported 'feudal rights'.

As we drove along in the half-light, Eoin and I had an orgy of such talk. It is like the talk that comes out of drink or a terrible sobriety. The old values are seen with a profound clarity. They belong to the mountains and glens, to the curve and flow of the land, to the gleam of the sea, to that which exists static and eternal, yet flowing, before our eyes. The silence is inspired with the far sound of it. It is closely akin to the vision of the modern young communist poet, except that he is moved by a sort of intellect whereas we were moved by a sort of memory.

And the memory provided us with actual stuff to go upon. And individuals, too—very tangible indeed. Like Mary Macleod, who liked snuff and whisky. Or Mary Macpherson whom the folk called Mary of the Songs; their hearts went beating with pleasure when her face showed round the door-

How not to Buy a Boat

jamb of the céilidhe-house. She was welcomed by the common folk as, farther south, Burns, of the same stock, was welcomed when he followed his greeting into kitchen or tavern. But little of the real stuff that enchanted her listeners has come through in writing: only enough to assure us of her original force: the rest is with traditional memory.

There was, then, most certainly this life of the folk, full of the warm human hungers, of fun and laughter, of labour-songs and pipe-playing and story-telling, a life that seems now almost dark and secretive, well hidden behind the clan pomp of feudalised chiefs, with their vanities and bloody little warfares, behind the history or 'romantic glamour' of Bonnie Prince Charlies.

The more solemn snatches of it we find gathered into Carmichael's *Carmina Gadelica*. Little of the same kind in modern poetry can equal in intensity of utterance and perfection of form some of these short hymns or invocations recorded by Carmichael direct from the lips of old men and women towards the end of last century (published 1900). The evidence is there—and, in the Introduction, evidence of much else. 'If not late, proverbs, riddles, conundrums, and songs follow. Some of the tales, however, are long, occupying a night or even several nights in recital. *Sgeul Coise Cein*, the story of the foot of Cian, for example, was in twenty-four parts, each part occupying a night in telling.' Against which, Shaw's *Methuselah* is a slight affair!

Possibly all this talk had some effect on Eoin, for when we arrived quite safely at his destination, which was an inn, I followed him down the passageway as if we were entering the old dark secret life of the folk.

And this, in a measure, we did.

There were young folk and fun everywhere, and good

27

drink. As we had eaten little that day, a craving came on Eoin for salt herring and potatoes. The sharpness of salt herring affects the palate as satire the mind: both live on what they consume with a hunger for more. Too many potatoes induce in some the flatulence of boasting. And a bit of boasting is needed when visiting legs are being pulled. The number of herring seemed large, but they were small and sweet behind the salt, and anyway we refused a second dish. It is said that the Celtic people, for all that they were the first to distil whisky, had only beer in the beginning. And after salt herring, beer still comes first.

There was no respite that evening. Every voice was ready and, in merriment, a trifle beyond itself. The day's worries and troubles were now rich with fun. Eoin knew his people, and a hundred others they all knew. Yes, he had met Tom Macleod. And did they hear about his boat? What! they hadn't heard how the poor fellow had lost his boat. 'Go on with you!' said Eoin; 'you needn't tell me you haven't heard!'

When he had them rocking with expectation, he told them the story, with a mimicry and stuttering that made it thick with life. But first he turned to me, the stranger, and said politely: 'In Skye and the Islands you will understand that the boat is one of the family. It is like a son. Should it chance to get wrecked it is mourned as a breadwinner. For it is nothing less. Indeed perhaps there is many a member of a family of far less use to the home than the boat.' He made this so clear that through restrained laughter the sea came to our feet; a truth so close that its intimacy might have embarrassed us had Eoin himself not been so simple and direct. Well, it appeared that Tom Macleod's boat had got a plank staved in on the rocks, just off the pier. A gust of wind had swept her into the swing of the tide and before his half-brother could get her nose to it, 'she was round on him—a thing that could happen easily enough to anyone'. But Tom and his half-brother were pretty quiet about it, for their next-door neighbour in the clachan, Mrs. Grant, had just died. A decent old woman. Now the minister, who was new enough to the place, didn't he in the first of the darkening come to Tom Macleod's door, thinking it the house where the corpse was. And knocked. (Three knocks gave Eoin.) The door opened and there was Tom.

'I am very grieved', said the minister, 'very grieved indeed to hear the sad news.'

'Och yes,' said Tom, 'it's s-sad enough.'

'Very hard on you, very hard truly.'

The deep ministerial sympathy moved Tom to make the best of things. 'Ah well,' he answered, 'it's maybe not so h-hard as all that. It's my b-brother that was mostly going about with her. And we have been th-thinking that with a good strong patch on her b-b-bottom she should be all right.'

Sometime before midnight Eoin suddenly decided that I must meet a special friend of his. (Wherever he goes he has special friends that you must meet.) So three of us set off, the slight bulge of a pocket denoting a friendly gift in tissue-paper. We felt sure the family would be in bed. But the light was in the window and Eoin followed his knock and greeting and we were welcomed with exclamations of delighted astonishment as if we were accompanying Mary of the Songs herself.

When toasts were drunk—the woman of the house touching the glass with her lips as I had seen many a time done in the northland—Eoin demanded a song. This was far too quick a demand, for song follows a natural mellowing of the mood. But Eoin, on the crest of himself, was well beyond the niceties of social usage. So being pressed in the argument to sing himself, he sang an old Skye Gaelic song. And

29

he sang it well, with the young lads of the household unable to take their shining shy eyes off him. In which mellowing of the atmosphere, Eoin was toasted.

And in time the man of the house sang. His voice might have been no better than my own, to put it kindly, but when he stood mid-floor, his eyes staring beyond the wall, his chest full, and his hands clenched, I lost all sense of time, hardly knowing whether I was myself now or a thousand years ago. The simple interior might have been a thousand years old, except that then the fire would have been in the middle of the floor, like a camp fire, or the fire of a million years ago.

How the eyes of the lads glistened when Eoin told his stories! They had been shy of their father's singing, but Eoin was the bard himself, carrying the strange birds of life about with him in his pockets. At any moment he could let the strangest one flutter in their faces. You could see the wings of excitement tickle their skin and flash in their eyes, while their thin arms circled their bodies like withies a lobster-pot.

But the great gift of the evening was the woman's song. It was as unselfconscious as the sea, and had a note of legend in it old as the earth. We were far beyond criticism of singing as singing. As though one should pause to criticise the tone of a cry of terror or joy, as though tragedy or beauty could express itself only through the mask of a perfect face! None of these art tricks, here, where the elementals lived unconditionally, and the queer fleering break in a harsh voice could set cold bird-feet walking on sorrow's face!

In the effect it has on the minds of native singer and listener there is something about this Gaelic folk-song that transcends purely musical or intellectual values, though that something may be impossible to define. Indeed the effect can be most disturbing, most profound, when the rhythm, sustained by meaningless or exclamatory syllables, repeats itself in a monotony growing so surcharged that it almost becomes unbearable (cf. *ubhan, ubhan* . . . in the song, *Grigal Cridhe*); so that it is no longer an individual song that we listen to, nor is the singer an individual singer. The song and the singer become oneself; then a faceless individual who sits bowed under it, nameless as a boulder in an immemorial landscape, about which the ever-shaping wind of destiny blows. Or like a rock that the sea swirls around, covering it, smothering it, to recede and come again in its undefeatable rhythm. More than this the living quick of the mind may not experience, because beyond it there must be surcease, a drowning, death.

I recall a night in an hotel on a little Hebridean island, many years ago. The hour was advanced and an argument on Fitzgerald's *Rubáiyát* intricate and challenging. On a purely literary appreciation I was not disposed to give in to my army antagonist despite his experience of India and Persia and the amount of liquor he had consumed. Until he leaned towards me, eyes distended, and asked, 'Have *you* ever heard *the beating of a distant drum*?' I had never been conscious of not hearing it until that moment. So I capitulated with all the grace I could summon.

We left that kindly house, after breaking bread, and entered a circle where the fun was more natural than ever. Songs came at intervals, but what sticks in the mind most is the subject-matter of some of the stories. Humour and vivacity and richness of texture. My sparse Gaelic was hopelessly insufficient to follow Eoin at his best, and he would turn and translate, saying, 'It doesn't sound nearly so bad in the Gaelic.' And I believed him, though it occasionally required some effort of the sympathetic imagination! The English translation was, by the normal social standards of mixed company, so shocking that one wonders whether Urquhart, in his great masterpiece, did yet achieve the translation of the social spirit that encompassed Rabelais. Clearly Eoin could talk of things in Gaelic to his compeers that were untranslatable into English without a complete loss of original innocence. Of this I have no doubt, because certain nouns were known to me in both tongues. In Gaelic, the old woman in his story could use a word by way of exclamatory objurgation that, if I were to translate it into the only English equivalent we have, would certainly worry the censor.

At that hour it was clear to me as a vision that such original innocence could come only out of a long tradition. It went back beyond original sin, perhaps all the way to that 'golden age' when the humours and practices of the flesh could illustrate a life story, as bubbles, rising and plopping, indicate a healthy ferment—with the assurance, when all is distilled, of a pure spirit.

But then I admit the hour was getting pretty early. At half-past five I thought I had better get to bed, for I had had only three hours sleep the night before, and the boat was still sailing her dark sea. So I left them to their songs of innocence and fell asleep, trying to bring her to a mooring.

The effort must still have been in my head when I heard the door open and saw Eoin enter carefully with a glass of whisky. 'Are you feeling dry?' he whispered. He sat on my bed. 'Take that, it'll do you good. I've been thinking about the boat.'

Solemnly there, and with the voices of conspirators, we talked about the boat and what she was worth and what should be offered for her. It was a long earnest talk. The hour was six-thirty, there was frost on the grass, and the sunlight, bright in its morning innocence, was watching us through the window. We came to extremely intricate yet perfectly clear decisions regarding methods of procedure, and as there was nowhere to set down the glass (there may be a greater abomination than whisky at such an hour, but I do not know of it) I drank it, and it did me good. In fact I got up and dressed.

Skye was a poem that the poets have forgotten how to make. It held me to the window, startled more than a little, as if I had just missed the passing of silver wings. The brightness they had left behind held the magic that, in after thought, one believes to be no more than the deceptive by-product of a mood, but that at the moment provided the strange and almost terrible certainty that one should never recapture it.

After breakfast we bade goodbye to our charming hostess, and set off for the place of the boat.

I was never much use at bargaining, finding it easier always to say yes or no. Yet true bargaining is a fine art and requires character. To see two Irishmen bargaining over a horse at a Kerry fair is one of the liveliest and most heartening things in life. I can just remember the old hillmarket at home, the scoffing, the sarcastic witticisms, the derisive toss of the head, the walking away, the coming back, up to the spitting on palms and clasping of hands, and the withdrawal to the long white tent where healths were drunk with cordiality and mutual esteem. As boys, the spectacle to us was of the greatest mirth, with a thread of admiration in it for the finer points.

I could not hope to achieve anything like that, yet the owner and I walked away from the others, and after courteous preliminaries I found myself obliged to name my figure.

How not to Buy a Boat

Absurd! Impossible! No use talking! For that matter he did not want to sell the boat at all! No, no! On my part I explained truthfully how at the same figure I could obtain a bigger and stronger boat in Lewis and offered to provide name and address. However, if he was not selling, of course that ended the matter. We became distant and even more polite. We rejoined the others. We entered his house. The talk went to and fro, detachedly, as if boat-selling were a matter of remote interest. Until at last the two protagonists regarded each other across the table and the owner said, 'It is the old custom: let us split the difference.' I gave him my hand.

Down to the sea we all went and inspected the boat. Assurances were given regarding painting inside and out and the fixing up of the engine so that I could take her over in a sea-going condition before the beginning of June. I asked her name, for it was not painted on her, and was told it was *Thistle*. There was a smile at this for I had been somewhat concerned with Scottish affairs for years, and Eoin thought it a good omen! The owner had only had the boat about a year, and had not got her original particulars, but so far as he knew the engine was not more than twelve to fifteen years old. Old enough in my view, but not hopelessly old for a poppet-valve Kelvin. So the new ownership was toasted, and sometime after midday Eoin and I started back for Inverness.

We stopped at Portree to send off a telegram, advising the purchase of the *Thistle* and our return about six o'clock, for we were expecting some guests at that hour.

Neither of us is ever likely to forget that run, for lack of sleep and many toasts can induce a state of being in which the flesh grows tenuous and the mind floats like thistledown in a white wind. The fevers and greeds of living are understood and all one's enemies forgiven; not at all to be confused with the mood of never climbing up the climbing wave; for it is so full of brightness that it sees even optimism as half-blind struggle.

We saw a man on a knoll winnowing grain in a gentle wind. This age-old picture so affected us that Eoin without a word drew up the car to light a cigarette.

From the rhythmic motion of the riddle, we watched the good grain fall to the earth and the chaff blow on the wind. The man on the knoll stood against the sky.

In the northland, the generation before mine used to winnow thus in their little barns, the winds blowing in at the small window and out at the door. As they used to do it in the country of the Loire away back in that sixteenth century when Joachim du Bellay wrote, *D'un Vanneur de Blé aux Vents*. 'It is a song', says Pater, 'which the winnowers are supposed to sing as they winnow the corn, and they invoke the winds to lie lightly on the grain.' The song that begins:

> *A vous troupe légère*
> *Qui d'aile passagère*
> *Par le monde volez . . .*

and ends:

> *Cependant qui j'ahanne*
> *A mon blé qui je vanne*
> *A la chaleur du jour.*

'One seems to hear the measured motion of the fans, with a child's pleasure on coming across the incident for the first time, in one of those great barns of Du Bellay's own country, La Beauce, the granary of France.'

Older than the barns of La Beauce, this figure on the hill— in a land, too, that had songs for all its labours. Yet the virtue of the picture lay in its gathering together in human kinship all men who have winnowed grain across all the fields of time.

How not to Buy a Boat

As we went on, the Black Cuillin rose up white before us in an impressiveness, a massive symmetry, that on this sunny afternoon would have been incredible, did I not know that the imagination in its utmost reach for fantasy could hardly achieve so towering a spectacle. Some perfect angle of approach, some trick of light on the snowfields, some grouping of lines and planes and perspectives towards aspiring pinnacles, achieved for a moment this unearthly effect. There was silence for a long time, then Eoin said quietly:

'When sleep takes you, where does it take you first? Is it in the eyes?'

It was a matter that had to be weighed thoughtfully. 'No,' I decided; 'it takes me in the head.'

'Do you know where it takes me?'

'Where?'

'In the hands. My arms and hands go jerky and queer. You see the turn there in front.' It was a fairly sharp turn to the left. 'My hands will want to turn to the right.' If his hands had their way, the only craft that would thereafter interest us would be old Charon's ferry-boat. We waited calmly to see what would happen at the turn. The car was a 30 h.p. V-8 Ford, and when the sole of the foot fell with the lightest negligence on the throttle, the whole mechanism charged like a Spanish bull. After flawlessly negotiating a few more bends, we drew up and got out. Eoin stretched himself on a hillock—just to ease his legs for one minute, he said.

His snoring was the most magnificent I have ever heard. It induced reverberations of laughter in the coping of a small stone bridge. The bog quaked. I could hardly read my watchface for snorts of mirth that issued from some obscure but happy benevolence within.

At Kyleakin—Haco's Kyle—we had to wait an hour and a

quarter for the ferry boat, which seemed bent on demonstrating the scientific curve of timelessness with the two off piers as axes of co-ordinates. And very convincing it was, for our wits were sharpened by the knowledge that we were now to be at least one hour late, and we followed the graph with close attention and occasional exclamatory remarks of admiration. A car had shut off its engine behind us. From it, in a lull, came an explosive voice: 'What the damthing wants to keep jiggering about like that for, God knows!' But we had not the energy to form a committee.

Often in following weeks was I to curse this absence of time in the West, a state or condition for which there is no human warrant. It irritates supremely the active man who wants something done. I swore that one day I should have my revenge.

The cod at Kyle of Lochalsh were forgotten. And all Eoin's friends passed by. The long trek across country was accomplished in marvellous time. For we took turn about at the wheel, the one who was relieved climbing into the back seat and curling up in a half-sleep where the body was softly tossed by trains rushing backward, by the screws of heaving steamers, by a certain small motor cruiser, twenty-seven feet over all, refusing to give way to beam seas. And we triumphed, for when I bade good-bye to Eoin at the gate, our guests had not yet arrived.

'You've bought her?'
'Yes,' I said, acknowledging her smiling welcome on the doorstep, 'and you are hereby engaged as the whole crew.'

II

Fitting Out

With copies of the *Motor Boat*, the *Yachting Monthly*, and similar periodicals (not to mention cruises in book form of small craft on most of the seven seas) lying about me, I realised that I had gone against every authority and precedent in first buying my boat and then proceeding to find out the sort of boat I should have bought. I was a stranger to this sea-cruising world, with no knowledge of its technical needs, and with a very indifferent stomach for its heave and roll, yet I hadn't even invited lists of second-hand vessels from the Clyde yachting yards, and so have ensured certain positive aids in the way of equipment and comfort.

As a Caledonian, I should presumably blush to mention this, but in my desire to help other men who, equally ignorant with myself, may yet have the sea in their blood, I must leave the hard-headed myth to its place of origin. I did things first and met the consequences after. And as this is largely a record of these consequences, I must set them down as they arose.

I soon learned—particularly from catalogues of yacht equipment, like Simpson, Lawrence & Co.'s of Glasgow—that my boat was, beyond all argument, the merest shell. The engine was in the cabin, and I knew only too well what internal combustion engines are capable of in the way of fumes and noise. The cabin was unlined, and the more the Crew pondered the lack of locker accommodation—for there was nothing beyond the pantry-box—the more disturbed I became. Smooth water and sunny days are not altogether the rule on the West. While as for gear, the total outfit consisted of two anchors and some chain and even these were not galvanised. There was no navigation equipment; no place for cooking, no galley. And, of course, no dinghy.

Assuming the fifteen-year-old engine broke down in a stiff sea with rocks on a lee shore, what then? I knew how the tides could swirl through these western narrows at anything up to seven or eight knots, and, against the wind, what jabbling infernos they could kick up, not to mention rips over sunken reefs. Curiously enough, I was never afraid of being able to handle the vessel, if only I could contrive to keep her under way. I should always know what to do so long as I could get the bow pointing the way I wanted. To be broken down and helpless might not only be perilous in the extreme, but would brand the seaman a fool, if, with the seaman's foresight, he had not made such arrangements as he could. One can resign oneself to an Act of God, but hardly to the dilemma of a fool.

For some weeks my investigations, after working-hours, were carried on with the greatest interest. Mostly this consisted of long lazy meditations where some visualising processes went on that every now and then had to be checked by reference to catalogues or charts. No other writing had the slightest interest, and often I found myself astonished that people should read novels or plays or daily papers (apart, conceivably, from the advertising or financial columns). The possibility of a world war was a little upsetting, but the vision of a kettle of hot water upsetting over the Crew, if there were no gimbals, faded it out easily.

Fitting Out

I walked with the sea and boats. The Crew remembered how once, as a little girl, she had prayed for a bicycle. But the pleasantest sarcasm was unavailing, for somehow the whole idea sailed best of all in a breeze of laughter. These were happy preoccupied weeks, and out of them let me try to get some order.

And first the sea itself, for if your boat keeps going, you must take her somewhere, against wind and tide, beyond headlands, by reefs, round islands, into inlets, until you come to a safe anchorage. And here I record my first gift— two Admiralty charts covering the whole west coast of Scotland (nos. 2475 and 2515). They were presented, duly inscribed with a gallant verse of poetry, by an Orkney Saga-man who has charted the more dangerous human reefs as far a-sea as America and China. I got a third chart of the Hebrides, from Barra Head to Scarpa Island (2474), and a fourth of the north from Thurso Bay to the North Minch, including Sulisker (1954). These more than covered the whole of any possible cruise, and though the scale is small (about two and a half miles to the inch), I found the one book to help it out, namely the *Clyde Cruising Club Sailing Directions for the West Coast of Scotland*.

The easiest way for me to praise this book is to say that for any amateur yachtsman on the West Coast it is indispensable. Simple and direct in statement, with details of coasts and buoys and large-scale charts of many anchorages, it does not forget to tell you where to find water and stores, a post-office, a telephone, an inn. Its tidal information is particularly useful, as we found, for example, when, lying in Oban, we thought we should like to tackle the Falls of Lora. I got the new 1937 edition (8s. 6d.). Along with it, I purchased *Brown's Nautical Almanac* (3s.), so that by certain calculations I should be able to tell the times of high and low tide fairly accurately on any day at any place. Most of its information went over my head and therefore thoroughly astonished me, for the knowledge man has got of the sea is very marvellous.

The Admiralty charts (4s. 6d. each) held an unending fascination. Hours were spent following imaginary voyages, checking up anchorages from the *Sailing Directions*. Nothing of all this remained in mind, though possibly a certain familiarity with the idea of sailing routes was engendered. The only other books I got together were two or three on bird and plant life and on geology.

Meantime the Crew had been arranging for the purchase of a good and suitable camera. She finally left the choice to our friend Fritz Wölcken, who does marvels with a Leica, and he got her a reasonably priced little box with which she was delighted, particularly as she did not require to remove it from its slung leather case while taking photographs—a useful consideration when scrambling over rocks or trying to keep upright on a plunging deck.

But photography is an art and we hardly knew the beginnings of it. Moreover, as we kept moving about from place to place, the Crew could not get her spools developed and delivered in time to benefit from her failures. Landscapes and seascapes that had looked magnificent to the eye turned out to be quite undistinguished in the print. And the whole realm of the constructed arty photograph remained—perhaps wisely—unexplored. On the whole we derived our greatest amusement from what are doubtless photographic failures, as most of the prints in this book make quite clear—and thus, perhaps, contrive to illustrate the story of the amateur.

Of course, in the beginning the Crew did not believe there were going to be many failures. And these she would offset by a first purchase of twenty spools. The spool used was an

Afga Isopan, and the camera, by a special numbering device, took twelve pictures ($2\frac{1}{4}$ in. × $2\frac{1}{4}$ in.) instead of the usual eight. A notebook with proper headings, showing the number of the spool, time exposure, distance, lens, was duly and neatly prepared (even if, in the stress of circumstance, entries were not always kept posted!). Finally (for she had her own catalogue hunting to do) she was delighted to discover that for the sum of 3s. 9d. she could send the undeveloped spool away and receive back the developed spool together with twelve photographs (enlargements) measuring 5 × 5 inches.

Meantime I had to bestir myself to the serious business of fitting out the boat, and the first problem was that of a breakdown. We had to carry something that might take us out of a difficulty and the only conceivable thing was a sail of some sort. The high house of a motor cruiser precludes sails in the ordinary way, so that though I had read controversies on the Bermudian rig (only one halyard, me boy, and stowed in a moment) *v.* the gaff rig, I did not get much help. In any case, my type of boat would never tack against a wind. All I could hope for was a sail to give me steering way when running before it, so that with enough sea room I could reasonably hope to fetch a convenient anchorage.

So one day I set off for Andrew Noble, the sailmaker in Burghead, and on his knees that skilled and genial man drew my boat to scale (1 in. to 1 ft.) in blue chalk on the floor of his once busy premises, and set the fourteen foot mast in its place. I had come to the conclusion that a gaff sail would be unsuitable for a high-decked boat and that, though not elegant to look at, a triangular sail would keep the centre of gravity low and do its work. Mr. Noble agreed and solved the two problems of rings and a boom by suggesting that the canvas be laced to the mast by a single rope which could be

42

pulled taut in a moment once the sail was up and that a double sheet be provided without any boom. I was so pleased about this that I also got a foresail to lace to the forestay, with sheets running aft to the cockpit.

The height of the sails was twelve feet and the foot of the mainsail about the same length. For a twenty-seven foot motor cruiser these are just about the right dimensions (and here I add our own experience to what I have read). Halyards and sheets were to be fixed all ready for use and the whole sent to Duntulm in Skye. Two blocks for the top of the mast and various cleats, shackles, and odds and ends, I bought from Mitchell & Co., Inverness, the owner seeming to welcome my innumerable visits and difficulties, for he was an enthusiastic yachtsman himself. Often did we bless him for the double-acting gimbals from which our primus stove (No. 5) was slung. In truth I was surprised to find the number of persons who were keen on boats. Our banker—frequently in my mind those days—took me into his parlour to tell me about the one he had had for years. Here was a new brotherhood.

The little galley was to consist of a small platform for the primus, with suitable shelving, lined above and at the back with enamelled tin sheets. The important business of locker accommodation would have to be seen to in Skye.

Catalogues were searched for lamps, lifebelts, and other gear, while I spent an afternoon in John Macpherson's Sporting Stores, trying out more personal material, from oilskins to beds and sea-fishing tackle. A detailed list of utensils required for the simple business of dishing up a meal rather staggered me, so I refused to have anything to do with it, beyond giving the cross measurement of the gimbals as $8\frac{1}{2}$ inches. I had thought an irreducible minimum meant two or three articles that could be sort of wrapped round and carried under the arm. 'Strike out what we don't need.' But I was not being caught as easy as that. 'Strike it out yourself,' I replied. And if, after that, I became a bit reckless, I must at least mention one particular purchase, for its comfort had the perfection that knows no reservation. I refer to those shaped inflatable beds, made of some sort of rubbered twill, that weigh only a pound or two and can be stowed in an attaché case. Luxuriousness is not their sole virtue, for water, salt or fresh, refuses to penetrate their thin hygienic skins and the price of those we had (Li-lo) was seventeen and sixpence each. They never let us down—or not so far but that a pumpful or two of air restored the desired floating effect. I cannot conceive of anything better, laid on the laced canvas of a yacht's folding cot. But then perhaps I am talking of pleasure cruising in confined spaces, not whaling in the Arctic. In any case, I must have presented an unusual spectacle to the young lip-sticked customer who came upon me, sans jacket and boots, extended inside a blue sleeping bag on a red Li-lo upon the top floor of Mr. Macpherson's shop. For I was penitently trying to amend my practice of buying first and trying afterwards.

Finally there were the compass and aneroid. There is a very good little article on the weather glass in *Brown's Nautical Almanac*. I paid more than I had intended for the compass with its four-inch card in a simple teak box. But it is a beauty. A very good one, however, can be got for about forty shillings. And if mine cost nearly double that, I did at least make an effort to get one second hand. In comparison, the aneroid was very cheap (if it had cost so much per tap, it would have ruined us).

Meantime no news was coming from Skye, but I felt sure that the engine would now be running like a sewing machine and the hull glistening in new paint. I had reckoned without the timeless West! On a chance visit, several weeks after I had bought her, Eoin discovered her to be still untouched, the old paint flaking in the sun, the seams opening like daisies, the engine scattered on the grass. There were high words, I understand, and counter orders, and Eoin arrived back fuming, far more annoyed than if the boat had been his own, for he felt his folk had let him down before the stranger!

Letters and telegrams—and a couple of weeks later Eoin and I were on the road again, assured the boat would be launched and ready.

May and June are, as a rule, the most perfect weather months in the Western Highlands. Early spells of cold wind, bright sun, and flying cloud, invigorating days, running into weeks sometimes without any rain, are followed by June warmth and the endless June nights.

Of all months, give me June, though it can be fine to go through May to reach it, May of the green leaves. As Eoin and I set off on an evening in mid-May the birches were out, tentative as young love, quiet as thought. For in Glenmoriston the birches in the evenings are cowled a little, like forest acolytes, their shoulders drawn together, their heads slightly bowed. As we returned two mornings later, with the sun turning every tender leaf translucent, they were pure aspiration, living green fires, holding to the earth by some miracle whose harmony took our breath.

It is a great run, by Loch Ness, up Glenmoriston, past Cluanie Inn, and down the long green defile to the Seven Sisters of Kintail and the shores of Loch Duich. If we travelled at as high a speed as the narrow twisting road would permit, it was because we had to. Besides, there is the positive exhilaration the diver gets between a high rock and the deep water, or a salmon between the deep water and the sky. And then the West again. In the evening light its grey timeless spirit came towards us and flowed in behind.

But we knew about that timelessness all right! We were not deceived any more than by the treacherous turns up Mam Ratagan, though our attention was claimed by the young forest already clothing in green that noble hillside. How magnificent the Western Highlands will yet be when afforestation has come into its own! These young trees had all the hope and sap of invincible youth.

There was a brave new ferry-boat, too, at Kylerhea, with a 30 h.p. Kelvin engine, which defeated the swift tidal current with such ease, that we tried to amuse ourselves by wondering what Boswell would have struck out of Johnson had they been here now.

As a lad I had many a time pulled my row-boat smartly into the current and then lain back to be floated away towards Glenelg. There was a Christmas memory, too, of carrying a pushbike on my back up the hillside through the snow and down the steep slopes to the shores of Loch Duich. But what sticks in the mind most persistently is a boyhood day spent on the moor beyond the stiff climb from Kylerhea.

To Eoin, this climb presented no difficulty, for he had learned the wisdom of changing down to bottom gear before tackling the two short steep slopes near the top. Not to do this is to invite stalling and temporary difficulties.

It was deep gloaming when we emerged on the moor and followed the road that winds by the little stream towards Broadford. A whole summer day the boy had spent there, guddling yellow trout, looking over the silent moors, seeing no living soul. It had been a day of such curious and intimate loneliness, so withdrawn from all practical ways of being and thought, that I can afford to wonder if it happened to me in this life, or indeed if it happened at all.

There are many stories in the West of fairy gold. The stories are very circumstantial and the gold quite real. I should be inclined to doubt, all the same, the adequacy of practical research in the matter, whether by mineralogist or folklorist.

But I should never doubt the fellow who found the fairy gold—once I had glimpsed his eyes.

It was quite dark by the time we were at Broadford, and after midnight before we had knocked up the mechanic. There was a long confidential talk on the roadside, during which we learned that the boat had been launched but was not yet altogether ready, what with cutting the peats, putting down the harvest, and one thing or another. However, he would be up at six o'clock in the morning and send off a telegram by the school children advising us of his arrival some time tomorrow, without fail. That was the best he could pledge himself to, so we said *Sláinte!* over again and departed amicably.

These long confidential talks in the dark—they would induce the hind leg off a donkey, so friendly their conspiracy, so warm, so pleasant. That no one is much deceived does not matter.

'Do you think we'll see the boat tomorrow?' I asked Eoin.

'Yes,' he said. 'By one o'clock.'

I smiled in the dark and laid a bet that it would not be before four, for that was the hour at which we must depart.

The following morning was all bright loveliness and the sea shimmering and irresistible. We set a net between Hulm Island and the first rock on its north side and then explored the island for loose stones to weight the net. But they were difficult to find, for the volcanic rock was dark, pitted, and solidly fused. On the steep seaward ledges and on the grassy inland slope, seagulls were preparing their nests. We found one egg with dark blotches on its olive shell. There were masses of celandine in full bloom, while here and there were violet, seapink, and yellow trefoil. In the shallow western cave, where shags stuck to their nests until the very last moment, we came upon a marvellous display of sea-urchins, spined like the hedgehog. Their colouring in the clear water was very attractive, while ball-clusters of bright white and yellow adhering to the rocksides Eoin assured us were their young. After many attempts, we managed to balance an urchin, round and big as a tennis ball, on the blade of an oar and take it up and into the boat. It was low water after an exceptionally high spring tide, and the tangle-weed exposed their drooping fronds in miniature forests.

At one o'clock Eoin's voice called across the island, 'Here she comes!' I rejoined himself and the crofter in the boat and gazed as directed into the far sea haze but could see nothing. Eoin kept telling me to wait, as he had seen her all right. The crofter wasn't quite so sure. After many minutes, I suggested he had seen her wraith, for he has an undoubted gift that way.

'And what about the telegram we were to have had in the morning anyway?' I gently probed.

Whereupon, digging his oars in, he grunted his criticism of those who let him down.

Above us were the ruins of Duntulm Castle and I had pointed out to me the three knolls: The Justice Knoll, the Rolling Knoll, and the Hanging Knoll. Here in times past the Macdonald of the Isles had sat in judgment with and on his people. When a man had been condemned on the Knoll of Justice he was taken to the Knoll of Rolling, put inside a nail-studded barrel, and trundled off. If he had the fortune to survive he was deemed innocent, for they had a proper respect for miracles in those days. When true Christian culture came from the south, however, it brought with it the gallows, which was given a hill all to itself, the Hanging Knoll. It did away with miracles. When it was first set up, Macdonald and his intimates were greatly taken with it and wondered just how it would behave. The story goes that they saw an old man and called to him. Such recognition by the mighty fairly set the poor old man hurrying towards them, and when he arrived he was seized and strung up. The contraption worked perfectly. Whereat they were properly astonished and laughed heartily.

I asked Eoin, still muttering threats against the absent, what he would do at the present moment if he were Lord of the Isles, with control over the three knolls. We laughed heartily at the things he said, and obeyed his instructions to cast the empty net on the south side of the island, so that it might catch such fish as chose to come in on the first of the flood. There and then the net was well anchored with three heavy stones and had lead sinkers all along its base line as well, yet it was later dragged by the tidal current right round the inshore point and in front of the sunken wreck of the steam drifter. It was my first practical demonstration of what can happen to ground tackle in the pull of a sea and I was to remember it very soon.

We poked about the wreck, which shows a barnacled gunwale above spring low water and which should be given a comfortable berth by vessels coming to anchor. I was told a war-time story about this wreck, but am not sure enough of the law of libel to repeat it. We tried to disclose the tons of coal which are said to be sunk with her but succeeded only in shoving an oar through the rust-rotten side of a latrine. The hold of the vessel was now a rich marine garden, with its scavenging eel as a fair understudy of the serpent.

Sails away towards Fladdachuain (Fladda of the ocean) attracted our attention, a white sail and a brown sail on the one boat, and we waited her coming on the flat rock that slopes slowly into the sea below Duntulm (the ridges in this rock, said to have been worn by the keels of Macdonald's galleys, are still quite clear).

It is difficult to think quickly of anything ever made by the hand of man more beautiful than a sailing boat. A racing yacht has something of art for art's sake about it, but the lobster fishers' boat on that bright sea gave art its warrant. They hove to between the island and the shore and sank their lobster catch, then came on to be drawn up by all of us above high-water mark. She was a long open boat, what they called an Irish skiff, and she had in fact been built in Ireland. I had seen her kind in Kerry. There was shamrock-green paint on her, too, and she had those simple subtle lines so difficult to define, holding within them reticence, deceit, and all man's knowledge of the treachery of the sea.

Eoin's eye had meantime caught sight of the crabs creaking against the bottom boards, and the friendly skipper told him to take as many as he liked for they were of no value to him. The four men had spent the whole night on Fladdachuain Island, but, as it happened, without much success. Not that you would guess it from their mien. This traffic with the sea may be a despairing but is also a fascinating business, for it is a gamble not only in its catches but in its markets, and as the summer went on it claimed our attention more and more.

The skipper told us how to distinguish between the male and female crab. The last flap of shell that folds like a tail over the breast is pale and narrow in the male and purple and broad in the female. He himself would eat only the male. So

Eoin and I gathered five or six males and went back to the hotel, where he insisted on having them cooked. It was now five o'clock, with all hope of seeing my boat gone and our minds committed darkly to departure. Indeed we should have been gone an hour ago. Eoin was cracking his last claw with a ruthless hammer when the telegram came advising us of the boat's arrival that afternoon. Whereupon someone walked in saying the boat was in the bay. We went to the front door and there she lay calmly at anchor, beyond the wreck. And through an inexplicable and disturbing warmth, I thought she looked very well.

It turned out that the telegram had been handed to a schoolboy in the morning, but the schoolboy had handed it to a van-man, who had carried it on his rounds back to Portree, and thus, in a very close finish, the yacht had beaten it.

As we backed out, I was about to swing the head of the small boat against the sun when the crofter stopped me; so I immediately swung her with the sun and headed for the yacht, while Eoin's voice assured us that she was bonny and sat the water like a swan. There are less heartening things than optimism and a kind eye. The dark mood of disappointment and irritation was lifting from us, but still a few direct words might be said. And they were, for as we stepped aboard a voice with a slow sarcastic drawl remarked:

'You were surely in an awful hurry.'

And we found ourselves without an answer. In fact, though all that had been done to her could, to my inexperienced eye, have been done in two or three afternoons any time in the last six weeks, I was made to feel guilty and did my best to explain that we were anxious to take advantage of the presence of a carpenter about the hotel who would put in some shelving and locker accommodation. A floor board over the propeller shaft was missing, and I was told the owner would have put a new one in had I not been in such an inexplicable haste. I expressed my sorrow for that. Moreover, there had not been enough time to stow the ballast properly or quite finish the painting, while the engine throttle still needed a spring and one or two other things needed adjustment. Besides that, the old magneto had been damaged by salt water, but there was a borrowed one in her and she was going well enough. By salt water? Had the boat's plug been left out? Hsh! said a shaken head.

Feeling confused and more guilty than ever, as if I were altogether to blame, I tried to put everyone at his ease, for perhaps I had been in too great a hurry, and anyway this was my own boat and I had not yet got to know her. So we lifted anchor, the mechanic swung the flywheel, and there was a roar.

After the soft hush of a motor car, it was an impressive, an obliterating sound. I sat beside the mechanic in the cabin and tried to catch what he shouted into my ear and sometimes succeeded, though a dumb show of feeling the circulation system and cylinder heads, pointing to the oil-drip feed and the throttle, indicating forward, neutral, and reverse, was more immediately intelligible. Then he gave her the load, and as I stepped out to the cockpit, we were under way, with Eoin at the tiller and the small boat in tow.

The land began slipping past. We were headed for Flad-dachuain, confused once in the remote past with Tír na n-Óg, the Land of the Ever Young, the Gaelic paradise.

But we did not land there. We were hardly prepared for Tír na n-Óg yet, despite all our experiments with time, so we put her about and came back to Skye, the basaltic masses of the Quirang behind Ruadha Hunish—a magnificent side-face of rock running into the sea, with the coastguard's look-out perched on its brow. She was going well, steady on the helm, as I brought her in between the rocks off Hulm Island and so back to her anchorage.

The two anchors had folding stocks and we decided to put both out, for this can be an uncomfortable berth when a sea-wind comes down the channel. With the larger anchor, some difficulty was experienced in getting the pin into its hole in the stock. It was hammered, but went little more than half way home; which might have been far enough, I thought, if only the binding wire had been fixed more securely. But unfortunately I said nothing. Eoin and I then took measurements inside for the use of the carpenter. By the time we had finished it was eight o'clock.

So there could be no Inverness that night. There was, however, the still unsolved question of a dinghy, and after we had toasted the day's work, we set off.

I liked the look of the dinghy when I saw her in the half-dark. About nine feet long, and beamy, with bottom boards. And a grand sea boat, I was told. So we decided to try her. She was no sooner in the water than the sea came pouring in through her seams, and five yards from shore she was about half full. So we hurriedly leapt to dry land, emptied her, and hauled her up. I accepted the assurance that there was nothing wrong with her but the seams, which would take up after a few days in water. As it happened, she belonged to the man from whom I had got the motor boat, so we repaired to his house, where there was talk and bargaining in two tongues, until in the end the one cheque was written for both boats, and the owner asked me if I would like to rob him of his suit of clothes as well. By that time he was tearing the tissue paper from a bottle of whisky, a beverage with a long history in the Island and still not unknown, despite its vindictive price.

Some time about midnight it occurred to Eoin and myself that we were expected in Inverness more than two hours before, so we had to hunt for a telephone and found one in the inn where we had spent the pleasant night. No one was in bed and I was now no longer a stranger.

When between four and five in the morning we left Duntulm, the mists were curling up from frost. Beyond the castle ruins, two Loch Fyne boats were ring-netting for herring and we remembered the oily patches on the sea's surface the day before. The evolutions of the boats were slow and friendly, as if they were playing a game. The two buoys of Eoin's net, which he had forgotten to haul, were still athwart the invisible wreck. (The crofter would perhaps haul it sometime.) Beyond, lay the *Thistle* at anchor. I thought she looked very well. I turned again and had another gaze at her. She was so peaceful there on that quiet sea in the silver morning that she might well have been wondering what on earth I was going away for. I suggested as much to Eoin. 'I don't blame her,' said he.

And so on through Kilmuir, once the granary of Skye (did not Pennant find the fields 'laughing with corn'?) with enough peaceful and bloody and romantic history between the ruins of the monastic establishment on Columba's Loch (long since drained) and the sheep-disturbing siren of a Ford V-8 to fill a whole shelf with volumes of Transactions.

And long before the time of St. Columba, strange ongoings resounded down there by the shores of Loch Snizort. When Finn MacCumhail (or Fingal) and his men lost touch with the deer, they sent Caoilte, the Thin Man, to find them, while they resigned themselves to gather limpets and make a hash of them with milk from the grey-cheeked cow.

Caoilte was so swift, it was said of him that he could appear as three individuals; just as Bran, Finn's dog, could appear simultaneously as a separate dog at every opening or gap around. A conception of speed which is still a trifle beyond our age.

But the truth of it can be read on a rock, for one day when Caoilte, sent to find deer, let out his mighty shout, a Fian (or Fingalian) on the shore spewed out the limpet hash on a rock in front of him. With its grey splotch, it is known in Gaelic to this day as the Rock of the Mouthful. And the grazing fields of the grey-cheeked cow may be found on the modern map both in Gaelic and in Norse. A philologist once told me that in Skye for every two place names in Gaelic there are fully three in Norse. Already I had seen more than one mountain-top where a princess of Lochlann had elected to be buried.

Who would blame her on a morning like this? The rising sun flashing up through the hollows of the hills; mist not all-pervasive but here and there in snow-white clouds clearly defined as the skylines; the quiet moors with their enchanted cottages, the arms of the sea, the sea itself, the Ascrib Isles, Fladdachuain, the far Hebrides. And beyond the seas, over the foam—Norroway. There is something more than the eagle in a spirit prepared to fold its wings on a mountain-top. But what that something more may be we seem to have forgotten, though it moves us still.

Then suddenly, right across Skye, we saw the serrated tops of the Cuillin. Pale in the morning sun, they seemed at an infinite distance, like guardian mountains to a strange and fabulous country.

It was not difficult to believe in that moment that the warrior Cuchulain had performed daring deeds there in the crossing of the Bridge of Cliffs, in war, and in love. Cuchulain, 'the small dark sad man'—what is there, in the designation, of strength and insight and love, that still has its grip on the imagination? Dunscaith, on the other side of the Cuillin, was his castle. But with troubles brewing in Ireland—an old story—back he had to go to the wars, leaving his 'lovely sunbeam of Dunscaith' to look in vain across the sea for his return.

But, like MacCrimmon, he never returned.

Dunscaith and Borreraig are both in ruins.

Crofting and fishing are still the main occupations in Skye, though they have been declining for years into the grey economic decrepitude that has overspread most of the West. Here and there houses have been enlarged for tourists. One comes, particularly in places like Broadford, on roadside signs displaying the word BOARDING, with an initial surprise that quickly enough fades into indifferent acceptance. And why not? Why not Broadford as well as Blackpool? High time that antiquarian sentiment was abolished in these things. Yet the effect the historic change has had on the living creative spirit that lured Cuchulain to Dunscaith and the MacCrimmons to music in the piper's hollow at Borreraig, is a matter for long uneasy speculation—particularly in the bodiless hours of an early summer morning.

By the time we came in sight of the Red Hills the sun was rising beyond them and turning their hollows into fiery chasms. The hills seemed to emit a red granitic dust that splintered the white shafts of light and dissolved them in molten air. I had never seen anything in landscape so startling, so magnificent. The chasms, too, appeared to be of an immense size and the hills themselves heightened and etherialised. By comparison, the Cuillin, standing back on the right, were now pale and insignificant. Rarely does the witchery of light perform so astonishing a miracle. And I hesitate in mentioning it here because I know how unexceptional, apart from their pink (and not very attractive) colour, the Red Hills normally appear. But that is the whole gamble of sight-seeing in Skye or, for that matter, anywhere on the West. The miracle is come upon unexpectedly and seldom if ever repeated.

That morning the Red Hills gave life to geological time. Though one realised in a flash that here the word time had no more meaning than the convenient word ether. It was something in which immense geological periods had a certain relation to one another. Skye, for example, was mostly a manifestation of the last or Tertiary period, at the beginning of which molten matter welled up quietly through great surface cracks and flowed over the land, filling up hollows, until there were formed those basaltic plateaux we had come upon in the north. This out-flowing happened many times, not only in Skye but right down as far as the north of Ireland, and in Mull to this day one can count as many as thirty terraces on the mountain side, thirty layers one above another, to a depth of about 3,000 feet. In between these eruptions were quiescent ages lasting so long that they still have evidence of plant and animal life.

But such out-flowings did not exhaust the reservoirs below, and when the heavy blankets of basalt tried to keep the molten matter down, it searched for the weakly cemented spots between the basalt and the rock it lay on, and heaved. Down in the Cuillin area this rock—or skin of the earth—was fairly tender, and the molten mass of basic rock, called gabbro, shot upward through vents or pipes until it heaved the basalt sheets into a dome, as a boy makes a 'tent' of his bedclothes with his toes. Under the strain the sheets cracked, and the gabbro thrust itself into the cracks, and having done all this more than once, it found such relief that it let its topmost anger cool—and solidify. Then through long ages (in this recent geological period) the basalts were weathered or worn away and the gabbro was laid bare in those shattered, angular, fantastic precipices we call the Cuillin. And being coarse-grained and tough, it makes for grand climbing.

Ages later there was a similar sort of disturbance in the region of the Red Hills, and molten masses this time of a granite-like rock (hence the red and sometimes yellowish colour) were thrust up through both basalt and gabbro, and, after more ages of denudation, showed themselves with some of their ancient fire to us on a summer morning.

And all this, including the complete weathering away over vast areas of the whole 3,000 feet of tough basalts, took but a short while in the immense space of time that goes back to the formation of the Lewisian gneiss now exposed in Sleat.

Against such conceptions of time the thought of the length of a human life draws a smile from that odd detached wisdom that comes one knows not whence.

And taking everything into account, particularly the recent pattern of our rather hectic doings, the smile was decidedly 'on me'!

For here was I, suddenly become the owner of a boat— with the prospect of three weeks' cruising! Three weeks! It sounded like some love relation, rather than an adventure into—or out of—time! In fact, bad weather might very easily prevent our going to sea altogether. What then?

What had really prompted the buying of the boat? Was it that I wanted to outdo the folk of the West in their disregard of time ('You were surely in an awful hurry'), to have some sort of revenge on the monstrousness of time itself?

Facile speculation, perhaps, that yet could crystallise into a definite picture—as vague hope generally does in the lazy mind. For I could always become haunted by one very clear picture: a sea-loch, the boat at anchor, evening passing into the peace and glimmer of summer midnight, with a sea-bird calling along the shore to intensify the quiet.

That at least was no vague dream. It was a piece of reality that I had experienced more than once. I knew it in all its intricate detail of thought and mood and sound and silence and sight, flowing and merging; too intricate ever to reproduce, to do more than hint at.

It is easy, of course, to dismiss the picture by calling it the escapist's dream, and difficult to defend it, without pretentiousness, by an excursion into speculative thought on the condition of human affairs in the world to-day.

Have we, in this sense, grown afraid to escape, become dominated by the idea of a social duty that must keep our noses to the human grindstone, the grindstone that an ever-increasing mass hysteria keeps whirling with an ever-increasing madness of momentum? Work, records of unemployment, misery, conflicting politics, wars, and the lowering nightmare of a universal war, until sensitive beings can hardly listen in to the wireless news, so grisly its tales of disasters and mass human destruction. Are we in social honour bound to increase this ghastly momentum by adding the thrust of our own forebodings and fears? or has a time come when it may be the better part of courage to withdraw sufficiently far from it to observe with some sense of proportion what exactly is taking place? Not to mention the purely personal point of view that one has only one life to live and that, before shuffling off, a little peace may be necessary in which to exercise one's mental attributes and try to get some glimmering of what all the madness is about, or even of what is due to oneself, despite all the man-made duties in the world?

For at least nothing seems more certain finally than the loneliness of one's own self, which no mass hysteria, or political creed, or religious faith, can save from the last lonely departure that is death. It seems more than a pity to go out into that final dark without making some sort of effort to discover what glimmerings of harmony may visit the mind if we give it a reasonably receptive chance.

When the average man goes away in his yacht, be he wealthy or poor, what is the driving force behind his desire? And when his brother who cannot go envies him, why the envy? What is being searched for beneath all the ordinary human reactions? What has been lost, what is being missed? And, anyway, how can one answer honestly *for oneself* without time for personal experience and dispassionate thought?

Time again! Then one night Eoin called on me about midnight in Inverness and took me apart with the air of a man at a funeral. 'I wanted to tell you by yourself,' he said. 'I have just had a 'phone message from Skye. The *Thistle* dragged both her anchors yesterday in a terrific gale and went ashore on the rocks of Hulm Island.'

III

Cutting the Painter

Those jagged rocks, fused dark and hard as iron, beneath the brown weed. My spirit sank in me as I looked at him.

'No, they got her off after an hour or two, I'm told,' said Eoin, 'and she hasn't been greatly damaged, though I cannot say how much.' He seemed sad and disappointed about it. We discussed the matter back and fore and then went in and told the Crew.

Within a day or two I got fairly accurate information. Her rudder had been broken and one side scraped, but by some miracle the hull itself was sound, not even a plank having been started. The slimy cushion of brown seaweed must have helped.

The trouble had lain not only with the storm, but with the heavy anchor, for when I came to investigate the matter on the spot, I discovered that this anchor had lost its hold because the stock had shifted—when the pin came out.

A carpenter from Kilmuir, who had served on ships in his time, got on to the job, and in due course I was informed that she was sounder than ever.

But my restlessness was increasing. There had been nothing but delays and trouble ever since I got her, and a feeling was beginning to grow that nothing would go right until I took her over myself. All along, too, I had been disturbed by the age of the engine, and the mechanic's report that two of the gudgeon pins were perhaps not too tight did not help. Fifteen years is old even for a Kelvin, but I had the faint hope that I might get word from the makers, to whom I had sent the number of the engine, that she might be no more than ten. On the back of the news of the beaching on Hulm came a letter from the makers informing me that the engine was installed in 1912. Twenty-five years old!

Seventeen or eighteen years might have induced wrath or despair. But twenty-five so belonged to the realm of fantasy that we could do nothing but laugh.

New gudgeon pins might do no harm! And even a new bearing or two. The mechanic was told to go right over her from the beginning again and replace whatever was necessary. Then word reached me that the beaching and salvage had been officially reported to the Receiver of Wreck. She was not insured.

The only way to meet all these fantastic happenings, it seemed to me, was to be even more fantastic, and when a man came out of the blue and asked me if I was selling my house (the rumours of our going to sea must have been spreading!), I said yes. Within an hour of our seriously discussing the price, we were in a solicitor's office and the house irrevocably sold.

That night the Crew and I thought it might be as well to discuss matters realistically, so we figured out our resources and our hopes, and the following day I went to the chief of the Civil Service Department in which I worked and handed him my resignation. His initial surprise turned to consternation and he spoke to me for a long time in a fatherly way, for he has a humanity that no red tape can strangle. Did I realise that I should not only lose my salary but my pension, towards which I had worked for over twenty years?

Cutting the Painter

For though it is commonly believed that a Civil Servant's salary is smaller than it should be because of pension rights that accrue, in actual fact a Civil Servant is not deemed to have any legal right to a pension. A pension is a gratuity graciously granted by the Treasury after forty years' service. Should one elect to retire after thirty-nine years' service, there would be no pension. There is here the characteristically delightful indefiniteness of British institutions whereby the individual is deemed to have rights—until he actually tries to act upon them—when he finds he hasn't quite got them, not in his way, in fact not at all.

To make sure of this, I applied for a pension, including in the application certain personal considerations which I need not detail here, and forwarded it to our Departmental Board in London. In one sentence, curtly accepting my resignation and refusing even to lay my case before 'the Lords Commissioners of His Majesty's Treasury with the view to the award of a pension', the small matter was economically disposed of. Which was that!

But I was touched by the friendly consideration of our northern chief, who did his best to point out the madness of my ways and the uncertainties of literature, particularly (as he tactfully if not very hopefully put it) when not of the commercial kind. I trust that when he retires in two or three years he may draw his pension for a period long enough to make up in some measure for the pension I did not get!

And if there is any excuse for such a personal irruption, it may lie in this: that after these two days' action, our only abode was a boat in doubtful condition, and that if we had lost all visible means of support we had at least gained a little control of time.

63

Cutting the Painter

So one fine and cloudy morning the Crew and I packed our small car with a miscellany of household gear and set off for the West. The sun was shining in Glenmoriston and we went past the oaks and the birches in the happiest mood. How complete a change had come over our earthly fortunes since, a few weeks before, Eoin and I had taken that first jaunt to Skye! The old boat had won out.

We had a few minutes' anxiety near the crest of the steep hill behind Kylerhea when the engine, pulling away on bottom gear, suddenly roared and the car began to slip backward. I held her with both brakes until the Crew got out and fixed large stones behind the rear wheels. Three men working on the road came to our assistance. They were obviously used to this sort of trouble. I felt sure I had stripped my gears. But the oldest cheered me by saying, 'The steepest part is still in front of you.' They got their shoulders to the bodywork. I let in the clutch with no hope. The car moved away from them. In a flash I realised what had happened: under the continued vibration of low-gear work, the lever had of its own accord jumped into neutral.

The relief from this experience—for I had visions of hopeless delays and expense—heightened the pleasure of the day and we arrived at Duntulm in great form.

And then our troubles began.

The engine was not in the finished condition I had expected, though the job had been on hand for some two months. The floor boards were awash, though she had been dried that morning. When we tried the old pump it would not work without priming and then ejected about as much as a peashooter, so we baled her out with a bucket. Eoin had warned me about this pump, and some two weeks before, a new pump had been despatched, but had arrived without the

64

two extension pieces of piping and so no effort had been made to put it in. The drip-feed box was absent. Wire was wound round the cylinder block. The two new lockers were upright shallow shells without shelves, and no storage room had been put in beyond the forward bulkhead. The dinghy was still unpainted and on daylight examination looked anything but the wholesome job I had thought her in the half-dark. A local fisherman hesitatingly believed 'she might do if her bottom was heavily tarred'. The Crew could not find her primus stove, our only cooking fire, but we ran it to earth in an outhouse, where it had been used as a blow-lamp for plumbing.

In short, between one thing and another, I was disheartened to the point of despair, except for the moments when I internally cursed the sloth of the West generally and one or two Skyemen in particular! And what I should have to pay for all this, heaven alone knew, for there had been no contract.

There followed four days of unceasing toil. I had the boat beached again and the carpenter sent for. When the tide left her we found a bad leak from the lavatory outlet pipe, which moved bodily as the handle was worked inside. The carpenter made a perfect job of fixing this pipe, and after some attention to the pumping mechanism, we had no further trouble from the lavatory: a point worth making, perhaps, against small-yacht owners who have written uncomplimentary things about the functioning of this modern contrivance. Not that I am prepared to go into details of use and wont in the wilds. But the contrivance worked in a civilised way when called upon.

But the shining porcelain wash-basin—it was a fraud, for when it was tilted up the water merely ran on to the floor. The extension pipe from the zinc pan beneath had at some distant time been torn away. Before going to sea, we got a piece of flexible piping and made quite a respectable job of fixing it underneath to the hole in the zinc, with just enough length to reach the lavatory pan.

The real saga of these four days, however, was the hunt for extension pieces to the new bilge pump. When I think of it now I smile, but at the time the humour was very intermittent. It covered the whole social and individual background of Skye, including the religious (for a watch had to be set on a half-holy day while work went on behind closed doors).

It began by my 'phoning the plumbers in Portree to find that they did not possess $2\frac{1}{4}$ inch piping in lead, iron, copper, or any other substance; the size was apparently an unusual one. For two days we went through the Island in a car, in quite a fair emulation of Caoilte after the deer, hunting blacksmiths, garagemen, joiners, or anyone remotely likely to have anything to do with piping. For the delay that would result from having to send to Glasgow or elsewhere on the mainland was at this point simply intolerable to contemplate. The weather was bright and pleasant—splendid sea weather, that one could not reasonably expect to continue, after such a glorious May. A break was overdue—and it might easily last a fortnight. As we flew along the coasts, the sea mocked us with its brilliant sparkle.

Then on the third day someone heard of someone who knew someone who was close neighbour to someone who had purchased some surplus piping some time or other from the Board of Agriculture, and would it be worth while going to enquire? I was in the mood to go to Timbuctoo, as long as I could go myself; so off we set and duly arrived. While the mechanic was going across fields and ditches towards the croft house, I sat in the car beside the neat-handed lad from the hotel and offered him wild odds in shillings that the piping, if any, would not be 2¼ inch. He contemplated the bet seriously, and then declined it.

The farmer and mechanic appeared from the croft house coming leisurely towards us, their hands in their pockets. We smiled ruefully. Presently they stopped—and waved to us. We went across. Lying at their feet in the grass were lengths of piping sufficient for the needs of a small village— and with threaded ends. We measured a diameter. It was 2¼ inches. Not quite believing this, I sent for the pump. The threaded end of a pipe screwed well and truly home.

While two short ends were being cut off by the hacksaw— for we always went prepared for such a miracle—I asked the price and got back the inevitable reply:

'Whatever you say yourself.'

'But I have no idea of the price,' I answered.

'Oh—well. Whatever you say.'

'But I simply do not know,' I protested, and suggested he must know because he had bought it.

'Whatever you say,' he laughed.

So in desperation I named a price. He did not laugh. I doubled it, and we shook hands. Whereupon we set off in triumph with our treasure.

And then our real mechanical difficulties began, for this rusty piping had to be bent into the shape of the boat's hull beneath the stern-seat, and, above, turned at right-angles through the planking. An expert blacksmith might do the job. No one else could. Someone suggested road contractors who were busy in the neighbourhood. We got in touch with the chief mechanic, an invincible man from Nairn, who went to no end of trouble in his off hours to help. The blacksmith joined in and worked on the wire plan I had carefully made, heating and fusing and hammering and bending like an artist. He treated my wire plan seriously and we were both completely justified in the results obtained. That pump, which never required priming or any further attention and which threw out the gallons in solid continuity, proved as great a comfort as the inflated beds.

Meantime, however, the engine was still needing a bolt, and in fact it appeared that water had been seeping into the works. Late on Saturday night that invaluable mechanic made and threaded a bolt for me which fitted, and I dragged weary bones to bed, wondering what next, but vowing in my own mind that before that next happened we should be at sea. For a fatalistic feeling was growing in me that we might never get to sea, and that all our reckless doings might peter out in miserable fiasco. If we even got one day at sea and fetched a quiet anchorage, I should be happy and feel justified and would lie at that anchorage until some sort of peace was got hold of. After that—we should see.

The twenty-gallon petrol tank was full and the water tank nearly full. I had a spare tin with about four gallons of lubricating oil. I fixed seven o'clock on Monday morning as the hour for getting the boat finally ready. Everything now depended on the weather.

Sunday was a good day and I strolled over to see the Coastguard Officer who had attended, I was told, the salving of my boat. I wanted to thank him and whoever else had done me so friendly a service. He was a pleasant southern Englishman and when I expressed my gratitude I could see he was embarrassed. Then I learned that he had not only officially reported the salvage of the vessel but named in his report the nine men who had assisted. In short, the matter was still in the hands of the head Receiver of Wreck and he wondered whether legally the vessel could not be detained pending a settlement of all salvage claims!

A stroke quite as thrilling as the age of the engine! So I

smiled, and as I had once had occasion to act as a Receiver of Wreck myself, we discussed the matter in all its bearings and implications.

Before I left him he put me through my paces in weather lore, and asked me if I had distress signals, rockets, or similar gear aboard. I confessed I had none. This shocked him and he told me to remember, whatever else I forgot, that I could always soak rags in paraffin and make a flare.

At six on Monday morning I looked out of my bedroom window and saw a sea of glass. For some reason, I had slept very little. I was by this time almost completely short of ready cash.

The West has so long been run by landlords, shooting tenants, dukes, and yachtsmen, that anyone with anything in the nature of a cruising vessel is inclined to be included within the moneyed class. There are, in fact, whole villages mainly dependent on this summer yachting business. The men run yachts during the season and then have the winter at home and appear at church in fine clothes and bowler hats like Glasgow professional men. The yacht owners for the most part are very kind to them, and I heard of one seaman who last year returned home in a motor-car which his master had presented to him.

Unfortunately for me I did not belong to this kind of owning class. And there was this business to settle with the Coastguard Officer. So at seven I got up, and, with the hotel lad, carried down our gear to the dinghy, which the Crew had painted, and which still leaked despite the copious tar a local skipper had smeared on her bottom. For an hour and a half we were very busy starting up the old engine—with once a backfire of pure flame over the carburettor—and heaving the two anchors. We had as much as we could do to get the heavier one aboard, and I realised then that I could never hope to heave it alone. However, nothing was going to stop me now. We came nearer the shore and dropped the light anchor. Then I left the lad to putty up round the exhaust outlet of the bilge pump and do one or two still unfinished jobs while I went off to the coastguard station.

There I fixed matters satisfactorily and the officer on his part promised also to convey to the nine good men my deep sense of obligation. As I bade him good-bye, he asked me if I remembered what he had told me.

'Yes,' I said. 'When the sky is green or there is a swell on a calm day, look out. Long-drawn clouds betoken wind and—'

'No, no,' he interrupted me. 'Do you remember about the paraffin and the flare?'

A conscientious officer, a helpful cheery man, and I liked his southern tongue. He had a good word to say for the strangers he dwelt amongst and felt he could assure me that such simple arrangements as I had made would be properly received.

A quick breakfast and I was down to the shore again carrying more gear. There the skipper of the local lobster boat was waiting to say good-bye. We had had pleasant talks together, especially about the present economic position of the lobster fishing and what could be done to improve it, and as I had nothing to do now but wait for the Crew with the last of our personal belongings, we sat down on this calm lovely morning and talked together.

The immediate difficulty here at Duntulm, as I had already found it in the northern mainland, was one of transport. The accommodation on a bus carrying passengers is limited. The freightage charges on a single box of lobsters, from passenger bus to final rail delivery, is so considerable that it is often crippling and always out of anything like reasonable proportion to the fisherman's returns. What was necessary here to begin with, we decided, was a two- or four-ton truck doing the loop from Portree by Staffin, Duntulm, Uig, etc., back to Portree, two or three times a week, and collecting en route from all the creeks. Mass consignments would reduce transport charges by nearly half and be an incentive to production.

The individualism of the Highlander is deep-seated and inclined to suspect grandiose schemes. Yet the whole past basis of his social life has been communal, and the folk will still help to cut one another's peats or plough one another's land and even find a sort of holiday pleasure in the process. But all at once extend that process to the pooling of the surplus resources of many villages and to the sharing out of profits *in hard cash*, and in due course there would be quarrels, mistrusts, and disruption. There must be a transition period. The four-ton lorry would help.

Roads would require widening and building up here and there, but even this might be done if a real economic case were made out for the authorities who spend so many millions of pounds with no ostensible purpose beyond helping the smooth passage of the tourist car.

As Mr. Nicolson and I talked away in this strain, the lad came ashore in the dinghy, and now descending from the hotel were the Crew and the lady who had been our perfect hostess for several busy days.

In the height of summer it was a lovely place and the wind was laden with the scent of honey. From the knoll where the castle ruins stand, the Crew had on one occasion returned after a short time with a written list of thirty-two different kinds of wild flower. But now she and our hostess came laden with the last odds and ends of our belongings and soon we were in the dinghy pushing off for the yacht.

Inside, the scene was a piled-up drunken fair, but I at once got the cover off the engine, primed her, swung the handle, and produced the roar. Within a few minutes I had all four cylinders firing, but found that the throttle attachment was not working. I fixed it for the time being, got on top, and soon had the light anchor up. Then back to the engine, increased the roar, and let in the clutch. She nearly spluttered out as she took the load. The Crew had the dinghy painter in hand, for on one thing I had made up my mind, namely, that I should never allow the rope to get round the propeller. My Inverness yachting friend had assured me, against all my protestations, that this was bound to happen once. I was to prove to him that it should not. 'Hard over!' When the engine beat was established, I joined the Crew at the tiller. We were under way, with the dinghy properly in tow, and after a sweep round the bay, passed well clear of the wreck and headed for sea.

It was a good moment. We waved farewells until the ancient ruin on the rock shut out the white walls of the hotel and the figure of our hostess. Ten miles away Waternish Point lay low to the sea in a faint haze. We set a straight course for it and committed ourselves to our adventure.

IV

Out to Sea

On such a lovely morning the adventure seemed full of promise and in a very short time we were conscious of being in a new world. It is difficult to explain how deep the meaning in these last words. Two elements composed it, I think: the first, the novelty of being on the ocean making for anchorages we had never seen, assisted by small-scale charts we were unaccustomed to read, for the truth (as may have been gathered) was that neither of us knew anything about navigation or the handling of any craft beyond a row-boat; the second, the strangeness, the wonder, the beauty of the scene itself. We had both travelled in steamers and I still have a vivid memory of the mountains of North Africa rising out of the sea (with their suggestion of elephants and tropic jungles and hinterlands of burning sand), but never—and I had visited the Hebrides and traversed their length and breadth a few times—had natural features and atmospheric effects combined to make of the world, as far as the eye could reach, a place of such still enchantment that at moments its beauty was profoundly sad.

The clear blue of the overhead sky passed into the haze of the horizon out of which the hills rose in dim purple, full of distance and legendary peace. I had never realised how mountainous Harris was, and I gazed at the Clisham, on whose steep road an insignificant buzzing figure on a motor-

73

bike had once nearly broken his neck. Southward the eye caught the saddle-back of Ben Lee and the cone of Ben Eval in North Uist. South of that, Hecla, Beinn Mhor, and the hills towards Loch Boisdale in South Uist. And finally, remote, out of the mist, a nipple against the sky, insubstantial, inclined to vanish, that could only be Heaval in Barra. Land outlines and sea inlets in between were guessed at or perhaps imagined, so uncertain were they in the opalescent haze.

Above these lands, at no great height, hung a continuous ridge of puffed-out cloud, like the angel clouds in Renaissance pictures. Their whiteness had an internal warmth, a suggestion of pink, that tinted the sea to a gleaming hue, and the water undulated slowly like sheeted iron. A similar cumulus formation hung over Skye, but there it was Arctic white, like puffed-out snow, while the land beneath faded away in sunbright haze.

The water changed continuously in colour, and over its vast waste birds worked singly or in little coveys, black guillemots, large guillemots, puffins, fulmars, while a single gull made us feel truly at sea by following us from side to side and sometimes passing overhead and throwing a startling shadow on our hands.

As we came abreast of the Ascrib Isles, we passed quite close to a school of basking sharks. Their triangular dorsal fins, showing full above the water, looked like the mainsails of miniature yachts, only the fins were black and moved to some other caprice than the wind's. They cut in and out in sudden swirling circles as if they were playing an amusing game or worrying some hidden life to death.

But within this visible world, I was haunted by my own particular worry, and every now and then I got up and felt the circulating pipes and cylinder heads. Occasionally new noises developed to my ear, thuds and thumps and queer irregular beats. Yet the engine was going steadily and I was afraid to experiment either by giving her more throttle or moving the ignition lever. We had left Duntulm at 10.30 a.m. and at 12.7 Waternish Point was abeam, so we were doing about six knots, and if in that time we had had the last of an ebbing tide in our favour, on the other hand we were towing a dinghy which though small was heavy. I was not dissatisfied. With the broad entrance to Loch Snizort behind us, the first step in our journey had been taken. It was a new anchorage now, whatever happened. At last we had won through the web of circumstance, with its decisions and clinging obstructions, into freedom. We set a course for Dunvegan Head, which lay in the sea like an immense squatting animal with its snub nose out of the water.

As we came abreast of Loch Dunvegan, still going steadily, I abandoned my half-formed plan of entering and anchoring between the islands of Mingay and Isay, where there is good shelter, as a Waternish man had told me, and where we could have devoted the rest of the day to getting things shipshape, particularly in the piled-up mess that was the cabin. To tell the truth, I did not care to let the Crew remain in the cabin while the engine was going. I did not feel like taking any chances until I knew my mechanism a bit better, for I could still see very vividly the flash of that naked tongue of flame over a wildly flooding carburettor when we had started her up in the morning. There was a hatch over the forecastle, through which one could push up on to the deck in an emergency, but in the event of such an emergency arising it might not be altogether wise to complicate its pattern with fore-hatch acrobatics.

Moreover the day was fine, and all that wild shore, with its towering basaltic cliffs, that forms the north-west coast of Skye, might be a good place to get round while the going was good, particularly as it is exposed on the south-west to the full force of the prevailing swells and provides no sheltering anchorage of any kind.

I asked the Crew how she felt about it. She smiled and turned away, and all in a moment I saw she was so sick with excitement that her dry lips refused to come adrift.

The sea's depth had got her, a depth so near that she could have leaned over and put her fingers into it; and nothing between her and it but thin planking upon which some hundredweights of defective metal beat its devil's tatoo. A sense of insecurity so awful, so imminent, that sheer sick apprehension kept her head up—lest she see the distant bottom too clearly. And for the rest, she had absolute reason to have confidence neither in the navigator nor the boat.

Some understanding of this came upon me in a wave, and I laughed. She had encouraged me in my mad courses! And I could see by that smile that she was not giving in now. It was faint perhaps, a trifle wan, but game. I rallied her, pointing out our perfect security. The day was so fine that if the boat sank under us, we could row ashore in the dinghy. But she moved my talk aside and pointed to a great dark-hulled steam yacht, her varnished lifeboats swung out on their davits, now coming out of Dunvegan Loch. We watched until we could clearly see three white caps on the bridge and the steady stare of faces that must have wondered and smiled. The Crew gave a salute, and three caps were lifted. The courtesy of ships that pass on the high seas!

The yacht disappeared towards the distant haze of Harris, and we settled back into our own world. The sun was very hot and we took off our jackets. I brought the compass into use for the first time. I had had to stand to see over the high deck of the cabin. I now got the bearing of Dunvegan Head on the compass and sitting in a corner of the low cockpit extended one arm along the tiller and the other along the rail. The Crew made herself comfortable in the other corner.

Never in my wildest dreams had I imagined so perfect a day, so full of wonder. It was as if we were floating on a coloured bubble. There was that air of the intangible, the incredible. And at odd moments it did bring a feather of something to the throat.

We played games at trying to name the colours of our enchanted world, but it was a difficult game that tended to pass into long silences. Every now and again I rose to see that nothing was in our way, then subsided.

Shortly after two o'clock we were abreast of Dunvegan Head; then laying our course on Meall a Veg Head, I decided the time had come when we must make up our minds where we were going.

We settled on Loch Bracadale, in the west of Skye, and for anchorage on Portnalong at the entrance to Loch Harport. The name Portnalong was quite new to me, and our decision here, as in all other cases, was reached after a study of the chart and the *Sailing Directions*. Never had either of us any personal knowledge to go upon. A rough calculation showed that we could not hope to arrive much before six o'clock. I increased the oil drip-feed of the engine for luck. Neither of us worried about a set meal. The Crew spread out biscuits, cream cheese, and a cupful of milk in the cockpit. I ate with relish and she with deliberation, while the rocks moved slowly past and the sound of the engine was almost forgotten.

The sun beat down upon us and upon the sea yet not glaringly but, as it were, modified by the distant sombre haze. There was induced, too, an insidious lightness of the head, not unpleasant, a sort of etherialised intoxication due in some measure, I suspect, to eddying whiffs from the engine! The roar of the engine in that world of ineffable quietude became itself a comment of the purest fantasy—for which there could be no acknowledgment but a smile.

As we passed the 'Merchant', a basaltic column near the head, Neist Point lighthouse stood out before us and the Crew became interested in the magnificent rock formations that rose up one behind another in varying degrees of shadow and light. She got her camera ready and we debated the question of exposure, for with a calm sea under a clear sky we recognised that there must be a tremendous amount of light about, far more than there could ever be on any landscape. The camera does make one look at things, though whether one gets it to reproduce what one sees is entirely another matter! And those white fingers of light that man has set up to guide him round the danger spots on his charted seas can have a remarkable fascination, for there is something more than a facile symbolism here. Enterprise, endurance, a continuous vigilance. If there is anything amongst the works of man that may conceivably give him a feeling of pride, even of nobility, it is surely a lighthouse. There was no movement about Neist Point lighthouse, yet we felt human eyes watching us. The white paint and strong clean lines, set upon the dark rock, had a fine austerity. The Crew had an impulse to salute with her horn that watchtower as we passed, but she did not dare.

Suddenly I observed seaweed around us, floating masses of it here and there, in a sort of vast still pool, and did not know what to make of it. I grew a trifle anxious about the propeller, wondered even over the possibility of submerged rocks, as I steered between the masses. Yet I was certain there could be no rocks, so certain that I had to make sure by a quick glance at the chart—and there, opposite Neist Point with its orange spot for the lighthouse, I read: 'Streams meet or separate.' The westernmost point of Skye, where the tides divide or meet. We were certainly at sea! So we had another smile, as the weed fell behind us, and the lighthouse.

All the coast we had hitherto passed was quite clean, but now between Neist Point and Idrigill Point, a reef of broken rock ran out into the sea for a mile and a half. I tried to work out the state of the tide here, for the *Sailing Directions* discussed in cable lengths possible passages between the Big and the Little Mibow Rocks; but decided finally to stand out round Dubh Sgeir, the outermost rock, and take no chances, consoling myself with the thought that by so doing we should lose very little distance in making Loch Bracadale. Yet I had the urge to try those rocks. Indeed this desire to attempt difficult passages for the first time grew with the days, and is, I should say, one of the finer pleasures of cruising. But I did not know yet what I could do with my engine, and moreover I here discovered for the first time how woefully insufficient is a small-scale chart for inshore navigation. I could not make out the lie of the rocks properly, nor could I draw up, as it were, by the roadside and explore the surrounding territory, but must keep on ploughing ahead at six knots.

Dubh Sgeir was unmistakable for I knew it should show sixteen feet clear at top of the stream. A light breeze was now darkening the waters to blue, but the day remained perfect.

Abreast of Dubh Sgeir, and quite close to it, the Crew got a real fright, for the engine missed a beat or two, spluttered, and then, without any attention, re-established the one-two-three-four. Everything had gone so well that she had begun to forget the uncertainties on which we depended.

And the rock, as its name told (Black Rock), was black enough, black as coal, with a small-columnar formation that looked at once fascinating and sinister. I could hardly take my eyes off it. Seabirds used it for resting. Cormorants had dived off it as we approached. In a regular sou'-wester it must stir up a devil's broth. 'I wouldn't go any closer,' said the Crew. Whereupon the first missed beat came dramatic as a hammer stroke.

Now I began to look for the Macleod's Maidens. Long before we had reached the reef, we had seen three rocks of curious formation inshore, not very big-looking, in fact so slight against the cliffs that I had thought them the inner end of the reef itself. But they had receded as we came up, and with the reef behind us were still two or three miles ahead. They were in fact close to Idrigill Point and proved to be Macleod's Maidens, those three basaltic columns that rise sheer out of the sea. We stood in to have a good look at them.

The largest was like an oversize statue of Queen Victoria, well bustled behind, rather than any sea maiden of a clan chief; but the two smaller ones were maidenly enough, one stooped a little as in meditation. It was only when we discovered that Queen Victoria was two hundred feet high, and the others each a hundred feet, that we properly realised how massive were the cliff-walls, reaching at one place to over six hundred feet, against which we had sailed most of the day. The Crew surveyed them from all angles while I steered for Wiay Island in the entrance to Loch Bracadale. Beyond the cliffs of Wiay lay Oronsay Island, with its face of rock like the wall of a medieval fortress, complete with arched door in the centre. I gave the two low spits that run out from this island a respectable berth and then headed for Ardtreck Point, round which should lie Portnalong and our anchorage.

Meantime the Crew was drawing my attention to many

things—a habit she developed as the days went on, and a not unpleasant one, for there was as a rule plenty of time to contemplate the unusual. And the grass that rippled over Wiay and Oronsay had certainly the velvet-like texture of a living skin, while the sheep that clung so precariously to the very edges of the precipices might readily be mistaken for small grey boulders.

'Do they ever fall off?'

'Oh, a few of them now and again. Their thrill. And the bite just beyond reach—pretty sweet. As a sheep, would you have an urge to get such a bite?'

'As a sheep, I have had such an urge in my time,' she replied, looking at me pointedly. She was picking up!

I told her to keep her eyes on her work, as we were now about to perform something that might be very much more exciting to us than standing on a cliff-edge is to a sheep.

'What is that?'

'We are about to come to our first anchorage,' I replied.

At that, sobered by imagination, she stuck her head into the chart. 'Is that Ardtreck Point?'

'What else can it be?'

'Is Portnalong round that?—it isn't named on the chart.'

'No', I answered, 'but it's named in the *Sailing Directions*: read it out again.'

So she read what was there printed thus: 'Sheltered anchorage, except for a short carry from the east, in four faths. close in-shore. This bay is free of dangers, and affords splendid anchorage to W. of pier, the holding ground being very good. The pier shows a fix. red lt.

'Stores. Small store. P.O. ¾ mile up road. No Tel. Water. Tap behind shed at head of Pier.'

'It seems queer to think that all that's round that point. Do you think it is?'

'I doubt it,' I answered.

'What'll I have to do?'

'Wait till you get your orders.' And then I remembered she had not been with me when I was told two very impressive stories about Skyemen coming back with motor boats for the first time from Gairloch or some other near spot on the mainland.

'The trouble was the same in both cases,' I explained: 'no member of either crew had thought of finding out how to stop the engine. When the first crew reached their home bay, they were sure only of one thing: when the petrol was all used up the engine must stop. So round and round and round the bay they sailed her, all through the night and into the morning, while the folk on shore kept watch, until the strange brute stopped at last, and they rowed to land.'

'That's not true?'

'But the second crew, going to a different place, were not so patient. They surveyed the hot whirling roaring mass with cold unfriendly eyes. Moreover, what if the thing never stopped? What if it never stopped at all? They considered the matter gravely, for if they touched some little sticking-out thing, what guarantee had they that they wouldn't get some awful shock or that the whole thing wouldn't whirl into flying bits that would sink her? After all, they knew it was as strong as sixteen horses. And even fourteen horses are no joke, as we know. So it was a very real problem to them. And in the end they solemnly decided the only thing to do was to smother the whole sixteen at once. "We'll try it whatever," said the skipper calmly, and when each man had his suit of oilskins bunched against his stomach, he gave the word to fall on, and the five of them fell bodily upon the mechanism, jamming home the oilskins as they did so. The sixteen horses gave one gasping cough and died. The men stood back. "That seems to have settled them," said the skipper. "You can get out the oars.'"

'Did Eoin tell you those stories?' asked the Crew.

'Well, maybe he did,' I admitted.

She kept on laughing, but half in excitement, for here we were at Ardtreck Point (as in Admiralty chart; but Ru aird Tearc in *Sailing Directions*), and now we were round it, and there in front of us—the bay and the very pier itself.

The Clyde Cruising Club had worked its big magic!

It was a moment for belief in man's—but gratitude was knocked out of me by the Crew, who, all sea-depths forgotten, was crying to me to look at Portnalong against the Cuillin. I looked, and in that afternoon sunlight it was indeed one of the prettiest sights I had ever seen. The scattered white-washed croft houses ascended the green slopes from the pier and were backed by the Cuillin at full stretch, each jagged peak cut clear against the sky. It might have been an arrangement by some giant theatrical producer, who went in not only for impressive effects but for light and happiness. But the Crew could not get her camera on it because of the mast and stays in the field of vision—and this was part of the job for which she had signed on—yet at the moment I could do nothing to help her, for I was all alert and more than a trifle excited myself. If there is one fool who justly calls down upon himself the derision of all onlookers it is the skipper who makes a landlubber's mess of coming to anchor. I knew this in my bones, but I had no knowledge at all of how the engine was going to help me. And I could take no risks. Nor could the Crew be of any assistance. While ducking my head into the cabin to get at the controls I, of course, lost sight of where I was going. And these controls! But with a quick spanner I did get her slowed down a very little, and then stood in for the 'splendid anchorage to W. of pier'. I decided to try to get into neutral in good time—yet not too early, lest the engine stop altogether. The moment came. 'Keep her going like that,' I said, and ducked, caught the gear handle, and pulled—and pulled—and tugged—and wrenched—and swore—with every ounce of energy I had, but the handle refused to budge. There was nothing for it but to shut off the petrol. I did so, and before she had right stopped I was on top of the house and beside the anchor, which I had all ready to drop. She lost way more quickly than I had expected, and when the anchor got a hold she swung to it slowly. Not at all bad—except perhaps that we were a trifle nearer the pier than I had wanted to be, for I reckoned we were in about four fathoms of water (the chain was not marked) and I should have to pay out about ten fathoms for comfort, which would mean a fair swing. Two or three small boats anchored just inside the pier had attracted me, and I hailed a grey-bearded man working with a net in one of them and asked if I was all right. He said I might be all right but it would be better if I went 'west a bit'.

Very good—west I would go. I fitted an extension piece on to the gear handle. The Crew had a long-handled floor brush. With the brush as battering ram, I let drive at the extension piece. At the second shock, it gave. (I should have used a heavy hammer on the drive-coupling, but I did not know that then.) I fed and swung the engine; went aloft and heaved the anchor; put her into gear to go west a bit, and after a few revolutions tried to get her out of gear. She stuck. I tugged and wrenched—and again had to shut her off and vault forward. The fisherman was already signalling me to stop. As if it were a simple business! I dropped the anchor—indeed in my haste I threw it—overboard. She swung to it, however. Had I gone a bit too far? Couldn't be much for we were still nearer the pier than the opposing side of the little bay. The fisherman stood looking at us, silent. I paid out chain, made all fast, and sat until the gentle north-easterly wind got the high tide lapping about us. Then I joined the Crew. As we looked around we felt pleased with ourselves, and, taking everything into consideration, a little incredible. It could blow now if it liked! We had arrived.

V

And it did Blow

B ut the moment for complete relaxation had not yet arrived. There was this donnybrook of a cabin in front of the Crew. I boxed in the engine until nothing was seen but a smooth piece of furniture, though why the builders gave it a curved top we never could understand, for had it been flat it would have made an excellent additional table. Meantime the floor had been cleared for the laying down of a thick fibre mat, weighing about a hundredweight and measuring eight feet by four. It was one of Eoin's incredible second-hand finds at three shillings, and it fitted beautifully, covering the space between the engine and the forward bulkhead and giving a sense of comfort beyond all our expectations. We could sit or lie or walk about on it on feet or knees. The primus stove was soon hissing away, though after its plumbing efforts it was anything but brisk. The swinging table was fixed by its brass arms to supports under the skylight and in a very short time we were enjoying our first hot meal on board. And we did enjoy it, and lingered over the coffee, and smoked a cigarette, and thought that life on the whole was a very marvellous affair.

But I was soon cleared out into the cockpit, where I uncovered one of our deep-sea fishing lines and, taking off the hooks but leaving on the lead sinker, used it for sounding. We were in two fathoms. Not too bad, even if the tide was still ebbing and the weeded shore looked uncomfortably near. The wind was freshening somewhat from the north-east and therefore crossed the 'short carry' referred to in the *Sailing Directions*. It did not seem so very short—a good couple of miles into Loch Beg. But the glass was steady.

So I went ashore for milk and left the Crew to her glory. Calling at the first cottage on the right, I had a talk with a pleasant woman who said she would be milking at half-past eight. It was almost an hour before I came in sight of the boat again—to find the Crew trying the lead line! I smiled, but kept hidden. There was now a gentle breeze blowing and the *Thistle* was slowly swinging through a considerable arc.

How transformed, the cabin! Where the pile of stuff had disappeared I could not see, but certainly here at last was something like a home. I pumped up the two red Li-lo beds, let down and fixed the frames of the cots, laced on the canvas, and soon our bunks were ready. At low tide that night I took the depth. A little over one fathom. The weed was very close. The wind was increasing.

Our beds were so comfortable that we decided to cele-brate in two hot carefully compounded drinks. Whereafter I was able to explain how, even if the boat did drag her anchor, we should be in no personal danger, for she would merely go ashore and then we could jump. Quite simple. It was sub-sequently alleged that I fell asleep while still talking—and certainly in the last day or two I had expended more energy than I usually did in months.

But at 3 a.m. the Crew got up and tried the depth—though I did not discover this till many days afterwards, for I awoke at a reasonable hour—to find the wind disturbingly strong. Clearly something must be done about getting into deeper water, for the lee shore was so close that there was little mar-gin left for a dragging anchor. So after breakfast I decided to start up the engine, engage the forward gear, jump for the anchor, carry it a bit, drop it, jump back and switch off. I tried this mad manœuvre but completely failed, for the boat got under way with astonishing speed. Against the grain, I therefore had to reconcile myself to the Crew's suggestion of getting advice or help from shore.

The grey-bearded fisherman came out with me and surveyed the position. He walked the top of the cabin with ease, got hold of the chain, and began laying on it before I had the engine running well enough to take the load. On his knees he waited for me and then signalled to go astern. Yelling to the Crew to get hold of the dinghy's painter, I put the lever in reverse. She began going astern, but slowly and would not back into the wind. He signalled to go ahead. My relief was great when the lever came out of reverse, but very short-lived, for when I tried to engage it forward it would not go home. The Crew was shouting that the painter was caught. One quick glance and I realised that that had happened which I had sworn should never happen: the rope was round the propeller!

It was a moment of chagrin so intense that I could have wept, and probably did use emphatic language. For I had not forgotten the possibility of such a thing happening. It was simply sheer bad luck that, as the Crew had pulled the painter, the heavy rudder had swung round and nipped it against the stern-post, whereupon the reversing propeller in a moment had sucked the slack and coiled it round its shaft as tight as iron.

The fisherman let the chain go and the boat swung round into her original position, for he had not, he said, actually weighed the anchor—for which I inwardly blessed him. We were still afloat.

With a knife lashed to the end of the boat-hook, I tried for a long time to cut the rope clear, but in the heaving sea this was impossible. 'You will have to beach her', said the fisherman, 'when the wind takes off.'

A quiet wise man, to whom the Crew took immediately. But I said I would strip sooner. 'Are you a good swimmer?' I had to admit I was not very good. He shook his head and asked us where we had come from and where we were going to. I told him, approximately, for I had private designs on the Outer Hebrides. He stared at me. 'Are you the only man on board?' 'Well, there are two of us,' I suggested. Whereat he shook his head more profoundly and with not a little wonder. 'You should have another man,' he said. When I went forward to get a dram, he repeated this to the Crew in a way that impressed her.

All the same, I made up my mind that I wasn't going to beach the boat. She had been beached far too often already. It would soon be a bad habit. However, nothing further could be done at the moment and Mr. Macleod went away.

But in the afternoon we saw him return with another man, get into his small boat, and with an oar apiece they pulled out into the wind and then came stern first down on us. Throwing me the end of a rope, he told me to tie all the rope I had to it and then make fast. Out into the wind again, pulling all they were able, for it was now blowing pretty stiff, they paid out rope until they had gone a considerable way. To their end of the rope was an anchor which they dropped overboard; then, tying up astern of us, they came aboard.

All three of us pulling on the chain could not get our light anchor out of the water, it was so foul with weed and stone, and at last Mr. Macleod got into our dinghy and began the laborious and precarious business of clearing it: while we heaved until I thought my heart would burst. When it suddenly came away we both sat heavily on the deck and laughed.

We now lay on the rope and slowly pulled the *Thistle* away from the shore until she was in the spot where Mr. Macleod wanted her, and then I received my first real lesson in how to let go an anchor. Long after he had carefully got bottom he continued to pay out the chain foot by foot. There could be little doubt but that in my haste in dropping anchor, I had fouled the arms with the chain and gathered half the sea-bottom within the tangled mass. Had there not been such good holding ground, we might well have been in a worse plight than with a fouled propeller. I had learned that lesson, and never again forgot it.

Altogether this had been a very neat manœuvre and the lead showed us to be in a comfortable five fathoms. That evening the wind took off, and I fastened the big clasp knife securely to the short stern flagpole, got arms and shoulders bare, and though the dinghy was still heaving away, I could now and then get a glimpse of the rope on the shaft. I had put a fine edge on the blade and started in to cut, guided by the soft feel of the rope. In twenty minutes I had the propeller clear.

Lying in our comfortable bunks that evening, peace descended on us. The boat swung slowly round and back through a wide arc while the water lapped audibly the clinker sides of the dinghy. The skies were grey. There was no one on the pier; no human being visible anywhere. Through the open cabin doors we could see the shore, and it passed before us like a slow-motion picture, in which all the small things seen took on a reality of their own and even composed themselves into a pattern, like a story.

First the pier with its grey massive wooden piles and dark shed. Then the shore and the seaweed, with two boats hauled clear, one freshly painted black and white with an orange bead and the other black and white with a white bead and blue gunwales. Beyond them, a crofter's cottage, white in the evening light, and two dark sheds. A small stream coming down from the crofting lands and spanned near the sea by a little square stone bridge. Dark stones along the shore and wet brown weed. A low black skerry whitened with barnacles—a dangerous place to drag against—and a greyish-blue cow eating on the gentle slope beyond it. All the land rose and dipped in flowing lines of easy beauty to a ridge against the sky that could not be more than a mile away. The grass was browned with ling so that the patches of bracken were greener than it. The undersides of the bracken, turning over, let you see the wind running on pale green feet. There were no trees except two small birches overhanging a near bank with a ghost-white rock beneath it. Grey fence stobs against the sky, and then slowly coming into view a ruinous thatched cottage, a green boat beside it, and a tarred one showing its stem round a gable-end, sheltering there, too old to go to sea. But the old red cow was still eating, with the industry of all the working mothers in the world. Through the lapping of the water against the dinghy came the song of a lark. It was exactly ten o'clock (summer time), but we had heard a cuckoo at Duntulm after eleven. The lark's song was piercingly sweet and earth and sea were suspended from it; until suddenly a sea-bird's cry ran along the shore, and in the sound of it were the swift feet and the dipping tail.

Moving along this little landscape, knitting it together, giving it some obscure meaning, at first near to the shore, then curving in and up and over a rise, to reappear on the far shoulder to the right, before curving up and over that, to disappear we wondered whither, was a small brown road.

Portnalong we found a very interesting place, for it sums up in itself much of Highland history, certainly of economic history. The houses are all built to the same pattern: stone gables, corrugated iron sides with front-door porch, and roof of grey artificial slate. With rare exceptions they are freshly painted or white-washed, look very well, and fit into the landscape. Inside they are lined with wood, preserved with a light-brown varnish, and those we were in appeared snug and comfortable—more comfortable in their one story than many of those bare windy two-story houses that stand so gauntly by old thatched ruins. We were surprised, however, to find the dwellings all of the same build and obviously fairly new. Had all the old thatched cottages been demolished by their owners in a sudden burst of prosperity? And then I noticed something I had never seen in Skye before, that each cottage had its weaving loom.

As we went up the road in the early evening we heard the *klak-klik-klok* of the looms—each housed in a timbered hut beside its cottage. And then, like offerings to whatever gods may pass by, we saw here and there a chair by the roadside, unattended, and covered with tweed, stockings, socks, and scarves. There were no tickets of sale. Just the articles in silent offering. If this was Skye then we had never before seen the real island! The potatoes and corn were springing up in small but healthy patches; milch cows were everywhere; and from the absence of sheep around the crofts we deduced —correctly as it happened—the existence of a club sheep farm. Our Gaelic was good enough to know that Portnalong meant the port of the ships, and though the three small boats by the pier might not imply much in the way of sea-fishing, still there must be something in a name. Another significant thing—the Crew had already talked to an elderly woman who had not got one word of English, and even the young married woman from whom we continued to get our milk had clearly to think into English as a foreign tongue, so that instinctively one mended one's linguistic manners and spoke simply and correctly. As for Mr. Macleod, who had already been of such service to us and with whom we were presently on the friendliest terms, he was not used to a daily exercise of the Sasanach tongue. However, I put my questions to him sitting in the lee of a hen-house he was building, and the mystery of Portnalong was laid bare.

Thirteen years before—1924—sixty-six families, he told me, had come from Harris and Lewis, but mostly from Harris, and settled here under a Board of Agriculture scheme, taking over the existing stock at a reasonable figure. The Board had the crofts fenced off in, roughly, twenty acre lots, with a black wooden hut (now housing the loom) as a temporary home until proper dwellings were built. Money and material were advanced on very favourable terms for the building of these dwellings, and tenants had the option of buying the wooden huts at something like half the original cost. The newcomers had each chosen his croft and settled in, and as far as an outsider may judge was enjoying a decent livelihood. There were certainly no signs of poverty or distress, and if a cynic at Carbost later told me that many of the young fellows were on the dole, well, doubtless they had earned the right, and the cash must have added to the comfort of the township. It certainly in no way interfered with courtesy and kindness, and in this respect, amongst all West Highlanders, it has long been my opinion that the Harris folk take a lot of beating.

I was surprised to find that they do not take much interest in their club of some 1,300 sheep, worked by two shepherds, for elsewhere in the Highlands these club farms are a source of trouble and agitation. In recent years, of course, prices have been very bad, and now that prices are going up interest may be quickened; though there is, I think, a fundamental difficulty that these individualists have never quite got over, and that is an ownership vested in nearly seventy persons. Effective supervision is difficult and the paying off of the initial large debt is never an exciting business. However, I do know of clubs where the debt has been cleared off and where the individual income therefrom is now a very important item in the crofting balance sheet. When this stage is reached, personal interest is roused and communal attention properly concentrated on management. A nebulous ownership struggling against debt and bad prices naturally enough becomes disheartened.

I was anxious to find out the general attitude to the Department of Agriculture over the complete settlement business, and, as far as I could make out, though some grumble over difficulties, on the whole they feel that they got a good and, in some respects, a generous deal. The rent of each holding is round about £4. Peat fuel is close at hand and a main water supply runs through the township. The mainstay is the croft with its produce and cattle, but there is hardly a house where ready cash does not enter by way of sales from tweed, Old Age and Contributory pensions, and army pensions. It is difficult to think of destitution here. And the settlement is considered (locally, at least) one of the best in Skye.

(Later, I heard that a few years ago, in the worst of the depression, many of the crofts experienced considerable hardship if not, indeed, some degree of destitution, but the folk themselves never complained, and no outsider could have guessed their plight. The old Highland pride that kept the head up, clothes clean, and eyes steady! I have heard that Skye men affect to look down on Harris men. Let it be ever so delicately suggested that the same eyes might not suffer by an occasional effort at looking up.)

But however one may argue or discuss the merits of the

present settlement, there can be no doubt of the happy contrast in which it stands to the same land under the dominion of the old lairds or chiefs. Less than a century ago Portnalong was cleared of its inhabitants, the houses burned down, and the folk herded to the shore and there placed on two ships—the port of the ships!—that transported them to America. But the ships, I was told, could not carry them all, so those who were left had to build houses for themselves along the barren coast towards Fiskavig. The ships came back and took them away too, and the ruins of their fourteen houses may still be seen.

As we wandered in the hilly lands about Portnalong, towards Carbost on the one hand and Fiskavig on the other, we came on the new houses everywhere, in sheltered hollows, on sunny slopes, and their bright faces seemed like the mind of a folk who throve for untold centuries, and would thrive for centuries more, if the greed and egoism of the landed or plutocratic designers of our worldly affairs gave them half a chance.

I have so often heard it said that West Highlanders are evasive, deceitful and unreliable. The marvel is that they are not cut-throats—instead of the kindly, honest, decent men and women whom we met in Portnalong. Every year in August they hold a fair of their Port-na-Skye tweeds in the long green shed by the pier, and buyers come, we are told, 'from all over'. If they paid no more than we did for their socks—loose and tough and excellent for knee boots—they got bargains.

At the post office we bought some fine hill mutton, bacon (machine sliced), a wash basin, ginger beer, white enamel paint, bread, toffee, a water bucket, tea, Danish butter, tomatoes, but decided against a suit of dungarees, though I was now a variegated pattern of engine oil and chain rust, after we had sent off a telegram for our letters and arranged for a late telephone call. (*Sailing Directions:* There *is* a Tel.).

Altogether I could see that the Crew was not at all displeased that the wind, now blowing from the north-west, ruled out any further seafaring for the time being. 'I could stay here for a month,' she said. And it did seem at the moment as if the hiring of a suitable boat—I could think of cheap fishing boats for those who liked to rough it—and the coming to a more or less permanent anchorage in some desirable sea-loch might make for one of the most interesting holidays imaginable.

Round about, the Crew found the plant and bird life that made a walk with her such a lengthy affair. The larks were very friendly and kept leading us on from post to fence post. The yellowhammers, gorgeously fresh in colour, evidently throve on their *little bit of bread and no cheese*. Birds of the warbler size were everywhere and our knowledge of their individual notes being often uncertain, we did a lot of stalking and sadly missed not having a proper bird glass. But the plant life could be handled and examined. There is a pleasure in finding the unusual, but there is a fonder pleasure in finding the familiar in some slightly unusual guise—as, for example, the milkworts, which seemed larger in size and deeper in blue than on the northern mainland. One bank, covered with them, had from a little distance the sheen of a bank of wild hyacinth. The orchis, too, were brilliant, particularly the deep purple, while we came on one hollow of pure white ones of an unusually large size and rich flowering. And when we straightened our backs, there lay Skye around us, its low green hills generally ringed by basalt ridges, as if their flattened tops had been built up for some circus performance in the remote days of the Fians, while always there was the sea, glittering deep blue in sun and wind, and brooded over by massive headlands.

Across the sea loch beyond our boat, little settlements or townships were scattered here and there, and individual dwellings; and in the vast treeless area that the eye covered everything was static, so that each house looked wind-swept and very quiet, while the landscape itself took on a dream quality that had in its stillness something incommunicably sad. As we sailed round the wild north-west coast, this effect had been particularly strong. It is an effect, no doubt, entirely in the mind of the beholder, but surely there is, too, that extra-universal feeling of the essential loneliness of human life and even something of the mystery of its being and doing on a planet of so remote and incredible a geological past. For looking thus on Skye we did, in truth, get the effect of looking on a planet, on one small curve of the green hide that formed over the forming structure of the earth. And to feel as much does not lessen the sweetness of wind and sun on the face, or the pleasure of seeing the plant life or watching the birds.

And as for birds, we certainly were provided with every opportunity of studying the herring gull, for one insisted on being companionable. He generally rode the dinghy while waiting for food, but if we took no notice of him, he dropped on the edge of the cockpit, gave us first the benefit of one yellow eye-ring, then of the other, reformed the perfect lines of his pure white neck, splayed his webbed pinkish feet more comfortably, opened his yellow beak with the blood-red spot near the tip, and in a strong, impatient voice, said 'Skoo-awk!' But the real instinct of the wild was in him, and it was interesting to watch the internal struggle that went on when a crust landed in a position where he could see it but where he would for a moment lose the instant use of his wings. To do him justice, he never allowed his greed to overcome his instinct.

Sea-bird life was, however, not very plentiful and the only other regular visitor to our little bay was a black guillemot that showed a pair of red heels when you looked at him even from a distance. There were night cries along the beach, some of them young and wavering and sorrowful—though not, one imagined, unduly distressing the breast of the mother bird. It was never quite dark. In the middle of the night near things loomed and far things were clear against a sky from which a certain pale light did not fade. Then a curlew passed over our heads, calling in the long tremulous whistle that as boys we had always said brought rain. A dark curtain came about the world and the rain descended.

The rain, and then the wind rising.

For three whole days we were in the grip of a storm that for two of these days prevented our going the fifty yards to shore in our dinghy, so that we were finally without milk and very nearly without matches. Since our arrival the glass had been steady at 30.40, without any inclination to waver, and though the wind had been strong the weather had been invigorating. The change was complete, the wind coming suddenly out of the west and the rain driving in sheets across the water and over the hills. It grew cold, too, and at five o'clock in the morning the primus was pumped for hot drinks.

During the day, as the wind increased, we became anxious about our holding, for the anchor was no more than twenty pounds, and as the boat swung wildly in the terrific gusts from the hills, the light chain over the stem roared like thunder inside the cabin or snubbed so violently that the whole vessel shook. One of the ventilators had been lost on Hulm Island, the shaft that held the other one loosened, and though

And it did Blow

I thought I had both shafts fairly tight, they began to drip badly. The double skylight, despite a rather smeared evidence of new putty, also began to drip, while high up the sides one or two small trickles appeared. Fortunately we lay so near the windward shore that no sea could get up to increase our troubles, and if we broke away and were lucky enough not to pile on the pier, I had a good mile in which to get the engine going before visiting the smoking rocks on the other side.

The second anchor of at least sixty pounds, presented an intermittent nagging problem, which I tried to work out in every conceivable single-handed move. At last I decided to leave it alone, and trust to a perfect holding ground and to a chain in which I had fair reason to believe there could be no weak link. We set a watch during the night.

But the following night, with the force of the wind much increased, we smiled at these early anxieties. In the fierce gusts, the sea boiled to spindrift, while the spume thrown up by the rocks on the other side hung on the air like curtains. Several times during the long vigil of that second night I thought we were dragging. Out of the midnight gloom, in the wild swing of the boat, the pier would loom up menacingly upon us. More than once it seemed so close that I was certain we were going, and got ready to jump—but she always swung away again, though for a time we were convinced that she had dragged a bit. That pier, coming and going in the sheeted rain and roar of the wind, fascinated the Crew to a steady stare. I asked her if she was frightened. No, it was not exactly fear; but a sort of dumb deep-seated anxiety. It was an anxiety that was quiet, anyway, and companionable.

When the daylight came again (it was here was developed the intermittent habit of hot drinks in the very early morning), we were relieved, and though the glass was now down at 29.24 and still falling, we felt we were holding our own. The weather had turned very cold, and what with our wet clothes and Skye a lowering world of gloom and driving clouds and mist and incessant rain, and the fact that we were worn down by two days and nights of dull anxiety in a small and very unstable boat, we might have had some excuse for doubting the wisdom of our ways.

Then suddenly came a lull. The glass fell to 29.14. So I knew we had to look out for something. The wind was changing, from sou'-east probably to. . . . It took the thought out of my mind in a roar from the north-west, and we were tossed with the spindrift like a cork. There was over a mile of carry now and quite a presentable sea running. As hour followed hour through the long day it became very wearing. I would stand now and then in the cockpit, hoping to see someone, some life about the shore. But the pier was deserted, and when a figure appeared near one of the crofts it was always with bowed shoulders, hurrying through the white drifts of rain. Once a man paused on a near rise and seemed to look at us. I gave him a wave. He hurried away and did not reappear. Afterwards we heard that some of the folk were concerned about us, and more than once Mr. Macleod had had a glass on us during the day. But at the time, the only thing that seemed to be near was the black spit of rock with the white barnacles and the whiter sea. Somehow I should hate to lose the boat now. And if she did break, nothing could save her, for the spit was only a matter of fathoms away.

However, a sleep we must get this night though the heavens themselves fell, so I decided to do something with the sixty (if not eighty) pound anchor, and about nine o'clock that night I hoisted it on to the top of the tossing house, got up after it, and on hands and knees pushed it before me to the bow, the Crew paying out the chain behind. Flat on my breast on the narrow triangle beyond the mast, I passed the chain through the channel against the stem and let the anchor go. I had waited my time until the boat had swung up to and away from her own anchor, so that, in the swing back, by keeping a strain on the new chain, I might prevent any fouling of the heavy anchor. After paying out a few fathom I made fast, with a final couple of hitches round the base of the mast. If the first anchor gave way, the second might take hold in time to keep us off the rocks. This was all I could do, and though it did not seem to be much or very satisfactory, yet when it was done it relieved the normal tension in quite a remarkable way, so that we brewed a strong drink and celebrated cheerfully.

Shortly after that the gale reached its height, a whistle and a whine in it, with the rain-tautened halyards slapping the mast at express speed. (I had meant to try to lace them up when putting out anchor, but had forgotten.) As I looked out of the cabin door, a sea-trout leapt six feet in the air and the backs of three porpoises showed by the pier going up Loch Harport.

I knew where they were going. I remembered the fright one of them had given me off Talisker Distillery, some four miles farther up, many years ago. I had been out in a little canoe, fishing for haddock and flounders to a stone anchor. The wind was freshening and every now and then the water lapped in over the canoe, so that I knew it was dangerous to linger, yet could not tear myself away from the fishing, for I was having a fine catch, despite the light greedy mouths of the whiting. Then, as my anxiety was all worked up to an edge, there came a terrific snort behind that lifted me a foot off the seat. A porpoise! I saw the living brown of his body—

brown in that green water anyway—at full stretch passing under me, and I was so angered that I caught up one of the light oars and jabbed it at him. How I was not upset I still do not know, for I certainly had to paddle home sideways like a crab.

At eleven o'clock we turned in and within a few minutes, despite the multitudinous noises, I was sound asleep and didn't awake until five, when it was still blowing but not nearly so hard. We both complained of the wintry cold, though we had kept our jerseys on and covered our bunks with our oilskins. After a cup of steaming Bovril (I almost liked the stuff) and when the Crew had got a hot-water bottle against the damp patch in her bedclothes next the hull, we went to sleep again. By the forenoon I was trolling a minnow round the boat in a calm innocent little bay.

That afternoon the Crew had been able to fulfil her promise to take some photographs of Mr. and Mrs. Macleod and their grand-daughter. Mrs. Macleod, who was over seventy and did not use the English lingo, was quite excited and specially prepared for the occasion. She spoke volubly in Gaelic and had a happy manner full of bright touches of humour and could hardly believe us when we failed to catch her meaning. When she saw the Crew in her blue flannel trousers, her eyes twinkled; then she gave her a playful skelp behind and said, 'Och! Och!'

We were getting to know the folk now, and that night I had a little adventure after my heart. A boat, a net, and a wise old seaman who said that God had created all the fish in the sea for man, and made no reservations of special kinds for special men. I devoutly agreed. So about eleven o'clock we set off.

Though the weather did not smell very good, it was a calm night and the moon, near her quarter, came up in clouds of glory, while over the hill-ridge to the south, in a misty blue, Sirius hung large and red. Indeed I had never seen the redness so pronounced, and from the stillness of the night and the leaden glitter of the water, my eye would be drawn to where the red eye of the dog star watched our proceedings in a cryptic mood.

I have pleasant memories of that night, apart from the cares and excitement of it. I was on the oars and was directed by the movement of a hand or a quiet word, while the old man set the net. In his eagerness, he was pessimistic. He did not expect anything. The weather was too cold. There was no fire (phosphorescence) in the sea. But it would do no harm whatever to give it a trial. So we beat up the water, he with mighty sweeps of the boat-hook and myself with wild splashings of backwatering oars, until we must certainly have frightened whatever lay in the seaweed between the net and the mouth of the stream.

'Did you see anything?' he asked me.

'Nothing.'

'I told you!'

So I backed her up to the inner end of the net and he began hauling.

'I'm feeling something,' he said. (That nig-nig-nig on the back line!). 'It'll be just a mackerel,' he whispered, taking the net in fast. 'Get the skummer—aft there.' But before I could move he had stooped over the side of the boat, swift as a gannet, and brought up a meshed white fish. And, strange to say—and how were we to blame?—it was no mackerel. It was a fine sea trout, caught by the gills, and by the time he had got it out of its entanglement, it was dead. So what could we do but make the best of our misadventure? 'A good one!' said he, in a husky voice, his face all lit up with a smile.

And it did Blow

It was, under the moon, the expression of a boy, quick and eager and lovable. 'I cannot help it,' he said. 'It is in my blood.' And it came over me that if blood were never created for anything better than that moment, it might still be enough.

When we had set the net in a new place, we drew to the shore and talked quietly. He told of the bays and rivers of Harris that swarmed with salmon and how he went down from his house to the sea and hauled a bagful when they were on the run, 'many's the time that'; how as a young man he had gone to the herring fishings. 'You will be thinking your boat is small with that big cabin in her, but I have been to the winter herring fishing in Loch Hourn and the whole four of us slept in the fo'castle, which was just seven feet long, and narrow. There were no motors then.' The sea was in his blood as it is in the blood of all the Harris men I know —mostly men of medium build, very agile, with strong bone.

That very day I had gone up to see another Harris man who had a small galvanised anchor of about twenty-five pounds stuck in the grass beside the hauled boat with the blue gunwales. As a second anchor, it would suit me very well, if I could manage an exchange with him for my heavy one. However, I did not blame him for considering my anchor far too heavy, and, in the course of conversation, I asked him how he liked the change to Portnalong. He replied that it was well enough but he himself had nothing much to do. 'In Harris there was the herring fishing and the white fishing and the lobsters, too; but here there is just the land. You could always be doing something in Harris.'

In that moment I had seen the profound difference between the real sea-fisherman and the crofter, and understood how it came about that the fisherman left the working of 'the bit croft' to the woman as her responsibility—for which so many casual observers have so readily condemned him. The sort of testy niggling business of attending to animals, cleaning and milking them, of hoeing up stolid rows of potatoes, or trying to deal with refractory beasts, was hardly enough to hold the real attention of a man. Give him the winter fishing in Loch Hourn, in a seven-foot fo'castle, amid incredible discomfort and continual danger, with days of labour that have no set beginning or end, governed by tides and storms, and he is all alert and alive, finding occasionally a high exultation in beating death to the nearest headland. After that, thinning turnips or feeding a calf may not claim his full interest, so he is inclined to leave these curious pastimes to the women.

It was fine and friendly there, talking and having a quiet draw at the pipe, about one o'clock in the morning, for at the height of summer, midnight in the Isles is no more than a deep shadow in which sea and sky take on some permanent aspect and the hills assume their abiding lines.

When we had drawn the net again (and if a net is left for an hour or so one may find many things in it—like the two half-grown lobsters we got), we pulled for the *Thistle*, whose porthole lights welcomed us in a way that made me feel ownership and hospitality. With the grey of the morning on the hills, my companion pushed off for home. I listened to him tying up his boat in the black shadows of the pier. He would certainly see that everything was ship-shape. By the time I heard the nails of his boots on the iron rungs of the ladder, I had a half-dozen fish gutted and cleaned in salt water. Then I put the two glasses away and turned in.

The following afternoon I set off for Carbost for our letters. Under Carbost, the *Sailing Directions* show: 'WATER.

And it did Blow

—At Talisker Distillery.' I had a memory of the water being particularly good there. Whisky cannot be bought in the ordinary way at a distillery, and Talisker certainly cannot be bought at Carbost (though a good dram of it is sold at Sligachan, some miles away). But I had an island friend who welcomed me hospitably, after I had got a lift from a commercial traveller, who stayed with us for a time and discussed these western seas on which he had travelled for the last thirty years. He had, he said, a sure cure for sea-sickness and he reckoned—and we agreed—that if it worked on the S.S. *Hebrides* or *Dunara Castle* it would work the seven oceans over. It was very simple and consisted in regulating the breathing thus: as the vessel rises you draw in your breath and as it descends you let it out. That is all. And he assured us out of a wide experience that it never fails. But wasn't this a very difficult exercise? we asked. Apparently not, for after a time you did it quite automatically. As the Crew and I had not been afflicted by sea-sickness, we were unable to put the matter to a test; which was perhaps as well, for in such weather as we experienced in our small boat we should have had to breathe very quickly out and in, and sideways as well.

In Carbost I saw the first newspaper for about a week and was relieved to know that the European war had not started. Indeed the trouble in Spain seemed to have taken second place to sport, and our hostess described with what thrilling excitement she had been listening in to an endless bout between Austin and Von Kramm.

I had the distinct feeling of coming from another planet and of being told of things that happened in some previous incarnation, distinguished by a queer hectic sort of futility. At such a moment one becomes obsessed by a curious awkwardness, until the old trick of quick converse is simulated again. And to complete this provincial attitude, let me confess that when I did finally, in the quiet of the little bay, get down to the newspaper, I turned it over, page after page, and then back again to the beginning, but could not find whatever it was I had hoped to find. It wasn't there, and though I was vaguely disappointed, yet again I didn't mind. It didn't matter. The only news I really wanted was of Spain. It alone seemed immensely important; and still at the back of my mind was the battleship we had seen steaming slowly north, the day before we had left Duntulm.

My favourite of all single whiskies is Glen Mhor of Inverness. When you get it good it is clean and very palatable indeed. But if you get Talisker good, and get it in Skye, it is really surprisingly fine. Whisky, like all the other good things in life, must be taken with moderation and at the right time. There is, of course, the case of long abstinence and a burst; but that is very difficult.

As I walked the four miles home by the western shore of Loch Harport, I read some of my letters. They, too, were a little distant, though now and then one of them came near the heart. I could see that this absence or escape could make one very sensitive to real values, with a quickened capacity to distinguish between the warmest expressions of social usage and the direct true feeling from an individual mind. It threw into a momentary but clear light what was real in the old argument of the individual versus the mass.

When I got back to Portnalong my old friend was 'barking', or soaking with pitch, his best net in the big iron pot which Mrs. Morrison used for her vegetable dyes. The operation over, he turned the pot upside down 'lest the little one should fall in'. The little one, two years old, was trying in Gaelic to get the black cat to wait for her, but *a' phiseag dhubh* was wise.

And it did Blow

The Crew had been greatly interested in this business of collecting wild flowers and roots and lichens for making cloth dyes, and had taken a pencil with her, determined to jot down the Gaelic names of the various plants. But she was disappointed. They did not seem to know the names of the flowers and in fact used very few of them, because most of the dyes in synthetic form could be bought at the shop. But one could see that a generation or two ago all the dyes were got from plants and the crotal-brown is still got from lichen gathered off rocks. A layer of wool, a layer of crotal, a layer of wool, a layer of crotal, and so on till the pot is full. But in the case of pink, the woman said that she first boils all the pink clover flowers, including leaves and roots rolled into a ball, in the pot and then dyes the wool in the juice. To deepen the pink add more clover. Ragwort and one or two other plants are still used, but the convenience of the ready-made article at the shop is naturally, and rightly, very attractive. The Crew was amused by the belief that the little tormentil grew up into a buttercup. Here was the disintegration, the gradual dying, of an old art based on an exact knowledge, and the Crew, though seeing the inevitability, regretted it, too.

The wool used is mostly from the club sheep farm, so that, apart from some shop-bought dyes, the cloth, stockings, and scarves are products of the place. It is a common sight to see a woman walking along the road, looking round about, and knitting away, the sock held no more than waist high. When she meets a neighbour and talks, the needles keep going, though they have their dramatic little pauses.

This evening the *Dunara Castle* (a tenth-day visitor) came to the pier with her cargo of goods from Glasgow and her 'towrists'. Mrs. Morrison could have sold all her scarves if only the young man she had left in charge, while she went on a visit, had known their price. But he did not know or had forgotten, so he didn't sell one. Whereat she and the Crew laughed merrily.

But always behind our pleasant life in Portnalong had been the wind. The glass would go up only to fall again; a calm was no more than a lull. Here is a note I made lying in my bunk:

'Now and then beyond the low dark clouds scurrying and tearing from the sou'west, we catch a glimpse of a sunlit blue with small white summer clouds high and still, before the whole is blotted out again.

'Last night from sou'sou'west, the breeze increased to gale force and woke us with its violence about three o'clock. Terrific gusts boil the sea white and curtains of rain obscure the pier at fifty yards. The glass is falling steadily and slowly. I tap it often but always to be disheartened. We have not yet reached the worst.

'At noon it is as bad as ever, and looks as if it might last for ever.

'I think there is no force in nature so wearing as the wind. And though out of fear, as out of all elemental emotions, there emerge moments of great exaltation, yet there is no outlasting the ruthless persistence of the wind, because even the persistence is not steady but (near land, at least) subject to swift shrieking violences, when every plank in the boat shakes, the anchor chain goes *crack!* and for a moment one wonders if everything has gone. Actually at times it seemed that some malevolent force caught the boat by the stern and shook it.

'At two o'clock the glass remains steady at 29.50. I imagine the wind is lessening in force, but it is difficult to say, for this business of staring at the sea becomes hypnotic. In half an hour the glass has risen a point. A change of some sort is coming. I forecast a lull, followed by a change of wind to round about nor'west and a more violent storm than we have yet experienced.

'The herring gull rides the dinghy and as I stare at his yellow eye and dead white breast I see him like the Ancient Mariner's albatross. There are moments when a gull has an almost terrifyingly dead look. And being white, he is not lucky. I throw him a monster mackerel. He is on it at once, but can neither rise with it nor swallow it. The wind drifts him towards the pier, while he struggles with outstretched wings. He manages to keep on flying a yard or two out from the piles until at last he actually rises with the hard heavy fish to the top of the pier. A common gull comes along—or perhaps a lesser black-backed gull, for the wings seem darker than our herring gull's—but does not interfere. Then over the water are swift sharp cries and about us all at once is a cruising company of terns. How graceful they are with their leisurely wing-beats and swallow-pointed tails! The moment of poise—the dive: and up and off again.

'A skylark is singing strongly in the rain (contrary to our book's belief), which at last is coming straight down, for the wind has died.

'There is something ominous in the lull. Yet I see a cormorant coming down Loch Harport and heading out to sea. And sea-birds can be a surer indication of weather than a glass.

'The small boats by the pier are swinging round a little. The wind is changing. In the quiet, the rain beats heavily on the deck, and though I had spent a whole forenoon renewing some of the putty in the skylights and fixing the ventilators, there is still a drip here and there. The sort of small thing that can be very annoying.

And it did Blow

'Our herring gull is wiping his beak on the end plank of the pier. He has a careful look round, picks up specks here and there—the last of the monster mackerel, bone and all—takes off, settles in salt water and nuzzles it cleansingly, then alights on the end of the dinghy, now half full of water, looks straight at me, and says, "Skoo-awk!"'

In this lull, we dared not risk going ashore, for weather conditions were similar to those which had preceded the previous gale. The gull alighted on the edge of the cockpit, more deathly than ever. Vigorously I shoo'd him off, for certainly he had proved himself a bird of ill omen for us. But immediately we heard his feet overhead, where he made a mess. A second cormorant came down Loch Harport, and I blessed the bird. The glass had moved up two points. We went ashore, where I met the carpenter coming down to work on the pier. He promised me some tow for caulking the dinghy and I asked him what he thought of the weather. 'I'm afraid the summer is over,' he said. 'We had all the good weather in May.' I had discovered one or two doubtful bolts about the engine. The prospect was gloomy enough, so I got hold of my old friend and an outboard motor, and that night in the straight rain we went away with the net.

I still hear his voice as he stooped for the first white gleam: 'Mackerel!' And for the second: 'Maakerel!' And for the third: 'Maaakril!' A fine crescendo of disgust it was by the time we had landed a few dozen of these fish. But we had our good luck, too, and the incessant downpour gave things a friendliness. The stage is reached where rain no longer matters, a certain easy pleasure is got from it, a real sense of freedom. And a pipe smokes with the bowl upside down about as well as any other way. When at last I heard the footsteps die away on the pier, I turned in and slept like a stone.

And it did Blow

And then in the morning, lo! a breath of wind from the east and the glass still rising.

We would go!

Up at six o'clock, we soon had breakfast over and things fairly sea-shape. I cleared the engine and primed her. She roared first time. I could but hope that no damage had been done to the shaft or clutch. At nine, we went ashore. I wanted Mr. Macleod to help me haul the big anchor. The two chains had got foul.

Far to the west there was a break, showing a touch of blue, in the heavy clouds. The day might turn out all right. There were very few smokes about. The wise folk were not yet out of bed! So I went on to the post office and sent off a telegram requesting our letters to be forwarded to Eigg. That settled it! The postmaster, an obliging intelligent man, said he would come down and give a hand with the anchors.

As I was on the way back to the pier, a shaft of sunlight pierced the clouds and all the air about me ran with light, and all the land of Skye. Green and lovely it looked, a siren island. Here and there cattle were slowly being put to pasture. How leisurely awoke this rural life in the freshness of the morning! An exultation came upon the mind, all the keener for the previous hopelessness and gloom. There was a contrast here that runs in the character of the people. I saw it and understood.

Meantime the Crew was getting milk and oatcakes and scones from Mrs. Morrison. She was allowed to pay for the milk, but for naught else, being overcome in the laughing argument. Here was the old Skye. So the Crew took photographs of them all and promised to send them (which she did), and we made our farewells.

Mr. Macleod and the postmaster soon appeared in their own boat. The wind, alas! had shifted to the west, which meant there would be a swell outside. Mr. Macleod was not at all sure of the weather; though it might keep up for a bit, it was not settled. There was stuff on the sky yet. However, if I couldn't face it outside I could always run back, which I must be sure to do. He was obviously not very happy about the size of the crew! but I had made up my mind that we were going, for in the last day or two there had been growing a curious feeling of being trapped in this place, and I did not want any such fatalism of the West to take hold.

The heavy anchor was soon up and stowed in the cockpit. As they were hauling the light anchor, I got the engine going. The boat was now facing the shore and they stood off ready to help. The painter was properly shortened! I put her in reverse. She took the load. Now for it!—and I pushed the gear lever forward—and it went, into neutral and then into full speed ahead. There was a moment's desperate hesitation before she took the forward load, but she took it, and I joined the Crew at the tiller. The Crew was charged with controlled excitement. But we were going—if not confidently enough yet to give the men a wave! They were already pulling for the pier and we were opening out the Cuillin—shrouded in tremendous cloud. Portnalong was in deep shadow. As we rounded Ardtreck Point, we waved farewell to a place where we had spent ten days of a new pleasant life, not the least memorable part being the storms, which Mr. Macleod had said were the worst summer storms he had experienced since coming to Portnalong. Which was something!

And then we met the sea—and the swell.

VI

How we Arrived at Eigg

The Crew had never encountered this motion of the sea so directly. In a steamer it is different. There one is high above the sea, with a great company around to inspire confidence and with a proper captain and crew. Here in our small boat the whole ocean came at one in rounded hills, as if (said the Crew) it were being heaved up from below. And there was about it the suggestion of a living restless force seeking all around to do something, to be violent, and yet with an immense and even more sinister power of restraint. If the restraining power were removed—what destructive forces would be released! The 'pulse of the sea' is a poor image for this massive on-rolling imminence.

Down the cliffs on our port side, a waterfall dropped sheer, its white vein smoking here and there. To starboard the surf was breaking on the two spits of Oronsay Island. Beyond were the cliffs of Wiay—and then, to the horizon, nothing but the ocean.

The sun was obscured by cloud, but round it I saw a wide halo, a complete circle of stormy rainbow colour. So that the Crew might not see it, I asked her how she felt.

'Fine,' she answered.

'Like a smoke?'

But she shook her head and made a motion with her lips. They were dry and sticky. The knuckles of the hand that grasped the cockpit rail were white. She smiled. 'I am not used to it. That's all.'

I explained how lucky we were in having such a good sea, but when we got out of Loch Bracadale and headed south we would bring the swell abeam and so would be inclined to roll a bit. She nodded and asked me where we were going.

As I wasn't sure myself, I began to expound a general plan of campaign. I would first head straight out of Loch Bracadale into the open sea, so that if the old engine broke down, I could rig up a sail and try to fetch our starting-point under canvas. We must accordingly keep a long distance off shore, because our particular kind of boat would, under sail, do little more than run before the wind. We could never tack into it. Had the wind been in an easterly direction, we could have fulfilled our first intention of making Soay Island and getting into Loch Scavaig beside Loch Coruisk (where it might have been interesting to spend a midnight or two). That was now ruled out. We should therefore bear presently for the island of Canna. And beyond that we need not for the moment think.

The engine was going steadily, the circulation pipes were cool, and the oil drip-feed was working. We were doing fine! Soon we had opened out Macleod's Maidens and the hills of South Uist and were looking towards them, when a cable length ahead I saw a yellowish scum of water. I thought it tidal but kept my eye on it. And then I got what was our first real scare at sea. A heavy thirty-foot beam of wood, no more than just awash, was directly in front of us, broadside on. I put the helm hard over; there was a swaying lurch as the sea came at us, and we passed clear. What would have happened if we had hit that stem on, I do not know, but I imagine it might have been pretty bad. I smiled at the manner in which we had navigated by the compass and with no look out for long distances on the way south! No more of that, and I peered over the high house at the wind-darkened sea. Yet despite a keen lookout, I missed a second log altogether and only saw it as it swished past at arm's length. Clearly the recent gales had taken toll of some deck cargo.

The western edge of the sun's halo was thinning, as were the seaward clouds, and though over Skye behind us immense cumulus moved and burgeoned upon dark ominous underbodies, the day seemed to be lightening. I went inside and tapped the aneroid: 29.68 and, if anything, going up. The wind was not increasing; lessening, in fact, I thought. And without any warning a feeling of exhilaration, of a rare gladness, came out of the air, and I put her straight on Canna.

The mountains of Rum rose to the left of Canna, and beyond Rum, in the haze, the Scuir of Eigg. We were a week overdue at Eigg, but as the Scuir was some forty miles away and the boat doing barely six knots, we could not bring ourselves to believe we should get there. If we fetched Canna, we should do well.

The wind became intermittent and the colours in the sea varied and fascinating. Towards the west, where the blue sky was widening, the water was living amarynth; east and south it was a leaden rolling waste. The cloud formations were of great complexity, from pure white puffs in the distant blue, airy as meadowland dreams, through snarls and wind-drawn angers overhead, to the sombre pall that lay on Skye and the inky gloom that blotted out the south-west. A gannet lank and white, like a dead bird re-arisen, passed overhead. Puffins, scuttling out of the water, disappeared as by magic over the edge of the next swell. There was a splendid exhilaration in this width and expanse, an expanse rendered all the vaster by the hazed islands and the immense stretch of the mainland highlands now rising out of the thinning clouds far to the east and south'ard. Something here very much grander, more impressive, than any circle of horizon when no land is seen.

Canna, lying low to the sea, became more defined as we drew nearer and presently we could make out the flat shelf of Sanday Island at its south point, between which and Canna was the harbour. I began memorising—and visualising—the entrance and anchorage from the *Sailing Directions*.

All sea directions are necessarily against dangers, but the detailing of rocks and reefs (particularly those that may be covered by the tide) and tortuous channels and depths does not make easy or pleasant reading. The sea's teeth seem everywhere and even a very few tons moving at six knots can make short work of thin planking. Not but that one could circumspectly face up to any danger—with an engine that answered promptly. But when there is a feeling that the lever may refuse to come out of gear, that the engine may stop altogether in an attempt to slacken speed, and when one knows, over and above, that wind and tidal current continue remorselessly, then the coming gracefully to an unknown anchorage is a bit of a thought.

The Crew was looking at Canna and remembering or paraphrasing some words by the Rev. Kenneth Macleod in his Introduction to the *Songs of the Hebrides*. When a man on a journey landed on Canna he might stay only two or three days if he was in a hurry, and then the farewell to him: isn't it the great pity that you are going instead of coming.

'Going we are,' I answered, for the wind had fallen to a light breeze, and with Eigg still in mind, I thought we should chance making for Loch Scresort, the only decent anchorage in Rum. We were now far enough at sea to be able to make Loch Ainort or even Loch Brittle, in Skye, under canvas, should the old engine conk out. Always as we went along these computations were made. It was a conjuring with many possibilities, and when we felt we kept a reasonable balance, it added the zest of a game.

Rum was impressive in its hills. The two peaks of Ailbemeall and Aisge-mheall dominated the whole, with Aismheall topping a high ridge to the south. It took us two hours' steady going to come near enough to see the brown sandy bays on its eastern shore. The green of the slopes were deeply tinged with brown. It looked a desolate land.

It is, too, a desolate land. Once Rum carried a population of about 400, all crofters and fishermen. Now there is neither a crofter nor a fisherman on the island. Apart from the mansion house of the proprietor, there are only some six families, all thirled to 'the estate'. The whole original population of Rum was evicted. Sheep in thousands took their place. Now there is not a single sheep. The whole island is preserved for sport and no Rum native treads its soil.

It is the perfect example of what the clearances, and, following the clearances, sport, have done for the Highlands. It is perfect even to such minor details as that one never encounters either a domestic pet or a paying guest.

Some amusing stories are told about visitors who, having business on the island, try to land there—mostly, of course, visitors engaged on some official affair of the Post Office or, in the case of wreck, of the Board of Trade, as it is difficult for any other kind of visitor to land, except from a private yacht, because the ferry-boat that goes out to meet the steamer is estate-owned. As a private individual, you may buy a ticket from Messrs. MacBrayne for Rum, but what would happen when you wanted to get ashore is another matter. And even if you did manage, what next? For every door would be shut against you and you would have nowhere to spend the night except on the beach. What would happen if you boldly took to the hills amid the wild goats and the wild ponies, I, however, cannot say. But don't depend on ground game, for there is neither rabbit nor mole on the island.

I know of men, landing there on official business, who have been promptly told to clear out (when, the steamer gone, the only place to clear into was the sea) and who ultimately won a temporary footing on the soil by the production of a commission which empowers an officer to call on all liege subjects to assist him in time of difficulty in the public execution of his duties. There was once a crew in a disabled ship, lying off shore, who had at last to be permitted to land in order to move a warp. At once they lined up and expressed, in a way of nature, solemnly and ceremoniously, that instinct of independence and freedom in man which, despite all oppressions, will find a suitable outlet. But the stories are many and amusing and the best of them true. At this time of day, all this may well sound incredible to one unacquainted with the history of these parts. To such a one the adventure remains open of trying to make himself at home on Rum.

Loch Scresort, about one and a half miles deep, is the island's one decent anchorage, and being exposed only to easterly winds, would suit us very well. So we laid a course on the headland that guards the northern entrance. But as we brought this on our beam, the island of Eigg beckoned more strongly than ever, for we were going well and Rum was at least protecting us from the westerly swell. As we opened out Loch Scresort we saw the walls of dwellings, far in the shelter of the inlet, that had obviously never been designed by or for crofters. I experienced a strong desire to go in and land there, but as we had had a fairly rough fortnight on board our small craft, we thought it might be wiser first of all to keep our appointment in Eigg, which might then be used as headquarters for foraging expeditions to islands round about, should the weather behave itself at all.

And it was undoubtedly clearing up. The Scuir of Eigg, that remarkable formation of hard pitchstone, had its elevated backbone so clearly cut against the blue that one could see all its knobbly joints. The massive clouds had lifted a little off the Cuillin and the western peaks were just clear. Soay Island could be made out, but the fierce gusts for which Loch Scavaig, behind it, is notorious reconciled us to a postponed visit. For the time being we did not want anything worse than we had experienced at Portnalong! There is a good natural harbour in Soay itself, and we still had it, as it were, under our lee bow. And some good history of the eviction times, as can be gathered from the evidence led before the Royal Commission in 1883. If I may be permitted to quote once on this subject, I should like to give the reply to the Chairman of that Commission by a cottar and boatman, not so much for its economic as for what one may be allowed to call its Imperial aspect: 'My great grandfather served with the army. My grandfather was forced to go to the army, and his bones are bleaching in a West India island. My father was in the militia; my brother was in Her Majesty's navy till the time of his death, and now the grandson of my grandfather is on a rocky island that is not fit to be inhabited. In Soa we pay £3 of rent. At first the agreement was that we were to have four milk goats, a cow, and ten sheep. The farmer by degrees reduced the number of our cows. He did not reduce the rent a farthing. There are twenty-three families on the island. The crofts are on bogs and rocks. When you put your foot on some parts the ground shifts so much that you would think you were standing at the foot of Mount Etna.'

How we Arrived at Eigg

Soay had been uninhabited until these families had been compulsorily removed to it from good holdings in Skye. And the evidence of the next witness, described as 'cottar and fisherman', also suggests Imperial travel or travail: 'My present house is built on the sea-shore, and the tide rises to it every stormy night that comes. I have to watch and put out all my furniture, such as it is. A sister of mine was employed last winter putting out the furniture, and she was sickly and died in consequence. I tried, by carrying some peat soil on my back, to make a bit of land, but it defied me. The ground is so soft about me that I had to pave a way with stones for my cow to get to the hill. I never saw a place in Scotland, Ireland, or France so bad for man to live in.'

This is the Soay that was in the news recently, trying to get better steamer connections.

East of us, the Point of Sleat, and round it Sleat Sound, which I knew so well, with Loch Nevis, Loch Hourn—that deep wild loch, Isle Ornsay, Glenelg Bay, and so to the Kylerhea narrows and Loch Duich. Southward we could see the headland which covered Mallaig, and down from Mallaig the long indented coast of the famous white sands. Behind, stood mountain range on mountain range, and here and there in hollows dim distant peaks in the heart of Inverness-shire. As we opened out Eigg, Coll lay to the southward and east from it the long headland of Ardnamurchan. A noble country, and worth surely a better modern story than the evidence from Soay.

Between the two islands, we caught the western swell again, but now its surface for minutes at a time was completely unflawed by wind and we saw what appeared to be the machinery of the sea in motion. There was such fascination in watching it that the eyes were held and slightly dazed. Glistening alternate movements, smooth sliding movements, of light and dark, coming up to the boat, clearly defined as steel, into and out of each other, elusive and yet extraordinarily powerful—and noiseless.

At a little distance we saw a gannet asleep on this power, its head curved over on its back. As it heard us, it lifted its head and in a moment we saw the black tips of the moving wings. It made no sound, though an old fisherman told me that when you surprise one of them too closely it lets out an unearthly screech.

Small things or incidents like these were continuously surprising us, and gave the sheer living of life a vivid interest. It even quickened local history, usually so dull a subject, till its human movement took on dramatic values, till the universal was seen in fact as an extension of the local. And usually there was plenty of time for imagination to sift such a thought through, quite on its own!

But here at last was Laig Bay on the west of Eigg, and, somewhere near, the Singing Sands, that Hugh Miller discovered for print, and that Gordon Bottomley made a verse drama upon. The long waves were breaking on the brown sands. Soon we closed the bay and came over against the Sgaileach rock, showing the same basaltic formation that had been with us everywhere. A waterfall down its face was like a vein of quartz. But the chart was now being handled with some anxiety and the Crew was called to her reading lesson on our approaching anchorage:

'. . . Eiln. Castle shelters the N. or Flod Sgeir anchorage from southerly winds, though at times a considerable swell sets in, but it is rather difficult to enter for the first time, owing to the numerous reefs, almost all of which cover at H. W. Only two of these rocks are marked by poles . . . coming in from the north—'

'That's us,' I said.

'... the starboard hand perch is surmounted by a circle, and the port hand by a cross. . . . The best anchorage, which is sheltered from all but N. E. winds, is just off the jetty in three fathoms. . . . The passage between Eiln. Castle and the shore, through to the S. anchorage, is only ½ cable wide, and there is a bad reef on the Eigg side to be guarded against. The tide runs strongly through this channel. The S. anchorage is in the middle of the bay, in 4 fathoms. Off the S. end of Eiln. Castle the reef extends for 1 cable. . . .'

But there I stopped her. We should not go to the south end: we should have 'the best anchorage', with heaven's help and the engine's.

And then I made a curious miscalculation, misled probably by the strong set of an ebbing tide running with us and increasing our speed perhaps to round about eight knots. In our chart I saw a headland marked Rudha nan Tri Clach, on the east coast of Eigg, which I took to mean the headland of the three stones. I began to watch for this formation. Presently I saw a headland thrice-terraced in rock and assumed it was the one I wanted. But soon a doubt began to arise and I wondered—for distances at sea can be very deceptive—if what I actually saw was not the point of Eiln. Castle (or Castle Island) at the southern corner of Eigg, inshore of which lay our anchorage.

This it turned out to be. All too quickly the island came open of Eigg and we saw the rocks and reefs and tried to pick up the two perches. I dare not disappear to attempt a slow-down, and look as we liked we could not see the perches. Perhaps we had expected something more solid than thin iron rods. But suddenly the starboard perch leapt to the eye, and then—though it took a moment or two because the dark rod is not readily visible against the dark beach of the island—we picked up the port perch with its cross. And there, some white boats lying at anchor—off the jetty.

As we came dead between the perches, keeping a smart lookout, I glimpsed the shore rising to wooded loveliness against the eastern end of the Scuir and some figures on the jetty watching our arrival. Eagerness to make a tidy mooring rose keenly in me.

But alas! for human vanity. A strong tide was with us, the seaway was narrow, there were plenty of reefs about, and the bay to starboard was obviously shallow. I waited as long as I dared, then I ducked to the lever and gave it a tug; it came, and in neutral the engine let out a mighty roar. I throttled down the least bit; the engine stopped abruptly. I was told that my remarks were heard on shore. I swung the heavy flywheel to a spin; but the engine refused to fire and I had now no time to prime her, for we were being carried on the tide against a ten-ton motor boat in the middle of the fairway. Nothing could be done except fend off, so I eased the bump, and, hanging on to the vessel's rail, hailed anyone aboard. There was no answer, and slowly the dinghy swung round the other side of the vessel's anchor chain. We were properly fixed now!

Pretty maddening, what with our friends on shore and the sweat running into my eyes and down my nose. But the Crew held on nobly till I got the engine going again, reasonably, in neutral. Then we cleared the dinghy and the Crew stood ready to push off from the vessel's quarter as I went into reverse. We came away nicely, slowly round into the right spot, and the engine actually kept going this time in neutral while I dropped anchor and paid out foot by foot as she swung to the current, and waved to our friends ashore, and wiped my nose.

The Crew, of course, had been tensely excited over all

these complicated manœuvres, particularly as any order I shouted was generally drowned in the splendid roar; so that she had not had time to look at the engine; which was fortunate, or she might have collapsed, for as I stooped in at the door I was met by water being whirled all round the cabin with great velocity, and decided that at least one of the cylinders must have burst. After shutting the throttle (there was no switch for cutting out the spark) I satisfied myself that all that had happened was the rising of bilge water into the shallow pan beneath a flywheel doing its thousand or so revolutions a minute. So we got ready—I had a second pair of trousers which were supposed to be less oily—and rowed ashore.

VII

Egga, Ego, Ardegga, Egea, Eiggie, or Eigg

Our hostess, in white, looked cool and very clean, and welcomed us to her white home with its blue woodwork and cream walls, its lupins and gorgeous cabbage lettuces. This introduction to Eigg was somehow extraordinarily full of brightness. It was not merely that the sun was shining. There were trees, and braes with little hazel woods, and everywhere the fragrant white rose of Scotland. This is a delightful spot and during the five days we made it our headquarters we fell in love with it, even if the weather did not treat us well.

Our host—a writer—had the understanding of human needs that makes hospitality one of the pleasanter arts. In the cool room were bookcases and burning logs, and if he writes—which he threatens to do—a book about the Small Isles (Muck, Eigg, Rum and Canna), I shall place an advance order. If ever I come across a book beginning, 'When I tapped the glass this morning it rose to 29.98 . . .' I shall be held like the Ancient Mariner. And think of this for the beginning of a happy ending: 'The black needle, steady on 31, was pointing to VERY DRY.' Though I admit that may be carrying romance a bit too far.

But the feeling of ease and pleasure after the trip is very real. Happiness exudes not so much from the mind as from

the skin. One looks slowly at things and with a sort of be-
mused loving-kindness. One calls one's hosts lucky dogs.
Tells them this sort of blessedness is not fair. They laugh,
and after one comprehending glance at a wrung-out body, he
produces a tankard of draught beer with froth on the top.
There is something a little divine about all this. The body
breathes and lives in itself.

Outside, the Scuir dominates the scene, with its high per-
pendicular walls, and that evening we set off to have a look
at it. There were gates with 'Private: No Thoroughfare,' but
we pushed by them. The Big House was up in the woodland
to our right. The walks were trim and the banks neatly cut.
It all looked very prosperous and financial, but left upon the
air the suggestion or reality of privilege and superiority,
hardly the natural element in which a wanderer may feel at
ease. However, we kept going happily towards the near
base of the Scuir, intending to traverse its length (for now it
was like the deep upturned keel of a boat) and get on top of
it from the west side, whence the view would naturally be
very extensive. But the visibility promised not to be too
good and, in any case, we came on Gruiline which had once
been a settlement of crofters. The ruins had still about them a
feeling not of death so much as of ghosts—according to my
friend, whose city boyhood finds the place quite eerie and
haunted. Oighsgeir lighthouse was a thin white finger far in
the western sea and Barra a small purple hump. Coll and
Tiree lay to the southward and inland from them the Treshnish Isles with the crown of the Dutchman's Cap quite clear.
Then Mull, Ardnamurchan, and again the whole Western
Highlands. We asked the names of peaks that darkened
shadowily the ultimate haze. From land, I don't know that I
had ever seen anything so impressive, and when, that evening, I happened to pick up *The Countryman* and came on Sir

Muirhead Bone giving his favourite landscape as from Arisaig, with the Small Isles in front of him and the white sands and peach-black rocks at his feet, I was pleased, but felt it was not the only point from which to regard this marvellous land and sea.

But the Scuir is what meets you at every turn.

'The Scuir of Eigg', wrote Hugh Miller, 'is a veritable Giant's Causeway, like that on the coast of Antrim, taken and magnified rather more than twenty times in height, and some five or six times in breadth, and then placed on the ridge of a hill nine hundred feet high.'

And when we tried to find out about this wonder rock with its sheer sides, we were caught in one of those geological stories that have the air of pure fantasy. For it is really difficult to believe that it lies on the bed of an ancient river, that much higher rocks rose on each side of it, forming a valley, and that the ages have washed all these away, leaving the Scuir to its lonely glory, surrounded by the sea. Whence did the river run and where did it end? The answer given is that once upon a time there was no sea here at all, that all this was high and dry land, and that, as a guess, the river may have been the Tweed! But how can anyone know?—for 'caverns measureless to man' are much easier to imagine than that.

Geikie in his geological map of Scotland gives it a corner all to itself and describes it from the bottom up. Above the groundwork on which the Scuir rests ran the river, and driftwood and shingle may still be found to mark its course to this day. Just as in Skye we saw the lavas overflow and fill the hollows, so here the river bed was in due time filled up by 'the pitchstone-porphyry that is now the Scuir'. Then the valleys were removed, and the high lands, and in its appointed season—came the sea.

Not that all geologists agree on the point. Hugh Miller believed that 'the gigantic Scuir of Eigg rests on the remains of a prostrate forest' and is there by upheaval. But Geikie's river shows the vaster and, as it happens, the truer sweep.

However, those, like myself, who know little of geology, may be interested not so much in the likelihoods of the discussion as in the surprising fact that it exists; just as it might not greatly matter to us what exactly was the nature of the rock which troubled Hugh Miller at Ru-Stoir, to the east of the island of Eigg, as that it belonged to 'the age of the Plesiosaurus and the fossil crocodile'. 'I hammered lustily,' he wrote, 'and laid open in the dark red shale a vertebral joint, a rib, and a parallelogramical fragment of solid bone . . . I had thus already found in connection with it [Ru-Stoir] well-nigh as many reptilian remains as had been found in all Scotland before.' Banks of basking crocodiles and plesiosauri, here where the ancient river ran! And there could be little doubt of it.

And even in the quite recent story of man, Eigg provides a cross-section lurid enough to satisfy the most morbid curiosity. Our host, by way of illustration, led us to Uamh Fhraing (the Cave of Frances), now generally known as the Cave of the Massacre.

The tale of the massacre is widely known, for Sir Walter Scott has it in his *Tales of a Grandfather*, and other writers have debated its origins at length. That it is no legend is certain, for less than a century ago Hugh Miller describes the human bones as he found them still on the floor of the cave. 'The floor, for about a hundred yards inwards from the narrow vestibule, resembles that of a charnel-house. At almost every step we come upon heaps of human bones grouped together. The skulls, with the exception of a few fragments, have disappeared; for travellers in the Hebrides

Egga, Ego, Ardegga, Egea, Eiggie, or Eigg

have of late years been numerous and curious; and many a museum—that at Abbotsford among the rest—exhibits, in a grinning skull, its memorial of the Massacre of Eigg.'

The story is that of a feud of uncertain origin between the Macdonalds of Eigg and the Macleods of Skye. 'Some hundred years ago', wrote James Wilson, in his *Voyages Round the Coasts of Scotland* (1841), 'a few of the McLeods landed in Eigg from Skye, where, having greatly mis- conducted themselves, the Eiggites strapped them to their own boats, which they sent adrift into the ocean. They were, however, rescued by some clansmen; and soon after, a strong body of the McLeods set sail from Skye, to revenge them- selves on Eigg. The natives of the latter island feeling they were not of sufficient force to offer resistance, went and hid themselves (men, women and children) in this secret cave, which is narrow but of great subterranean length, with an exceedingly small entrance. . . . As much of the coast is cavernous, this particular retreat would have been sought for in vain by strangers.' After pillaging the houses, the Skyemen were going away 'when the sight of a solitary human being among the cliffs awakened their suspicion and induced them to return. Unfortunately a slight sprinkling of snow had fallen and the footsteps of an individual were traced to the mouth of the cave.' Whatever preliminary parleying took place there we do not know, but certain it is that a huge fire was set ablaze in the entrance to the cave and thus by 'one fell smoke' was the entire population of the island smothered.

But Hugh Miller gives 'one of the Eigg versions', accord- ing to which 'it was the McLeod himself who had landed on the island, driven there by a storm. The islanders, at feud with the McLeods at the time, inhospitably rose upon him . . . and in a fray, in which his party had the worse, his back was broken and he was forced off half dead to sea. Several months afterwards, on his partial recovery, he returned, crook-backed and infirm, to wreak his vengeance on the inhabitants, all of whom, warned of his coming by the array of his galleys in the offing, hid themselves in the cave . . .' to be betrayed by the fatal footsteps in the snow, whereupon 'the implacable chieftain' unroofed the houses and piling the debris against the cave set it on fire. 'And there he stood in front of the blaze, hump-backed and grim, till the wild hollow cry from the rock within had sunk into silence, and there lived not a single islander of Eigg, man, woman or child.'

Of the completeness of the holocaust there can be no doubt. Had any of the original inhabitants been left, they would never have allowed the bodies of their kinsfolk to moulder and rot in the cave, and in fact travellers of a later generation found that the new folk had no island traditions going farther back than their grandfathers. Hugh Miller mentions how the general disposition of the bones shows 'that the hapless islanders died under the walls in families, each little group separated by a few feet from the others. Here and there the remains of a detached skeleton may be seen, as if some robust islander, restless in his agony, had stalked out into the middle space ere he fell; but the social arrangement is the general one.'

A narrow path took us winding down the grassy declivity that, before giving on the beach, turns in leftward to an opening at the base of the hill no larger than would admit a dog with comfort. Indeed it looked like the entrance to an animal's den and certainly conveys no idea of the vastness of the cave beyond.

But we had been provided with candles, and, after scrambling in on all fours, stood up in the gloom. Ahead all was pitch darkness and when we lit our candles and stumbled forward, the darkness came about us in such an apprehension of substance that our hands went out against it gropingly. We could not see the walls until our fingers touched their dank surface and our eyes peered forward to glimpse the colour—or lack of it—that could so absorb the light.

To me the place was damp and wretched, with the sort of human wretchedness that tramps contrive to leave behind them in rotting wayside caves. I could not feel the tragedy that had been enacted here. Or perhaps the mind involuntarily refused the fullness of realisation, using a protective callousness to defeat anger—as if the deed had been committed not in the sixteenth century (as is generally believed now) but yesterday by men whom I knew to the marrow. And the Eigg version of the story that has the McLeod chief standing hump-backed and grim is like the truth. For his men would have been anything but inactive and grim; they would have been shouting in their lust for those within to come forth now. They would smoke them out, the badgers, the dogs! Unaware in the madness of their lust and laughter of the awful thing that was really happening. Incapable of realising it—callously not caring in the end—carried away by the very excess of their cruelty into cruelty's final frenzy.

For their earliest records show them as a home-loving people, given to hospitality, and with many of the graces of life, their music and poetry an active personal possession. The early Christian missionaries went all over Caledonia, unharmed, even by the Druids. Indeed amongst them all only one appears to have suffered martyrdom—and for that a queen is held responsible (it happened on Eigg, too). One seems to have to introduce chiefs or self-seeking egoists of some kind, men with ruling power and avid in their vanity for more, before sensitive decent men can be worked up to

blood lust on any senseless extravagant scale. It is not necessary to go back to the sixteenth century for proof of this.

The demoniac instrument here was the Macleod chief and
his grimness is no metaphor. For the Macdonalds gathered
in their pitiful little families inside the cave, as for the
Macleods outside—fathers and brothers and sons—we may
have some sort of baffled wretched understanding.

There is still another explanation offered of the massacre,
founded on historical record. In 1588 Maclean of Duart was
indicted by the Lord Advocate on the specific charge that he,
with a party of a hundred Spaniards from the Spanish
Armada ship, *Florida*, in Tobermory, sailed to the islands of
Eigg, Rum, Muck and Canna, burning the whole of the
inhabitants without distinction of age or sex. Maclean pled
guilty and the Privy Seal Records contain an entry covering
the remission of his deeds. But a strong folk tradition can
hardly be superseded as easily as that. Maclean was manifestly another chief out on a foray of his own, and as he
could not presumably rouse his clansmen to go with him, he
roused some foreigners instead and shared with them the
spoil. Before a chief could get his own men to rise, he first of
all had to create a feud or 'bad blood'. Just as nations have to
do to-day.

As we wandered in that inner darkness, there was produced one effect of tragedy, purely theatrical. The cave is 260
feet long, 27 feet at its widest, and about 20 at its highest.
After having picked my way over the stone debris—the bones
were removed some years ago—of the uneven uprising floor,
I turned to look back and saw the faces of the three women
coming behind, the wondering troubled faces only, haloed
in each case by the candle held aloft in a hand. Though in
truth the effect was far beyond anything I had ever seen in a

theatre, or imagined out of Shakespeare, or conceived in a cathedral.

We were glad to get back into the sunlight, for there was something in that dank dreadful interior that chilled the marrow.

Another cave, a little farther along, is called the Cathedral Cave, for here the Roman Catholics, in their persecution days, met to celebrate the ways of their religion. The deep stone ledge, which was used as an altar, is on the left as one enters; and around, there was certainly space for a considerable congregation. Through the high entrance arch the noise of the sea comes upon the ear, from the faint susurrus to the deep boom, as if the cave itself were a vast sea-shell; which in a geological sense it is.

To-day the population of the island is half Roman Catholic and half Protestant, but there is neither persecution in religion nor division in social life. They live happily together, and on occasions of great sorrow meet by deathbed or graveside in a common grief. The folk themselves prefer to live in this way and have always preferred it. It is man's natural instinct to like a pleasant life, to enjoy himself in merry gatherings of his kind, or to ease the burden of fatality by sharing the emotions it engenders. Were not this the blessed truth, the power-perverts would have destroyed the world long ago.

The first time we set out to cross the island to Cleadale we were defeated by the rain, but the second time we were more fortunate, and strolled on beyond the green fields of Kildonan, past little streams and grey sallies, through the hollow way, with the Scuir high on our left and slow-rising ground on our right, past the post office, and so to the edge of the escarpment that overlooks Laig Bay and its wide flat crescent of fertile land behind.

Egga, Ego, Ardegga, Egea, Eiggie, or Eigg

Of the eighteen crofts left on the island, sixteen are confined to this spot. Apart from farm lands belonging to the proprietor, the rest is a sporting estate, and though pheasants are reared it must be at a cost which precludes economic considerations, while the few bright charming houses on the east side are estate property (the architect—an Englishman, I understand—might with great advantage be consulted by Scottish rural authorities generally).

How pleasant it was to come into this crofting land and see the fields of grain and roots, to get the smell of clover from the hay-fields, and to observe children and barking dogs and cattle! There need be no fear of trespass here. I looked for boats on the shore but saw none. Across the water, forbidden Rum rose up, impressive as ever in its high barren mountains.

We came on the priest mending the road before his gate and he welcomed us with the courtesy that is native to the Islesman; and the overbrimming hospitality. It is pleasant to come from a long journey on foot into a living land. To be treated in the midst thereof to wine, and in the fullness of time to cakes and honey, does help to entrench the precariously held belief in human goodness!

Though when the talk got round to the past history of the Small Isles and I learned something of their vital statistics, the belief had all it could do to hold its own.

The clearances again. They dogged us everywhere we went, and at times the tale sickened us, so that we could have wished for something new, were it only some new variety of economic atrocity.

Rum, as has been said, provides perhaps the most readily intelligible example of what landlordism succeeded in doing to the Highlands and Islands. But it is doubtful now if it could ever be repopulated successfully under any scheme. It

135

is often easier to break in the virgin wild than clean the waste land that was once cultivated. It was a point that had never been put to me so clearly before.

Eigg and Canna are kindlier islands and certainly could carry many more good crofts. We heard rumours that Canna might be 'raided', for there is land there as fertile as may be found in the Lothians.

But these stories of the Small Isles being raided by men from overcrowded islands farther west wanting new crofts are now getting fairly hoary. I could have more readily believed in them if I could have seen in this crofting settlement of Cleadale a desire by the young and eager for more crofts on their own island. But this I did not see. What I discovered instead was something very different, that looked rather like the disintegration of Cleadale itself, so that if I were tempted to prophesy I should say that in two or three generations there will be no crofters around Laig Bay and all Eigg island will be one sporting estate. Not, here, by any particular compulsion of the present landlord, but from general social causes that have been active for a century, that have not generally been arrested, and, as things are, that are not likely to be.

Sad to think of this fertile spot without waving fields and human voices, without cakes and honey, a wilderness of rank growths and dead memories. Not a pleasant picture to contemplate in the company of one who loved the people so well and was in himself so hospitable.

We were guided down to the beach, that smooth wide sickle of brown sand, and along to its north corner, where, in the soft sandstone, hard polished boulders are stuck like plums in a face of cake. This is the place to study structural geology. One boulder that the sea had picked out was in every detail like a huge skull and it was exhibited to us like a

family heirloom. We would have gone along to the Singing
Sands, but Father Campbell told us they were too wet to perform to-day. Though what I should really have liked to have
done was to have followed the coastline north-about and
hunted for one of Hugh Miller's plesiosauri by Ru-Stoir.
And *that* I might have found—though not the shieling where
he was so hospitably entertained by the girls who lived there
all alone making butter and cheese in this same month of
July. 'An island girl of eighteen, more than good-looking,
though much embrowned by the sun, had come to the door
to see who the unwanted visitors might be. . . . I have not
yet seen the true Celtic interjection of welcome—the kindly
"Ooo"—attempted on paper; but I had a very agreeable
specimen of it on this occasion, *viva voçe.*'

Laig once had its inn, too. The house was pointed out to
us, and we were told that the first tenant of that house was a
son of MacMhaighstir Alasdair (considered to be the greatest of all our Gaelic poets). Of his son, again, a story was told
as we climbed the winding road up the escarpment. It appears that, returning to Laig one night, he was met on this
corkscrew by a giant before whom he refused to give way.
Perhaps he had been prepared by John Barleycorn for the
unequal and desperate contest. Anyway, in the end, he was
too much for the giant, and slowly forcing the great body to
the brink of the ravine, thrust it over. The following day the
Laig bull was missing, and, after search, was found at the
bottom of the same ravine with his neck broken.

There is a stream where the 'washer at the ford' may still
be seen, and if you are foolish enough to ask her what she is
washing she will tell you it is your own shroud. There are
young folk who would not care to cross it alone after sun-
down. And doubtless old folk, too. It is an innocent enough
looking stream. But there is a way of looking at it.

Egga, Ego, Ardegga, Egea, Eiggie, or Eigg

We talk a lot about superstition and the credulity of simple country folk, and for the most part with some reason, for the giant very often turns out to be the island bull; and when this happens the folk themselves delight in the story and tell it with so happy a gusto that one feels they are pleased not only with the humour of the story but with the relief of it.

For however often one can explain an apparent manifestation of the occult, there is always the odd time when one cannot. Sometimes I wish I had kept a record of second-sight or occult experiences told to me at first hand by men and women whom I should no more doubt than I should the evidence of my own normal senses. It is not a pleasant thing to have one of these experiences. One man, who sees funerals before they take place, is so affected that when the phantom cortege has passed he finds relief in involuntary physical vomit. He hates the 'gift', and would not readily speak of it even to his intimates. And occasionally you meet the man, scientifically trained, who is quite at a loss to rationalise what has happened to him, though he tries his best.

For example, here, in brief, is an experience told me recently by a man who has a science degree from a university and was born in the Long Island. He was visiting his sister, who held a professional county appointment on the mainland, and he lodged in a cottage of four rooms, two upstairs and two down, inhabited by two old women, who had their occasional misunderstandings, for one accused the other of 'wandering in the night'. This was repudiated by the other, and at night each locked her own downstairs door. He had arranged to have his meals with his sister and to sleep in one of the two upstairs bedrooms in the cottage. So far all was simple and clear—until just after he had fallen asleep on the first night, when he was awakened by footsteps coming up the stairs. They paused outside his door and he got up and

Egga, Ego, Ardegga, Egea, Eiggie, or Eigg

opened it. There was no one there, and he satisfied himself that the stairs, lit dimly from a roof skylight, was quite vacant. Presently, back in bed, he heard the footsteps come again, and this time after opening the door and seeing no one, he went into the bedroom opposite, searched its cupboard, hunted under its bed, and assured himself definitely that no one had entered and was hiding there. Then he went quietly downstairs and tried the doors of the two rooms. Each was locked on the inside.

He is not at all the sort of man to be vaguely afraid. He does not like vagueness, and, determined now to find out what caused this curious night disturbance, he lay awake, waiting, and when the footsteps started coming the third time, he arose at once. Just as they got opposite his door and he was in the act of gripping the knob, the knob turned in his hand. He swung the door open. There was no one there.

Now his brother—who had been delayed a day—arrived on the morrow and they arranged, for old time's sake, to occupy the same bed. When they had retired, my friend soon affected to feel sleepy, for he had not mentioned his nocturnal adventure with the footsteps to anyone and wanted to make sure, if possible, that he had not been the victim of some odd form of hallucination. For normally he does not possess the 'gift'. So presently he said good-night and composed his breathing for slumber.

In due time he heard the footsteps and felt the dig of his brother's elbow. 'What is it?' he asked sleepily.

'Footsteps—up the stairs—listen!' whispered his brother, all nervous tension.

Together they did all they could that night to find any possible explanation of these footsteps, but were completely baffled, and the following day they shifted their lodging.

Some time thereafter my friend was back in the same

neighbourhood on a visit, and actually attended the funeral of the 'wandering' old lady who had slept below him. Her body had been found on the ground beneath his bedroom window, from which it had fallen with fatal results.

He invoked Dunne's *Experiment with Time* and we traversed theory and practice generally, but of his actual experiences in that cottage there could be no shadow of a doubt.

That is a fairly common type of story. In fact it is by far the most common. The Brahan Seer and the Petty Seer saw remarkable things—and always *before* they happened. A very rare type is that which, while dealing with the present, invokes both past and future. Here is about the most interesting example of this type that I have encountered recently. It was told me by a medical doctor, and I may not, for obvious reasons, be more specific here than to give as locality the Western Highlands. The subject in this case was a young woman, cheerful and companionable, anything but hypochondriac, though confined to bed with what is normally a fatal disease. The doctor got his first shock when he went to a certain house where a woman was about to be confined. On the way, he was wondering how he would be able to get her to agree to go to a distant medical institution, for he knew it was just the one thing that any local woman would hate to do. Yet because of certain facts in the history of her case, he must get her to agree to go. Prepared for the most obstinate opposition, he was amazed to find none. Husband and wife agreed at once. But later he discovered that the bed-ridden young woman of the 'gift' had foretold his coming and his instructions and had advised the husband to go home and prevail with his wife to obey the doctor.

It turned out, as he had anticipated, to be a difficult case, and when they did at last resort to induced labour, it proved fruitless. Meantime the young woman back home told the husband that his wife would have a perfectly natural delivery on a certain day and give birth to a son. And that, in short, was precisely what happened.

Having heard enough about all this to pique his interest, the doctor called on the young woman, who was his patient, though he could do nothing for her, and in the course of conversation discovered that she never felt lonely, least of all at night-time, for then a dead neighbour would drop in for a céilidh and they would have a pleasant chat. She told him that his mother (who was dead) had called on her recently and had not sat on the chair or stool as the others did, but on the bottom corner of the bed in a way that he recognised as peculiar to his mother. Now this young woman had certainly never seen his mother alive, for his home had been in a distant place. Yet the people here had got it into their heads—by an understandable mistake, which need not be explained— that he belonged to another place, so that there was a certain puzzlement in the young woman's look when she repeated his mother's story of the true birth-place. She described his mother quite accurately. A forecast, by his dead mother, regarding the girl's recovery has yet to be 'proved'.

There is a third class of story dealing entirely with some past event, generally of a desperate or gruesome nature. The haunted room is the type of this story, but such experiences as have been related to me by those who have undergone them have been characterised for the most part by an ugly terror. Little of the cloak-and-sword romantic phantom or of the wailing of the banshee. In fact it could almost be said that it is not so much what happens as of the state of mind induced by the happening. A brilliant young Dublin woman is in the Irish West, walking along an Irish road with her sister, the place new to them, their minds happy, when all at once they are overcome with terror. They hear chains clanking behind them. They try to run, but their joints weaken in loathsome horror. They begin squawling. The experience was altogether horrible. As she tells it to us in her Dublin sitting-room, she shudders.

They found afterwards the true history of the clanking chains. It was a real piece of the past, and others had had a similar experience at the same spot.

This kind of horror story has its fascination for those interested in the physical content. The horror can be so awful that it not only terrifies and overcomes the mind, leaving it abject and degraded, but becomes so omnipresent that the very senses apprehend it, as they would a pervasive poisonous smell. The reaction is one of profound and bitter shame, not only for oneself but for our common humanity.

There is still another type of experience much more difficult to describe than any of the foregoing, perhaps impossible, for how can a unique experience, without tangible physical attributes, be conveyed at all? It is difficult, anyway, to conceive of its being conveyed at second hand, so the best the writer can do is to attempt the personal. I had been sleeping in the south wing of an old country mansion house when, sometime during the night, I awoke, sat up in bed in a room dim with starlight, and saw my door swing noiselessly open. The transition from sleep to sitting up watching the door open must have been almost instantaneous. I immediately went and stared into the long black corridor, but neither saw nor heard anything. Then I closed the door and went back to bed, but could not sleep, for I became aware—or rather I had an apprehension—of what I may tentatively call pure evil. Now strangely enough it did not come from inside the house but from outside, and not from the ground but from the air, from the vaults of space. It was not a being, a spirit, an imminent presence: it was a force; not a black magic but (if I may be understood) a black electricity. It was quite impersonal, yet not a mere death ray; an emanation from an active principle of evil, as though the old conception of two principles in creation, good and evil, were in fact true, and the evil was at that moment having an undisturbed innings. The method of its operation was disintegration for its own sake, a disintegrating of the mind, the personality, and finally of the body. Its purpose was to break up the tissue of what the good or creative principle had put together, and one had to strive against it with the utmost strength of one's will. This, of course, was something utterly beyond any consideration of social or personal morality, as it was beyond any jugglery of the door, which had conceivably been opened by a current of wind in the long corridor acting on a catch not quite closed.

However, we are now reaching the point where discussion is as fruitless as it would be for two born-blind men to discuss the colour red. A little knowledge of such obscure forces does help one, all the same, to appreciate the feelings of the young girl in Eigg who is still afraid to cross a certain stream lest she see the 'washer at the ford'.

Some of the western islands are remarkable in ways other than superstitious or geological.

Our host in Eigg had amassed a large amount of curious knowledge about his island, and one evening he took us over to Kildonan, with its ruins of an ancient monastery. It was here that Donan, contemporary with St. Columba, had his cill or religious cell. There is the early recorded story of Donan's visit to Columba or Columcille with the object of making him his 'soul's friend', and of Columcille's reply: 'I shall not be soul's friend to a company of red martyrdom; for thou shalt come to red martyrdom and thy people with thee.' The virtue of this reply is presumably meant to lie in its prophecy, which was duly fulfilled, for it is surely strange that Columcille should refuse friendship to one whom he foresaw would be martyred for furthering the Cause to which he himself had dedicated his life. There is something in that early attitude to fate that is a trifle elusive to us now. For no question of courage or loyalty can be involved. Again and again in the records of these times one comes on a happening which has upon it the light of a remote paganism, with its taboos, and should some shutter of the mind lift for a moment one gets the ancient vision, and, in that necromantic moment, all seems understood.

The story of the martyrdom of Donan and his fifty-two monks is attended by one curious circumstance, namely, that when the enemy came to dispatch them, Donan, who was celebrating mass, requested them to refrain from slaughter until the holy rite was over, and at once 'they gave him this respite'. When it was over, Donan and his monks came forth and were duly slain, 'and all their names are in a certain book of the books of Erin. A.D. 616' (*The Martyrology of Donegal*).

Accounts vary as to the identity of the enemy. One record has it that the queen of that part of the world kept her sheep on Eigg and when she heard of the landing of Donan and his monks, she said, 'Let them all be killed.' 'That would not be a religious act,' said her people. But even in those early days apparently there were chiefs who thought sheep of more importance than men, religion or no religion, and so her will prevailed.

Yet to do the people of Alba justice, this is about the only real martyrdom of the early Celtic Church, and when we talk of savages and barbarians and the light being brought into their pagan darkness, it should not be forgotten that Columba and his men and their successors, over a long period,

Egga, Ego, Ardegga, Egea, Eiggie, or Eigg

travelled the length and breadth of Scotland, to the Orkneys, to Ultima Thule, talking and preaching to folk who not only must have listened to these pervertors of the ancient Druidic faith, but manifestly must have fed them and given them hospitality. Indeed if we go back to Ninian (one hundred and fifty years before Columba), the founder of Candida Casa on the Solway, we have a period of several centuries when strangers with a strange gospel penetrated the forests and mountains and glens of Scotland not only with immunity but amidst surely a remarkable tolerance. For if the practice of the Druidic religion, then certainly more than one millennium old, centred round the burning of human beings in wicker cages, as our school books told us, it seems odd that all this human material, wandering like destructive birds into the dark Druidic cage, should have been spared. Pagan Rome promptly devised the sport of tossing Christians to the lions. Christian Spain achieved the monstrous cruelties of the Inquisition. And it is not so very long ago since Scotland suffered the incredible ferocity of 'the killing times'. Compared with the religious barbarities of the modern age, these early centuries have an air of halcyon calm, of kindness. Even this martyrdom of Donan in a contemporary record is put down to 'pirates of the sea'. And in yet another it is recorded that the queen had to call in 'Latrones' to do her bloody work, because her own folk refused.

Towards the end of the eighth century Norwegians and Danes started their murderous inroads, and from then on the old sense of peace and security vanished in that lust for land-ownership and power which is still with us.

There is a round-headed tomb let into a wall of the old monastery and it is believed to contain 'the bones of the prince of pipers, Raonall MacAilein Oig, the author of the most celebrated pipe music in existence', according to one

writer on Eigg (Dr. MacPherson), though what all the fans
of the MacCrimmons and MacArthurs and Mackays might
have to say to that I do not know. Certainly the run of
vowels in the name is music itself and half persuades me to
believe the learned antiquary.

In the evening light, as we turned away from the tomb
with 'its Celtic notions of heraldry' and came out on the
grassy promontory towards the sea, we were in a mood to
hear the learned voice continuing: 'Thus have we glimpses of
island history for a thousand years from the martyrdom of
St. Donan to the death of Ranald the piper. But who can
assign their true dates to the flint, the iron, the bronze, the
amber, the jet, the timber, not one of them products of the
island . . . yet they are not only found in the island, but
specimens of each one discovered in a single tomb.'

At our feet white sea-shells were round the green mound
of a child that had recently died on the island. Older the
meaning of that decoration than we could fathom. In front
the lush grass was thick with yellow rattle and rising out of it
was an ancient Celtic cross (or at least parts of the original
cross cemented together). To the right, two old graveyards
were overgrown with nettles, in that condition of complete
neglect so often encountered in the Highlands. Further to
the right, the land dipped and rose and went down through
the little hazel woods and the short braes where the white
rose of Scotland, with its incomparable fragrance, grows in
greater profusion than anywhere else I know. Below, the
water moved in slow tiny impulses over the pale sands of the
flat shore, and in the shallows between, the seagulls waded
across.

In the deepening gloom the learned voice grew faint: 'There
is still in the Island an old blind man who chants Ossianic
poetry, never yet published, which he received by tradition.'

Egga, Ego, Ardegga, Egea, Eiggie, or Eigg

But the old man is dead, his poetry gone with him, and what have we, who come after him, to set as a light in the gloom?

At that moment our eyes, lifting to Castle Island, were held by the flash from the lighthouse, not yet full-bodied, with a twilight elfin green in it. It came upon us like pure magic—but the magic that in a moment held some secret assurance, perhaps a little pride, and certainly hope. Our hostess's involuntary smile seemed to suggest that perhaps we, too, have tried to do something after our fashion.

Stepping into a dinghy is a simple enough matter, if done with decision; but to put one foot out and then hesitate is to ask for close communion with the sea. Kit, not being used to small boats, adopted the hesitating precedure, and the dinghy slowly left the pier wall with one of her legs while the other remained desperately ashore, until she gracefully sat on the ocean, and would have quite disappeared but for the attentions of our host, who effected a spectacular rough-and-tumble rescue. This was not a very auspicious opening to our projected descent on Rum, particularly following an earlier visit to the *Thistle* which had been interrupted half way and when the floor boards were awash in an effort to find the missing cork. Of all ways of bailing a small boat, the easiest is by hauling the boat ashore and pulling the cork out. Only it is as well to make a habit of seeing the cork is in before taking the water again. Not that there is any real danger so long as one knows where the draining hole is and can readily get at it. Those not used to this sort of misadventure can, however, become quite disconcerted when, at some distance from shore, they suddenly find sea-water pouring into their shoes.

The visibility was very poor as we stood out between the beacons, but we hoped that the fog might lift around mid-

day. I had made up my mind to land on Rum and climb one
of its hills and inspect its terrain for myself; and, more particularly, see what steps might be taken to prevent me. In
fact had the weather permitted, the Crew and I had intended
to anchor in Scresort Bay for a day or two and then explore
fully.

But we were destined never to land on Rum. The weather
proved too much for us. As we went along shore, the rock
faces of Eigg to within a short distance of the water were
shrouded in cloud and mist, and we could not see much more
than two hundred yards ahead. The skerries were crowded
with birds and one mysteriously moving rock point turned
out to be a seal. Ru-Stoir was really impressive in that magnifying gloom, and the sea was surly, though there was not, as
yet, much wind.

We set a compass course for Rum into stuff thick as a wall,
and only when Eigg was disappearing behind, and the sea,
opening between the islands, threatened to be nasty, did I
fully realise the folly of our expedition; for even if we found
our anchorage, what could be seen by landing on such a day,
and in the event of our being storm-bound, how deal with
five grown persons on one small boat? We held council, and
as it was now after midday with the fog showing no signs of
lifting, it was decided to return. Yet it was with a deep
reluctance that I pushed the tiller over in that lumpy sea and
once more fetched Eigg out of the mists. It was our first
taste, however, of attempting a new anchorage through fog,
and though we were baffled it was not because we could not
have made the passage. Sailing into fog is an eerie experience,
and must, with the siren going, become wearing to the nerves
of any navigating officer. Fog on a dirty sea in cold wet
weather can become unpleasant to anyone. It was cold enough
with us.

Egga, Ego, Ardegga, Egea, Eiggie, or Eigg

We got safely back inside Castle Island and, with five willing pairs of hands, made fast to our two anchors fairly creditably. Our disappointment eased as the weather worsened.

The night before leaving, a working engineer happened to be about and he had a look around my engine. Of the four bolts that held it to the boat, two were so loose that they could almost be picked out. They went round and round and could not be tightened.

'I shouldn't worry about that too much,' he said, '—until you get two bigger ones.'

He then took off the two inspection plates to the oil chamber. 'Once', he explained, 'we were at sea with a one-cylinder Kelvin. There was no splitpin beneath the locking nuts to the big end, and didn't the nuts work loose and come off. There was one *dunt!* and that was the end of that engine. She was smashed beyond any repair. I have never forgotten it.'

His hand was meantime feeling around the big ends. 'Some of your splitpins are missing,' he said, in the same conversational tone. 'You should have eight. I can only feel two.

'Do you mean six are gone?'

He groped all over again to make sure. 'Yes. Six splitpins are missing.'

'Sounds pretty bad.'

'It's not too good.'

'Any to be got here?'

'No. I'm afraid you'll have to wait until you get to the mainland. Of course, she might run without them for long enough.'

'And she might not.'

'That's so.'

VIII

To Arisaig and the Sands of Morar

We waited for the 10.30 a.m. broadcast to shipping—some day a great or simple man will give the B.B.C. its high due—and were told that the visibility would grow less and the wind freshen. So by eleven we were trying to disentangle the anchor chains in the midst of a nest of boats, for a pretty red sailing yacht had come to rest dead astern, blocking the north passage. The sixty-pound anchor I managed single-handed to break out, haul over the bows, and stow astern; then, with the engine running, I felt for the small anchor, waited for the swing round of the boat, hauled away rapidly, and dived for the engine. Mercifully, she took the load and we threaded our way for the south channel against the tide. I had lost a good hour and a pint of sweat, but we waved to our friends gaily and so bade farewell to the bright island of Eigg.

We had already seen that there was a bit of a sea running outside, but in a rash moment we had arranged to meet friends at Arisaig, and go we must, while going was possible. A squall struck us as we came off the south corner of Castle Island and we rolled heavily, shipping some water over the high deck. The wind was certainly freshening and there were white caps ahead. This was the first time we had encountered a heavy sea, and as we came broadside to it, the Crew had to hold on with both hands. For a time the plunging roll was fairly violent, and I had to crawl forward on hands and knees, warily, to lash the anchor, while the Crew struggled valiantly with the tiller. It was then I got the feeling that she was a good sea boat. Subsequent events proved this, but even on that day if I helped her at all she rose up and bowed as pretty as you like. And she needed help sometimes, for we did, in truth, get a bad tossing. The rain showers came in squalls from the south, not only whipping up the seas in an ugly way but blotting out the mainland, until at last we lost altogether the landmarks by which we were to know the entrance to Arisaig. I suppose I kept nosing up to heavy seas more than I was quite aware, and when the Crew had performed her trapeze act past the engine into the cabin, and returned with the compass, I saw we were heading considerably south of east instead of points north of it, as we should be doing by the chart—though it was now not an easy matter to consult it properly, for we had no shelter and the helm required all my attention. There had been one very alarming moment, when I had heard a rush of mechanism and felt a sudden vibration under my feet. But before the trip was over I got used to this racing of the propeller, and the old engine refused to take the prank seriously.

The rain set in steadily and the mainland was almost continuously blotted out. It got very cold, too, and the water looked anything but an inviting element. I had one or two nice problems set me for the first time. For instance, I *felt* I was going in the right direction, and wondered if the compass was being affected by the near vicinity of the heavy anchor and chain. I tried vainly to test this by shifting the compass, but it was hardly the moment for experiment. I trusted the compass, of course, and presently satisfied myself that we were heading for Loch nan Uamh, south of Arisaig Point, between which and the island of Luing Vore lay our entrance. And here the *Sailing Directions* had one of its capital little notes, for it said of this island that it was 'the only one in the vicinity which shows trees on its summit'. We therefore simply could not go wrong.

But we soon realised how different is an indented mainland coast, with islets and rocks off it everywhere, from an island in the ocean! We held north but could neither be certain of Arisaig Point nor of any island conforming to the size and appearance of Luing Vore. Yet by our time, we should have had the Point abeam before this. I was completely baffled and stood along the coast, with masses of floating seaweed here and there, and, rising out of the obscurity ahead, a nest of large rocks spouting spume. I could doubtless make Mallaig or Loch Nevis but I wanted to make Arisaig, and none the less so that the *Sailing Directions* considered a detail chart essential! 'Written instructions would only confuse, as the coastline is so broken up, and the rocks and islets are bewildering. The detail chart 2817, is the only sure guide, and it would be well to make this harbour for the first time at L.W. or soon after, when the reefs are showing.' But it also mentioned the trees on the island and said there were poles to mark the 'very narrow and winding' channel to Arisaig, even if 'the marks are on the highest parts of the rocks and not on the shoal water'. Which sounded clear!

Though it was impossible to stand without holding on, the Crew was doing her best with the glasses, but in the rain and haze they were useless. However, suddenly she drew my attention to some Scots firs on a low summit well behind us. I was now quite certain that we had passed Arisaig Point, even if we hadn't seen the island. I had yet to find out that when a coastal island lies between you and the mainland, it is generally impossible to distinguish it from the mainland. I had observed those trees before coming to them, but, as they had seemed to be well inland, hadn't given them a second thought. Now, however, as we glanced back, they at least appeared somewhat isolated, and as the engine was behaving very well, I decided to have a proper look at them.

I watched my chance in the seas, and she came round beautifully. I was delighted with this manœuvre, and though there was a mighty difference between running before the sea and plunging into it head on, I found the difference very exhilarating. The spray came flying over her bows, but actually we shipped very little. She really had a gallant way of going into it, and when she heaved and plunged and did a complicated rolling-sliding movement as well, you never doubted the central stability, just as you never doubt it in an acrobat, even when the heart is in the mouth. And an extra good effort did call for applause! 'A pretty good boat, this of ours!' I shouted to the Crew. She smiled, clearly at the stage of nearly believing it, but still with a certain pale reserved judgment. I was surprised to find that my own lips were a bit dry and sticky; but then added to the excitement of the boat's motion was, I suppose, a deep-seated anxiety as to reaching our anchorage, while if anything went wrong with the mass of mechanism, minus its splitpins, we should certainly now be in a nice plight. Yet somehow this state of exhilaration produces an unconquerable optimism, and all one's muscles are alive to the last cell. I had heard of staid phlegmatic fishermen, in an all-in fight with the sea, develop an incredible activity and instancy, become truly inspired. In the end, the skipper does not speak: he moves a hand.

We came abreast of the trees, still looking as if they were on the mainland, and kept going, always with enough room about us in which to manœuvre, for I had to bear in mind the possibility of having to set our small sail and run before everything for Sleat Sound. At last I stood in for the place with the trees, keeping about half a cable length off some rocks at the south corner, where the chart (assuming this was Luing Vore—or as the chart spells it *Luinga Mhor*—for the variety of Gaelic spellings in the *Sailing Directions* and Admiralty charts must be enough to make a real Gaelic scholar forever despair) shows seven and eight fathoms, and then made over for the opposite shore, where the sailing depth ran inland from what was presumably Arisaig Point. After going for a mile or so, the place with the trees did begin to look like an island and I felt convinced that we were right. It must have been about half tide or more, for much of the shoal ground was covered. And so began the hunt for the guiding poles—those with a cross for our port side and with a circle for starboard, after first of all picking up a plain perch.

But we never picked up that plain perch—and we were now on the inland waterway, with rocks and shoals and land everywhere. We could not keep going full speed ahead, and I did reduce our way a little by retarding the spark, but I feared as yet to touch the throttle. When we saw a house ahead of us and a hill behind it, we searched despairingly for a pole or even any decent sign of a continuous passage, but could find none. We must stop. Which meant trying to get her into neutral until we should have time to see properly where we were. Which might mean—resort to the brush handle, or worse, in a narrow tidal way. I did actually dive to the engine, put my hand out to the throttle and then draw back, deciding on a further hundred yards and one last look around. It was a successful look, for I picked up a perch with a cross on our port bow. It was a pleasant moment, and a complete triumph over the Crew, who prides herself on a true far-sightedness. 'They're no use,' she said, putting the glasses away.

It was great fun after that, picking up pole after pole—for they are widely spaced—on the three-mile channel winding its narrow way amid innumerable rocks.

When at last we emerged, the rain gone, and saw the houses and trees of lovely Arisaig, we felt masters of the situation. The sheltered waters were little more than darkened by the wind and we began looking for some sort of harbour. The chart showed 'Arisaig Harbour' right in on the starboard hand, but we could not even see a jetty. However, when we picked up a red buoy lying well inshore, I put her at it, and in due time I resigned the helm to the Crew, reduced the throttle speed nonchalantly, pulled the lever without any difficulty into neutral, ran her on the last of her seaway up into the wind at a reasonable distance from the buoy, while the Crew took a sounding of nearly two fathoms, dropped the anchor carefully, paid out chain at my leisure, then stopped the engine, as if we had been doing this sort of thing perfectly all the days of our lives! It was worth some laughter and, in truth, we were as delighted with ourselves as children.

There is, by the way, no pier or jetty. You go ashore in your dinghy and scramble up over the weed. But there is an excellent shop where you get everything, except perhaps two of the most indispensable of all things—fresh vegetables and eggs. In any case there were none for sale when we were there, but this was a lack that dogged us all over the West, even in busy tourist places. No wonder the Crew had exclaimed, like a traveller in a desert, at sight of the oasis of cabbage lettuces in Eigg! And such lettuces, with such hearts! Is there any place in the British Isles—excepting certain areas of Ireland—where more succulent vegetables or sweeter flavoured berries can be grown than in the Western Highlands and Islands of Scotland? And is there any place where they are grown less? But one would at least expect in a nor-

mal tourist centre, such as Arisaig, that some local gardener
or crofter would try to meet a seasonal demand, even if he
was not partial to such cow fodder (as I thereabouts heard it
called) himself. Apparently not, for when we accidentally encountered some Glasgow friends, they said they had hunted
green food in vain. We never did manage to buy West Coast
fresh fish on the West Coast—but then there may be no
fresh fish there (apart from those that deliver themselves up
to trawlers). But of that again, for meantime I had got in
touch with the hotel keeper, a true host, who made no more
difficulty over cashing a cheque than over providing a large
tankard of true and frothful draught. He had lettuces for
table, too—and grown, I should say, in his own garden. May
it increase. Then I wired an old friend, Maurice Walsh, news
of our landfall, as we had had a few adventures in our day together, and he and his wife were anxious to see what ploy
we were up to now. I had no sooner done that than we ran
into a poet and his wife, who entertained us right splendidly.
Had we met Mr. L. A. G. Strong? He had a house thereabouts. Oh, a real writer's haunt. And artists, too. . . .

After the few nights on a shore bed, it was surprisingly
pleasant to be back on the water again, feeling the swing of
the boat, hearing the night birds cry, and watching the glass
falling. The rain was terrific that first night, and at 3 a.m. I
was back at the old game of stopping a leak and making a
hot drink (and liking its flavour no better). We both slept
profoundly and awoke to a windy sea.

Presently a ship's dinghy, bobbing like a cork, was discerned making its way towards us, and when I was handed a
telegram, I only thanked the thin dapper grey-clipped man,
with the yachting cap. He saluted and swung away again,
shipping little more than a broken wave-top, and so danced

back to land. Quite a remarkable performance, and in my astonishment I had shown a lamentable lack of hospitality. 'Pretty smart postal service!' said the Crew.

But I discovered him again on the beach, whittling a wooden stock for a small anchor, and we had a real sea talk. He asked me, in the usual Highland way, where I had come from. I told him and said it had been blowing pretty hard.

He agreed, adding, 'But of course you would know the passage in?'

'No, I came in on the chart—and was troubled a bit because the scale was small.'

'The Ardnamurchan to Small Isles chart?'

'Yes.'

He looked at me. 'You'll have a good crew with you?'

'Just my wife.'

The hands with the stick dropped a foot. 'You are the hardy gentleman,' said he. And even if he had meant foolhardy (which he didn't quite), I was still prepared to extract flattery out of it!

He had once been yachtsman to a certain gentleman on this coast, he told me, and had got him to build a special craft for it. She was fifty feet long but with no greater draught than three feet six inches. The right thing for some of these lochs with their shoal water, as I would understand. 'Well, one afternoon along he comes and says we were leaving for Oban at six o'clock that night. I told him we couldn't leave because it was blowing too hard. He laughed at me. So he was thinking I might be frightened, perhaps? I said no more. Very good. We set out. But rounding Ardnamurchan in the dark she would go over so far that you couldn't see in the world how she would ever right herself . . . I am glad to say it wasn't me only that was frightened then.'

This was very encouraging, but better was to follow, for

he told me that when he himself was in doubt or difficulty over an entrance or picking up a perch or a buoy, the strain upon him became such that he could not speak to anyone. As my sympathy was very real, he there on the foreshore re-lived the very mood, until words failed him, and half-turning to the sea he made a gesture with the wooden stick and shook his head. How I wished the Crew had been there!

But these men know the sudden moods of that western sea. And when he finished up with: 'You should have one other man aboard whatever', I realised, I think, the experi-ence out of which he talked.

When we met Maurice Walsh and his wife at the railway station, they were enchanted with their trip across country from Fort William, surely one of the finest pieces of natural scenery to be encountered anywhere. And in sun and cloud and a healthy wind, Arisaig was looking very well indeed. They were on their way back to Dublin, and I hoped to take them as far as Oban. But clearly we could not tackle Ardna-murchan Head—the storm centre of all this land—in this wind, so in due course we set off to explore the country be-tween Arisaig and Mallaig.

As you leave Arisaig and come over the hill looking down on Back o' Keppoch, the view is very striking, not only of the mainland but of Eigg with its thousand-foot cliff, Rum of the mountains, and, far to the north-west, the headlands of Loch Bracadale, which we now knew so well, with all Skye northward and the Cuillin and Red Hills in purple. Every-where white caps were racing on a glittering blue-green sea. We were gaining a little knowledge of this magical corner of the world, and inwardly I knew that months should be de-voted to it. The restless desire to keep on visiting one island after another was wrong. No corner of the earth yields its secrets to the tripper. There is the first dramatic look, exquisite and forever memorable, but the crowding of one such moment on another is a form of cinematic debauch that in the end kills the deep motive powers of wonder and curiosity and puts a surface taste for crude sensationalism in their place.

How lovely that Morar country is! I don't mean merely the famed sands—though we counted every variety of sea-colour over them, from a real yellow, through browns and greens, to a sparkling blue—but the moors, the turns and twists of road or path, the canna blowing in the wind, the wealth of wild flowers, the little strange intimate corners of peat bog; there, a red cow eating can convey the idea of Egyptian timelessness. And the hills, their lines flowing and merging. Morar River has its spell where the green water breaks into white over the cascading rocks. To spend a day there on one's back, with sun and warm wind for happiness, or grey gloom for strange thought, might be an experience worth having stored away against the day when life seems drab and mechanical.

The herring nets, set to dry on the roadside fences, met us about four miles from Mallaig. I have heard Mallaig spoken of as an end dump. And it can look uninviting enough on a wet day, and such architecture as it has may not be exactly a tribute to its situation; but still it deals with the sea and deep-sea fishing boats and is a depot—a famed name—for fishermen in these western seas. They can 'make for Mallaig'. Which should be enough for anyone. The miles of net guided us all the way in till we saw the town down below, the water breaking green round the rock off the harbour entrance, a few small yachts at anchor in the basin, in front of them two drifters with mizzens set, the *Lochmor* at the pier, a train engine puffing, a crane cranking, and a great crowd of screaming gulls. There was something very bright about it.

Our friends were delighted with this sudden evidence of life and work at the end of so lovely a road. A man was packing mackerel in boxes with ice so busily that he had no time to speak to anyone; clearly the mood of one avid to make money out of a not very hopeful speculation. There was a gutting machine that could gut and wash and split over sixty herring a minute for kippering; a very neat piece of mechanism, though I prefer the product smoked rather than dyed in vats. Then I ran into the engineer whom I had met in Eigg and he took me to a marine shop, where I got a supply of splitpins, sparking plugs, and two holding-down bolts. Thereupon we adjourned to where many seamen were gathered together, and I discovered the other side to the bright picture.

For the herring fishing was a failure. At this time of the year there should have been fifty or sixty drifters lying out there instead of two. Mallaig is an all-the-year depot for deep-sea fishing.

You could feel this lack of life, this concern with a box or two of mackerel, where there should have been a throb of life round gutting stations overflowing from good shots of herring, everyone working at high pressure with the excitement of taking part in a magnificent game of chance. In the old days of the sailing boats, what a nimble-footed throng, what jostling and rustle of women gutters' oilskins, what gaiety!

'Aye, and there were the local seasons, too. Think of the Tiree fishing bank itself, for cod and ling. The East Coast boats used to go through there, even from small places in Caithness. They had little huts and lived there while the season lasted, catching their fish, splitting them, and drying them on the rocks. Nothing of that now. They say the trawlers have cleaned the banks out.'

To Arisaig and the Sands of Morar

'They say anything, but dammit if the West Coaster had any spunk left in him, he wouldn't go blaming the trawler. The only thing he's good at is getting the dole, and he's a dab hand at that.'

There was a short laugh, for stories of 'wangling' the dole by a clever 'faking' of insurable employment provided a touch of humour in most places, though one could always feel the underlying spirit of condemnation.

'Well, I don't know,' said an old fisherman, whose sea days were manifestly over, 'but it was a hard life in the old days. We had our good times, but the life was hard. Take the small line itself. You were no sooner home than you had to start in to redd the line, then to put on tippings and lost hooks, then to shell the mussels, and then start in to bait the six hundred hooks. And after that a few hours in bed—and off again. You have your engines now—no calms, no hanging on the oars, no head winds. And not a hook to bait. It's fair pampered ye are, if you ask me.' And his old eyes twinkled.

'God, I don't know,' said a fine limber man of about forty-five, obviously a skipper, with the grey salt of the sea on a fold of his blue jersey. 'Even the seine net is as hard work, and more constant, than the old winter-fishing small line. You're at it the whole time. The engine merely compels you to work the harder. You've got to keep going. Why? For a reason you never had in the old days: overhead expenses. The Bank won't let you off your interest. And it sees you pay your insurance company. And your gear—it doesn't stand up to the wear and tear long. And if you run an engine, you don't run it on air. You had hard times in the old days certainly. No one is denying that. But you hadn't this—threatening thing—behind you.'

'That's so,' said the old man quietly. 'But we often had our own debts and they seemed heavy enough sometimes.'

'That's so,' said the skipper soberly. 'When things are going against you, it's bad enough, whatever the age. We've got to do with it as it will do with us.'

'Unless you go in for the dole,' said the man who had already referred to this topic. He was a youngish, red-necked, strong fellow, and obviously had a story to tell. He did tell it, too; about three fellows who were employed to barrow stones, so that when their wealthy employer decided to build a dyke round his house the stones would be all in one place.

'Digging the old hole to fill it up again!'

'Never mind. Their employer—'

'Who was their employer?'

'Their employer was an Old Age Pensioner.'

There was a hearty laugh at that.

'Come on, you'll have another glass of beer,' added the red-necked man, who had clearly a humour of his own.

'No, no, Dan,' said the skipper. 'It's high time we were off, boy.'

'Where were you shot last night?' asked the old man.

'Off the north end of Skye,' answered the skipper. 'Three baskets of mackerel—that was all. I have never seen the herring scarcer.'

'Oh, man?'

'Yes. And I have never seen so many squeeb about.'

'Ah, that explains it,' said the old man. 'I remember . . .'

IX

Round Ardnamurchan

From Arisaig to Moidart is a land of sea lochs, shoals, rocks, sands that gleam like surf to distant eyes, hills, glens, and Jacobite history. But it would need, as the Arisaig yachtsman said, a special yacht to itself and most of a summer; while the land running out from Loch Moidart to Ardnamurchan Head—comparatively little known—has always had a special attraction for me.

But I resist the temptation of even touching on the history, with its 'Pickle the Spy' stories, or on such aspects of the country as I knew from previous contacts, for the Walshs had to be in Oban in two days, if they were to occupy their berths in the Glasgow-Dublin boat. It looked an impossible job for the *Thistle*, with the wind blowing, as we returned from Mallaig, and we gave up all hope of it. But in the morning there was a calm under heavy skies and I went ashore, roused them out of bed, and got them on board. With luck we would round Ardnamurchan that day and make Tobermory in Mull. We should see they got to Oban in two days somehow.

This was more like the thing! The previous evening Maurice and I had got the six splitpins and the two holding-down bolts where they should be. I swung the flywheel and off went all fourteen horses to a splendid start. Up the anchor and we were under way. Now I felt happy. And Toshan

Walsh was a sound woman to have on board, for she looked round about her and saw the sea in all the subtle varieties of that colour which blind people call leaden, and saw the land with the still houses and the still trees, and us going away from them, and the mountains hazed to an insubstantial pageant, and the islands opening, until she grew silent at the wonder thereof. And even Maurice himself admitted, listening to the engine, 'I like her beat.'

'Like her beat! If the barbarians of Kerry saw us now they would think it was the grand Day of Judgment.'

'They mightn't be far wrong,' said he, and touched some wood.

We had no difficulty at all coming out, except for one anxious moment—the tide was full and the whole look of the entrance altered—in picking up the last pole. I knew we had to stand in round the hump of land that projects on the port side, but the hunt for the pole gave everyone some excitement. Then we found it and in due course opened out the Small Isles and encountered the long slow roll of the open sea.

The yachtsman at Arisaig had suggested my keeping her on the island of Muck for a bit and then wearing round until we picked up the Bo Faskadale light—a red buoy, which we must comfortably clear to port. Soon the Ardnamurchan Head lighthouse raised its thin distant finger, and wearing off Muck we put her on what we took to be those rocks at the northern point of Coll, called the Cairns of Coll. But look and spy as we would, we could not pick up the Bo Faskadale red buoy. The hunt for it became a game with charts, land marks, field glasses, and compass. A real amateur's hunt, and with an ear for the engine, I enjoyed it.

But when we had crossed the line of Moidart sands and Castle Island (Eigg), it was high time somebody was seeing something, and when we opened out Rum between Eigg and

Muck, manifestly we should have the buoy abeam. On a direct course from Ruadh Arisaig to the Cairns of Coll one should almost run it down. When at last Maurice picked it up well inland, we all saw it. I had held on to Muck too long.

And now for Ardnamurchan, about the wildest spot on the whole West Coast, and notorious for its stormy seas; the one spot every amateur is warned against. And here we were heading for it on a long slow roll pleasant as slumber. An old-world sailing bark was rounding it under a full spread of canvas, and in the distance looked like a miniature craft that the keepers might be amusing themselves with. I was prepared, all the same, to give the Head a comfortable berth, but as at last we drew near I stood close in, for the Crew was wanting to experiment with her camera. We were gazing all eyes, the engine forgotten, when it missed a beat or two and was obviously going to peter out, but I dived quickly and opened the throttle, which staggered her a bit, until she resumed her beat again. Some drops of rain fell. A long black thundercloud lay out from Eigg. It was any sort of weather next, with the glass perceptibly falling. Southerly wind came freshening the water. Slowly that weather-worn headland with its grey-dark twisted strata fell astern. We could see no bird-life, except for an occasional gull floating like wind-blown thistledown against its immense southern wall. The scene at the height of a winter storm, passing into the dark of night, must be about as near to an inferno as the mind of man can conceive.

The Crew produced one of her celebrated light lunches, and we entered the Sound of Mull to the most plentiful bird life we had so far seen. Long lines of puffins, with their yellow parrot beaks, moved swiftly over the water, while guillemots came upon us like advance air columns of armies, low to the water, at a great speed, and in perfect formation.

They were obviously fishing up Loch Sunart and carrying their catches—we could see what looked like herring fry laid crossways in their beaks—to their young, possibly on the Cairns of Coll or still farther away. Once more we saw a solitary gannet. It rose between us and that pleasant looking settlement of Kilhoan behind Ardnamurchan Head. 'That's our lucky bird,' explained the Crew.

Loch Sunart penetrates so far inland that it comes within a few miles of making the land of Morven an island. We took an interest in finding the lie of the Red Rocks, the New Rocks, and the Stirk Rocks, that guard the southern entrance, and picked up the red buoy that marks their western reach; though by this time we were more concerned with the clear view of Runa Gall lighthouse, two or three miles beyond which should lie Tobermory.

We were soon abreast of Ardmore Point, where there used to be a tidy crofting hamlet, before it was cleared for sheep. This crofting area is interesting because, as I was later told in Tobermory, it was one of the last places where the ground was worked on the run-rig system and the whole farmed out on a communal basis. Each crofter was finally responsible for a single plot, after lots had been cast yearly over the subdivision of the common land. The system worked harmoniously over most of the Highland area, and if we may now think that the land was not put to the best use, we are judging from a standard of crop rotation and production that is universally quite modern. In these days rent was paid in kind and in labour. Even MacCrimmon's fees for teaching the bagpipe were expressed in terms of cows, and that did not lessen the coveted value of the diploma which he sealed with his own seal after it had been won. Another thing I was told about Ardmore: that it is a very good example of land, once cultivated, going back to a wilder and ranker state of nature than before it was originally broken in. The sheep paid for ten years. Then they didn't.

As we rounded Runa Gall lighthouse, glistening white and spick and span, the old anxiety over making a decent anchorage began to heave itself up. It was all very well struggling away in front of some crofters' houses, but a famed yachting centre, with its piers and daily steamers and smart yachtsmen with their smarter women and still smarter craft—with little else to do, likely, but watch a poor devil, struggling with the malignant demon that inhabits a thrawn bit of machinery, and misunderstanding the situation with the interest that demands amusement anyhow—that was a different kettle of fish entirely. Not to mention a very natural desire to do the thing decently before our friends. There certainly was no need to put them to shame, too. If only she would repeat her behaviour before Arisaig, I, on my part, promised myself a quite professional performance. But already—wasn't that a queer knock? There again. I refused to listen. The Arisaig yachtsman would certainly not have been able to open his mouth now! There it was again—a rat-tat-tat of metal. Let it rat!

For we were opening out the bay. I'd better try to reduce speed. I gave Maurice the helm and made to ease back the spark, but immediately got the impression that she would stop if I touched anything. Something was wrong—and pretty far wrong. We daren't stop here. And when I pushed my head up, there, still, was the bay, but where were the piers, the houses, the yachts? I actually consulted the chart—as though the blessed engine had hallucinated us.

I was told a story later by an engineer in Tobermory of a certain man who had bought a motor boat from a landed proprietor of this part of the world and on coming at full speed to anchor for the first time, went to pull the lever into neutral at the appropriate moment and while still a considerable distance from shore. But the lever, to his amazement, wouldn't budge. It is all too easy to imagine him tugging at it and tugging at it in an ever-mounting wrath while the smart craft sped on. Easier still to say afterwards that he might have done this or that. I, mercifully, had always closed the throttle. He forgot so simple an expedient, and his vessel charged up the distillery burn and became a total wreck. That he tried to get redress from the previous owner proves that he had a sanguine temperament. At least I could avoid the burn—and there it was (for Tobermory is tucked round a corner) with the distillery (now a wreck itself) beside it. And the houses along the front, and the two piers; but, by the grace of God, no yachts. A schooner lay at anchor off the inner or old pier and I made to pass outside her. Now for it! and I went to put the engine into neutral. At the third tug the lever came. And in the same moment it was as if a machine gun had gone mad in the cabin. The rat-tat-tatting at a terrific velocity was deafening. I shut her off. And she shut, and was quiet, and nothing more came from anywhere.

'What's gone wrong?'

'The whole bag of tricks, by the sound of it.'

A fellow on the schooner was idly watching us. I shouted, asking him if we would do where we were. But he cried us to come in. I got into the dinghy, tied the end of a rope to the seat I sat on, while Maurice got a hold forward, and rowed away. She came like a penitent lamb. Not that that softened me. She had taken us here. She had never let us down. What if she had gone phut off Ardnamurchan? I was not interested. When the man on the schooner indicated that we were right, I got on board again and we let go the anchor. 'You're fine there,' he shouted. 'Thank you,' I acknowledged, and dried my sweat. We had arrived once more.

X

An t'Eilean Muilleach

We had anchored about fifty yards inshore from where the Spanish galleon had been sunk, and when we landed and went, by chance, to the Mishnish Hotel on the front, the proprietor showed us a piece of African blackwood which had once been part of the sea-going might of Spain. For after the defeat of the Armada in 1588 many galleons had come up the west coast of Scotland, and in certain outlying islands there are supposed to be discerned in some of the inhabitants to this day physical characteristics of a somewhat Spanish cast.

A legend of grandeur and knightliness centred round that old Spain, and you can see the process of transition into the folk conception in the song *The Spanish Lady*, which I had heard only in Ireland—until, the night before I bought my boat, Eoin had sung it in Skye with all the Irish vivacity. Curiously enough he had first heard the song sung by his mother in Skye when he was a little boy, and she certainly had never been in touch with Ireland.

Now to give a true scholar's interpretation of this word 'folk', I should like to quote from the Introduction to *Popular Tales of the West Highlands*, orally collected by J. F. Campbell, himself a great traveller and student of the folk-lore of many lands. '. . . it may be said that there are hundreds of other books as well known in England as those mentioned above, of which neither I nor my collectors have ever found a trace. . . . There are no gorgeous palaces, and elegant fairies; there are no enchanters flying in chariots drawn by winged griffins; there are no gentle knights and gentle dames; no spruce cavaliers and well-dressed ladies; no heroes and heroines of fashionable novels; but, on the contrary, everything is popular. Heroes are as wild, and unkempt, and savage as they probably were in fact, and kings are men as they appear in Lane's translations of the *Arabian Nights*.'

Mr. Campbell collected his tales round about 1860, so he did not know of our fashionable novels which do in fact attempt to bring to life well-known figures from the past, and even to translate them into the present, whereby, say, Helen of Troy may be readily understood in Mayfair. But being done in an ultra-smart fashion and with the witty idea of debunking greatness, the result is perhaps a trifle anaemic; certainly nothing like this:

The Spanish Lady

As I walked down through Dublin City
At the hour of twelve of the night,
Who should I spy but a Spanish lady
Washing her feet by candle light.
First she washed them, then she dried them,
O'er a fire of amber coal,
In all my life I ne'er did see
A maid so neat about the sole.

Whack for the too-ra loo-ra lady
Whack for the too-ra loo-ra lee,
Whack for the too-ra loo-ra lady,
Whack for the too-ra loo-ra lee.

An t'Eilean Muilleach

As I came back through Dublin City
At the hour of half-past eight,
Who should I spy but a Spanish lady
Brushing her hair in broad daylight;
First she tossed it, then she brushed it,
On her lap was a silver comb,
In all my life I ne'er did see
So fair a maid since I did roam.
Whack, etc.

As I went down through Dublin City
When the sun began to set,
Who should I see but a Spanish lady
Catching a moth in a golden net;
When she saw me then she fled me,
Lifting her petticoat over the knee,
In all my life I ne'er did spy
A maid so blithe as the Spanish lady.
Whack, etc.

The galleon had sunk in Tobermory Bay after an explosion, and was believed to hold treasure to the value of well over a quarter of a million sterling. Three hundred and fifty officers and men are said to have gone down with her. She settled in clay to a depth of thirty feet, and many abortive efforts were made to recover the treasure, until, in 1912, modern salvage gear did fish up some goblets, dishes, and coins, if not the vast treasure itself.

The landlord being not only a good host but a very knowledgeable one, Walsh and he were soon deep in a discussion concerning the disposition of the Highland clans in this part of the world, Macleans, Clanranalds, an' all. Mull is Maclean land and, besides its interesting history, is reputed to be one of the most beautiful of all the western islands.

An t'Eilean Muilleach

Many a time in a spirited céilidh had we roared out the chorus of

An t'Eilean Muilleach (The Isle of Mull)

The Isle of Mull is of isles the fairest,
Of ocean's gems 'tis the first and rarest;
Green grassy island of sparkling fountains,
Of waving woods and high tow'ring mountains.

Tho' far from home I am now a ranger,
In grim Newcastle a doleful stranger,
The thought of thee stirs my heart's emotion,
And deeper fixes its fond devotion.

Dr. Johnson: 'A most dolorous country.'

For ourselves, after spending many days on its coasts, we sing the song with greater fervour than ever, even if we missed the fountains.

The water front of Tobermory, with its sickle of houses, has a slightly foreign appearance—but this may be due to no more than that it was deliberately built as a fishing station in 1788. The streets on the steep slopes above the front are well laid out and very clean, with red postal boxes and tidy gardens. Trees are everywhere around the bay, which is wide and spacious and an excellent anchorage, being protected on its exposed or eastern side by the island of Calve. By the northern entrance yachts and steamers of all sizes come and go. Our concern over our guests reaching Oban the following day was immediately dispelled when we discovered a twice-daily steamer service to that town—on one trip the twenty-four miles being covered in about an hour and a half. So we stretched our legs on the steep slopes of the town and, proceeding inland, discovered an undulating wooded country not unlike that of the south-west of Ireland.

An t'Eilean Muilleach

We had some excellent fresh fish for supper, and congratulated the landlord on such evidence of local enterprise, telling him of our difficulties in this respect on the West. He smiled. 'Unless a trawler drops in, we get all our white fish from Aberdeen. That's from Aberdeen.'

So he had the laugh on us. Once up in Kinlochbervie I explained how I had seen crofting housewives buying Aberdeen fish from a roadside van, while some friends were out in a boat in the bay getting quite a good catch. 'How nice it must be', said the Crew wistfully, 'to have plenty of money.'

Towards evening several yachts came in, all under auxiliary power, white, blue, lovely craft. They floated in with assurance, took soundings, slid ahead, found the desired spot, dropped anchor, and, with a boil of reverse, paid out chain. So quietly, so efficiently done! I felt we had no right to be here at all. What to us was a long-drawn-out anxiety and excitement was to them a normal performance, like taking a booked seat in a theatre. And when at night they lowered their flags and hung out their riding lights, humiliation could do little more than have an amused smile to itself. Having seen a three-light navigation lamp on board, I had in these early busy days possibly assumed the existence of a riding light. But there was no riding light. We had, however, a three-and-sixpenny storm lantern (or so it was called) and about eleven o'clock at night, when I thought nobody was looking, I stole out and hung it up on the forestay. There was a thick smirr of rain, a heavy sky, and a moderate wind. I watched the wick flutter till my head got wet. Then I ducked into the cabin and with an electric torch—the only other light on board—saw the Crew's concern for my difficulty; whereat we both laughed, and the water being hot in the kettle—it had a habit of being hot about this time—I brewed such a soothing draught as no other craft could produce in that bay, and we drank it as we lay in our bunks looking out through the grey light of the open doors.

This last hot drink with a slow cigarette was the day's luxury, its perfect all-reconciling end. We envied nobody anything. We realised, in the warmth of that beneficent concoction, that yachting with two or three white-capped professionals, who know every anchorage, was doubtless very pleasant, but also very easy. God bless them, we were doing grand! And we had lured our two friends through some of the finest scenery in Scotland in order to take them round one of its stormiest headlands, killing in the process any tendency towards either boredom or museful rhapsodizing by making them hunt rocks and buoys, study charts, and hope for the best. The engine lay in a bad, perhaps a ruinous, condition, and the boat was making far too much water for comfort, but, after all, we were here, and with luck and decent weather we might go farther. The weather had certainly been broken, so there was always the chance it might mend. On Eigg last year they had had months of perfect weather, blue skies and sparkling seas, until they had thought it was never going to end.

I went out for my last look around. The lights were still bright in the Mishnish hotel, where our friends were safely housed. Farthest out in the bay, the *S.Y. Killarney* was a blaze in every porthole, and as I stood there the orchestra played 'God save the King' to its army of trippers. Very wonderful she looked in the grey night light with its smother of fine rain. Not far from her a puffer had come to anchor. A sailing yacht of ten to fifteen tons, all white and beautifully lined, lay light in the water as a seabird; and in from her, a blue yacht of about the same size, was already asleep. Other craft, larger and smaller, swung to their riding lights; and our friend the schooner, a dark hulk on the grey water, lay in a friendly way close to us. The contrast between puffer and schooner on the one hand and the pleasure craft on the other was strangely marked, and one's heart went out to those toilers who do so much to keep the whole show going. I glanced at our own light, an uncertain feeble flicker, but burning still. 'What are you smiling at?' said the Crew. No one could see anyone smiling in the dark. But there are moments when she is like that.

I ran into the skipper of the schooner the following morning. He was a disappointed man, though with the undemonstrative toughness or endurance that goes with the Glasgow accent. In such an encounter, you can read the whole history of the Clyde. The accent may not have what is deemed polish or suavity, but it has pith and nearly always a natural gaiety or optimism. It is the speech of men of brains who make things with their hands. Fine obliging men to meet, too, prepared to be friendly, and at their best doing you a good turn. There is a similar sort of gaiety or optimism in the Cockney, perhaps; though he may have lost that toughness of fibre that naturally enough characterises the engineer, for metropolitan shopkeeping has other needs. The schooner carried a hundred tons of coal and supplied lighthouses and odd merchants in outlying places. The previous Saturday, when I knew there had been a good swell running, she had actually gone into the narrow rocky fissure that is the harbour for Ardnamurchan lighthouse.

'Surely you had difficulty in getting in?'

'No. There's a foot or two to spare on each hand.'

'But the swell?'

'Ay. Ye've got to watch that.'

That wasn't his trouble now. At six o'clock this morning he had set off for Kilhoan with a few tons of coal for a merchant—to find that the puffer had beaten him to it, and as two vessels could not unload at the same time, there had been nothing for him to do but come back and wait. The loss of a whole day! 'If only I'd guessed, I'd have been off at four,' he said, a philosophic grudge in his voice. He had a 40 h.p. Kelvin engine, reconditioned four years ago. 'No; no trouble,' he assured me, 'and it has done thousands of miles now.' He deserved that piece of luck.

Lying at the jetty was an old smack with the lovely name of *Anna Bhan* (Fair Anna). She was being tarred all over before running forty tons of gravel to Coll.

So Tobermory presented its contrasts.

Altogether it was an island of contrasts. Once Mull carried a population of 8,000, I was told, whereas now it is little over 2,000 (2,388 in 1931), and of that total Tobermory itself accounts for 800. How did the population diminish? I wish I could think of some new answer. And the attitude of the inhabitants themselves? Those of the older generation will tell you that the young will not stay. It is not only now an economic problem, but a defeatist or psychological problem. And that lands us back in history again.

For Mull is indeed a self-contained island garden when compared, say, with the Faroes, a group of a score of islands lying away towards the Arctic Circle some two hundred miles north-west of the Shetlands. But in these treeless isles with their deep fiords and dangerous currents, there is an industrious and thriving population of nearly 26,000. Yet their total area is only 540 square miles against Mull's 350. In the last ten years the *increase* in the population of the Faroes is about 50 per cent. greater than the total Mull population. It is the sort of sum in arithmetic that those forever crying for outside aid might ponder before delivering themselves positively of the right answer.

Our visitors departed at four o'clock for Oban by the S.S.

King George V, and once the vessel had slid from the pier, the Crew turned away saying it was not lucky to stand and wave. Perhaps it is not very easy, when you are sorry to see good friends going.

So I tried to get hold of the mechanic who had been recommended to me, and, by one of the coincidences that are stranger than fiction, discovered it was he who had sold the *Thistle* to the man from whom I had bought her in Skye. Incidentally I found out a great deal more, in particular the date of the sale, the price paid, and the age of some of the gear. I felt a bit of a fool. Though, after all, I had no one to blame but myself, for I could have checked up details before concluding my bargain. But that would have been tedious, and life is short.

The engineer and I spent a day and a half on the engine. He was trained in a Glasgow engineering shop, and it was interesting to see how he set about the work. What had been done and what had not been done were made perfectly clear. He remembered the very bolts he himself had put in and demonstrated how they had been misplaced. The chain on the reverse gear was so stretched that it was inclined to hit the casing. He had a good second-hand chain, and in his workshop he made a bolt for it, threaded the bolt, holed it for a splitpin, and fitted the lot satisfactorily. With rusted bolts, he had a slow persuasive way, and they all obeyed him. Our ultimate fear was the discovery of a broken ball race, for in such a case we should undoubtedly be held up for many days, as Glasgow was our nearest depot.

At the end of ten hours' concentrated labour on that first day, with most of the engine adrift, we discovered that the terrific machine-gun racket which had heralded our arrival had been caused by the flywheel hitting a small projecting part of the tin pan underneath it and could have been put right by a decent kick!

However, we also discovered so many things done badly that the long labour was worth while. I was feeling pretty tired from the continuous cramped stooping, and, on tightening the coupling bolts of the shaft, let the spanner slip under strain, and so came full tilt against the engine, splitting a temple and piercing my left ear. After a time I got the bleeding stopped and felt that now that the brute had had blood, she might behave more reasonably. On the trial trip, the following afternoon, she again stopped suddenly on coming to anchor. The engineer took the pilot jet adrift and underneath the gauze found the accumulated dirt of years. No wonder slow-running had been difficult!

I paid my bill with pleasure, and would suggest to any yachtsman in trouble with his engine in Tobermory that he need not despair so long as Mr. Ogilvy is there to assist him. With sufficient time and scrap, he might even build him a new one!

So we were due a day or two's holiday. I felt like going to sea with the lobster fishers, but the time was unfortunate, for they were 'making nothing of it'. They were fishing from beyond Ardnamurchan to well down the Sound of Mull, and one man, to whom we spoke, after a last fruitless round had taken all his creels home with him in despair.

The weather worsened, too, and the bay was soon filled with yachts. The Highland voices of the crews came across the water as they made all shipshape and here and there put out a second anchor. As we lay inactive in a downpour that lasted nearly two days, the sight of such wealth somehow became depressing. A thousand insignificant strokes etched the picture of contrasts. The island gulls were in great evidence; scavengers waiting for the buckets to be emptied.

Whenever one dived by a yacht's side, even at an empty match box, all the others were upon it. You could see their constant eager watchfulness lest they miss anything. A mute swan, also on the watch, would eat out of your hand. The black eye, snail-black boss on the beak, the reptile-like fringe at the sides of the mouth—a scavenger, too. Dependent on the tourist industry. I thought of the puffins and guillemots heading out of Loch Sunart in formation as of a life swift and clean and fearless.

An honest Glasgow voice told a story with simple wonder of an Islander who was so overwhelmed with pleasure when he saw his chieftain-landlord coming that he would throw his bonnet into the ditch and, bowing low, run eagerly to meet him.

'What ye'd call a serf?' he questioned.

'It's more complicated than that,' I suggested. 'Serfs don't usually run to meet their masters.'

'Unless—they think they're going to get something?'

'They didn't get much.'

'No, but—ach t'hell, anyway.'

'Quite so.'

And there followed a passage or two of history. The Scots are pretty good at history. Which, perhaps, is why most of them mistrust it. For it is full of facts, most of them ugly.

It is full of other things, too, but they tend to get lost or mislaid. Descendants of the MacVurichs, bards to Clanranald, may still be found in Tobermory, and a very intelligent merchant assured me that there is one who still extemporises poetry and recently produced a broadside of satiric contemporary verse that split his sides. Also one who knows all the history not only of this part of the world, with its clans and chiefs and battles long ago, but also of Ireland, thus uniting in himself the old seanachaidh, the complete

Gael. But the true inwardness here is difficult to penetrate, without time and some knowledge, particularly of Gaelic. For the normal tourist, it is impossible to penetrate, being beyond picturesqueness or the presence of unusual personal attributes, good or bad. For here, I suppose, nothing less than a whole way of civilisation got lost or mislaid.

When the rain ceased I picked out all the putty round the skylight windows with a chisel, while the Crew followed me, cleaning and reputtying. With the sun shining, the bay, tricked out in wooded slopes and shimmering yachts, looked a lovely sight, and life a dancing holiday. Gloom and sunlight: perhaps you need the one for the other, and whenever you get too much of the one, the other seems very precious. The Crew, with shattering extravagance, presented a young lettuce to the swan. 'After all the dry biscuits and things,' she explained. The swan agreed. Then she drew my attention to the beauty of the gulls, as they circled and heeled, very white in the sun. 'You had better give them some of your "Macnair's Crax" ', I suggested, referring to a private hoard of very special biscuits. But she only laughed. If she did not care so much for things that crept or leapt or flew or grew it would make life simpler often.

She had a new oilskin cloth sort of decoration for the cabin walls behind the bunks. 'Its pure white tones with the pantry box,' she observed. 'It will keep away any drips, too.' Clearly she had not been idle ashore while we had slaved away at the engine. If only we had been able to get the boat on to a slipway, we should probably have found the offending nail or two responsible for the bilge leak. However, the amount coming in was not alarming and the new pump was working effectively. Actually the boat had been very little used in her long life—apart from the last two or three years in Skye—and under Mr. Ogilvy's ownership she had been oiled and varnished so thoroughly that I at last understood why paint chipped easily off her hull. A simple all-round overhaul and she would still be an excellent sea boat. When my brother arrived for ten days, we were ready to give her a further trial.

XI

Round the Caliach

A westerly wind was blowing gently over Tobermory, but the sky looked stormy. A yachtsman of a ten tonner assured us that the west of Mull would be 'uncomfortable' for our boat; and, as it turned out, he was right. However, we wanted to be off, for we had now been a good week in Tobermory, and though we had enjoyed its variety very well, we felt we could do with a more secluded anchorage.

Not until we had rounded Ardmore Point and put her on the Caliach, did we feel the real sea. Here the white caps were racing over a vivid deep sparkling blue, and with the forward plunge—for the wind was about sou'west and head on —the passage was alive with exhilarating movement. And now I could enjoy it in the proper holiday mood, for my brother (whom the Crew dubbed the Mate) was used to heavy seas in a small boat, and I suppose responsibility does account for some leakage of vitality over a long run. Soon we opened out Ardnamurchan and the full length of our old friend, the Scuir of Eigg, with dents in its upturned keel. Then Rum, Canna, low to the sea, and, beyond, the hills of Skye. Westward, the Cairns of Coll, Coll itself, with a dull glitter on its bare rocks as they ran into Tiree. If, when we came abreast of Caliach Point, we should find a beam sea too uncomfortable for us, we had made up our minds to keep heading into it until we fetched Loch nan Eathar in Coll, where there is a good anchorage in a westerly wind.

But Mull had been playing tricks with the wind, and soon we found it blowing from about sou'sou'west. As the sun came out strongly, the breeze seemed to freshen, but the glass was going up and we could read the sky well enough to have no great fears. Yet we could see the Mate was restless, for he was working out in his mathematical head what would happen should the engine, of which he had heard things, decide to break down. This high boat, with its comparatively shallow draught, would certainly be uncomfortable if left broadside on and helpless. As we passed Loch Cuan in Mull, the rocks at its entrance threw white streamers which were wonderfully beautiful but not perhaps inspiring. And a long drift would provide an excellent close-up of the rocks of Ardnamurchan, which would be merciless enough to-day. But I liked the beat of the engine. It had never been so assured.

However, a trapeze act had to be performed to the forecastle and the sails brought forth, and in the cockpit they were carefully gone over until the Mate had the hang of their lacings and sheets. 'A light little gaff and simple traveller that you could run up in a second would suit me better,' was his comment. I defended; and we argued rigs until we found ourselves standing more closely for the Caliach than I had intended, for according to our *Directions* a tide rip extends outward from the Point for a distance of about two miles. As we were now on a tide ebbing strongly against the wind, there should be a nice jabble; but it was a trifle too late for a two mile detour, so we kept our eyes open and passed the Caliach about half a mile out in a short piled-up sea. But it was never more than thoroughly uncomfortable, and I was pleased to see the Mate gain some respect for the sea-going qualities of our craft.

Round the Caliach

As we bore south we brought the wind a few points to starboard, and though we continued to be tossed about a bit, there was never any danger. And the seas were really alive, a vivid pulsing blue. In the bright sun and flying cloud, the freshness was entrancing.

Calgary Bay looked inviting with its sands and woods, and south of it the terraced formation of the land was very striking. The terraces rose one behind the other in perfect parallels, as if they had been artificially made. The same old basaltic formation as we had met in Skye, of course, only very much bolder and more clearly defined. Each terrace represented an outpouring of lava, and when, as in the mountain of Ben Mor, which we could now see, the total depth of the terraces is about 3,000 feet, and when we recognised that such a depth—or height—must have extended across the area over which we were now sailing, the mind grew a bit dizzy at thought of the magnitude of the denudation that had gone on in what is spoken of as recent geological time. For manifestly *flowing* lava would not build itself *up* in neat terraces and ignore the gaping void below! It would naturally have searched for hollows to flow into, and these high terraces that now rise over the sea tell their own tale. They are green, and, as Ben Mor stood out clearly before us, we were very impressed. The cloud shadows lay on its vast bulk like sky starfish. The green became a sombre sage green, and over its immensities, unbroken by tree or jagged rock, was that imponderable air of the immemorial.

But the sea does not permit indulgence in land reveries, not for very long, for Treshnish Point was falling astern, and we had to make up our minds what we were going to do. The Treshnish Isles, opening out to starboard in their flat rectangular rock formations, low to the sea, were a continuous and ever varying attraction. The Dutchman's Cap, from an easterly aspect, is ultra-modern in the severity of its lines, compared with the island north of it (Lunga) in which the Crew from one point found a remarkable resemblance to Napoleon's hat.

But the Mate had discovered low on the horizon what he believed from the chart to be Staffa, while I wondered about a boss of rock obviously much farther away and a little to the west. It could not be Dubh Artach lighthouse, for that was much too far distant to be seen. Nor apparently was it the end of the Ross of Mull, judging from the configuration of the land. It did not look like an island but like a rock coming up out of the sea, and we could not find a likely rock anywhere on our chart. Every now and again this mysterious rock drew our attention—as it must have drawn the attention of Vikings and Gaels, pirates and pilgrims, throughout the centuries.

As the day went on we opened out Loch Tuadh, got Ulva Island on our port beam, and the Mate was showing a considerable degree of confidence in our general position. I watched him working out the game of chances.

'You see', he explained, 'if anything happened now, we could make one or two sheltered anchorages in the north of Ulva Island. I could sail her into them easily.'

'Fine.'

'And just round the southern point of the island, there's a good anchorage we could run into, called—called—'

'Gometra,' I said.

The Crew smiled. 'It's an old game now,' she explained. 'He always has a few anchorages up his sleeve.'

The Mate laughed, delighted.

I suggested that in fact I shouldn't mind landing on Ulva, as it afforded a quite outstanding spectacle of social devastation, consequent upon land clearances, and said that Dr.

Johnson and his Scotch satellite had been there and also in the neighbouring island of Inch Kenneth, where the Doctor was astonished to discover civilisation in quite shapely forms.

'So long as we know,' said the Mate, holding a steady southerly course. And they both laughed.

'Aren't you impressed by Johnson's visit?'

'Not particularly, at the moment. In fact the only thing that impressed me in the whole affair was the old boy's philosophic behaviour in dirty weather. Remember the night they made Coll? By heavens, it was a filthy night. And the old lad lay like a log, sick as a dog, and abused no one. Full marks.'

'And he really hated the whole show. How he hated it! It was somewhere hereabouts, wasn't it, that he confided in Boswell his real opinion. He would not wish not to be disgusted in the Highlands, he said, for that would be to lose the power of distinguishing, and a man might then lie down in the middle of them. He wished only, he said, to conceal his disgust.'

Somehow it sounded good, and we laughed merrily; for it was a self-portrait to the life.

A few months before, two English travellers, following in Johnson's footsteps through the Highlands, had told me how astonished they were to find little knowledge of Johnson's visit, and even less concern about it, in any part of Scotland.

In the modern phrase, Johnson had failed to register. His dislike of the Scots was made obvious enough, yet it never raised any real opposition. No legend of antipathy to the man has been created. Whether this is evidence of a complacency even greater than Johnson's own, or whether his prejudices were so strong that they became idiosyncratic and amusing, it is difficult to say. He would not wish *not* to be disgusted!

One thinks of him hanging on to it—and the laugh is out spontaneously.

The unfortunate weather was another matter, for when at last we drew abreast of Staffa we found that we could not land. Our disappointment was keen, but as we watched the seas heave from under us and rush on the rocks we realised there was no help for it. Had we known our ground intimately, we might have risked dropping anchor somewhere and then tried to have stolen ashore in the dinghy, and with this thought in mind we did keep tossing about the island for fully half an hour, but in our ignorance clearly the proceeding would be beyond a reasonable risk. In fact, once or twice I got my heart in my mouth, when I felt what I thought was the ground-swing of the water, for the Crew was anxious for a photograph and we all wanted to see what we could. The photographs turned out to be failures, apparently from over-exposure. They were all taken at 1/100th of a second, but presumably the lens should have been closed more, for the amount of light about was really extraordinary. The sea was dancing alive with it; the broken tops of the waves dazzled the eyes with their whiteness; and heaving into the caves went billows of green fire.

Usually the show places of a country are disappointing, but I must say Staffa was arresting. We had never seen anything quite like its pillared rock formation, for at first glance it struck in us an incredulous note, as if the southern rock face had been artificially carved into high-relief columns and then the whole erection given a slight tilt. It certainly did not look like a piece of work by haphazard nature. The economy, the precision, the regularity seemed altogether too human, and, from the sea, rocks rarely appear very large or massive, in the way, say, a cathedral appears from a pavement, or the rocks themselves from their crests. Staffa is not at all spectacular in the grand manner. It comes upon one with an air of surprise and wonder, like a work of genius in a picture frame. And what I regretted missing most of all was not a close view of the perfect symmetry of the columns, but the colours of them and of the seaweed and of the water in Fingal's Cave, with movement in the colours and in the underwater light. We could hear the modulated note of the booming wave, and remembered the old Gaelic name, *Uaimh Bhinn*, 'the melodious cavern'.

We had a look at the entrance to the Clam-shell Cave, with its twisted pillars, the Boat Cave, and McKinnon's, but when we finally put her about off the rocks on the western side and saw what seas were breaking there, we bade farewell to Staffa, for it was not the wind that bothered us but the sliding treacherous swell, on which, however, we had managed a few exciting moments—particularly the Crew. Perhaps the circumstances had been a trifle more dramatic than those that attend the usual visitors, and the wind and brilliant sun and flashing seas had given the rocks a glittering and memorable beauty.

So we consoled ourselves, anyhow, as we held south— and perceived at last, beyond doubt, that the mysterious rock which had guided us since we had rounded the Caliach was no other than the round hill of Dun-I in Iona.

At the back of all our possible landfalls on this day, Iona had been waiting, and now here at last it was, only an hour or two away.

'What about it?' asked the Mate.

But I couldn't see how we could make it. From what I had read, I knew that the swell must be coming right up the narrow sound between Iona and the Ross of Mull. There would be a tide too, and on the Iona side there seemed to be

Leaving Tobermory

Thistle, Skipper and Crew

Croft on the Isle of Skye

Rum from Eigg

Crofting landscape, Isle of Skye

McLeod's Maidens

Runa Gall

Tobermory with Maurice Walsh

Calgary Bay, North Mull

Fingal's Cave, Staffa

Iona

Bull Hole off Iona

Loch Etive

Hanging on in the rain in the Caledonian Canal

very little in the way of shelter. We had had enough movement and adventure for the day, and on the sheltered north
coast of the Ross there was one obvious anchorage, where
we could go to sleep in a quiet calm. I asked him to look up
Loch Lathaich.

Agreement was unanimous. From Loch Lathaich, too,
we could find out about the Sound. With our minds made up
and the old engine plugging away stolidly, we felt in very
good spirits.

It was at that moment that the Crew saw the cloud over
Iona, on whose northern rocks and pale sands the sea broke
white.

It was quite a small cloud, not much bigger than a good
puff from a railway train, at no great height, and the colour
of pipe tobacco smoke. It was the only low cloud of its kind
far as our eyes could travel, for high in the heavens were
cirrus and blue fields, and where it could have come from we
had no idea, for it was a real cloud and its tenuous blue was
irradiated with light. The Crew said it was a sign.

'A good sign?'

'It's a sign,' she said, with an enigmatic smile and a nod to
herself.

Here was evidence of the curious superstition that grows
in one against naming certain things at sea, and we laughed
and said she was frightened to say yes or no lest she might
'alter it'. But she would not be drawn. Along the Moray
Firth coasts there used to be many words that a fisherman
would never mention at sea, such as clergyman, salmon,
rabbit, and for these there were special words. The rabbit,
for example, was 'clever feet' or 'clever feeties'. When a
member of the crew took God's name in vain there was a
cry of 'cold iron', and each held on to the nearest bit of iron
until the danger passed. I can just remember, as a very small

boy, the strange shock I got on learning that the skipper of a certain boat had turned back one morning on his way to sea because he met an old woman who was reputed to be a witch. I knew her by sight well. She always wore a black skirt, a closely wound black shawl that came up over her head and framed her wrinkled face, and she was bent.

Now I have never been much influenced by such superstitions or taboos, unless indeed in a sort of inverse fashion, so that by passing under a ladder or taking the number thirteen or spilling the salt, I actually hope to attract luck. Haeckel and Huxley did have an effect on our early teens, and to this day I can repeat the lengthy advice to the seeker after truth to beware of the Idols of the Tribe, meaning thereby. . . .

To-day the advice tends to come from the philosophic economist, like Marx, and youth finds, possibly, a greater thrill in conning and remembering it, because of the revolutionary impulse that demands action.

Yet here, at sea, the mind slips momentarily. The certainties of our industrial civilisation are not always in evidence. Neither the Douglas Theorem nor the Marxian Dialectic would help us *if* the engine broke down. So we fall into the habit of using *if*. 'If we manage round into the Sound to-morrow, we should with any luck be able to . . .' When someone says, 'I know it is going to be a good morning,' we look as if we hadn't heard. We all inwardly believe, from the signs, that at long last it is going to be a good morning, but why say it? Why risk saying it? Why permit the boast of our knowledge to be, as it were, overheard? Very foolish, and indeed, in bad taste. To these old fishermen, beating west to Castlebay in their small part-decked sailing boats, the nearest of all the gods, the omnipresent, the incalculable, the terribly swift, was Death.

Before setting out each of us had written on a sheet of

paper what we hoped would pass for wills (for unwitnessed holograph wills are good enough in Scotland). Instinctively, I suppose, we felt it was as well to give the Old One respectful recognition.

So the Crew refused to say anything about the cloud over Iona, as we headed for the white beacon that marks the east point of a group of islets lying in the entrance to Loch Lathaich. We could pass this group on either hand, and decided on the eastern passage, so that the loch, which is one and a half miles long, could be opened up. In this game of approaching unknown anchorages, we had become firm believers in the wisdom of opening out the maximum that can be seen, before proceeding to a decision or final action. In this way it is astonishing how what had appeared rather alarming in the *Directions*, or impossible in the small-scale chart, lays its problem open for an obvious and even easy solution.

It was while we were on this course that we got a first view of that massive headland between Loch na Keal and Loch Scridain that rises in terraced grandeur to Ben Mor. It is a whole peninsula rather than a headland, and during the days we spent in Loch Lathaich, waiting sea weather, it impressed us in its ever-varying atmospheric effects more profoundly than any other place we saw. It came and went, loomed gigantic or withdrew in mists and twilights, primordial and everlasting.

We gave the beacon on Eilean Lathanach a fairly wide berth, and, being warned that the east side of the loch is very foul, crossed towards the west but not too close. We now discerned the two islands, Goat Island and White Island, towards the head of the loch and knew we could stand in behind the latter for an anchorage in two and a half fathoms. But when we had opened out this anchorage we also opened out a short arm of the sea, called Loch Caol, running west-ward, and saw a motor boat of about our own size or some-what larger well within what seemed ideal shelter. Our *Directions* did mention Loch Caol, but with the instruction to anchor in the mouth of it. We were going one better than that! So I slowed down all I could, while the Mate steered ahead, intending to drop anchor well short of the other boat. But within a minute the Crew was crying, 'Look at the weeds!'

It was an extraordinary display of the weed *chorda filum*. I could feel the cords gathering round the shaft, choking the blades, and slowing us up, so I promptly stopped the engine. Though we were in about two fathoms, the upper parts of the weed streamed along the surface, combed by the tide. We estimated the length of some of them at thirty feet, yet two or three dozen of them, hauled from the bottom, could be found adhering to a single pebble not much bigger than a pigeon's egg. They were about the thickness of boot laces, brown, tapering finely at each end, and tough. Many a time in the days and anchorages to follow did a minnow give a tug for the fisherman to observe laconically, 'Chorda filum.'

We could not see the propellors in their brown nest, so getting into the dinghy the Mate towed us back a little way, and we dropped anchor. The boat hook cleared the shaft in a short time, and, in any case, we decided the weed was slimy enough to act as grease! Moreover, we had had a great sea day and—we had arrived.

XII

The Ross of Mull

The hour or two after arrival provide a relaxation that is extremely pleasant. I had thought, before we started out, of long quiet evenings, when a man might get the size and balance of things. And evenings like these were given. I can still hear the thin piping note of a young oyster-catcher, haunting the still night with its plaint, like a new-born infant a darkened tenement, a spiring wail out of the gulf, a beginning in pain and fear carrying already the overtone of the end. On nights like these, things come whole into a silence that the brimming and choking and recession of the sea deepen unfathomably.

But the general picture of actual living conditions was much thicker or grosser—particularly in the hour or two following the making of a good anchorage, when the hissing of the primus stove and the smell and taste of food enwrap released bodies in a divine ease. One sits, feet out, and goes over the events of the day, and exhorts the Crew, now cook, and takes what comes, and feels the sun and the wind and the rain and the glitter all warm in the face and lazy in the shoulders and at rest in the legs; while the only touch of mystery or wonder is in the astonishing amount the other fellow prepares himself to consume. Good nature moves about this festival too lazy to laugh outright, but full of nods and sly sayings and frank remembrances. 'All that I am hoping', says the Mate in a doleful voice, 'is that I'll be able to get a blink of sleep to-night.' Now he sleeps exactly like an Egyptian mummy. But should a man who so sleeps chance to be disturbed for two minutes in some silent watch, the morning memory of it is multiplied like a reflection in a room of mirrors, until the whole night has become peopled with his restlessness. A luxurious picture of suffering that, once established, he does not readily give up. And particularly when it draws mockery from the Crew. 'I'm afraid I cannot take all this,' he complains, prepared with a forearm of defence. 'You just leave what you can't eat,' says the Crew. 'All right,' he agrees, resignedly.

However often these fatuous things are repeated, or suggested in dumb play, they never lose some air of drollery, something of friendliness caught from the rigours of the day. It is not the moment for wit, hardly even for humour, certainly not for seriousness: it is a moment for the body and requires some invention of drollery to be chuckled at despite oneself.

Then the question of to shave or not to shave, seeing we must go ashore, and the Book says, 'Shop. P.O. Tel. Inn at Bunessan.' The evening is fair and fresh and we can stroll there looking at all the new things on the way. If we shaved now, then we shouldn't have to shave to-morrow. Moreover, we never care about drinking direct out of the water tank, and after a strenuous and exciting day the body is, in sober truth, wrung dry. Finally the Mate carries a packet of blue blades that make shaving almost a luxury, and he is very generous with them. So we shave in the cockpit and wash in the salt water, and by the time the Mate has combed his hair —about which he continues to be particular—the Crew appears complete with milkpail, handbag, and creases in her blue trousers. And we sally forth on dry land.

'What's the time?' asks the Mate suddenly, for only the Crew carries a watch.

'Half-past eight,' she answers.

Lengthening his stride a little, he observes, 'I wonder why the fellow who compiled the *Clyde Cruising Club Sailing Directions* thought of inserting "Inn at Bunessan"? Why Inn? What, strictly speaking, has that got to do with navigation? I have been trying to think it out, but can make little of it.'

'Look!' says the Crew, and dives to the ditchside where some curious weed is growing.

'Marvellous!' agrees the Mate, absent-mindedly getting between her and the ditch.

'I hope', she says, 'we'll be able to get some milk.' And then she spies a croft house well off the road.

'But why get milk there now—then carry it into Bunessan —and then carry it back?' he asks with helpful logic.

But Bunessan is farther away than we thought, and by the time we reach the roadside public hall, we find that it is nine o'clock and that the district is *en fête* with a cake and candy sale. As we enter the village, the Crew asks a woman where she can get milk and is directed to the inn—'round the back'.

The Mate, shaking his head sadly at this conjunction, leads us round the back and we find ourselves in a crush of men in a dark passage. After he has had a few confidential words with a black-haired maid, we are led into the dining room in front, and there the Crew at last arranges for a bucket of milk.

After we had wished one another a continuance of good health, there was no great hurry, and in the shop that is also the post office, we got fresh stores, including tomatoes that were quite firm. And somewhere or other the Crew got new-laid eggs.

The Ross of Mull

There was a great press of life in Bunessan that night, for the cake and candy carnival was to be followed by a dance, and quite a bit of tartan was swinging around visitors' legs, while young women flitted from point to point in that sort of aimless excitement that is very catching.

Bunessan itself does not look a flourishing place. Decay seems to have touched a past busy-ness and left its mark on the untidy foreshore. It is finely situated, as indeed are all the villages and towns round the inner crescents of the bays of the West.

But to-night Bunessan is alive. The old native life has natural colour in its cheeks. After much anticipation, the excitement of an opening reel to the ancient music sets a healthy body clean daft. Hooch! and swing and set and hooch! again. 'That's the stuff, Davy!'

You can tell the visitors by the civilised way in which they mix between dances. They have not the old native manners that set the men and the women apart, like two opposing electrodes. The current of music, the flash: they miss that intensity of the flash. This easy familiarity is very civilised and pleasant; but its potential seems low. In a country dance, any-way. For there is something strangely attractive about a country dance. It may be the wide world outside that is strange, the stars, the mid-summer glimmer on the horizon, a greyer glimmer of sea with dark islands, and secret dark hollows everywhere. The meeting of the creative forces of the earth in a lighted room, like the manifestation of the earth's electrical energy in a dynamo. And there is something dynamic in a country dance.

A weather-lined face, thin, with an untidy moustache, leans towards Davy, catches him by the shoulder, for the good-natured mouth from the hills hasn't had time to take anything beyond a drink or two.

196

'It's not the dance, Davy. No—not only the dance—it's the walk hom'.'

'Wheesht!' says Davy.

It was getting dark enough by the time we took our own road home. We had to walk three miles. With the midnight glimmer on the water, we did not bother to light our lamp. We had seen enough to reflect upon as we stretched ourselves on our soft bunks. It must have taken me nearly a minute to go off, and in that time I asked the Mate something but got no answer.

All this western part of the Ross of Mull, from Bunessan to the Sound of Iona, is red granite, and in several places we came across evidence of quarries that were once worked. We admired the solid sea-wall of granite, as we left Bunessan the following night, and got the Mate talking on geology. The effect of sea-action was particularly marked on the foreshore just opposite our boat, where there are one or two small in-different bathing bays (and the warmest sea-water we struck on all the West Coast). The gradation from the solid granite boulders above high-water mark to the granitic sand, almost mud, over which we bathed provided about the clearest 'object lesson' I have seen.

Seaweeds were noticeably lacking in variety, being composed almost entirely of the two common varieties of bladder wrack and, below low-water mark, of the *chorda filum*. In fact we were struck every now and then, during many days we spent on the Ross, by an absence of life or, at least, of multitudinous life. Shell life was quite healthy, but lacking in number and variety. We fished all round these inner bays and caught nothing and saw only one native small boat on the water while we were there, and though we watched it for a long time saw no fish being landed. The

Mate, who knows much about the ways of rabbits and asserts that in July the young are tender, was certain from the greenness of bracken and undergrowth that 'the whole place must be crawling with them'. For there was little evidence of sheep and cattle on the ground, and less evidence than usual of obtrusive landlordism. But the total number of rabbits he saw was three. They ran at terrific speed. No gentle hopping and looking up. And where they disappeared one charge of dynamite would not have been enough. We saw no grouse at all and very little bird life. Though we hardly expected to see grouse in a deer forest. And we were too low to see deer.

The wind kept us in Loch Caol for over three days, and though we grudged the time, we had many fine exploratory walks. After Portnalong, no anchorage could be uncomfortable, and we resisted the Mate's sugestion to move into the shelter of a headland. The sun was bright, and on land the wind defeated the efforts of the only truly abundant life we found there, namely horse-flies or clegs.

All this land, however, was under an 'influence'. We could feel it without being quite able to explain it. Perhaps the cloud over Iona had a little to do with it, and perhaps it is possible that ages of pilgrimage do communicate something even to inert matter. Anyway, we were always aware that Iona was at hand and that in some fashion it drew life towards it.

Along the road an occasional bus could be seen with its load of passengers to Fionnphort, where the ferry is. For thirteen hundred years pilgrims had gone that way.

'We are now treading', says Dr. Johnson, in his celebrated passage on Iona, 'that illustrious isle which was once the luminary of the Caledonian regions, whence savage clans and roving barbarians derived the benefits of knowledge and the blessings of religion.'

The Ross of Mull

But Columba, who knew all the corners of his Caledonia, put the emphasis differently on that last day of his life when he climbed the little hill overlooking his mill and his granary and the enclosure with the simple round cells encircling the little church (what ear can catch the tread of *his* footsteps?), and blessed what he looked upon, saying: 'Unto this place, small and mean though it be, great homage shall yet be paid, not only by the kings and people of the Scots, but by the rulers of barbarous and distant nations with their people.'

Is it possible that the learned doctor would have been moved at the thought that he was perhaps fulfilling the prophecy better than he knew?

So the Mate and I set out on foot one day along the road, not as pilgrims but because we were told there were shops in Fionnphort and it was not much farther away from our boat than Bunessan. It was easy and lightsome going that road with the sun on our backs and a bracken switch for the clegs. It is an up and down road, too, with pleasant birch glades and unexpected turns. When we had gone a long way we came on an old man cutting hay in a field whose tall drystone dyke was built of red granite boulders, so we asked him if it was far to Fionnphort, and he told us, after laying down his scythe, that it was all of two miles.

'You haven't much of a hay crop?'

'No,' he said sadly. 'The deer tramped it down.'

'Do they jump these walls?'

'Oh yes—easy that.'

'Why don't you shoot them?'

'It's not my hay. I'm just working here. . . . Besides, it would get me the jail.'

He looked sad and worn and a little stupid, as if centuries of overlordship had drained the spirit out of him.

'Who owns all the land?'

He gaped as if he had not heard aright. Then he muttered something about 'The Duke', and breathing 'Aye, aye', by way of salutation and farewell, returned slowly and sadly to his work.

The benefits of knowledge and the blessings of religion. Aye, aye. But O for a touch of the roving barbarian and the clan savage that Columba knew!

We made a good two miles of it, before we went down into the hamlet of Fionnphort and stared across the Sound at Iona.

They are kind smiling folk in Fionnphort, with quiet voices and obliging ways. We got half a dozen eggs which the gentle lady of the shop could hardly spare. The 'influence' here was very strong. A brightness difficult to describe and full of peace. Doubtless Fionnphort (Fionn's or Fingal's port) like other little places, has its 'human dramas'. But it would be, I should imagine, distinctly difficult here to work up a pathological aptitude to run amock. Despite one's very best effort, the crest of it would tend to slide down like a wave, and slide down, and slide down, into the evening glimmer of calm. Or else one would clear out and be haunted remorselessly by the brightness of peace forever more.

Not so long ago I talked to a lady who had once worked here professionally, administering to the ills, ailments, and births of her generation. It was decided to buy her a bicycle with pneumatic tyres, and when it arrived it was the wonder of the place. The tyres, however, were flat, and though the more cunning detached the pump and applied it to the valve and worked it hard, they remained flat. In the end the contraption was brought before the minister, who examined it carefully, retired, returned with the manse bellows, and worked them right strongly but equally without result. So the committee solemnly packed up the pump and sent it back to the makers, requesting a proper pump in its place. But the makers merely returned the same pump together with the suggestion that, before using, it would be as well to withdraw the flexible piece of tubing from one end of the pump and attach it properly to the other end and to the valve. This they did, whereupon the tyres blew up, and she rode about to the admiration of everyone, young and old. But there was one who appreciated her riding above any other, and this was the minister's horse, for this horse had once drawn a cab in the mighty city of Glasgow, and when he saw the lady coming on her bicycle he would turn and trot away abreast of her, happy once more to be in touch with old days and civilisation.

But many wonderful things happened in Fionnphort a generation ago, and the district round about was well populated, for in addition to the active crofting and fishing life, there were the granite quarries where large numbers of men were employed.

But meantime we had encountered a man who spoke of the Sound as of a road he knew well. He confirmed our belief that there was no good anchorage on the Iona side, but said that we might lie with some comfort on the Ross side in behind Eilean na mBan in what is called the Bull Hole. We enquired about Martyr's Bay, mentioned in our *Directions*. Looking across at its white sands, he shook his head. 'Besides', he added, 'you might foul your anchor on the telegraph cables. The best on that side is Port-na-Fraing.' And he pointed up the Sound, northward. 'Do you see that house near the shore?'

'Do you mean that shed—'

'I should not advise you to call it a shed—not over there,' he suggested with a glimmer of humour. 'It is a house erected by ——' and he named a city firm of builders.

We apologised for the deficiencies in our sight, due to the very considerable distance, and parted still smiling.

We got a lift in a car which was hastening to Salen on Mull Sound to pick up a load of tourists from the steamer. I kept looking around the countryside because if I looked ahead at the turns on the narrow road I might sprain a tendon putting on imaginary brakes. 'This is all over the clegs,' said the Mate nonchalantly.

But, for our courage, the woman in the farmhouse just beyond the road on the south side of Loch Caol introduced me to her garden. The farm may not have had a notably prosperous look, but the garden was a marvel in that land. Lettuces were growing in abundance, and cabbages, carrots, leeks and similar green things, all young and of a ravishing tenderness. I got whatever I wanted, including milk and eggs, and smiled at my astonishing luck and was ashamed of the small cost.

In our absence the Crew had dressed ship with a washing and a gay sight it was, flapping in the breeze. So we ahoyed jocundly. Our gifts were received with proper avidity and in a very short time we were deep in a salad that was crisp and succulent and full of the pleasantest surprises. It was enough for a whole meal in its tempting variety quite apart from the more solid fare, and the cream cheese and biscuits and fresh butter that the Mate proceeded finally to toy with merely kept him, he explained, from drinking his coffee while yet it was too hot. As for fruit or fruit in jelly—later, perhaps. After walking in a hot sun, one should, above all things, be abstemious.

'I have a hard time of it with you both,' said the Crew.

The Ross of Mull

By Sunday morning we were really anxious to be off, but the weather was not too good and the glass depressing. We might just as well lie here as in the Bull Hole. It began to spit rain.

We decided to climb a hill-top to get a better view of the weather. As we ascended, curlews and terns kept calling out over the water beneath the overhanging gloom. We crossed a wide marsh of bog asphodel in flower and another of bog myrtle that scented all the air. Behind Bunessan a loch lay in the hills. A livid light shone down on the inner waters of Loch Scridain, and low headlands went out into it and created a phantasmagoria of the nether world. The green terraces—I think we counted over twenty of them once—were shrouded in mists, while Ben Mor and all peaks beneath it were lost in dark cloud. But to the north of the promontory a headland was caught in a diffused light that the gloom turned to a strangely ominous pink. This sabbatical light touched an end of Inch Kenneth, but, beyond, Ulva could be no more than vaguely discerned. Staffa we had come to call the ship, for from Loch Lathaich it looked very like a battleship raked clean. It was still menacingly at anchor, bearing on the Dutchman's Cap, which, in the thick weather, came and went like the Flying Dutchman of legend.

As we stood there, the wind died quite away into a listening calm. In the crofting land beyond Loch Lathaich a cock crew, and the sound was very forlorn. Out at sea, but invisible, gulls were crying. From far away in the hills came the lowing of a cow.

Our eyes fell to Eilean Lathanach, and there, amid the encircling gloom, uprose the white finger, man's beacon light.

We decided to go.

XIII

Hii, Hy, I, Ia, Io, Y, Yi . . . or Iona

Under way, the Mate insisted he was going to rig up the mainsail, and as we came down Loch Lathaich he sat into the mast. There was now a slight sou'westerly breeze and, when we had passed inside the rocks at the entrance to the loch, up went the white canvas for the first time. There was a cheer at that, for this was, in fact, the very first time we could reasonably have used a sail on our type of boat, for either there had been no wind or it had been against us. Back in the cockpit, feeling the pull of the sheet, the Mate was delighted, and we had to admit that the sail both steadied us and added to our speed. To please him we had to feel the pull on the sheet. His hair was everyway. He smiled to himself and offered us cigarettes and then dislodged me from the tiller. If he had to choose between a sail and an engine—'a sail every time,' said he.

The shore on the north coast of the Ross of Mull is very barren. We passed some salmon nets and a strand of yellow sand, and the Mate regarded the salmon nets thoughtfully. Northward, the lowering gloom still held. The weather showed little signs of clearing up, and the waves were smashing on the rocks off the north end of Iona. Soon we opened out the pale white sands of Iona itself, the red roof and white walls of its first house, the cathedral so dull and grey that it was scarcely distinguishable, and, well down the

Sound, the clustering houses of the village. Dun-I was now seen to stand above the slopes of a pleasant land, green and cultivated. One cornfield, yellow with charlock, gave us a feeling of home.

A steady small rain was carried against us, and up the Sound with it came a considerable swell. Though the weather looked anything but promising, the glass was steady at nearly 30. Very reluctantly the Mate took down his precious sail, and we entered the Sound of Iona.

We had intended anchoring in the Bull Hole, of which the *Sailing Directions* gives a very helpful chart, but now as we passed it on the north side and saw it hemmed in between gaunt granite rocks, it looked dull and anything but inviting. Manifestly, too, in a northerly wind it would be anything but comfortable. But that was not what was worrying me at the moment. I had the feeling that, having come into the Sound at all, we were in courtesy bound to land first on Iona. I should like to do it, anyway, and when we saw the modern dwelling, which we had inadvertently misdescribed, I suddenly made up my mind to land at Port-na-Fraing. It was not shown on our chart, but we headed for the house and discovered the anchorage just a little south of it. A short reef of black rocks half-guards its southern side, and the slipway of wet sand looks smooth as cement. The Mate, standing over the bow, could tell the depth of water at a glance, for the bottom was white sand and brown weed. He signalled me inside the outermost point of rock, just clear of the tide race. I could almost find time to be amused at his easy air of assurance.

But the engine, going slow, showed an entirely new belief in discipline. She accepted neutral, went ahead again, reversed, and remained running while the anchor was let go. It all seemed like a fairy story, and with proper solemnity we

attributed it to some miraculous influence from the Island.
The Crew took the depth—a couple of fathoms, with about
two hours of ebb to run. Perfect—with good holding in
tough weed. The heavens acknowledged our gratitude, drew
the mists about us, opened their gates, and let the rain
descend solidly. We had reached Iona.

In oilskins and long boots, the Crew and I got ashore at
the sandy slip, and using a half-broken oar as a roller, pulled
up the dinghy clear of the surf. The sand, composed of the
pulverised shells of land snails, was so fine that it stuck to our
hands and coated the rope. In striking contrast to the Mull
shore opposite, where the broken-down granite remains
sharp-edged, here the pebbles were smooth and rounded and
beautifully and variously coloured. There was immediately
the feeling of landing on a different, almost a strange and
foreign, shore, though it was yet more intimate, as a shore
of tradition, or dream, or actual past experience is intimate.
On the right hand the conjunction was seen in a massive
rugged boulder of red granite lying on smooth greenish-blue
water-worn rock. At the head of the little slipway, where
two row-boats were drawn up, springs of water came
through the clean pebbles, and the scent of clover was in the
air. Masses of ragged robin gave way to eyebright and
buttercups. As we went up by the hayfields and over the
fallow ground, we saw that this was a fertile island, and
suddenly the rain was warm and soft. The barley was green
and heavy in the ear. The root crops hid the soil. The fields
were well barb-wired, but we won through to the pasture
lands at the foot of Dun-I; and there, on impulse, we decided
to climb this rock which had so attracted and baffled us from
beyond the Treshnish Isles.

We took a rather steep face, but in time we reached the

cairn on the top and opened out the west side of the island, the green machair land, the sandy bays, the innumerable rocks, with the swell breaking on them and throwing its spume high in the air. Here at last was the true Atlantic roar.

When, after a long interval, I come upon such a scene, my mind goes back to Benbecula, to a picture of great waves on its western strand, a herd girl sheltering against a stook of corn, wild geese on a stubble field, in a grey day of small rain. What virtue there is in that picture I cannot tell, but it has already much of the force of legend, and the human feeling in it is made the more intense by a long-thoughted conception of human destiny, ironic and tragic perhaps, but not without its own worth and a certain underlying, evasive, and even defiant happiness. It is the mood of human comradeship, quiet and simple, but strong. It is the smile that acknowledges Fate—and no more.

The rain seemed to be getting heavier, if that were possible, and we sheltered for a little in the lee of the cairn. In many ways it was a typical West Coast day, with lands and islands vaguely looming and disappearing in the mists. Being properly clad, the rain could not wet us nor the long grasses get over our boots. And this in itself provided a pleasant freedom. The rain, too, kept all folk indoors, so that we saw no human being. We saw the isle itself, and in its coloured fields and soft air, in its sheep grazing here and there and its cattle, we saw also, perhaps more clearly than if the day had been fine, that it was a delectable isle. How wisely Columcille had chosen his ground!

For I feel sure, despite the legends, that this was no case of Columba's having just happened to land here—as early European navigators happened to land on a West Indian

island. Iona was an important centre in that early Druidic
world. The usual scholar's or historian's talk about the
savages and barbarians who inhabited the land in Columba's
time is very misleading. In this respect the Christian ethic
certainly prejudged the Druidic truth. We do know, for
example, that one king, Fergus, went to Iona for his coro-
nation; and in that same isle he was buried, a generation
before Columba landed. We learn, too, that the isle had a
great number of standing stones, and late travellers talk of
the existence of a Druidic temple of twelve stones, each with
a human body buried beneath it. These wise early missionaries of Christianity did not believe in violence and destruction. They sprinkled the pagan monoliths with holy water
and carved on them their Christian emblems. As one French
writer put it: 'They baptised these idols in order that they
might continue to be adored.' That was in Armorica; for the
practice was general, and in Scotland to this day we find great
menhirs with a Cross on one side and the Pagan emblems on
the other.

The Synod of Argyll pursued the contrary method, and in
1560 A.D. decided that the 360 sculptured stone crosses of
Iona were 'monuments of idolatrie' and were therefore to be
cast into the sea. Possibly this Protestant Synod did more to
destroy the accumulated spiritual riches of Iona than all the
Viking ravages put together. But some of the stones were
rescued and carried to the mainland, while it is possible that
at least two of them may still be found on Iona itself.

But out of much undisciplined reading about that ancient
pre-Christian world, what has always struck me is the
extremely wide, if not universal, practice of what may be
loosely called the standing-stone or Druidic religion. Even
the attempt over many centuries to make of Europe one

unified country of Catholic culture and religion, seems a small affair when set against the actual Druidic unification of that older world existing over a period of time so great that we hardly dare to compute it.

For example, the 360 *sculptured* stones of Iona make one traveller (C. F. Gordon Cumming) think of the Kaaba at Mecca. 'The Kaaba at Mecca (which to all good Mahomedans is as sacred as was the Holy of Holies to the Israelites) had, from time immemorial, been accounted by all the people of Arabia, to be the very portal of Heaven. Until the time of Mahomet, it was surrounded by 360 *rude unsculptured monoliths*, which, to the degenerate Arabs, had become objects of actual worship, and in presence of which, they were wont to sacrifice red cocks to the sun (just as the people in these Western Isles have continued to do, almost to the present day, though of course in ignorance of the original meaning of this ancestral custom).

'More unflinching than the Christian reformers of Iona, Mahomet would admit of no compromise. Like the Synod of Argyll, he resolved on the destruction of these "monuments of idolatrie", and so his iconoclastic followers did his bidding, and destroyed them utterly.

'Nevertheless, he still allowed his converts to retain their custom *of walking seven times in procession round the Kaaba itself*, in reverence for Abraham and Ishmael, who had rebuilt it after the deluge, *but he reversed the course of circuit.*'

That Columba and his brethren, who built their little church of wood and its surrounding cells of wattle and daub, so that now nothing remains of their habitation, should also have reared these 360 stones is manifestly absurd, even had we no collateral aids to judgment, such as the remarkable twelve-stone circle, with its radiating lines, at Callanish in Lewis.

Moreover, until quite recent times, Highlanders spoke of Iona as the 'Druid's Isle', and long after Columba had landed on it, the Irish continued to call it by that name.

One further thing has struck me, too, in this matter, and that is the obvious feeling of respect that these early Celtic missionaries had for the older faith. There was manifestly no bitter rancour, no outflowing of righteous wrath against a degenerate creed. As he made the cross on the monolith, so Columba in one of his written prayers calls Christ his Druid: 'mo drui ... mac Dé' (My Druid ... son of God).

As we stood there by the cairn, three oyster-catchers came crying against us for disturbing their peace, and as I watched the flash of the black and white plumage and the orange beaks, I remembered the wrong I had done to these servants of Bride or St. Bridgit. For once, long ago, while out hunting, I had shot two of them, and the man who had prompted me to do this carried them home to my landlady, who had been cook to a university professor in Edinburgh. She presented them browned on toast with the suggestion that the breasts only be eaten. They were very good.

In Gaelic they are known as *gille-Brigde*, the servant of Bride. And here again we are back among the old gods. I (or its variants) by which Iona is known to the ancient writers means The Isle. So the Hebrides are the Ey-Brides or the Isles of Brighit or Bridgit. This Brighit was a Druidic goddess, and, attended by noble vestals, her special care was the sacred fire. They had great reverence for fire in those days, and would hardly blow out a candle without a prayer that the light be given them again from heaven. They stuck to their sacred fire in the grove so obstinately that St. Patrick sent his convert, Bridgit, to deal with them. Now just as the Columban brotherhood found it more fruitful to bless than to attempt to destroy the standing stones, so Bridgit found it possible to convert these virgins only by allowing them to continue together in a community to look after what now became a Christian fire. And so it was done, and they were the first Christian community of women, and the temple of Bridgit at Kildare became a great convent.

Columba himself did not hold much by women. Tradition has it that he would not allow them on Iona, and any island workers with women had to keep them on Eilean na mBan (Island of the Women), that small barren granite isle which shelters the Bull Hole. Indeed, he did not even allow cattle on Iona, saying, 'Where there is a cow there is a woman, and where there is a woman there is mischief.'

Altogether he was a remarkable man. Tall, well-featured, with long hair falling to each shoulder from the temples (for the early Celtic priests shaved the front of their heads), he had a commanding presence, and was, in fact, full of a restless energy, passionate and impetuous. He had that quality of voice which does not appear to be raised when speaking to those at hand and which can yet be heard clearly at a distance. A statesman, an organiser, he was almost continuously on the move, over land, by sea, daring any peril, unsparing of himself, teaching, converting, founding, succeeding.

He succeeded very well indeed—so well that his own folk, the Gaels or Scots (Ireland is called Scotia in the old records), who landed, as he landed, on the Argyllshire part of Scotland, managed in time to give their kings to Scotland, their tongue, and their particular methods of church government. All that was distinctive of the ancient Pictish Scotland, strong enough in its time to repel the Romans, faded away before this Columban energy and statesmanship, leaving scarcely a trace behind. It is the great mystery in Scottish

history, so that to this day scholars debate the identity of the
Picts, what tongue they spoke and how they were governed
in church and state. Statesmanship that is so successful has
doubtless its own reward, even if suspicion of doubtful
dealings be not inevitably aroused. In any case, I was inclined
to be one of those who felt no great urge to pay further
tribute to Columba and Iona; who, in fact, would rather
learn somewhat more of our real forebears, the Picts, and give
his proper place to that Ninian who was a missionary in
Scotland one hundred and fifty years before Columba
arrived. In short, it seemed unnecessary to swell the vast
ranks that every year pay homage to the Iouan Island (Iona).

Perhaps the critical eye went a bit deeper, too. There is so
much scholarly talk of the Gael as the tall, aristocratic, con-
quering type, generally golden haired and blue eyed, that
up against the visible appearance to-day of the folk themselves—one wonders. Moreover, if the Gael was the fighting
extravert type, whence the exquisite sad music of Hebridean
melody? And from melody to poetry, courtesy, instinctive
good manners, and that gift for spontaneous gaiety in a
natural communal life illustrated so well by the céilidh?
Priestly energy, statecraft, power, dominance—until a whole
folk, with all their intricate ways of life, including the very
syllables of their tongue, fade away like the poet's insubstantial pageant.

Nearly all writers agree that in Scotland, and particularly
in the Highlands of Scotland, we were a savage and barbarous people, until Columba changed our hearts. Yet how
tolerantly we received Columba, though he walked amongst
us as an open perverter of our Druidic faith. Our Druids
disputed with him, but offered him no hurt. King Brude at
Inverness even confirmed him in his possession of Iona.
Were these northern folk so civilised that they could not see

Hii, Hy, I, Ia, Io, Y, Yi . . . or Iona

in Columba the emissary of a new power in church and state
that should finally usurp and destroy their own power?

In a word, I was prepared to be prejudiced to the hilt
against Columba. But, unfortunately, Iona is the last place in
the world to help a prejudice. If one doesn't forget it, at
least one cannot be bothered with it for the moment, not in
the rain, in the soft air. Presently, perhaps, should some
loud-voiced person be filled with Iouan unction.

For one can also see that other half of Columba's character, the affectionate part, full of warmth and understanding. It had the nobility from which, perhaps, all his restless
energy received direction. Tolerance, temperance, kindness,
simplicity, obedience, forgiveness—we know the rules that
governed their lives; but, above all, from their religion they
got the conception of charity, of love. It is the ancient goodness of the human heart, the primordial goodness. And a
religion that enshrines it will always persist. Those who have
this goodness in them are aware of life in the same way as
they are aware of light. Truly, life itself is an inner light.

And, at its best, it is a universal light. Columba loved the
birds, and the white horse that carried the farm produce bore
Columba a special affection. Indeed, as Adamnan relates in
his *Life of St. Columba* (written at Iona towards the end of
the seventh century), the white horse wept on taking leave
of its dying master. Which may be an exaggeration of the
truth; but still—of the truth. And that wise and scholarly
men of his age believed it to be the simple truth shows at
least what they wanted to believe. Which is the essence of
the matter. Beyond miracle and morality and theology, they
desired this goodness. And kings and priests and murderers
and perverts of all kinds went to Columba in Iona to find
again the peace of that goodness.

Hii, Hy, I, Ia, Io, Y, Yi ... or Iona

The most remarkable thing I discovered in Adamnan's remarkable record is this preoccupation with light as the manifestation or symbol of this goodness. The miracles are the light in legendary form. And many of them—particularly those relating to prevision or 'second sight'—may not be so legendary as all that.

The simplest and perhaps the best expression of this conjunction of light and goodness may be found in the story of that which happened to the brethren on their return to the monastery after toiling all day in the fields on the west side of the island. When half-way home with their burdens, each had felt within him 'something wonderful and unusual' but had not cared to confess it, until at last it could no longer be hid, and one tried to express it thus: 'I perceive some fragrance of wondrous odour, as of that of all flowers collected into one; also some burning as of fire, not penal but somehow very sweet; moreover, also a certain unaccustomed and incomparable gladness diffused in my heart, which suddenly consoles me in a wonderful manner, and gladdens me to such a degree that I can remember no more the sadness, nor any labour. Yea, even the load, although a heavy one, which I am carrying on my back from this place to the monastery, is so lightened, I know not how, that I do not perceive I have a load at all.'

Columba, 'mindful of their labours', had sent his spirit to meet their steps.

Gladness, then, is the keynote of the experience.

Adamnan knew of it in its many manifestations, and at one point writes: 'St. Columba, as he himself did not deny . . . in some contemplations of divine grace he beheld even the whole world as if gathered together in one ray of the sun, gazing on it as manifested before him, while his inmost soul was enlarged in a wonderful manner.'

Hii, Hy, I, Ia, Io, Y, Yi ... or Iona

We came down from Dun-I through the fenced fields towards the modern cathedral. The first Celtic Cross we saw stood in a walled bed of fuchsia and was erected to a wife of a Duke of Argyll. The Crew tried to get at it to see why, but was prevented by iron railings. Remembering the acts of a past Synod of Argyll, one could not resist certain ironic reflections, though they gave little pleasure.

As we entered the cathedral ground, two lambs—one white and one black—came running to meet us. The Crew smiled at that and welcomed them, especially the black one. We wandered round the ruins of the old cathedral, but when we wished to enter the new building found the doors shut against us for it was Sunday. However, we were fortunate enough to meet a young man who allowed us to go in alone for a few minutes.

The interior had more than the bareness of the usual Scottish country church, for the walls themselves were bare stones, yet from those stones there came a real effect of light, wonderfully heightened by what appeared on that dull day to be a long low altar of greenish-white glowing stone. Midway on this altar stood a narrow brass vase of flowers—white irises and blue and pink delphiniums—so perfectly arranged that they were a burgeoning of light and colour, an aspiration, a loveliness. The Crew could hardly take her eyes off them, as we stood in the nave at some little distance. And in truth I must confess I have rarely encountered so direct a manifestation of ineffable harmony.

But the harmony of the whole interior was destroyed by two massive recumbent effigies in white marble of a Duke and Duchess of Argyll occupying almost all the southern transept. One hesitates to write one's full thought about it. At the best, how sad and hopeless this heavy effort at immortality compared with the spirit that fed the birds or even the nameless hands that had arranged the flowers. Perhaps, but for these two in life, the modern church or cathedral would not have been there. We did not inquire.

Outside again, we stood before the great Cross of Iona, dedicated to St. Martin of Tours, the friend of St. Ninian. It has the easy incomparable grace of the true Celtic Cross, strong, sure in workmanship, and at rest. You could feel the harmony behind the chisel that hewed it.

Then we followed the road down towards the village and came upon the ruins of the nunnery, for Columcille's attitude to women did not withstand the fret of time. The Crew was delighted with the blaze of colour, mostly from red and from white valerian, growing not only about the well-kept grounds but out of the old walls. And when she had seen the nooks and crannies—for apparently the commonest blossom can be a distinguished friend at times—we went down to the village, which strings its little houses along the sea front.

The rain had taken off while we had been in the cathedral, and the oasis of blue we had seen towards Ireland was now enlarging itself in so wonderful a manner that it brought forth visitors from the houses, who looked at it and called to one another. Clean-shaven faces and bright faces and fine shiny silk stockings and creased and white and coloured clothes; so very clean, this community of the Washed, that we felt a little like bedraggled seabirds, with a hanging pinion or two, so I looked carefully at the anchorage off the pier, which was crammed with small boats, and at the anchorage a little farther down, which is Martyr's Bay, and satisfied myself that, for Iona, we were in the right spot. All the little shops being closed, we turned back, following approximately the ancient Street of the Dead, along which kings and chiefs and other important men (never a woman) were brought, after being landed at Martyr's Bay, on the way to their burial at Reilig Orain. Though Martyr's Bay itself is so named from that first slaughter of the monks by the Danes in 806 (Columba died 597).

The rain had now quite passed away and the air was so full of a soft brightness and warmth, that we had to stop by Maclean's Cross and strip off our oilskins. This is the second interesting cross on the island, and the carving on it seems to have been done about the fifteenth century, though how long its shaft of characteristic bluish schist has faced the sun upright is another matter. This is the spot, we learned, where Columba rested as he returned to the monastery on the last day of his life.

When at last we turned to go down through the fields, the fragrance of the clover and wild flowers and young grass was indeed 'of a wondrous odour, as that of all flowers collected into one'. What, in the reading, had perhaps appeared to be a trifle overstressed, was now perceived to be wonderfully precise, and we were in the silence of this when all at once the cathedral bell began clanging its summons to evening service. It rent the air to a shivering agony. Peace threw a cowl over its head and ran, bowed, seeking shelter. It was the bell of the 'killing times', of Covenanters and Calvin and the wrath to come. A city bell, to clang above tramcars and the clatter on the cobbled closes of slums. The monks might have rung such a bell as a warning of the coming of the murderous Danes, and a dying hand have rung it after to tell the tale. But never would the hand of Columba have clanged it for his services of faith and peace.

Perhaps we had become, after these weeks at sea, a little over-sensitive to peace, and when, having got aboard again and eaten, we heard the sound of military music, marching with precision to the beat of drums, invisible, but traversing the island, rising to a near high note and falling away to 'the tread of infinite cavalcades filing off', we might easily have believed ourselves forever after to have been the victims of a strange delusion, had not the Mate, who had stayed with the boat, been so positive that he kept time to the invisible feet.

In the evening the three of us went ashore and wandered along the sands until we came to the rocks at the north point of the island, where we watched two thousand miles of sea throw its fountains in the air. As we faced westward, there was no land between us and Canada, the home of the evicted.

Iona was full of visitors. We now encountered many of them. A man in his kilt, his wife with a Celtic brooch, and their two or three children following dutifully behind; a young man quietly dressed in his clan tartan, his face spiritual and aloof a little; several young men, more or less spiritual, athletic and clean; some young Glasgow women, just refraining from having a good laugh; boys bare-legged, with bathing suits; a group wandering aimlessly seeing what they had seen before; and suddenly, as we came down over a grassy knoll, an encampment on the western side, consisting of two splendid marquees and over a dozen bell-tents in army formation, to explain the martial music. The young men of the tents were playing football, deck tennis, and other games. Yet through it all the peace of Iona persisted. It is as if everyone were conscious of it. It is in the air. So that one wonders how they are affected privately by it now and then.

I remembered the lot of talk there had been in recent years over building a Celtic college in Iona. The United States had got involved, and there had been the usual—apparently inevitable—wordy battles in the Highlands. I confess I had scoffed at the idea of a college in Iona. We had had enough of that western, blue-rolling, rhetorical, impractical, sentimental, Celtic-twilight nonsense to last us for a century or two, and certainly until we had rigged up some half-decent way of getting bread and butter. If there must be such a college, let it be in Inverness; and, failing Inverness, well, all right, let it be in Oban (which was pretty handsome of one living in Inverness).

I saw now that I was quite wrong. Iona is the place. Here the things of the spirit would have to be uppermost—or a man might go mad. You could see it in the lack of noise, of shouting. It is a dedicated land. Which sounds perhaps a trifle solemn and oppressive, but which *might* sound: 'I perceive some fragrance of wondrous odour, as of all flowers collected into one; also some burning as of fire, not penal but somehow very sweet; moreover, also a certain unaccustomed and incomparable gladness diffused in my heart, which suddenly consoles me in a wonderful manner, and gladdens me to such a degree that I can remember no more the sadness, nor any labour.'

I do not know. All we can be sure of is that these words were written in the seventh century of men who lived in the sixth, and that if there is anything at all in the conception of evolution we should be able to add something to the 'incomparable gladness' in this twentieth century of the same era. Whatever the nature of that something, it should at least be as remarkable as the recorded experience of the monks. Out of a Celtic college in Iona, it might be as remarkable. Even the Marxian dialectic might look for it there as an expression of background. But I doubt if it could come out of any Highland town on the mainland.

And the island has no anchorage for large yachts; is never by any stretch of the imagination likely to become a Society pleasure ground or meeting place. In fact, when we returned to our boat at Port-na-Fraing we found her rolling very uncomfortably and knew we could not sleep there, while if anything like a real sea got up, we might quickly enough find ourselves in difficulties. The Mate was still inclined to rub a shoulder, for he had got tossed out of bed, after we had first gone ashore, by a sudden sea impulse for which there had been no visible cause—probably the tail-end of some ninth wave dying in the Sound.

The entrance to the Bull Hole is from the south and not readily discernible until you are near the Mull shore, as the opening channel is barely a hundred yards wide. Hold by the Mull shore, for half-way up the channel there is a rock that shows only at low water. It lies about thirty feet S.E. of a very obvious rock on the Eilean na mBan side, opposite which the land on the Mull shore comes out to a point. At this point the south-going stream tends to be bottlenecked, and one can encounter for a short distance a disconcertingly strong current in a very narrow channel. The interest of making a new anchorage caught us up, and it was not lessened by seeing a yacht many times our size taking up all the available and recommended holding ground a cable-length beyond the point on the Eilean na mBan side. But as the channel widened we turned to starboard into a little bay, where there is deep water right into the very shore. After two attempts we found the mathematically perfect spot, which kept us out of the main run of the tide, while giving a reasonable clearance of each arm of the rocky bay. 'Two fathoms,' said the Crew. There was hardly a movement on the water and we slept a perfect sleep.

We got quite an affection for this little anchorage of the Bull Hole, which had, behind its northern rocks, looked so forbidding, and carried out all sorts of deep-sea fishing experiments, though with little success. The Mate was particularly fertile in making night lines and using many kinds of bait from crushed partan to boiled limpet. And when a seal came to visit us he was more than ever convinced that fish of some sort were about. Occasionally in the days that followed, a cobble, with outboard motor, threaded its way in through the northern rocks, and saluted us as it passed southward to meet the steamer with whatever salmon the nets on the north of the Ross may have yielded. 'It's easy seeing what the seal was after,' said the Mate, who made me pull that dinghy until there were blisters between my fingers, while he ran the gamut of all my rubber eels, spoons, and minnows, and with a few gull's feathers turned my bare hooks into mackerel flies.

The Crew in a way was to blame for this tyranny. 'Now', she had said to him, 'your job is to provide the boat with fish.'

'That's easy,' he had smiled, in his element.

'Accordingly,' she had added, 'if you don't catch fish and I have to buy them, then you'll have to pay.'

'Pouf!' he had agreed. 'Turn out your whole stock of fishing gear.'

He evolved a scheme whereby his fish could be run over to quiet Port-na-Fraing, landed, and sold from door to door by me on a fifty-fifty basis. 'All you have to do', he explained, 'is just to continue not shaving, and even those who didn't want fish would buy them out of pity.' I had often a very hard time of it.

However, beyond one or two negligible small codling, he caught no fish. And, in truth, many a time on our cruise did I regret not having a net. Never again, I vowed, would I go without one. How gladly often would I have sacrificed the

Li-lo itself for that midnight apostrophe: 'Maaakril!' I explained this to the Mate, and got some small pleasure from seeing conflicting emotions tie him in a knot; for he is really pretty good with a net.

'I doubt it,' he said. 'For there's no fish in this barren spot. And that's the whole sum and substance of it. How would the bait on that night line be fresh and untouched in the morning if there were any fish about?'

'There's the salmon cobble anyway,' I suggested mildly.

'I'll give you a sixpence', said the Crew to him, 'for each fresh fish you catch not under six inches.'

That rather staggered him. And I had my laugh there and then, before he could take it out of me.

We got to know that bay and the surrounding inlets very well. One side of the inner corner of the bay is built up into a pier with huge granite blocks, and we saw that granite quarrying had been carried on here in recent times. Now the steep shore, with its great boulders and outcropping rock, looked barren enough, yet when we came to examine it closely we discovered little pockets of fertility everywhere. For example, in the face opposite to us, we gathered ripe blaeberries and cranberries while the Crew carried off a bunch of honeysuckle, whose odd whiffs surprised us for days. The place was fragrant with bog myrtle and meadow-sweet, and under the jagged stones we picked up young crabs and large winkles (for which the Crew concocted a special sauce, discovering in the process that any strong flavour is fatal). Beneath some boulders we exposed a world of hundreds of young sea anemones, their red nipples like blood spots of pain: an astonishing sight. In fact, if I made a complete list of each individual thing we saw in that small corner, it might well surprise the more curious. The Crew suggested a pastime: land for ten minutes, observe, return, and then in rotation have the usual knock-out game with the objects seen. 'I think I'll go fishing,' said the Mate.

Until the morning came when we went over to Port-na-Fraing, anchored, turned off the engine, and were getting ready to go ashore when the Crew said, 'Listen!'

Very distinctly from within the body of the mechanism came an intermittent hissing, like the sound of a drop of water falling on hot metal.

I heard it with profound dismay, and opened the four priming caps. Sure enough, out of cylinder number one came a little jet of steam as each drop sizzled internally. We could hardly speak. For how could the drop get in except through a cracked cylinder casing? And if such a crack existed, with the boat in so remote a part of the world, well —obviously—we were through! The cost of the repair, even if it could be done, including mechanics and gear from Glasgow ... we decided solemnly that it might be cheaper for us to sink her where she lay; and I actually found myself looking around for what might be a deep spot out of the way of traffic. After all we had been through, it was desperate luck. We went ashore profoundly dispirited. There was a motor boat at Iona, for we had seen it, and there might be a mechanic; we must investigate; but we had no slightest hope.

'It would need one of St. Columba's miracles,' said the Mate.

And the Crew answered simply:

'You never know.'

Her words took our breath, for to such a moment, fraught with such ruinous consequence, they seemed almost indecently insensitive. With some restraint, we ignored them, and walked up through the fields. It began to rain.

We discussed the crops. A light friable soil that should be very good for potatoes, assuming an absence of prolonged drought. The crofts looked very snug. Not many worries attached to living here. The Crew side-stepped to pick up a flowering weed, as if there wasn't a broken-down engine in the whole world.

We held on until we came to the village, and there we entered a shop of modern Celtic silver work and carved Iona pebbles. Some of the old designs were attractive, and it was suggested by the Mate that the Crew might help herself to something. But she shook her head. This was apparently the sort of expensive moment that she could appreciate. 'You may as well see first how deeply you are involved,' she suggested mildly. And the efficient saleswoman told us of a man of skill in the village and came and directed us to his house. The Crew went shopping.

The more gentle dreams of Iona were in his eyes, and his courtesy was equalled only by his deep interest. On his palm he drew engine designs with a black-lead pencil. But as to what caused our trouble precisely—that was a difficulty. He would come with us now, for if the whole engine were taken down, then . . . But I decided against that. There was another man, he told us, who actually had the solitary engine of the island, so perhaps he might have had this mysterious trouble himself. What about coming to see him?

This second man, bluff and agreeable, had had various troubles in his time but not ours. And I could see that, like myself, he was no believer in tampering. 'Keep her going on three cylinders', he said, 'till you come to some place.'

I was impressed by the excellence of this advice and thanked him. If our doom was written, at least it was not to be preceded by an undignified and unholy mess.

When the Crew met us, she said, 'There are no fresh eggs or lettuces to be got anywhere.'

'What did you expect?'

'But', she said, 'I have got fresh kippers—from Stornoway —MacIver's.' She looked at the Mate.

'Do you want the money now?' he asked.

'Oh,' she said, suddenly remembering. 'What about the engine?'

We walked in silence for a little way, southward and westward, for now there was no hurry. Indeed, I was aware of the tranquil feeling that is alleged to come upon those who have accepted doom. It is a subdued feeling, perhaps, but not utterly unpleasant. And it conjured up little compensations. For example, the boat had been making a good drop of water. Nothing disquieting. But two pumpings a day were hardly enough. Soon it would be three. And it's not better it would get. When we sank her—well, there would be no more pumpings.

But the real compensation was one of detachment in which, more than ever, was felt the Columban peace. This was the way the brethren walked to their work, over the back of the island, to the Machair in front of the great western bay. Somewhere hereabouts they had met the 'incomparable gladness'.

It was fairly easy to picture them in a general way, but I suddenly got an impression of the man whose words were reported so smoothly. Of medium height, he was thin and tough, the face lined, the dark-brown thatch of hair losing its colour, the eyebrows bushy, but the eyes of a lively and penetrating brightness. The creases in the face ran naturally into a smile that was the very net of irony. And the world irony was there, or the mind could never have passed to so expressive and comprehending a serenity.

And then we came back to the knoll where Columba communed with the angels. I could never quite see Columba's face. I could, in a way, but always, as it were, the outside face with its leadership upon it. Irony to serenity to the true humility, in which the flesh over the bone and the irises of the eyes are purified of the insignia of the boss—it is difficult to get the face of a leader like that, apart, perhaps, from the faces of one or two great religious leaders out of the East. And nothing less quite satisfies a mood grown weary of all the personal humours or manifestations of egoism. As though a modern voice cried with the agony of a pure spirit: 'Hell, let us be shut of all that egoism meantime.'

Inevitably there was a curious prying one amongst the brethren. He stole out behind Columba, against Columba's orders, and from a knoll near by watched the saint commune with the heavenly host. I found it difficult to see this man, for he has two faces. To one of the faces we have to return thanks for all the engines in the world, I said to the Mate, who deals in text-books and pure science.

'And to the other', he replied promptly, 'the broken-down engines,' and laughed, remembering my ordeal in Skye.

And there and then the sun came shafting out, and the rain, that had turned small and white, passed away.

The sun can behave with splendour at times; and now into its glory all the brethren were resumed like the grey rain. If the Crew had never been damped, she quite got on her toes at sight of the gleaming Atlantic breakers on the dark rocks. Photographs! We had to follow her down over the great green machair and had to shout to her to watch out as we saw a big one coming.

Suddenly the earth near us shook, as a stout lady hit it solidly and sent a little white ball a very little way. So the great machair was a golf course. We listened, but heard no words. What language *could* golfers use on Iona?

Or, conversely, if a retired colonel wanted a real kick out of swearing, was this the very spot? But such a thought lurking about in the jungle would be enough to put his eye out. Moreover, there were three persons walking on the sands, and only half a mile away could be seen at irregular intervals a high burst of spray from the Spouting Cave, while the obviously half-demented woman stalking waves round rocks as if they were sporting lions was enough to upset even the pendulum-swing of a putter. It is improbable that real golfers, men who know the rules, will ever come to Iona.

Over the rocky part of the island is Port-na-Curaich, where Columba first landed. There is a reef of green serpentine in the bay—the Iona stone, out of which the island pebbles are carved and polished.

Port-na-Curaich is interesting in other ways; but again it is difficult to get past Columba, for when he turned round as he landed here and could no longer see Ireland, where his tempestuous spirit had recently raised a war, tears came into his eyes. For he loved his own land of Ireland, as all good men love their own land, and being lucky in his he had the greater heart to feel the greater grief.

In the early evening we returned to the village and picked up our parcels, and stayed a while in the nunnery garden, for the Mate's benefit, while the Crew told the flowers, and wandered on to St. Oran's, where she left us to hunt milk.

As we went to enter at the gate of St. Oran's (or Reilig Orain) we were astonished to find it locked. As there was nothing to steal but the chapel ruins and the tombstones, and as nobody would steal on Iona, we decided some mistake had been made, so we vaulted the wall.

We had bought a guidebook on the island, a rather indifferent and uninspired affair—though, after all, so much is legend and tradition, that it is difficult to be positive about anything. Even the little roofless chapel, down in the corner to the left, and dedicated to St. Oran, the oldest of the ruins, is probably eleventh century. That Saxon and pious queen, Margaret, wife of Malcolm Canmore, is believed to have had it built as one of her efforts to civilise the savages of her adopted country. She stuck hard to her thankless task, yet with such success that good Scottish historians to this day bless her name. And as far as these Highland parts are concerned, her reforms slowly but surely spread until their feudalistic groundwork blossomed in the flame-bright flower of the Clearances. She was a pious statesman, whose sad and onerous duty, to herself and to God, was to spread the light in that heathen darkness where, long centuries before her redeeming advent, a benighted successor to Columcille was writing: 'At another time, while the blessed man was living in the Iouan Island (Iona), one day his holy face lighted up with a certain wondrous and joyous cheerfulness, and, lifting up his eyes to heaven, filled with incomparable joy, he was intensely gladdened.' They believed in those far days that 'when the heart is glad the face blooms'. Such simple and dogged cheerfulness must be a sad trial to any true reformer. But she did her best.

Yet perhaps the most astonishing thing about the burying-ground that lies before the chapel ruin (this 'awful ground', as Dr. Johnson called it) is that it contains the dust of forty-eight Scottish kings, the last of whom was Macbeth. Murdered Duncan was buried here, as Shakespeare, the incomparable, knew:

> '*Carried to Colm's-kill,*
> *The sacred store-house of his predecessors,*
> *And guardian of their bones.*'

Forty-eight Scottish kings buried in this tumbled grave-yard—*before* the Norman conquest of England in 1066. And to-day should a man be bold enough to refer to the Scottish nation, he is looked upon as a bit of a crank, and his brothers smile for him, with diffident humour, in apology. St. Margaret of blessed memory worked better than she knew, and certainly her husband, Malcolm Canmore, broke the Iona tradition by being properly buried in Dunfermline.

As late as 1594, the Dean of the Isles describes three tombs, 'formit like little Chapels'; *Tumulus Regum Scotiae, Tumulus Regum Hiberniae*, and *Tumulus Regum Norwegiae*. In the first 'ther lay fortey-eight crowned Scotts Kings'. In the others, Irish and Norwegian kings. 'Within this sanctuary also lye maist pairt of the Lords of the Isles, with their lynage, twa clan Leans, with their lynage, with sundrie uthers, inhabitants of the haill isles.'

There is little evidence of all this temporal glory to be seen now, though the two ridges—the Ridge of the Kings and the Ridge of the Chiefs—are clear enough, with the chiefs looking much more important than the kings. Altogether it is a small unimpressive place—to the mind looking for physical wonders.

But to a mind otherwise concerned limitless are the perspectives that open out. There can be little doubt, for example, but that Druidism and Christianity meet here, as the story of Oran so searchingly illustrates. When Columba and his brethren started building their first chapel they found that the walls were always being overthrown by an evil spirit. In his perplexity, it was revealed to Columba that a last sacrifice must be made. And then it was that Oran came forward and offered to be buried alive.

But at the end of three days, Columba, troubled in his soul, thought he would like to see how things were going with Oran, so he caused the grave to be opened: whereupon Oran promptly sat up and began to speak heresies, and, in particular, the heresy that Hell is not 'as it is said'. Which was

a nasty thrust at the priestcraft, and, lest he reveal still more
heretical things, Columba had him covered up again at once.
'Earth, earth on Oran's eye, lest he further blab,' became a
proverb in due course.

Until the Synod of Argyll destroyed them, three globes of
white marble lay in hollows on a stone slab beside St. Oran's,
and a visitor to the island had to turn the stones thrice sun-
wise—*deisul* (thus Druidically performing the rites of sun
worship on the way to the worship of God). The slab (Clach
Brath) is still there, with the hollows upon it, and until quite
recent times the natives used to turn three ordinary stone
balls in the hollows three times *deisul*, for luck, every time
they passed. But these later stones have gone too.

Leaving Reilig Orain, we decided to go into the grounds
of the cathedral, and into the cathedral itself, for I wanted
to verify what was a first impression by more exact observation; and in any case it should be a good place to rest for a
little before returning to face our troubles.

But we found the outer gate locked and the walls surmounted by barbed wire. Though we could have overleapt
these obstacles, we could also see that the door of the cathedral itself was locked. Just inside the gate was the box into
which on our first visit the Crew had dropped her shilling
for the restoration work. It was a small but very solid box,
heavily padlocked. It looked as if Argyll's Church of Scotland had less faith in all the moderns than Columba in his
savages and barbarians. Thus if the Mate did not see the
flowers and the light on the stone, neither did he see the
great marble effigies, so doubtless there is a compensating
balance in things. And, after all, there was nothing to be seen
that was authentically Columban, unless indeed the stone that
was reputed to have been Columba's pillow, now locked in
its little iron cage.

Hii, Hy, I, Ia, Io, Y, Yi ... or Iona

As we came down through the fields, the Crew was resting with her milkpail in a fragrant spot. I glanced away at the sea, and the heavy mood descended darkly, because the Mate had to get to Oban and now I could not take him there. Faith does not help when it comes to mechanism.

The crew, observing this gloom, smiled with 'wondrous cheerfulness', implying a faith so irrational that surely even a saint might be forgiven the movement within him of some slight exasperation. She did not, however, add to the offence by speaking.

Turning to the Mate, I worked out how by this time the top of the cylinder must have collected a fair drop of water. First of all we would have a look over the nuts, then turn the engine until the water was expelled through the priming cap. If after that we could get her going on three cylinders, we would try for the Bull Hole. It was a course of action, and helped the spirit a bit, so that I got the length of suggesting, with searching irony as I hoped, that we could hardly expect Columba to have a really deep knowledge of the internal combustion engine.

Whereat the Crew's smile merely became more cheerful. The swell was a bit nasty, and we experienced some difficulty in launching the dinghy, and finally I pushed off with the surf above my knees.

But we got aboard and tried all outward and visible nuts. Nothing moved, for I often put a spanner over them, except one sparking plug, which took almost a turn. So much for that. Now for the expulsion of the water.

I inserted the starting handle and swung the flywheel. Instead of water, clean vapourless air came hissing through. There was no water. The small orifice did not even show damp.

I swung again, with the same result. I looked at the Mate.

Nothing was said—except by the Crew, and she merely smiled. I primed all four cylinders and they went off in a splendid roar. The Mate broke out the anchor, I shoved the gear lever forward, and we headed into the Sound. Then the Mate took the tiller, while I, of little faith, stood by the engine.

When he put her about for the Bull Hole, we met a tide between the high rocks running strongly. Slowly but surely she nosed up through it, the propeller racing slightly as we were tossed from behind. She certainly could not have made the passage on three cylinders, for there was a moment off the point when I glanced ashore to make sure we were still going ahead. Anchored in the old spot, I switched off, and we listened in. There was no hissing. I opened the priming cap. There was no steam. Never again, in fact, did we experience the same trouble. We were in the midst of a debate, intricately hypothetical, as to what we had done to put the matter right, when the Crew said, 'If you get out of my way, I'll get the supper.'

But, if in a different fashion, quite as unexpected a thing happened to us on the morning we decided to leave for Colonsay. By six o'clock we had the engine oiled, greased, and spanner-tight. The glass stood at 30.05, the highest it had been for weeks. The morning was calm. Colonsay anchorage is exposed to easterly winds. Presently a westerly breeze would spring up to reassure us. We were just about to start when a gust of wind hit the water. The sky was clouding. By the time we had got to a hill-top, a strong sou'easterly breeze was blowing with promise of increase. Deciding to give it an hour or so, we returned to find the glass had fallen a point. The wind rose. We were stuck.

Not that we were simple enough to have expected more

than we had already got, still . . . it was a pity that we had
not got the Columban blessing complete.

The amount of water the boat had been making had become a bit of a nuisance. Nothing dangerous, as our pump
was good and strong, but the slow increase might become
disturbing. So we decided to have a look at her hull. The
Crew went ashore to hunt up some plant or other, so the
Mate and I heaved out the heavy mat into the cockpit,
stripped off the floor boards, and, starting at the stem, removed the iron pigs and examined planking and timbers
with an electric torch. The wood in her was really excellent,
sound as a bell. The Tobermory owner had oiled and re-oiled
the wood to some tune. We found nothing until we came
amidships, where the trouble was revealed. The water was
coming in copiously from beneath the cross-board on which
the end of the flooring next to the engine rested. We saw
that this board was nailed to the hull from the outside, and,
after thoughtful discussion, decided to prize it free. When
we had done this we observed four springs of water bubbling
up, each round a copper nail, loose in its socket. As we
pushed a nail outward, the spring increased; as we pulled
it tight, it lessened. These nails had obviously been worked
loose by uneven pressure of floor boards on the cross-beam
and not from any fault in the wood of the hull. Having made
sure of this, I bethought me of what I had seen coopers do
to a whisky cask leaking from a worm-hole (for there are
worms that penetrate an inch of whiskied oak stave with so
remarkable a neatness that one must assume relish). I made
four spiles out of a piece of hardwood, each pointed and
shaped to its nail; rubbed them with red lead, and, while the
Mate held the nail, hammered in each gently but firmly until
it naturally broke off in the nail hole. When the operation
was complete, not one drop of water came through.

With aching backs, we sat down there amid the rusty pigs and grease and oily slime and laughed heartily as at a piece of enchantment or miracle. Then we remembered the Crew—for we had been three whole hours engrossed on the job—and when we had the cabin shipshape went out to look for her and saw her seated amid the boulders and weed, patient as the sphinx. We brought her back. She smiled. 'Wasn't it fortunate that the wind rose,' she said, 'or now we'd be in Colonsay and the leak with us for the rest of the trip.'

So she made up a splendid lunch, and we had a drink before it, and when the rain descended upon us, and the wind increased, and the glass tumbled, we made merry in as happy a small home as was on the seven seas or maybe even on the seven continents.

All that night it blew from the sou'east, with continuous slashing rains. For the first time, too, we were troubled with one or two bad bouts of bumping by the dinghy. At seven o'clock in the morning the glass was down to 29.50 and I had to bail the dinghy with a zinc bucket. It was quite impossible to put to sea. The rain taking off for spells round about ten o'clock, we started for Fionnphort over very broken ground to fetch some fresh stores.

Going up the ravine from the Bull Hole, we came on a narrow green mound, with a low shaped granite stone at its head innocent of all writing. A few yards above it were the ruins of a cottage. In that barren place, the nameless grave and the tumbled walls made about as desolate a corner as I had ever seen.

Between the Bull Hole and Fionnphort there were extensive granite quarries that employed many men a generation ago. At Ardmore, half-way, there is a solid pier, with the double line for the bogeys or trucks rusting before the eye where it is not covered with grass. Immense hewn blocks of the red granite are still piled high here, and on the hillside nearer Fionnphort lies the largest single block ever hewn out of a British quarry (or so we were told).

No one could tell us exactly why these quarries were abandoned, though it is generally held that transport charges had become prohibitive. We had a long talk with the solitary fisherman at Ardmore, who works lines in the Sound just south of Eilean na mBan. He had his line all baited with slug worm, waiting for weather to get out. If he did not get out to-day the bait would go rotten.

He appears to be the only line fisherman on this coast, though there are a few lobster fishers, for the rocky nature of the ground is suitable for lobsters. But the great trouble here is the weather, which for long spells in the winter-time makes small-boat fishing very difficult if not impossible. It was easy to believe him, as we gazed southward at the heavy seas spouting towards the Torranan Rocks.

The Mate wanted to know why he had been so unsuccessful in his own fishing and was told that fish were certainly extremely scarce, though he could give no reason for this—apart from trawlers. He then related specific experiences, such as: he was making a fair fishing of small haddock last year in a bay round the northern point of the Ross, when one night a trawler dropped in, and 'after that I didn't see a tail'. 'They often come in at night, too, to the south of Iona over there, but they are a bit frightened I think to risk coming into the Sound itself.' He was a gentle quiet man with a young wife who obviously helped him with the fishing. He showed no animus against the trawlers. 'It's a fine spot this, isn't it?' he asked, with a Columban smile.

Lobster fishing apparently was coming on again, for white

fishing was valueless. 'At least the trawlers can't get the lobsters!' said the Mate.

He agreed, but said he had heard that trawlers could disturb the lobster spawn. I recalled the lobster fisherman in Tobermory, so disheartened that he thought of giving up. We did not know about lobster spawn, but it seemed reasonable enough to us that where fishing and spawning banks are cleaned up all sorts of life must be affected, for there is a balance in nature. One thing was certain, anyway, that if a man like this—and many like him I had met—were given half a chance to earn a livelihood from the sea, they would do their utmost. There is a point of despair where going on becomes impossible.

From Fionnphort the Mate telephoned to his home, and getting slightly disturbing news of illness, was anxious to be back by Saturday. It was now Wednesday, with the glass still falling. As we ploughed our way back to the Bull Hole, the sky looked anything but promising. There are times when Mull seems one of the most desolate lands on earth. There were no sheep on this southern part of the Ross and, more remarkable, we saw only two or three rabbits and these round about the deserted quarries. Peat and bog and granite. As we came down past the nameless grave, something sinister emerged from it all. We had hardly got on board when the broken skies closed over and the rain descended once more.

Towards evening our sheltered anchorage for the first time became very unsettled. The boat began to rock badly without any ostensible cause—until we found the wind had gone round to the west. If it went round still farther, towards the north, and began to blow, we should feel the sea in earnest.

So back again we went in the evening to try to pick up a

weather forecast. Fortunately we ran into the ferryman in Fionnphort, who, though he had not listened in to the nine o'clock news that evening had followed his invariable practice of taking the 10.30 a.m. shipping forecast, and he gave us heart. He explained that a depression had passed over, that the wind was changing accordingly to follow it up, that by the time we got back we might expect to see the glass rising, and that—if no other depression was following after!— we should have a good chance of getting away in the morning. His discussion of the situation impressed us and we enjoyed our talk with him very much. In his imperturbable way he described the bottom of the Sound and the course to take through the Torranan Rocks. 'If you find a heavy swell round the red buoy out there, do not mind about that.'

We thanked him and, much heartened, turned back. On the way, we saw the fisherman and his wife in the Sound off Eilean na mBan and were glad that his bait would not now go rotten. They were obviously having no easy time of it out there, while the young children would be waiting for them at home. We wished them and their stores well, for we could not help making the contrast between this life and the life of the house-letter. Indeed, we talked of it for the rest of the way and of the comparable life on the wild north-eastern coast of Scotland we knew so well. There, strong daring men use bigger boats—these East Coast men who have carried over some of the roving Viking spirit, who know Castlebay as well as Wick, Peterhead as Stornoway. The fisherman of Ardmore was not a native.

When we got back, the glass was still inclined to fall. The wind was freshening, and the yacht over against Eilean na mBan was pitching so badly that the sailor in charge was attending to his warps, of which he had two ashore (the owners all this time had been living on Iona). We decided if it was at all a sea morning to start at six o'clock.

We had a pretty restless night and could hear the wind and the sea outside. At six we made hot drinks. The glass was low but steady. Not liking the look of things we climbed our hill and decided to wait until ten.

By that time there were breaks in the clouds, and the glass, if it moved at all, moved up. We would go out into the Sound and see what it really was like.

XIV

The Torranan Rocks

As you go south through the Sound, there are two
conical buoys that must be kept to port. Opposite
the first one (after we had left the striped buoy to
starboard) we got the tossing the ferryman had predicted. If
there was to be nothing worse, we should be all right—provided the engine kept going, so we concentrated ahead. Distant rocks, encircled by spume, were opening out. It was the
region where Alan Breck and David Balfour had got
wrecked, and the farthest headland on the Mull side was
undoubtedly Erraid Island itself. Away south-west of Iona,
ringed in white, we could see Soay, 'the little island where the
sea-calves breed' (the seal farm for the monks), and we
practically kept her head on it, for comfort in meeting the
waves, though, of course, we were to take the passage inside
the Torranan Rocks. Glancing back at Iona, the Crew saw
the cruciform shape of the cathedral begin to rise against the
sky, so holding on with one hand, I tried to hold her with
the other while she took a parting photograph, but it was
difficult balancing in the running seas. The Mate was at the
tiller, while I clung to the cabin door ready to dive at the
engine, should there be any splutterings of rebellion. He was
happy at the tiller and felt for the seas with a sensitive yield-
ing hand. Our plan here was to make through the Sound
until abreast of Erraid and Soay, round to port from

roughly a sou'westerly to a sou'easterly course, and pass between Mull and the Torranan Rocks, keeping an eye for the sunken dangers. But it was not so easy as all that to-day, and for a long time the Mate kept her heading into the seas direct on Soay. It was while she was on this tack that she got one or two very heavy smashes, from which we afterwards discovered that a seam suffered. Because of the islands and rocks and the approach of slack water, the long Atlantic waves had got broken up into fairly short, tumultuous, and unpredictable seas. A pitch, a roll, and a slew round, all in one, was the comfortable order of our going, but when she stood on her tail and came down with a wallop, the smash and shiver put my teeth on edge. She was so game, so full of gallantry, that you could not help feeling for her.

In the midst of the seas, where white caps were hissing, the Mate shouted that he saw a salmon flash down from a high leap. But he was wrong. It was our gannet. We had always seen one and it had always brought us luck. Fishing those seas must be such an exhilarating business that it caused momentary wonder and a smile. The day was brightening; the wind freshening—but not much. With luck, we should make Oban yet, for once round Ardalanish Point, hardly an hour away, we should have wind and sea astern.

But meantime we were still heading for Soay Island and had to decide to put her about. To come beam on to the seas was not an experience to look forward to. I could see the Mate watching them and waiting his moment. I left him to it, and I must say he took us round with the minimum of discomfort. A nice piece of work, and full of relief for me, as I had not yet got quite out of the habit of feeling that I must do everything myself. If I remember correctly, I think that someone in *Kidnapped* says the Torran Rocks reach for about ten miles, and for a vessel coming in from the west side of

Iona, the foul stretch is long enough. But the Torranan
Rocks proper are thus described in the *Sailing Directions:*
'This is a cluster of rocks about 4½ miles by 2½ miles in ex-
tent. One of them, Ruadh Sgeir, the most eastern of the
group, is marked by a wht. beacon. Many of the others are
only a few feet below water, and there is usually a swell
setting in which breaks badly over them. The inside passage
is usually taken . . . and there are three rocks to be guarded
against. With the large-scale chart this passage should present no great difficulty. . . .'

Unfortunately we had no large-scale chart, and as we had
held to Soay too long (for the greater comfort when we put
about), we now began to hunt for the first rock, called
Bogha hun a Chuoil, which should be about right in our
course. It has six feet over it at low water and though that
was double our draught, yet in this sea (it was low water
now) the swing of the waves should expose it. And actually
we found no difficulty in picking up its great round lather
of foam. Several of the rocks mentioned in our *Directions*
were not named on our small-scale chart, but our instinct
for the lie of things helped us here. With the assistance of
the Crew, I was able, in the spitting rain, to glimpse the
chart and the *Directions*, and with an ear on the engine and
an eye ahead, I shouted to the steersman that he was doing
grand.

'She'll take anything—capital seaboat,' he cried back,
obviously delighted with her. 'Wait till we get some dirty
weather, and you'll see!'

The only thing that troubled us for a time here was picking up a twelve-foot rock somewhere between Dubh Sgeir
(not named on our chart, but referred to in the *Directions*
as 'a small islet off the Ross') and Eilean Chalman farther
south. For some reason I had expected this to be a conical

rock, and, anyway, from the angle of our approach its long back seemed to be completely out of the way. But Eiln. Chalman was clear enough and we knew that if we kept a cable length from it we could not go far wrong. The other unmistakably clear mark was the beacon on Ruadh Sgeir. Yet the rock Bogha nan Ramfhear, which dries four feet, and lies a few cables southward of Eiln. Chalman, and 'is the only real danger on the inside passage', evaded us in the breaking seas for some time.

The scattered Torranan Rocks, spouting to starboard, were now an impressive sight, but the Mull shore, a short distance to leeward, looked pretty merciless. It took a real romance writer to get a wrecked crew over these smoking skerries!

A landmark at this point, not referred to in our *Directions* but given to us by the ferryman, was 'three round humps of land open of Eilean Chalman', and when they were picked up away in the distance, they got a shout of welcome. Shortly afterwards, Bogha nan Ramfhear, well clear to starboard, was seen smashing and blowing like a demented whale. We were steering a fine course and the engine, round which I went every now and then, never even felt like missing a beat. True, she raced and slowed as the propeller heaved and sank, but there was never any dangerous hesitancy. When she took the load again she took it solidly, with a dour reserve of power. True, again, her vaporiser joints may not have been quite gas-tight, and I had put so much oil into her bearings that she was blue-smoking a little, and once for about a quarter of an hour I had to take the air in a light-headed condition, which the extreme tossing and pitching did not help, but she kept going, a tribute surely to the fine workmanship that had been put into her a quarter of a century ago. There is a slow solid beat about a real marine engine that is very heartening in dirty weather. What would it matter if we did foul a smart yacht or two, running with their showy flexibility on converted motor-car engines? Off the Torranan Rocks we were in the mood to foul a round dozen in the quiet waters of Oban Bay without undue distress—so long as we got there! For there was the better part of an hour when, if the engine had given up, there could have been no hope for the boat or, indeed, for ourselves.

Yet, as it happened, our worst spell came when we had cleared Bogha nan Ramfhear and set our course on Ardalanish Point, the most southerly corner of Mull. For three miles, with tide and sea behind us, we had an anxious time. The real trouble was the dinghy, a heavy water-sodden brute of a craft for her size, and leaky. I had meant to put a half-hundredweight in her stern to keep her head up, but hadn't, and now she was yawing and charging down in the most thrawn way. There was no cleat on our starboard side to which we could have fastened a second head rope, even if we had been able. As it was, she was being towed through a cleat some two feet to port of the rudder. When she was coming up the wave, the water in her rushed astern and she cocked her nose up prettily enough, but coming down the near side, the water rushed forward and she buried her stem to the tip. One slight thing helped here. Right round her rail I had tied a double stout rope and this perhaps prevented her from shipping those small lashings of water that in time would undoubtedly have sunk her.

The climax came when we ourselves, though making at least seven knots, were actually pooped. I then deserted the engine and with a small fender in one hand and an open clasp knife in the other, kept my eye on the dinghy ready to cut the painter the moment she filled. There was a good edge on the blade, for that morning, anticipating this particular emergency, I had surreptitiously sharpened it on a smooth granite slab in the Bull Hole.

I was now facing back on our course and, my eye lifting to the sky, was suddenly dismayed at the sight of clouds massing in darkness beyond the Torranan Rocks, that deep blue-darkness of a thunderstorm. I called the Mate's attention to it. He chuckled. 'If that gets us, we'll know about it!' Such a storm on top of the seas that were running— better perhaps to cut the painter at once and so get the extra speed to make the head and whatever grace if shelter might be beyond. I watched the sky anxiously. The wind was not directly astern, and the storm-centre seemed to be making its way towards Colonsay.

We had set our minds, days before, on going to Colonsay, then down the Sound of Islay between Islay and Jura, possibly staying a day or so on Jura to climb the Paps and see this new southern world, before proceeding up the coast of Jura and through the notorious dreaded Gulf of Coirebhreacain, for I had heard many tales about it from seamen in this part of the world—quite as hair-raising as its ancient legends. But my regrets were eased as the thunderstorm set in that direction, and at last we saw we should make Ardalanish Point before we got what would be no more than its outer edge. In our anxiety, we did not give it a wide enough berth and ran into a real nasty jabble of short slapping seas. I was learning that a headland can be something like a bottleneck for a wide bay, particularly with wind and tide behind, though along the Mull coast here the Admiralty chart had a note that some two or three miles off shore the tide rarely makes more than one knot, a note we had taken into consideration when we had first thought of starting at six in the morning. We now realised that a tide running at one knot *against* wind and sea (as it would have been, had we left at six) would have made a mighty difference to us at that moment, compared with this luck of having it running with us.

We rounded Ardalanish Point before the black edge of the storm touched us, and when it passed, we were heading for the Firth of Lorn with the dinghy still in tow and with the wind slackening behind. As if conscious of the blade that so recently had hesitated under the rope, that small craft began to modify her yawing tactics in a shamefaced way, and I got up from my wet, cramped position and had a look round the old engine, which was slogging away in fine form.

When I came out, the Mate regarded me rather challengingly. 'I'd like', he said, 'to try a little bit of sail.'

I knew fine what was passing in his mind. My old engine could bust itself now; with a bit of sail he'd make Oban though the heavens fell. So there was a smile all round and I took the tiller.

On hands and knees he got round the mast, took his time, and presently up went the triangle of sail. He drew the lacing taut, and, back in the cockpit, pulled with exaggerated effort on the sheet, so that all and sundry might observe this eighth wonder of the world. He turned, nodding humorously, delighted with himself. 'It can snow now,' he said.

The Crew, who had been under the strain of the weather, not understanding always what we had shouted at each other and fearing that we had been keeping things from her—for outlook cries for rocks and wild looks around and an open knife might conceivably make some sort of impression!—came to individual life again and did her trapeze act past the engine into the cabin where, on all fours, she made real juicy tomato sandwiches on heavily buttered good and thick brown bread (Beattie's Glasgow bread, which is got in the small places along the West, is palatable and keeps admirably if rewrapped in its own paper). Added thereto a raw egg dropped into a half-tumbler of fresh milk, with a table-spoonful of whisky, made quite a sustaining snack.

The Crew ate indifferently and confessed, on being probed, that she had felt a bit sick with excitement (sea-sickness never touched her), and for a time had actually had to keep her eyes off the seas. However, she also confessed that she would not have missed the experience.

The sail was steadying us beyond any hope of mine and must have been adding about a couple of knots to our speed. For the first time we began to take stock of our earthly environment, and enjoyed the relief that comes after an anxious spell.

For this was a new part of the world, after Skye and the distant Hebrides, the Small Isles and the Arisaig mainland. Heavy storm clouds blotted out the Paps of Jura and hung low over the ridges of Islay and Scarba, but the small Isles of the Sea had their rock walls glistening in a burst of sun. Far ahead the mainland was vague, and what looked like a dark cloud on the sea we assumed to be Kerrera Island.

But Mull was near enough for proper inspection, and the Mate, light-heartedly studying the chart, assured the Crew that the wide inlet she saw was Loch Buy.

'The Macleans of Loch Buy,' she remembered. 'So it must be in there somewhere—the Harper's Pass. Did you ever hear the saying they have on Mull: "Wasn't I the fool to burn my harp for her—or for him?" '

'No,' he answered. 'But I'll give you a cigarette if you'll tell it.'

'Well,' she said, 'once upon a time there was a harper in Mull and he was a very famous harper. Yet though he was famous, he was simple in his manners and affectionate. He fell in love with the flower of the island. Her name was Rosie.

And he married her. So to celebrate this great event, they set out for the low country to call on their friends—the three of them: himself, Rosie, and the famous harp, which wherever he went always went with him. Now as they came into a desolate part of the country, the sun sinking and the shadows gathering about them, Rosie got a cold fainting turn, and would have fallen to the ground, had he not caught her and held her. He wrapped her in his plaid and chafed her hands and tried to warm her back to life every way he could, but her hands remained cold and her face white and cold, and he didn't know what more to do. He felt she would die unless he could make up a fire, but though he searched for sticks or anything at all that would burn, not a scrap could he find anywhere. And then his eye fell on his harp. Now as he valued his harp only a little more than his own life, he quickly broke it into pieces and made a grand fire of it, and in the warmth Rosie recovered.

'In the morning, they set off again. But as they were going down a hillside, they met a hunter riding on a horse, and this hunter greeted Rosie as he would an old and familiar friend. Now the harper, as I have said, had delicate manners, and as Rosie had not thought of introducing him, he walked slowly ahead. But presently, as there were no sounds of Rosie coming, he turned and looked back—and there was Rosie being mounted behind the hunter on his steed, which quickly carried them over the hill and out of sight. So he turned homeward, saying bitterly to himself: "Fool that I was to burn my harp for her." '

'That's a good story,' said the Mate. 'And is the Harper's Pass really away in there?'

'Yes, it is. And now you tell a story.'

He thought for a moment and then he said, tilting his head towards me, 'We must go round with the sun.'

'If you look', I said at once, 'at the chart, you will find on that face of cliff to the east of the entrance to Loch Buy a spot marked "Lord Lovat's Cave".'

'Why, that's so,' said the Mate; then he stared at the cliff. 'And I can see the cave.'

'No sailor, man or woman, should be astonished at his chart. . . .'

'He's just gaining time to make up the story now,' said the Crew, interrupting.

'It was Simon Lord Lovat who hid in that cave after the '45. He was called the Fox. Now you would think when you remember all the lands we have passed, the desolate mountains, the glens, the great sea inlets, the endless moors, sky horizon after sky horizon, and still more mountains and corries and passes, with gaunt hiding holes everywhere, not to speak of little croft houses in forgotten places and wooded streams, and hillside forests, and granite rocks, you would think that no Hunter from the outside world would ever catch that Fox in such a land. Yet the Hunter caught him. He hunted him out of that cave, as out of many another cunning or desolate place, and you have only to look at it to see how persistent, how ruthless, he must have been.

'It was an extraordinary and bitter hunt, that rose out of the romance of Bonnie Prince Charlie, who merely wanted a crown for himself. The Stuarts were a strange family, and from their record you would say that it would matter less than a harper's tune to all that land we have passed and see still before us, even if Charlie did get his crown. For well the land knew that it was when the Stuarts were at St. James's that she suffered her worst religious persecutions, and suffered, too, within herself her most bitter division. In the old days the strife had been between two countries, and each had had victories and defeats, but at least they made

248

two sides, with wholeness of mind for the contest. But with the Stuarts in London, this land lost her wholeness and what harmony went with it. They say that if Charlie had won his crown, he would have done something. Well, he might have done something for a few chiefs—if the English had let him. But he was not likely to forget that they had beheaded his great grandfather, and if he wanted to keep his own head on his neck, he would have to play their tune. However, all that is as may be. He didn't win his crown—and the hunt was on, sounding over the red tartan on Drumossie Moor. It was never let up.

'They got the hunted Fox, too, and the Hunter trussed him up and took him on his steed behind him and carried him over the hills and far away to London, and there they let him have his say, and he said it right ironically, thank God, and so they executed him.'

'Do you think he made up that very well?' asked the Mate.

'No,' said the Crew. 'But maybe there's a great story lost in it. I thought you were going to end it by saying he had burnt his harp for Charlie.'

'I did think of it,' I answered, 'but it wouldn't be true. For now we come to the core of the matter as it touches this great and lovely land. Like Charlie, he burnt his harp for himself.'

We were now in the Firth of Lorn, with a favourable wind and a calming sea, and we debated whether we should cross over towards Sheep Isle and in due course take the sheltered sound inside Kerrera and on into Oban Bay. But the Mate was so set on his sail, and his arguments for the broad seaway were so strong, that we hadn't the heart to counter him and in truth we were ploughing along now in grand style, right pleased with ourselves and with this new country. Before we came abreast of Loch Spelvie we passed a white yacht, well inshore from us, making up the sheltered Mull coast in full sail. She was at least three times our size and we were astonished to see her pitching so much, and laughed in our astonishment when she plunged rather heavily and plainly took a green one in over her bows. With considerable complacency, we wondered how much she would take in off the Torranan Rocks! Not but that we knew the mighty difference between running before a moderate sea and taking it head on. Still, the sea now, compared with what we had come through, was calm, and I hope we were entitled to whatever innocent amusement was going. Anyway, we watched her for quite a time and chuckled more than once, I'm afraid.

Then the Crew pointed to a white finger in the sea.

'That's Lismore lighthouse,' said the Mate. 'On the way from Oban in the steamer we passed between it and the smaller lighthouse—do you see it?—a little this side of it? That smaller lighthouse is called Lady Rock. They say that four currents meet about there, and certainly there was a very nice jabble as we came through. I thought of your boat and wondered if she would stand up to it.'

'And what do you think now?' I asked.

'I'll take you through it, if you like, and we could keep the sail up?'

'Tell me,' said the Crew; 'why is it called Lady Rock?'

'I can tell you that, too—and without making it up either,' he answered, 'for it's a well-known story in these parts, though there are several versions of some of its happenings. In any case and in fairness, it will balance your story, for this is about the treachery of a man to a woman. Though in the case of the lassie with the harper—that is what is called romance, for what young woman, trudging the country with a wandering minstrel, but would be attracted by a hunter on his pacing steed?'

'Proceed,' said the Crew.

'This is a different story altogether. Do you see that old castle, by the Point? That's Duart Castle, where the chiefs of the Macleans lived. Long long ago, one of the chiefs married a girl called Elizabeth, and she was the daughter of the second Earl of Argyll. Now the Macleans had no love for the Campbells, and they would be damned, they said, if ever any Campbell blood ruled over them. They would sooner, they said, kill the lady and her young child, than that that should happen. And they there and then made a plot to kill them, and the husband did nothing to stop them.

'Well, one dark winter's night, they got hold of her and forced her into a boat, and choked her cries, and rowed with her over to the Lady Rock, which is bare at low water, and left her there.'

'Sorry to interrupt you,' I said, 'but I don't believe for a moment that clansmen, and especially Macleans, ever forced a chief to do anything so damnable. Now I saw somewhere —perhaps in Campbell's *Popular Tales*—that the actual position was that Maclean was carrying on with a Spanish lady up on the galleon in Tobermory. And now—and here's something sudden and bright!—we do know, from the Privy Council records, that the Maclean chief was in with the Spaniards, because he headed a squad of them and wiped out the Small Isles. What do you think of that? And perhaps the original "Spanish Lady" song was not about Dublin City at all, but about Tobermory!'

'Same number of syllables even,' said the Mate.

'Correct. And Elizabeth, being an Argyll, was equal to the occasion. She got the Maclean's own manservant to proceed privily to Tobermory and—no, not crudely despatch the Spanish lady but—blow up the whole ship. And the wreck is there to this day! Isn't that more like the thing? And the Maclean, who had laid waste the Small Isles, once he had wormed out the truth of the affair, wouldn't think twice of putting his own lady on the spot or at least on the rock. As a piece of cogent, if quick, reasoning—'

'You wouldn't mind if she drowned while you argued,' said the Crew. 'Will you please tell me what happened to the woman on the rock?'

'She cried and screamed,' said the Mate, 'but there were no fishers out there in that dark world; so the tide began to wash over her feet, and to rise higher, until she stood knee-deep in the icy water. And she screamed and listened again, but heard only the answering screams of the astonished sea-birds.

'The tide continued to rise, as the tide will, and when it was nearly at her breast, as the story goes—so it could not have been a stormy night—the dawn broke, and a boat, a small skiff, hove in sight. Though now nearly exhausted, she managed to attract its attention. The fishermen turned out to be Argyll's men and they took the woman off the rock and bore her away safely to her father's castle.

'And now the scene moves to Argyll—for something original and terrible in its cunning. You can feel it coming? It came.

'Argyll waited until the bereaved husband acquainted him of his great grief caused through the death of his beloved wife, the daughter of his lordship.

'Argyll was deeply affected, and sent an invitation to the Maclean to come and mingle a husband's sorrow with a father's. And Maclean with his kinsmen and followers, all dressed in deepest mourning, duly arrived, and was met by Argyll, clad in black. A solemn feast was spread in the great hall. They all took their places. Then the door opened and the Lady Elizabeth, superbly dressed, entered, walked to the table, and took the vacant seat.

'Maclean sprang up, and in his terror got as far as the castle gate, before the Lord of Lorn slew him. But the Earl stuck to the kinsmen—until the child which had been saved by its nurse was given back to its mother.'

'That is so terrible and dreadful a story,' said the Crew, 'that most people will forget in their minds that it is a story with a happy ending.'

'Can you tell me', I asked, 'what lighthouse is on the Mull there opposite the Lady Rock?'

'I heard about that on the steamer also. It has something to do with a monument to William Black, the novelist. But I'm not sure,' said the Mate.

A lighthouse to commemorate a novelist! It seemed too good to be true. And to dear William Black through whom the Highland rivers ran, whose novels had touched to romantic visions not a few of the days of our youth! Not a great novelist, so he had only a little lighthouse all to himself. I took off my sou'wester.

What more perfect memorial to a great man than a lighthouse! How superbly apt!

'Let us start,' said the Crew, 'by giving Ardnamurchan to St. Columba.'

Well—perhaps—seeing Stevenson had already collared Skerryvore.

'Hold on!' said the Mate. 'I have one or two scientists I want to fix up first.'

'Don't let us forget', suggested the Crew, 'that we have quite a lot of nice little conical red buoys.'

'And some with stripes on them', said the Mate, 'for the famous women.'

'No wrangling,' I ordered. 'Let us consider the great lights first . . .'

So I put the tiller towards the Lady Rock and we held over for the north point of Kerrera Island, round which lay Oban Bay.

The north shore of Kerrera is very indented, but after a little uncertainty we finally made sure of Maiden Island. Leaving it to port, we entered the narrows, and brought abeam a ruined ivied castle surmounted by the Blue Saltire, extended in the breeze.

'A royal welcome indeed!' The Mate saluted, and we regretted very much that we had no flag to dip.

We should have to make a decent anchorage after that! But there was Oban Bay before us, with its clusters of small boats and jetties and piers and steamers—and beside us the engine, with its turn for social satire. We forgot all about not caring whether we fouled anyone. Vanity rose up again to a fine pitch of excitement. Multitudinous detail was all about us in rich confusion. Our *Directions* suggested the town side of the bay, opposite the R.H. Yachting Club. Could anyone see the Club? Two or three small racing yachts were going through their paces right ahead. A steamer was approaching. Another was backing out from a pier. 'I don't like it here,' said the Crew. 'Neither do I,' said the Mate. 'I'll put her about,' said I. 'You've got to give way to sailing craft,' said the Mate, 'and that fellow is just going to put about: watch him.'

Out of compliment to the engine I let it salute the front for a little longer, then brought the boat round and headed for Ardentrive bay opposite, on the Kerrera shore, where all the big yachts were at anchor. I left the tiller to slow down the engine—and succeeded slightly. Steering a bold course between the fine vessels, I saw a vacant buoy away in the north-west corner of the bay. I shouted to the Mate, now standing forward, that he had got to pick it up with the boat-hook. Presently he signalled me to stop. The Crew took the helm and I the gear lever. Now for it! But she came into neutral like a lamb. Forward a little, signalled the Mate. And forward she went. I have got the hang of you now, my pretty lady! I tugged—and spoke harshly—and had to stop the engine. But instead of trying to pick up the buoy, the Mate let go the anchor, though I knew the bottom to be foul from centuries of junk. He indicated that the yacht next to us was riding to her anchor, and suggested we might have no right to use someone else's buoy. But my whole mind had been set on riding to a buoy. It was the secret desire of my soul. The force of this desire was so strong that it hurtled me into the dinghy, whose floor boards were awash, and rowed me over to a small fishing boat close by the low rocks on shore. There was an elderly man on board who spoke English with a strong Isles accent. No one had been tied to the buoy for many a long time, he said, and it would be all right. Back I went, and with an end of rope pulled off for the buoy and just managed to reach it, the Mate making fast the other end to the mast; whereupon he heaved up the anchor and presently we were riding all safe and snug to a real red iron buoy big enough for a liner. We had arrived. It was a moment of deep beatitude. When, leisurely, we turned and surveyed Oban in the westering light, we thought it the most beautiful town of its size we had ever seen.

XV

Oban

And Oban is a beautiful town, stretched along the curve of its spacious bay. Its house fronts, white and yellow and grey, brightly reflected the sinking sun. It would have stood comparison, we felt, with any classical town of the Mediterranean, and we wondered at a round building, high on the hill behind, like the Roman Colosseum. For Scotland, it had, in truth, a southern air, something captured from a brighter clime.

When we went to draw water from the well under the tall monument, to which the fisherman directed us, we lay on the grass in a perfect evening and stared across the many anchored craft. It was the perfect spot and perhaps the perfect hour for beholding this attractive town. Behind the sea-front, the ground rose steeply, deeply wooded, irregular, with fronts and gables of many fine houses. Even as we looked, we saw the smoke of a train approaching through a valley behind so as not to disturb the harmony. The passenger steamers, with their dark hulls and bright red funnels, swept from the piers at speed. Along the esplanade, the crowd sauntered slowly. Railway station, piers and fish market were all grouped together to the right of the esplanade and gave an impression of lively business, balanced in design by the uprising of wooded Pulpit Hill still farther to the right, with its irregularly placed private and boarding houses.

Oban

It was inevitable that a town should arise here, for such a situation must have been of social importance long before the days of recorded history. In digging foundations for houses, workmen have in fact laid open caves where the primitive hunters and fishers lived and loved and multiplied. Many strange craft crossed Oban Bay before King Haco of Norway entered it in the summer of 1263 and dipped his colours to the castle that is now an ivied ruin (though still prepared to wave a noble flag). Here he waited for his allies from the West Coast and the Islands before proceeding to the Clyde to teach Alexander III of Scotland a lesson he would remember. The grand fleet of 180 craft, with Haco's own *Christsuden* in command, must have been reviewed by the lads of Oban village with considerable respect.

And fine sweeping lines the vessels had, with high beaks, striking colour, and banks of rowers. The beak of the *Christsuden* was a gilded dragon's head; the hull was all oak and ornamented with more dragon heads overlaid with gold. And right princely courtesies they had in those days, too. Ewen of Lorn refused to help Haco, even though he held land from him; for he also held land from the Scottish king. Honourably, he offered to give up the Haco land, but by no persuasion could he be made to assist Haco. So Haco held on to him, until negotiations began between the kings, when Haco set him at liberty with many costly gifts; and on his part Ewen promised to do his best to make peace between the two kings.

But Dougal (of the ivied ruin) was all for Haco, who gave him fifty-five galleys to plunder Cantyre and Bute, which 'King Dougal' so thoroughly did, that by the time he had also plundered Loch Long and Loch Lomond he was too late for the Battle of Largs, where Haco was defeated, and as he thought he had better not take on the victorious Scots by himself, he followed Haco and met him again in Oban Bay. There they took their breath for a little, while the lads of the village did some private thinking, and then King Dougal convoyed the defeated king of all the Vikings as far as Tobermory, where he bade him farewell and returned to the castle, not yet with the ivy on it, to await the next move by Scotland's king.

In the well the water was crystal clear and we decided we should cleanse our tank of the brown moss of the Bull Hole before filling it with this remarkable liquor, so strangely without taste. Tall foxgloves grew about and large buttercups. But there was no hurry, so we climbed up to the needle monument and found it commemorated one David Hutcheson by whose energy and enterprise the West Highlands had received the blessings of steam navigation. A far far better reason than for being a landlord or even (as we had expected) a clan chief. Oh that we had his like with us now to amend the transport to suit the age! Still, a lighthouse and a monument, both for merit, in one day! And when, later, we investigated the Colosseum, and on a tablet over the entrance traced the words: 'Erected in 1900 by John Stuart McCaig, Art Critic and Philosophical Essayist, and Banker, Oban,' we were moved.

'*And* Banker,' murmured the Mate. 'What a conjunction is there!'

The more we thought, the more were we moved.

Alas that the building had never been completed, that it should be no more than the round shell of that strange conjunction! For what a project had been envisaged:

> *Statues he willed that his trustees should raise,*
> *His parents', brothers', sisters' effigies. . .*

Oban

We hurried to buy a guide book in the town, from which
I beg permission to quote a descriptive passage so admirable
for its conjunctive ease:

'When the Tower was begun, the half-dozen ancient
cannon, 32-pounders, which had long lain overlooking Oban
from their semi-lunar battery (which originated the adjacent
street name, Battery Terrace), were removed to the un-
levelled centre of the interior, where they lie derelict, objects
of curiosity to visitors. They were brought to Oban by the
second Marquis of Breadalbane, 'dear Lord Breadalbane',
Queen Victoria called him in her *Leaves from the Journal of our
Life in the Highlands* (written twenty-four years later on the
occasion of her Majesty's visit to Oban, 10th August 1847),
when on the Royal Yacht coming in sight, they boomed
forth a hearty welcome (Walk No. I). They were not again
fired till 1871, when there were rejoicings all over Scotland
on the marriage of the Princess Louise and the Marquis of
Lorn, eldest son of the Duke of Argyll. The Queen had seen
the Marquis as a child at his home, Inverary Castle, in 1847,
and described him as a "dear, white, fat, fair, little fellow
with reddish hair", never dreaming that in after years she
would have him for a son-in-law. It was of this marriage that
an old Argyllshire woman on hearing of it exclaimed—"And
it's a proud lady the Queen will be, whatever." '

If only John Keats on his visit to Oban in 1820 had left
us a sonnet our cup would have been full, but our wild un-
couth scenery inspired little poetry in that English wight.

And that was a little difficult to understand, for from
David Hutcheson's monument such magnificence was dis-
closed as surely must have touched to fugitive response that
most magnificent and sensuous of poets. Across the firth lay
Mull of the mountains: Dun da Chaoithe (the hill of the two

winds) over William Black's lighthouse; Mainnir nam Fiadh
(fold of the deer); Sgurr Dearg (the red sgurr); Creach
Bheinn (ben of the plunder); Ben Buy (the yellow ben), to
far Ben Mor (the great ben) veiled in mist; all ranging from
about 2,500 to over 3,000 feet. Southward the Firth of Lorn,
to the Isles of the Sea in its glittering waters. Northward, the
long island of Lismore (the big garden), with mountainous
Morven of the legends and the songs rising behind. Beyond
Lismore, the bright light on Loch Linnhe, leading to dark
Glencoe. And east of us Oban—and all Argyll.

There is a magnificence that can be terrifying. A vastness,
a grandeur, so removed from the conception of an inwrought
jewelled creation, that perhaps one can dimly understand the
reaction of so sensitive a mind as Keats's. Even over Mull, on
this fine evening, great shafts of slanting light penetrated
dark caverns, and as one gazed, the dark and the light reformed, so that one saw without ever quite catching the
moments of change: vast fade-outs and fade-ins as imper-
ceptible in transition as they were inexorable in effect. But
when sun and wind and cloud and rain set themselves to project on sea and mountain their best effort at a gloom fan-
tasia, the stage-thoughts of ten thousand human minds could
be drowned in the tail-end of its distant shower. Not used to
it, the human mind must rebel. Used to it, it can at least gaze,
and possibly appreciate, and even—for adventure is life—
criticise.

On this lovely evening, with the Torranan Rocks like
laughter in our minds, we came down to the well and filled
our buckets. From the fisherman's boat, blue smoke was
ascending. He was cooking his evening meal. Later, we
found that he lived on this boat all alone, winter and summer, occasionally shifting over from one side of the bay to

the other. During the time we were there we spoke to him frequently, and found him courteous and helpful, but did not care to intrude on his privacy, though I should have liked to have found the conclusions he had arrived at concerning life, explicit or implicit. Undoubtedly he had solved the problem for himself. On the second day he left us and went across to the Oban side by Pulpit Hill, and we wondered, with remorse, if our near presence had disturbed him. But in the evening he came back, his big sail of many patches and small holes bellying in the light breeze, anchored by the rock, and sent aloft his smoke. The contrast between his way of living and that of those of a tall-masted white yacht, with a string of fifteen portholes, indicated no doubt the progress of civilisation, but somehow not conclusively. His was a solitary life, but obviously neither morbid nor alone. When he wanted company, he commanded it, and spoke to his guests in a fine resonant Gaelic. But to our gross eyes in the darkening, his company was invisible.

The esplanade that evening was thronged, and we sauntered along like strangers returned to a life which is not quite real, its preoccupations and tricks of conduct and speech having a curious echo quality. That contact with nature (even if in her wilder moods, when emotions and capacity for action had been unusually quickened) for a mere handful of days should produce this effect is, I think, remarkable. We experienced it pointedly more than once. In fact we never lost it during the whole trip, and after two days in Oban we felt we had to move on again to things we could get a solid grip of. Even the food in the hotel seemed desperately reminiscent. We had been looking forward to a magnificent feed of quite a few courses; really doing ourselves well; and had joked about it in happy anticipation. And now out of the corner of my eye I saw the Crew, with an odd sort of dismay on her face, unable to finish her meat. She explained that she had been given too much, that it was a bit tough, with too many vegetables; too much on her plate. She was almost hurt, as if her toy had got broken. When the Mate, having finished all that went before, took a plateful of apple tart, with cream, she revolted. The coffee was quite good, but somehow still and oily, not with the steaming fragrant top we had got used to. Possibly we were too physically tired after our strenuous day (with the Crew unknowingly exhausted from over-excitement) to enjoy much eating. Whatever the reason, the feast was voted dull and stodgy.

'I never realised before', said the Crew, 'that man is just a cannibal.'

Though I had eaten pretty well myself, I admitted handsomely that I would have swopped the whole lot for one of her salads.

For what she does not know about internal combustion engines, she makes up on her salads. Like these weather effects over wide areas, they are pretty marvellous affairs, with a universal reach across the vegetable kingdom and a skill in selection and blending that would make any critic, pure and undefiled or gorged by cannibalism, offer up a soft sigh.

Basic ingredients may consist of lettuce, tomato, beetroot, bits of sliced date, banana and orange, with nuts, peas and other evasive pellets, until complications are introduced from grated turnip and carrot to parsley and mint, and whatever luck there may be with the more usual elements from onions to cucumber, not forgetting stoned raisins.

A revolting conglomerate, in turn? All I can honestly say is that it has its perfect moment, and not least when it is sweetened by the fruit to that point—and that point only—when the juices of the mouth naturally flow. And when anything is just so sweetened one is inclined to eat of it on and on. Just as certain unfortunate persons, finding a drink palatable, may drink on and on. And even on.

It was, in fact, the temperature of the drink that proved the hotel grand. We made acknowledgments there, and in the wide lounge, looking out on the sea front, we listened to the travelling world.

Two French women behind us had not been able to get rooms and talked much but not volubly. In front, the head of a family indicated an arresting sunset, for it must have been now about ten o'clock, but the daughter, slim and brown-haired with nails tapered and delicately pink as her flesh, hardly bothered to look out, as if all the beauty were a setting for that which her petulant brows suggested she hadn't got and for which she was so palpably prepared. A thin alert old man with grey hair talking of sunsets! And a thin bony-faced woman backing him up! She picked up a slightly soiled copy of the *Tatler*. Three men and two women discussed the dinner, which clearly had had its good points for them. One of the men read out of a newspaper, approvingly, about Royalty in Scotland to illustrate something. In a corner, male heads bent over a table and listened to a low voice and jerked back and laughed. 'That's a good one!' said one. 'Dem good!' A steamer arriving unexpectedly at the North Pier caused a slight commotion by a window. The Mate was still awaiting his telephone call, but we were in no hurry, and the waiter was a thoughtful young man. We had nothing to catch—or lose, and far away and multitudinous was the hum of the sea in our ears—even if the Crew implied that it was no more than the hum of our blood from over-eating. But she herself now and then put her hands to her cheeks to still the glow from the day that now, more than ever, she would not have missed.

Oban

With good news from the telephone, we rowed across the harbour in a state of pleasant well-being, glad to head for our own quiet corner, where we called a good-night to the Islesman and lit our lamp. The Mate pumped, and then put his head in at the door.

'Do you think', he addressed the Crew, 'that he has anything good in his heart? The well water is here.'

I never yet had a nice little private store of something very special but it was stolen from me.

In our short stay, we got to know Oban fairly well. Down a side street we found a plumber's shop with a smiling girl and obliging workmen. We had suffered nothing less than torture from the water tap. It had been hit by some wanton hammer in Skye and the cock, fitting badly, leaked, so that we had had to screw up the under nut very tightly, and as the handle of the tap was missing and the best-fitting spanner too big, drawing water was a matter of stresses and slips and barked knuckles. Often, too, when we got it opened, the spanner would slip when we tried to close it, and manners were temporarily dislocated as the precious water gushed over the flooring and into the bilge.

Though perhaps precious is hardly the apt word, for the Crew had reached the stage of rebelling against using the water itself, alleging impurities which I assured her were no more than gravel and healthy brown peat moss. So I had screwed out the tap, and then, I must confess, it took the Mate and myself the better part of two hours, using countless buckets of salt water, to clean out what must have been the accumulated deposits of twenty-five years. But let me draw a veil over that noisome business and get back to those plumbers who in no time ground in the cock, fitted a handsome brass handle with a black grip, and charged a shilling.

It was carried through the streets of Oban in triumph; it fitted perfectly; it turned with one finger; and the well water that came through was crystal. After that anyone would fill the kettle. Occasionally it does happen in life that one can purchase a shilling's worth of magic.

So we were disposed to think that everything in Oban was flourishing, but I knew I had yet to visit the fish mart, and there alas! was not even one phosphorescent scale of magic. What had once been the busy herring-curing stations was now a waste land boarded round and overgrown with grass. Of the first four of the fish-salesmen's offices, one sold ice cream and three were vacant. I had a long talk with a fish-salesman and his story was depressing. Already at Mallaig and elsewhere we had seen that the herring fishing on the West had this year been a failure.

'But what if a late herring season comes along?'

'Make no difference,' he answered. 'Mallaig and Castlebay will handle it easy—particularly as far as the Scottish boats are concerned.'

'You mean?'

'The Scottish boats are so much in debt that they can't fit out for a late fishing—very few of them, anyway.'

I asked him if the Herring Industry Board's report was out. In the same laconic voice, he said it was. Later, in the press, I read extracts from it and recognised it as the most desperate document yet issued on the subject, amounting in pith to little more than a statement endeavouring, by the aid of analytic reason, to show the inevitability of the early death of the whole Scottish herring fishing industry based on the system of the family boat.

It gave countenance, wittingly or not, to a recent press campaign against the Scottish system of family-owned boats and in favour of the English system of company-owned boats. And it was difficult logically to counter it, because, clearly, boats run by a shore syndicate, with capitalist resources to tide over difficult times, are bound in the long run to oust individual or family ownership, living from hand to mouth or at least from season to season.

We were seeing taking place before us the death of an ancient way of life that had many very fine qualities. For the skipper of the typical Scottish fishing boat has always been not only owner of his vessel but one of the crew, who called him naturally by his Christian name. He is one of themselves, one of a small company working for their common good, with powers of leadership and decision vested in him, and receiving an 'extra share' for the boat. Because of their common religious beliefs, for example, it would not occur to him to go to sea on Sunday—nor would any outside power compel him to go, whatever the material loss involved. To the dangerous business of the sea they brought the human factors that give to man his integrity and dignity, a matter conceivably of some significance for the world at the moment. For the universal problem appears to be: how to manage efficiently the economic machine and at the same time retain the maximum amount of individual freedom. The old Scottish system of family-owned boats represented perhaps the only great industry left in the world where some attempt at solving the problem continued to be made.

But it is a subject which I have dealt with elsewhere and I mention it now because of the depressing effect it had upon us on that quiet evening in Oban, with its gay visitors, and clean streets, and handsome hotels.

'What does Oban live on?' I asked the salesman.

'House-letting mostly. Though the shops do a good trade with the country round about.'

Two trawlers were unloading and a third manœuvring

for a berth. I asked him how it was we could not catch fish in the bays. I could not help smiling at his dry expression as he looked at the trawlers. I remembered the lonely fisherman of Ardmore.

'How much fish have they landed to-day?' I asked.

'I don't know to-day's figures, but on Monday last they landed two thousand six hundred boxes. Some days it's less.'

For one small quay it seemed an astonishing quantity of white fish.

That these vessels poached the inshore banks there could be little doubt. That the official effort to detect them was ludicrously inadequate there could likewise be no doubt. On our travels, we had once seen the Fishery cruiser. Giving her the West to look after was like giving all Argyllshire to one gamekeeper.

To blame the trawlers is to ask too much of human nature. In their position I should certainly do my utmost to poach. Indeed, as I looked at these iron vessels, their rust whitened by salt water and gulls, I knew I was looking at the most daring vessels afloat, manned by the finest and most intrepid seamen to be found on any of the oceans of the world. They have the air of buccaneers. No slacking or grousing against the Government here. They take their living out of the teeth of danger, in the worst seas fought by man, and a slowly meandering Fishery cruiser or the wailing of a pack of half-crofters is not going to trouble them much.

'Well, at least the trawlers bring a lot of business to Oban?'

But the salesman shook his head. 'They have the fish all ready in iced boxes and load them direct on to the train for the south. That's all.'

We watched this neat dispatch of business. The train shunted on the quay.

'Are there no local fishing boats from Oban?'

'There is supposed to be one.'

And there we were back at a sore point, back at the reputed laziness and lack of initiative of the West Coast man, at those tales of doles and faked employment, of constant demands for Government assistance, of a lost capacity to help himself.

'I want to buy some fresh fish,' said the Crew to the Mate.

Like a lamb he followed her into a fish shop. She chose a modest quantity for a single meal and the price manifestly staggered him.

'Are you sure they're quite fresh?' she asked pleasantly.

'Oh yes, madam. They've just come from Aberdeen.'

XVI

Glen Etive, where she 'builded her bridal hold'

W e left Oban at 8.20 a.m., round about high
water, having been informed by a man on
the slipway of the yard in Ardentrive Bay
(where we filled up with petrol and oil from the yard's
launch) that high water at Connel Bridge was about an hour
and a half after Oban. Though we could hardly be eight
miles from Connel, we were not astonished. In the Sound of
Iona, the ferryman told us that between the centre of the
Sound and inshore by the Bull Hole, a matter of yards, the
difference could run to an hour and a half. But it was easy
enough to check the information received. In the *Sailing
Directions*: 'CONST. for finding time of *High Slack Water at
Connel Falls* – 3hr. 6m. L'pool.' Turning up Brown's
Nautical Almanac, we noted the time of high tide at Liver-
pool on this particular morning, deducted the 3hr. 6m., and
found that the tide should be high and slack under the bridge
at 9.41 a.m. We should thus probably enter with the last of
the flood and certainly, all going well, were in time for the
slack water.

On paper it looked the most intricate piece of navigation
we had yet tackled, for we had heard in our time the roar of
the flowing or ebbing tide over the rock ledges in the narrow

channel spanned by the railway bridge at Connel Ferry. I hesitate to confess that it was the difficulty that attracted us, but I am afraid it must have exerted the major pull, for all our knowledge of the Loch Etive country was pretty well summed up in a few uncertain words of the song of farewell Deirdre sang—the most beautiful of all the women of the Gaels—on leaving Alba (or Albyn, as Scotland was then known). 'Glen Etive, O Glen Etive, where I builded my bridal hold,' as the modern translator interprets the simple words of the lovely one herself. Together with other vague historical odds and ends, but certainly with no idea of the astonishing past and present of the whole region.

It was raining slightly when we left Oban and the sky was heavy. There was no flag on the ivied ruin—that ancient centre of the Macdougalls (of whom I have never met a bad one). Passing Maiden Island to port, we opened out the coast and saw Oban's bathing suburb of sands—it looked attractive even in the rain. There was a real good roll to enliven us and remind us of the open sea. We gave the shore no more than a fair berth and were confused somewhat by our small scale chart, as, on this course, the entrance to Loch Etive is by no means obvious from any distance. We had made up our minds to go inside the island at the mouth, but having been misled by what looked like the channel and turned out to be the disappearing arm of a little bay, we stood off and finally passed the island to starboard and so opened out the entrance properly. To port now was the wide sweep of Lochnell Bay, with its legendary background to the Stone of Destiny. In the leaden-surfaced sea-roll and the rain and the gloom, it would not have been difficult to conjure strange figures out of a dim past. Dunstaffnage itself should be showing soon. So thoughtfully we asked the Crew to read a chapter.

Glen Etive, where she 'builded her bridal hold'

'The Island of Dunstaffnage', she read, 'and a small islet, Eil. Beg. N.E. of it, lie at the mouth, and the detail chart, 2814a, should be carefully consulted if going up, to avoid the shoal water off Ledaig Pt. and Ru ard nan leum, the N. and S. points of the actual entrance.'

'Get out detail chart 2814a.'

'Aye, aye, sir,' sang the Mate.

'About 1 mile farther up', the Crew continued, 'the channel narrows suddenly at Connel Railway Bridge, and the navigation becomes very difficult for sailing craft. . . . See sketch for passing through bridge.'

It was both an artist's sketch and a draughtsman's sketch, with an arrow descending from the second upright of the bridge on the south side. Admirable indeed.

'Close above the bridge, which spans the narrows, there is a ledge of rocks forming a submarine causeway. . . . There is 3 to 5 faths. at L.W. between the centre rock and the S. shore, the clear passage being straight and about ¼ cable wide. Owing to . . . there are many and various eddies along the S. shore, both on flood and ebb tides. There is also on that shore . . .'

'That's our shore.'

'Aye, aye,' said the Mate.

'. . . a ledge running out 3 or 4 yards from the rocks at the E. end of the channel, which only uncovers at L.W., dangerous because . . .'

'You take the helm.'

'Capital,' said the Mate.

I toured the engine, thinking she was a bit sluggish, but decided she was merely bored with the leaden day.

The Mate had now her head on the second upright of the bridge on the south side, going straight for the channel. We could no more than just see the dark ripple that denoted the

271

Glen Etive, where she 'builded her bridal hold'
submarine causeway. It was slack water. The books had
worked their magic again.

Up under the bridge we went, with the assurance of a
coastal tramp, and then—for the first and the last time—our
Sailing Directions (now called the *Book*) failed us.

'A mark', read the Crew, 'which will indicate when clear,
E. of the "submarine causeway", is when the west garden of
the second villa E. of the bridge, on the S. shore, is in line,
end on. The wall is conspicuous, and starts from the road, up
the hillside. When clear, keep to the N. shore until . . .'

As we came from under the bridge, the south shore was a
rash of villas, and three pairs of eyes, keenly concentrated,
could not pick up that conspicuous wall, however the villas
were counted or discounted. (We failed, too, on the return
journey. Though I should hesitate to suggest that the *Book* in
this particular needs revision.)

However, there was no difficulty in seeing when we were
beyond the sunken rocks of the famous Falls of Lora and so
we went over towards the north shore and faced into Loch
Etive.

It was now raining very heavily and the clouds hung low
on the mountains. The scene, stupendous and deep, held us
to silence, until the Mate said:

'I feel we are sailing west.'

The remark seemed more apt then than I can hope to
explain now. Actually we were going due east, but it felt as if
we were sailing into the very heart of the west in its most
arresting Ossianism. What fitful wind there was could no
more than slowly curl upward and reform the mists on the
mountains. Wild duck passed away from us, and on dim
shores we saw swans of an incredible whiteness. The rain
trickled down our faces, soft to the lips, and in the air around

Glen Etive, where she 'builded her bridal hold'

was, sudden as a memory, an immemorial fragrance. I dislike vagueness, but it is not always easy to be precise, to be able to separate with certainty the imaginary from the real. And even in the most elusive experience of this kind there may be something so overwhelmingly real that it transcends the personal and becomes old as history, the history of a whole folk, linking the historic process with a potency greater than may be found in its tongue or its music. Some folk music does search this out, but what it is in the music that makes the appeal I do not know.

We decided all at once that until the Mate returned a week hence, we should make this loch our home; and, rain or no rain, the prospect made us happy. For we were due a carefree rest, after what had been to us strenuous and anxious days.

'That sounds pretty good to me,' said the Crew.

'I'll come back,' said the Mate.

'More cheers,' said the Crew.

So what ho! for an anchorage. It would have to be a good one, sheltered, peaceful, and away from all human interference. The *Book* nobly rose to the occasion. Indeed it had obviously been keeping up its severe sleeve ever since we left Portnalong the word splendid. So we headed for 'a small bay which affords splendid shelter in 2 to 3 fathoms ...'.

'I think', said the Mate, 'you should make a special donation to the publishers.'

'We may yet', said the Crew, 'be invited to become members of the Clyde Cruising Club itself.'

'You certainly', said the Mate, 'have won your—uh—trousers.'

Which was a complicated point, because having worn out her grey trousers fore and aft through walking on her knees, etc., in the cabin, she had complained of a slight cramp amidships brought on by refusing to walk on her knees in the only remaining (and nicely creased) blue ones.

'Thank you,' she said. 'But there is an opening for you too. We could write to the Club and suggest that, excellent as their *Book* is, it might be made still more useful if to each anchorage was added a short note explaining where and how to catch fish.'

'It would do no harm', I suggested to the Mate, 'if you kept her straight on Airds Point—for that's it ahead.'

The little bay where we were to anchor turned out to be all that we could desire. Nicely wooded, with bracken and grass and a little burn entering its inmost reach, it looked remote from all the world. By the weed on the shore, we felt sure of the holding ground. The Crew took the sounding, the engine stuck in reverse, and the Mate towed her head to the perfect spot, while three oyster-catchers, two herons and a whole string of curlew told a silent world that we had arrived.

The rain increased until it was coming down in torrents. We tried to gather from the chart our general direction from Taynuilt, but the chart misled us, for which you couldn't blame it, as the village itself is not on the coast. In the afternoon the Mate and I set off inland, heavily oilskinned, through cataracts of woods, over low hills, and across swamps. Once, lifting my head, I saw what appeared to be the Mate surrounded by a dark aura violently in motion. It was the perfect illustration of the scientific conception of atoms or molecules hurtling around one another to compose matter, with the extra conception of electrons hurtling round nuclei thrown in. But when I opened my mouth to laugh, some of my own buzzing aura entered, and I had to spit the brutes from my throat. They were house flies mostly, and if they had stayed still for a moment, we could have sliced them. By

274

the time we struck the railway line we had had two Turkish baths each, but when we stood for a moment to let the steam moderate, the flies were upon us again.

But the rain was taking off, and indeed if we could not have located the sun we should not have known which way to turn. After two or three miles of the line, our oilskins, wetter inside than out but swinging behind us now in a gentle breeze, we saw Taynuilt ahead, with the great Ben Cruachan behind. The station-master hunted up all sorts of travelling information for the Mate and then directed us to the hotel. We entered and groped down a dark passage, where a bar window was slammed down against our faces. 'I thought you said this was the way?'

'It's all right. Ssh!' said our informant.

But there was no conspiracy about the beer, when it came in pewter pots.

Taynuilt is an airy scattered place, with reasonable shops, an obliging postmaster, and agreeable folk. As we returned to the station, we heard one or two explosions from a great scar on the mountain across the loch. We sat beside a work-man on the platform, who told us that the scar was Bonawe Quarries, 'the finest granite in the world', and he pointed to a house close by of bright grey stone.

'Where do they send it to?' I asked.

'All over the universe,' he replied.

He was quite clear on the subject of the weather, too, being certain that the summers had deteriorated since the Great War. Before then splendid sunny summers—now rain, rain. 'When I came first—'

'When was that?'

'In 1887. The summers were long and sunny then. . . .'

Granite must have agreed with him, for he did not look

old enough even to have been born in 1887. He had a lined humoursome face, with hair the exact colour of grey granite dust, and chuckled when we told him the way we had taken into Taynuilt. He pointed out a pathway over the wooded hill that could be seen even from the railway station. I thanked him as the train came in and he and the Mate went away together.

That evening, as I took the path over the Point, by birch and hazel and oak, with Loch Etive down below and more freshness and beauty around than the brain had the energy to think on, the refrain of the song *Deirdre's Farewell to Albyn* entered and took control. For there are old Gaelic tunes that in the right atmosphere do take control, and subjugate and tyrannise over and hypnotise, until the mind itself falls in love with the drug and the emotion or harmony it engenders. And though this particular air may be neither old nor traditional (rather, in fact, like *Clementine*), yet the subject matter so influenced the cadences that the fume from the drug arose in its soft tide and floated the mind.

For the subject matter was clear enough, as clear as the story about Helen of Troy at least. To English classical men the story of Helen of Troy is the great story of the world.
Hers was

> *The face that launched a thousand ships*
> *And burnt the topmost towers of Ilium*

and when English lips mouth the familiar words gently, you see the fume being created.

Yet with the air always of 'classical' legend, of something half-intellectually conceived and poetically remote, with the glimmering outline of Greek statuary, inducing a nostalgia behind the port, but ever so delicate and even well bred; a

Glen Etive, where she 'builded her bridal hold'

nostalgia, perhaps, not for Helen so much after all as for something that oneself has lost, like youth.

But to the Gael, Deirdre is not a lovely woman of another race: she is flesh of the same flesh and bone of the same bone, and at the words 'Deirdre the Beautiful is dead', the head is bowed and the mind blinded.

What befell Deirdre and the Sons of Uisneach is one of the Three Sorrows of Gaelic story-telling and the best known of the three. There are many versions of the story, the oldest being found in the *Book of Leinster*, a twelfth-century MS. It tells of individual and social life, of taboos, of love, of escape, of a woman's intuition of treachery, of man's obtuseness, of journeys by land and sea, and of final tragedy.

It starts in Ulster, with Conchobar, the king of that land, at a great feast given by his story-teller, Feidhlim. Everyone of importance was there. Such a feast lasted weeks or months and while this one was in progress, news was brought that Feidhlim's wife had given birth to a daughter. Whereupon the Druid had one of his moments of vision and told the terrible evils that were to afflict the realm of Ulster on account of this new arrival. So impressive was he (they knew with what accuracy his 'second sight' worked), that there and then they seriously discussed the wisdom of taking away the young life. But Conchobar said no, leave her to be reared by me, and I'll make her my wife.

So he put her into one of his forts, with a nurse to rear her and a tutor to teach her, and orders were issued that no one must go near her except Lebarcham, who was the king's 'conversation woman'. And no one went, until she had grown up and was 'in beauty above the women of her time'.

One winter's day the tutor killed a calf, and when Deirdre saw a raven on the red and the white snow, she said to Lebarcham that she would like to have a husband with these

277

colours; raven hair, and red cheeks, and white skin. And in the idle way that women have of precipitating the destiny that is their undoing, Lebarcham answered, 'I know a man in Conchobar's following who is just like that. His name is Naesi.' 'O Lebarcham,' said Deirdre, 'get him to come privately, so that I may see what he's like.'

Lebarcham did this, and in a little while Deirdre was telling Naesi how thrilled she was by all the wonderful stories she had heard about him—and would he take her away by stealth? In the end Naesi agreed, 'yet reluctantly, for fear of Conchobar'. So he got his two brothers and other heroes to help him, and together they abducted Deirdre and fled to Albyn or Alba. They navigated the Falls of Lora (without aid from railway bridge or villa garden; possibly they had a pilot) and came up past Taynuilt (the wood the Mate and I went through is still mapped as Coillenaish or Naesi's Wood) and went on past the spit opposite Bonawe Quarries and so up the loch until they reached that spot where she built her first house. They had many adventures and once went as far as Inverness, where the high king of Alba lived, for Naesi and his brothers were mighty warriors and were prepared to give service for their new land. A great feast was held at Inverness, whereat, it is related, there was a considerable amount of drinking, for even in those days they drank out of glasses in the northern capital. (As, indeed, they do to this day, and the distillate is still the best.) Well, from one drink to more, the high king could not keep his stricken eyes off Deirdre, and so she and Naesi had to fold their tent and steal away. Thus, with one thing and another, the happiest days of Deirdre's life were spent in Alba.

Meantime, old Conchobar was at another lengthy feast (for they believed in making the happiest use of their time long ago). The musicians and poets did their best, and fine songs were sung, and all the people were merry and in the highest spirits. And then, like a great actor, Conchobar stilled the throng. 'Young men and heroes of Ulster', cried he, 'is there here any fault or blemish or want?'

'Not any, O king!'

'I know of a great want,' said the king: 'the three torches of valour of the Gael, Naesi and his two brothers.'

Whereupon the joy of all rose to a pinnacle, for this very want had been in their thoughts, though they had been afraid to confess it.

'I shall have messengers sent,' said Conchobar.

But whom? For Naesi was under a *geasa* or vow not to return to Erin except in the company of Fergus, or Conell Cearnach, or Cuchulain.

So in due course Conchobar got hold of Conell privately, and flattered him, and suggested, 'What would you do to me if I should send for the sons of Uisneach, and they should be destroyed for me—a thing I do not propose to do?'

'I'd kill every Ulsterman I met—without exception.'

'Now I understand that the sons of Uisneach are dearer to you than I am.'

And so he sent for Cuchulain and that warrior replied without hesitation:

'I pledge my word that if you had that done, though you fled eastward to Western India, it would not save you from falling by my hand.'

Fergus, the third, said he might spare Conchobar himself, but no other Ulsterman.

So Fergus was sent, and we hear no more of him until he arrived in 'the fastnesses of the sons of Uisneach, namely Loch Etive in Alba'.

At the time of his arrival, Deirdre and Naesi were playing chess.

'That was the cry of a man of Erin,' said Naesi.

'Nonsense,' said Deirdre.

'There it is again!'

'That's the cry of a man of Alba,' said Deirdre.

But when the cry came the third time, and Naesi's brother went out to meet Fergus, Deirdre confessed she had known all along it was Fergus's cry.

'Why did you conceal it, then?'

'I dreamt', said Deirdre, 'that three birds came from Emain Macha with three ships of honey; they left the ships of honey but took away three sips of our blood.'

'And the meaning?'

'Fergus has come to offer peace from Conchobar, who has a design against you; for sweeter than honey is the peace message of a false man.'

When Fergus and those with him came in, there were happy greetings, and Fergus said that he brought Conchobar's peace and pledged himself upon it.

Deirdre argued against Fergus, but Fergus said, 'The sight of one's own country is better than vain fears, and what is prosperity to the exile?' And Naesi heartily agreed with him.

Nor could Deirdre change her husband's mind, for he had a man's simple belief in goodness and brotherhood, particularly when his own desire led him that way. She forbade him to go but he could see no reason in her woman's fears. For a little time the struggle went on between them. Then Deirdre saw that nothing would persuade her husband to stay, so she bowed to his will and prepared to go with him, though she knew they were going to their doom.

As they sailed away Deirdre looked back at that eastern land of Alba, and said, 'My love to you, O eastern land. Grieved am I to leave you; delightful are thy harbours and thy bays, and thy clear beauteous plains of soft grass, and thy

Glen Etive, where she 'builded her bridal hold'

cheerful green-sided hills; little did we think that we should leave you.'

And then she made her great song of Farewell to Alba (or Albyn), mentioning in it all the places she specially loved:

> *Glen Etive, O Glen Etive,*
> *There I built my first house,*
> *Beautiful its woods on rising,*
> *When the sun fell on Glen Etive.*

or

> *Glendaruadh, O Glendaruadh,*
> *I love each man of its inheritance,*
> *Sweet the sound of the cuckoo on bended bough*
> *On the hill above Glendaruadh.*

So they went back to Erin, and from the moment they landed there things went wrong with them. Deirdre foresaw each treachery, but Naesi being a warrior would not see it, and in any case was not now disposed to turn his back. So at last they came to Emain Macha and Deirdre gave them a last sign: if they were asked to go to Conchobar's own house, all would yet be well; if they were sent to the knightly Red Branch, all would be over. They went and knocked on Conchobar's door, and they were sent to the Red Branch.

All this time the king was wondering about Deirdre's beauty, for if she had lost it he would be sorry to sacrifice a good fighter like Naesi. So he sent Lebarcham to the Red Branch to find out. And Lebarcham went and greeted her darling, and told them, in tears, to barricade the windows. Then she returned to the king, sad that all Deirdre's beauty was gone, including her shape, and lamented, blaming the rough life in Alba and the weather. Which pleased the king, until his jealousy made him doubt, and he sent a young man who had no reason to love Naesi. And this young man saw

Glen Etive, where she 'builded her bridal hold'

Deirdre, in beauty greater than she had been in Erin, before Naesi threw a chessman that smashed his prying eye. Then the Red Branch was surrounded and war was on.

There were such deeds performed that night, that Conchobar in the end had to call on the aid of the Druid, who put Naesi and his brothers under a delusion, so that they were captured. Then did Conchobar break also his word to the Druid and the three great sons of Uisneach were slain.

Moving distractedly about the bloody green of Emain, Deirdre met the hurrying Cuchulain face to face, and told him of the treachery and the tragedy of that night, and when they came to where the sons of Uisneach lay, Deirdre spread out her hair and drank Naesi's blood, and made her great widow's lament for the dead, and killed herself upon his body, and was buried with him.

In the fume of the old immortal tale, I arrived back at the boat, where I tried out a minnow, and was astonished at the behaviour of a swan which came towards me at great speed. Though full grown, she looked young and slim and was clearly very frightened, for she crossed over my line near at hand without apparently seeing me. Greatly wondering at this, I turned round and saw a male swan also coming towards me, but with his wings lifted to an Elizabethan ruff about a head curved back in angry dignity. He came also at great speed, but without permitting the strong slow alternate sweep of each paddle to degenerate into haste. His reptilian eye never even glanced at me, and when the female swan struck the shore, she turned away making now for the Point. My rowing course led me naturally to intercept her, but she feared the dignified terror far more than she feared me, and in her terrified haste almost paddled herself out of the water.

Glen Etive, where she 'builded her bridal hold'

When she had disappeared the male tyrant lowered his ruff, and even stood up a little in the water to flap his wings, as a man might dust his palms. That was that.

Deigning at last to give me a glance with his round black eye, he paddled slowly back towards a second female swan, which had been following him at a distance, lingeringly, uncertain. Was this the mother of the daughter that was being driven from home? There was certainly something of that in her attitude, of holding aloof, of regret, following yet not following.

Meantime the ruffian himself must have had suspicions, for presently he deliberately paddled to see what was going on round the point. All at once up went the ruff, and off he set, the mother following more uncertainly than ever. Finally, all three passed from view.

Two days later, the tyrant and his wife reappeared, but without the daughter. Sometimes the Crew would wonder about her, and about the lonely anchorages she would make at night. 'For it is different—a daughter leaving a mother—from a son.' (Unless, of course, it was 'the eternal triangle'!)

In the deep dusk that night, between ten and eleven, an uncertain wind flawing the surface of the loch, there came across the water the slow notes of a pibroch played on the pipes. I knew the theme but could not name it. The wind brought it and bore it away, in the doubling, the trebling . . . and finally the slow profound statement of the theme again. It affected us like a spell, and when it had ended all the night was quiet.

XVII

Landlord Rampant

Off we set for stores to Taynuilt on a fine morning. The glass was going up. The good weather was coming. We tied the dinghy below high-water mark, for the tide had to ebb, and walked along the obviously ancient path, over the wooded hill and down to the bay, by the cottages, and up the stream to the Post Office, where we got our letters. Then to the hotel, where we refreshed ourselves and read the strange miscellany that a fortnight will gather together.

The sun was warm. We were in no hurry, did our shopping leisurely, and lay on a bank looking at Cruachan, wondering if we should tackle him some day. The goodness of life entered in at the pores. A week of perfect weather now and living might assume a dream-like beatitude. A woman in a shop had got lettuces from a private garden for the Crew. Tomatoes. A cabbage. Reaping machines were humming in the fields and the new-mown hay scented the air. 'I think she'll get me some fresh eggs, too,' said the Crew drowsily of the woman with whom she had left her milk pail.

The woman duly produced the eggs and the Crew talked to her so long that I all but fell asleep in the shade. Then we came to a cottage, ablaze with roses and hydrangeas, and the Crew stood and stared, until the owner came, removing his old panama, and spoke to her.

Landlord Rampant

They wandered about the little garden and into the little cottage, which all looked like the picture of a lovely memory. Which perhaps it was. For there was no woman now in that place.

Then I thought I should go and ask him about anchorages farther up the loch, and he told me there were a few, particularly one or two near the head of the loch where men went to fish.

'Fish for what?' I asked.

'Trout,' he answered.

'The landlords, you mean?'

'No, anyone. The landlords had tried to stop it—but had failed. It's the sea.'

'It's paradise,' I murmured.

Free fishing! The times were looking up. The landlords were growing wings. How pleasant and novel an exercise to write a sonnet in praise of landlords—by way of change from the miserable habit of girding at them or of stumbling over the ruins they had so lavishly scattered about the Highlands! We had trout rods and tackle with us. This very night, when the piper had finished, I should write the first sonnet in praise of landlords. And even if they had tried to stop folk fishing, still one could overlook a little thing like that.

So I bundled various parcels about my body, and, picking up the petrol tin of paraffin, led on, the Crew bringing up the rear with milk and eggs. I had the honey.

We had still about three miles before us, and we were a trifle sticky at the shoulder, before we saw our boat through the birches and the dinghy over the bracken. Mutely waiting for us in the quiet bay.

'There they are!' cried the Crew, and saluted with the eggs. The petrol tin rumbled response like a tom-tom. 'Isn't it lovely getting back to our own place?'

And behold! lying on a seat of the dinghy, a letter! A white envelope superscribed:

'To the occupier of the Launch.'

An invitation, probably by a landlord, to dinner! We did not want an invitation by anyone to dinner, however . . . I tore open the envelope, withdrew a sheet of paper, and read:

'———— *House*,
Taynuilt, Argyllshire
July 27*th* 1937

'As [the Landlord's] unwelcome guests have not had the courtesy to call upon him, they are now compelled to do so as the oars are at the House.

'The nuisance of bathing in front of the house having been added, the launch and the crew will be so good as to remove themselves forthwith.'

I was trying to make head or tail of this invitation, when the Crew said:

'The oars are gone.'

And they were gone—including the broken third oar which we used as a roller.

But who on earth was this Landlord? And where his House? It was a pretty esoteric sort of practical joke. I read the note a third time, and the spirit beneath the phrasing came up and hit me.

I now remembered having once seen a large house standing back from the sea. But before the occupants of that house could see us they would have to walk a considerable distance! Then the Crew remembered the woman and children who, the day before, had passed along the shore and stared at our boat. We had assumed no more than the usual and natural curiosity.

Landlord Rampant

In a white heat of anger, I started off for that house, the letter in my hand, and in due course came in sight of the house and of a man walking in front of me.

'Pardon me', I said, 'but can you tell me if that is the House?'

'It is,' he answered, 'and I am ————.'

'You wrote this letter?'

'I did.'

And so the debate was joined.

It lasted all the way to the house and for some time at the house. There was thus ample time to go into the relevant points, and even some irrelevant ones, with considerable pith and precision. In some persons, curiously enough, a white heat of anger rising from a sense of injustice can occasionally induce a logical drive as notable for its restraint as for its ruthlessness. Nothing trivial, so to speak, is allowed to deflect the fine edge! For a time I toyed with the idea of attempting to detail that conversation here, but was dissuaded for several reasons, not least that, the important facts being on my side, it was, in the film phrase, relatively easy for me to register. Though I do regret the loss of certain passages touching our social life, because of their redeeming humour.

However, in so far as this may be considered a matter of public interest, perhaps I should mention at least two of these important facts. First, then, I was anchored in a sea bay (an anchorage, as it happened, recommended by an official book of sailing directions—a book on public sale). From such an anchorage, no landlord had the right to order my removal, either forthwith or at any other time. Fact second: the foreshores, like the bays, of our country are still a common heritage and possession. My dinghy was tied below high-water mark, and while she lay in that position no one had any right, legal or otherwise, to interfere with her in any way, much less remove her only valuable gear, namely the oars.

One fact on the personal side: we had not been 'bathing in front of the house'. Actually we had never even entered the bay in front of the house. Therefore we had not committed 'the nuisance'. (Later, we discovered a bathing pair who had doubtless been mistaken for us.)

For the rest, in such encounters—especially for those, like myself, who hate them—the perfect retorts are thought of afterwards—and generally in sleepless hours. This stands out as one of those happier occasions to which I still find I could have added nothing.

I marched away from that house with the three oars over one shoulder and probably well cocked in the air, for the final passages had not altered the temper of the occasion. Hm! had been a frequent comment. Hm! indeed!

'Hm!' and the Crew emerged from behind a tree.

She had been following us up, afraid of the worst.

'I heard your voices,' she said, with a valiant effort to meet my high mood. Then she burst into laughter and caught my arm. 'You didn't do bad,' she said, and shook again. She looked as if she might dance. Clearly our little altercation had had its amusing side.

And by the time we reached our own shore I was laughing with her, so we sat down above high-water mark.

For there was something at the back of my mind, beyond the personal, that had to come out. For years past in every part of the Highlands we had met the young on foot between youth hostel and youth hostel, and thought it the most heartening sight in the world, for these young folk were laying up memories, most of them to lie in the subconscious, that would be of incalculable potency in all their after life.

Something deeper than feelings of freedom, of health, of its being their land, their country; something that goes to the primordial roots.

And now here is the second part of their country—the sea, infinitely more changeable and exciting than the land, giving a new aspect of the land, wedded to it, yet dangerous and subtle and distinct, calling out instancy and exaltation in a way the land never does.

If our trip was to have value for anyone beyond ourselves it must show how two persons, with no previous experience of handling a sea-going boat or reading charts or coming to strange anchorages, yet managed in their fashion to do these things and to have one of the most memorable of holidays, so that what we had done others could do as simply. All attempts to stop us therefore must—

'I wonder what would have happened', said the Crew, 'if the letter had got blown off the seat before we came back? Or suppose we *had* climbed Ben Cruachan and returned at three in the morning, dead beat?'

So we laughed all over again as we rowed to our boat, where I put up the fishing rods; for trout from this quiet bay—if the anchorage had not been too much for them— might taste good.

That evening, when we had finished fishing (small timid trout) and the piper had finished his playing, the beauty of the deep night assumed a supernatural character. Where the sun had disappeared, a dream memory of gold and yellow hung in the north-western sky and was reflected in the loch's still water. In the gulf of the north-east there was an uprising brightness as of the coming of morning. Eastward, a cloud over Ben Cruachan turned to silver, and the blue beyond it was all radiant light, heralding the rising moon. In the south,

Venus hung very large and bright, and in some faint movement of the dark water her lamp became a Chinese lantern. The black hills were inverted in the loch and the sea's margin lost. It was the beginning of our first spell of good weather.

A touch of frost in the morning, followed by brilliant sunshine, and soon we were in our dinghy rowing for Taynuilt. Before setting out, we locked our cabin door, a thing we had never thought of doing in the most thickly populated crofter area. For all the rest of our time in the bay we had the uncomfortable feeling of eyes being about, and this prompted us to do things and take precautions for the safety of our property, that we sensibly told ourselves must be absurd. The one positive thing achieved by the recent interference was this insidious destruction of harmony with environment. It had destroyed the completeness of peace. It is not that we feared what any man could do. In that material region we were prepared for diversion and, the issue now being joined, might have enjoyed it. It was the spirit that had been evoked and lay at the back of everything, as if waking into a joyous holiday one could not quite rid oneself of something sinister behind an absurd nightmare.

Six white galleys making down the loch two or three miles away, large and beautiful, like the escort to some fabled queen, knocked most things out of our minds. We blinked our eyes, but the vision remained, stately and slow-moving. In that direction lay 'the fort of the sons of Uisneach, which is at Loch Etive in Alba', and is 'commonly called Beregonium'. Down there was the very core of the whole world of the poems of Ossian. Great warriors and beautiful queens and stately halls. Fingal and Darthula and Selma. The galleys were setting towards the Falls of Lora. 'He hears at last the sound of Lora, and exclaims with joy "Selma is near".'

Then the mirage effect passed and six swans at no great distance reached still water by the western shore. The illusion as to distance and size had been so complete that the Crew now doubted the swans themselves!

On the thickly wooded slopes above us as we rowed along were a few old Scots firs, rising over the oaks and the birches and the hazels, their twisting arms warm as with ruddy firelight, nursing grey-wrapped bundles that turned out to be herons. Sheep scraped little beds for themselves in the shingle and settled under the shadows of boulders. A flock of curlew rose up and flew away silently. A wood pigeon, pecking among the stones, showed no fear at our near presence. Old Ben Cruachan had still a nightcap above his head—that slowly lifted even as we looked.

We came to a house with a little private stone jetty in front of it, and we felt we might be allowed to tie up here, for it was a small house. So graciously was the permission given that we were almost made to feel we were conferring a favour!

So we now had the day before us and the dinghy safe.

The adventure with the oars helped, too, for in our endeavour to find out if the path through the woods was a right of way, we were sent from one person to another, who told us so many strange things that local lore, often so prosy and tiresome, inspired us to historic hunts.

One old man said that most of the Houses are comparatively new and in more than one instance have been built on what was once crofting ground. For all this land had belonged to Breadalbane, but now it was broken up into small estates, and perhaps the new owners were 'worse than the old, for in the old days at least you could go anywhere you liked. Parties used to go over to your bay for picnics. No one ever challenged them—except once, and that was in the time of the previous proprietor and he tried to turn off the minister's wife. But she dared him to his face. "Ha!" she said, "this is just what I have been waiting for. Make a case of it," she challenged him.'

'And did he?'

'No. You see her husband was all for the crofters and the Land League. And her husband's brother, also a minister, went to prison for them. So I suppose he was frightened.'

Then he told me so complicated a story about the history of the salmon rights, invoking kings and chiefs and centuries and charters, that I wondered how any ordinary mere man could have squeezed the right to throw the tiniest trout fly.

'It's not settled yet,' he said. 'But in view of all the circumstances the Crown itself does not feel confident enough to force an issue. Your name and address may be taken, however.'

'One gets used to giving that. So this was all Breadalbane —Campbell—country once?'

'Once—but not now. You know the old prophecy about the Campbells?'

'No.'

'That an old grey horse will one day carry all they possess over the ridge of Tyndrum.'

'You make me see the wind in its grey tail.'

'Myself,' he said, 'I have always found the Campbells very nice folk.'

'But pretty good politicians. The grey horse is not likely to be foaled for a little while yet. So we can hold our sympathy even if Breadalbane has lost a few acres.'

'Perhaps, perhaps,' said Mr. Macdonald.

The matter of the right of way was inclined to get lost in these excursions, and presently was forgotten altogether when a learned antiquary pointed toward Ardchattan on the other side of the Loch and said, 'It was over there that Bruce held his last Gaelic Parliament.'

'I thought that was all Deirdre—Ossian—country,' I said, astonished.

'It's that, too. But Wallace passed along here before Bruce. And each of them fought a battle back there in the Pass of Brander.'

'Really!'

'Yes. And Cumberland passed this way after Culloden. It was some of his officers who saw all this fine wooded country and thought it would be the very place for smelting iron— with the charcoal.'

'It was a great thought.'

'Yes,' he said. 'The English were always good at making money.'

'And at using it, too.'

'That's true. Not so long ago they dug up some old coins over there at the Priory at Ardchattan. They were the coins of Edward the First.'

'You mean English subsidies against Bruce—even then?'

He smiled at my surprise. 'Oh yes,' he said. 'They were great politicians, the English.'

'Not greater than the Campbells?' I asked, jealous for my country.

'Well—not greater perhaps,' he said. 'Just bigger.'

'But tell me, they didn't actually come and start smelting iron here?'

'Oh yes. The foundries were working in my time. If you come over to this knoll, I'll point them out to you. Sailing ships used to bring in the ore. But look—do you see that standing stone on the hill there above the village? That stone was put up by the furnace workers to celebrate the Battle of Trafalgar. It was the first monument to that battle to be put up anywhere in the world.'

'In Taynuilt in Argyll! They are a very great race, the English,' I said, deeply moved.

'There's not much goes past them,' said my friend.

'Can you tell me the name of any book dealing with all this history about Loch Etive?'

'Not any one book I can think of. But there's a book dealing with the Deirdre period you spoke of, a very fine and scholarly book it is, called *Loch Etive and the Sons of Usnach*, by Angus Smith. You should read that, if you want to get some idea of the culture that should have come out of our own past. It deals with every old corner around the loch.'

'Very few folk,' I said, having made a note of the book, 'know about Deirdre—apart from the modern song. You know the song?'

'Yes, I have heard it. What you say about folk not knowing is true. The clever ones go to college and learn about the Hebrews and the Greeks. And very wonderful people they were, too. Very.'

I felt the wonder in his pause.

'About the song—yes, I have heard it,' he resumed. 'Though I wonder if the verse about Glendaruel [old Glendaruadh] refers quite to the place Deirdre was thinking of. Up the loch, there, is a place called Dail or Dal. There is a glen behind it with the colour *ruadh* on the hillside, sort of reddish-brown. It is a fairly common termination. For example, there is a hill on the right before you come to the head of the loch called Stob an Duine Ruaidh—the Stob of the reddish man. So why not at Dail—Glen-Dal-ruadh?

Deirdre's garden is about there. However, that's just an idea, for Glendaruel is away in Cowal.'

This suggestion so deeply interested me that I realised, with a shock, how antiquarianism might take hold of a man. Historic places as such had never really had any deep appeal for me, whatever I may have pretended. Yet here I was promising I should even hunt out the cave where Campbell cut off Makfadyan's head and presented it to Wallace—a story I had not hitherto even heard of!

'I think a few real long walks would do us good,' said the Crew, game for the next thing that might happen, as I pulled the dinghy home, taking advantage of every eddy by the shore, for the tide was against us. 'And there—our old friend *chorda filum*—to tell us how the current runs!'

'And there—look!' I said.

A shapely young woman poised on a boulder in a bathing dress, and a young man taking her photograph. Their boat was drawn up beside them.

'The mystery is solved,' I suggested, 'of the bathers who committed the "nuisance".'

'If only they knew how they were trespassing on that shore now!' said the Crew.

'Should I tell them?'

'What do you think?'

'Might be a pity to introduce the serpent into their idyll.'

'True,' said the Crew. 'Besides, they might go and bathe yonder again.'

The weather continued lovely during all our stay in Loch Etive. Now and then, I grudged not being at sea, for this was the cruising weather we had dreamed of, and I had hankerings after the Gulf of Coirebhreacain. But we had promised the Mate to wait for him here. And if we went to sea, who could forecast where we should heave to, or for how long?

And the sun—was due a little quiet worship. So we wandered idly round the neighbouring country enjoying small personal adventures of no interest to anyone but ourselves. We got all our stores in Taynuilt. The milk was half cream. And there was amusement even in buying stores. For example, one day, when the sun had brought back our lost youth, the Crew got a sudden craving for a certain sort of liquorice she used to buy for a halfpenny. Hatless, wearing blue trousers and dark sun glasses, she looked so unlike a figure anxious for a half-penny worth of liquorice that I challenged her to buy it.

She always accepts any challenge of that sort, so straight-way entered a respectable shop in Taynuilt and said seriously, 'I want a halfpenny worth of liquorice, please: the kind you tear off in strings.'

The man, who was not old, regarded her earnestly, anxious to serve but obviously at a loss.

She repeated her request. His face cleared intelligently. 'Oh, I see,' he said. 'You want it for your bowels.'

There was a really splendid silence. Then I went out.

From a solitary excursion, she rarely came home without an odd encounter and a strange saying, some of them local and pithy, as of the old lady who remarked of certain indivi-duals: 'The trouble with them is that they have nothing to do but eat their bums out.'

Then word came that the Mate was held up a further three days.

'We have never climbed Ben Cruachan, we have never hunted the cave in the Pass of Brander, and we have never gone up Loch Etive,' said the Crew.

'I was merely wondering', I said mildly, 'if we could manage the Gulf of Coirebhreacain.'

'You know we can't. And I have been reading all about the cave. Now listen. Here's my synopsis. Are you listening?'

'Yes. Where did you get it?'

'Out of that book called *Wallace, the Hero of Scotland*, by Paterson. Will you listen?'

'Is it long?'

'Wallace', the Crew began, 'after the treachery and desperate retribution—*it was terrible!*—of the Barns of Ayr, had moved rapidly. He was resting at Dundaff when news reached him that Atholl, Buchan, Menteith and Lorn had risen against Argyll in the interest of Edward First of England. Neil Campbell of Lochow had defied Edward and stuck to his—my writing is not too good—'

'Lands and heritages. Stout fellow!'

'Heritage. That's it! One Makfadyan, a low-born Irishman, had obtained a gift of Argyll and Lorn from Edward with the view of bringing the more inaccessible portion of Scotland under his control, and "false Jhon of Lorn", having been made a lord in England, concurred.'

'Wasn't Edward a marvel! Talk of astuteness, political genius! And that touch of introducing a low-born Irishman—'

'Duncan of Lorn, however, still struggled for the lands and joined Neil Campbell. They had against them therefore this Makfadyan, supported by four lordships, and by Makfadyan's own considerable army supposed to have been brought out of Ireland. "Many of them"—to quote—"he had brought out of Ireland and with characteristic savagery, they spared neither women nor children . . .".'

'Stop!' I said. 'I just can't stand that. I don't mind political astuteness taking a fellow's land from him. Edward's cleverness may have been diabolic but at least it was something the other fellows didn't possess—and would probably have

liked to have possessed. But this propaganda—already—
against the Irish! It's low. It's an ugly sin. For if one thing is
certain—and history is there to prove it—it is that the old
fighting Gaels never killed women and children; they were
chivalrous to an almost idiotic degree. Even in our own
country, take the Prince Charlie rising and the march on
Derby. Not one single little atrocity all the way from Moidart to Derby and all the way back to Culloden. The thing is
phenomenal. As Cumberland proved within five bloody
minutes. Or take Edward's sack of Berwick and slaughter of
the women and children. It's remembered there to this day.
What I'm getting at—'

' "Thai bestly folk"—this is Blind Harry, the Scots poet,
on the Irish—"could nocht but byrn and sla".'

'Go on,' I said. 'Edward knew. Divide—and destroy.
When you can't fight the enemy, get him to fight himself.
And there's always money.'

'Neil Campbell retired before Makfadyan to the head of
the Pass of Brander and broke the bridge behind him.
Wallace, having taken Stirling Castle, decided he had better
have a look at this business in the west and set off with 2,000
men and Duncan of Lorn for guide. And in due course they
came to the Pass of Brander and the fight took place in that
narrow defile, high rocks behind, and in front "watter depe
and wan". It was a desperate encounter, for Makfadyan's
men fought stubbornly, but in the end Wallace prevailed,
and Makfadyan jumped into the river Awe, held on to a rock
until he got his armour off, swam across, and climbed up into
a cave under Craigmore. But Duncan of Lorn went after him,
and slew him in the cave, and brought his head back, which
was stuck high on a rock for "honour of Ireland"—which I
think was pretty savage,' finished the Crew.

'Hm. The irony, yes. Let us go and see that cave.'

'Are you sure you wouldn't rather go to the Gulf of Coirebhreacain?'

'None of your Edward tricks on me. Come on.'

So off we set on a sunny day. And within the first mile or two of that public road, under repair, the sweet-smelling peace of our boat was brought forcibly home. Dust, petrol stinks, flies, sweat; vehicles bouncing past, eyes concentrated on a highway fenced in with barb wire. And we used to enjoy this!

The volume of water in the Awe surprised us. A large river, with salmon fishers here and there upon it. We watched a graceful if not very expert young woman until her fly stuck in the bottom, which I had prophesied would happen, and I was wondering whether I should risk telling her how she should set about getting the fly free, when she broke. Then her gillie came up and she handed him the rod, amused.

It was such a lovely stretch of water, too.

'Would you like to try?' asked the Crew.

'See these cairns—on the other side. They must be the graves of the dead.'

'You don't sound very reverent.'

'But the bridge that Campbell broke behind him—is manifestly still broken, so we can't go over. Shall we go on?'

'Yes. We'll get the train back. Look, there's a railway house on the line. They'll tell you about the cave.'

I climbed the embankment and came on a small platform and one or two houses and the usual tall signal box, at a window of which I saw a man.

When he had told me I could not get a ticket, I asked him about the cave.

He laughed. 'Who was tellin' ye?' And when I had spoken, he laughed again. 'That's his stock in trade! We've searched for that cave whole Sundays—and haven't found it yet.' The

irreverent Glasgow voice was infectious. 'I don't believe the
damned cave is in it! Ye'll catch a train at Cruachan Falls, if
ye step out.'

I joined the Crew, feeling reassured and modern again.
'We have to step out for Cruachan Falls.'

But the small railway station at Cruachan Falls looked
dilapidated and was completely deserted. There wasn't even
a railway bill stuck up. Had the modern failed us, too? We
hunted round about and shouted. Echoes, only.

So we resigned ourselves to the beauty of the Falls and
presently threw off the grip that time had been fixing on us
again, ate wild raspberries, and the Crew found some
flowers that pleased her.

'I read a verse—by Barbour, I think it was—describing
this Pass,' said the Crew. 'And somehow the old Scots words
looked exactly like this place. He first of all tells you that it
was an evil place so straight and narrow that two men
couldn't ride together.'

Then (for she looked up the words later):

> *The nethir half was perelous;*
> *For a schoir crag, hye and hyduous,*
> *Raucht till the se, doun fra the pas.*
> *On the owthir half ane montane was*
> *So cumrous and ek so stay,*
> *That it was hard to pas that way.*

'That would be about Bruce's fight here?'

'Yes,' she answered. 'But I don't remember much about it.
All these chiefs mix me up. He won anyway and went on to
Dunstaffnage and put a garrison there.'

'In the Wallace affair, I must say Lochow and his Campbells did right nobly. If they hadn't gone political so early,
the Campbells might have been a great crowd.'

'And how is Glencoe explained?'

'No one can explain it. It's there like fate, a tragic play of immortal treachery. Yet think—one can parallel it with hundreds of instances of treachery from other countries. But in these countries—Greece excepted—any individual instance of treachery seldom attained tragic dignity. Why?'

'Go on.'

'I know it's obvious. Treachery does not sear the mind of a folk for centuries—unless that mind had nobility for to sear. The Campbells had been playing with politicians greater than themselves, and so were inevitably herded into being the figures of awful destiny. Which, in a sense, was tough on the Campbells.'

'It was tough on the Macdonalds, too.'

'I was thinking in terms of Greek drama.'

'Hm,' said the Crew.

I looked around the road, for this tendency to collapse a discussion in sudden laughter was becoming an alarming manifestation of our new freedom. Two or three boy scouts on pushbikes did pull up—and told us that Loch Awe station was perhaps three to four miles farther on. After we had walked many miles a bus overtook us, and, as we sank back in our soft seats, for it was a magnificent bus, the Crew smiled. 'I always liked riding in a bus,' she said. 'This one feels like a chariot.'

'A chariot was a hard racketing—'

'Still, it feels like a chariot.'

It must be some rightness in a thing that makes one laugh at the wrong moment.

'Ssh!' she said. 'They'll think you're English.'

For she can be quite merciless when she gets you going.

But at Loch Awe station, she merely smiled when I told her of the church the antiquary had described to me. I was rather hazy about it, it is true, but I had the distinct impression of a church built of stones carried by chiefs. Perhaps for their sins? A remarkable thought, anyway, and when I began haltingly to interrogate a railway man, he at once said:

'The church? See that red shed? Well, it's beyond that. Enough time? If you hurry,'

'Good-bye,' said the Crew.

It was three times as far as it looked, and when I arrived I knew it must be the wrong church, for this was a large modern affair in grey granite. And when I got down to it, the doors were locked. I found two Englishmen round the back, dodging flying buttresses, looking for any opening.

'Isn't this truly Scotch?' said one.

'Every blessed door locked!' said the other, exasperated.

Silently, if none the less heartily and sincerely, I agreed with them. When suddenly a woman appeared, with a tall conical black hat, a slight stoop, and a bunch of keys. We followed her silently in at the main door. She had a quiet gentle voice. She knew everything. And had silence as a pure gift.

It was a remarkable church interior, containing so much extraordinary detail that I dare hardly be sure of describing one item correctly, for I have deliberately made no effort to find out more about it. There was an effigy of Bruce, the face and hands being of alabaster and the rest of wood. In front of him a chest, containing one of his bones, and to his left a great bell from one of the lighthouses of our western ocean. There were astragals from a window of the old church in Iona; coats of arms of many clans; something here from Edinburgh and there from India; cloisters of a kind, too, with upended gridirons used long ago to defeat the body snatchers. And a hundred other astonishing things.

The large windows and the grey granite filled the interior

with light, so that it felt like a church on an immense bal-
cony. Yet despite its architectural peculiarities (it must have
had some feature of every mode) and its conglomerate interior, it achieved a unity that affected the two English
critics, for one remarked softly to the other, 'When I turned
round there I expected to see the high altar.' While all he saw
was a bare table.

'The communion table,' said our guide, and her quiet
voice went over its austerity like a reconciling hand.

I hardly heard half of what she said, and have forgotten
that, for facts did not seem so important as the feeling of
unity that embraced the whole. And when I thought the
guide said that the builder was a Campbell, who had devoted
his life to the work, I began to understand. For here, written
out in stone and ornament, was the clear story of one man's
soul.

And the story, too—I wondered—of the whole Campbell
soul in its centuries of dealings with the Church, in its desires
and its repressions, its acquisitiveness and its aspirations, its
catholicity and its narrowness, its ambitions and its compromise, its effort at a Protestant Church universal achieving
—this individual story in stone.

I was so impressed that I forgot to hurry back and after a
final sprint just caught the train, which stopped at Cruachan
Falls.

XVIII

Farewell to Deirdre's Garden

W e had seen the little white passenger boat go throb-throb up the loch and down each day until it had become a friendly sight.

'Wouldn't it be a great thing', I suggested to the Crew, 'to be on a boat where another man had to look after the engine?'

So she led the way, and, from the ruinous wooden jetty at Bonawe, climbed a wobbly ladder with calm ease. The engine was a semi-diesel Gardener, and the polish on the brass was unbelievable and the engineer very friendly. When the skipper rang his telegraph, the engineer dodged down his head, turned a couple of levers, and things happened with the awful certainty of fate. Then up came his head again and the broken sentence was completed.

If ever (I thought) we have a marine engine like that, we shall start it and stop it, go ahead and go astern, glide up to little wooden jetties and reverse to a standstill alongside, quietly, without any fuss, yet with the accuracy of music. How is it that no poet has ever written an ode to an old Kelvin, or one breath-taking sonnet to a new? Free-verse moderns have, of course, attempted praise of mechanism and speed, but they are a trifle dashing, inclined a bit to worship their own emotionally vague mood induced by speed; their cylinders, vast and shining, tend to be confused with pistons, moved by the same mysterious violence as moves themselves.

Farewell to Deirdre's Garden

There is a lack of definition, arising out of a lack, one fancies, not only of exact knowledge but of physical handling. At the best, their mechanism is their servant and they would ride it as God rides the whirlwind. Or it suggests workers and social injustice and is thus not a thing in itself but a text for something quite other; something admirable and splendid and to be desired; but not an engine.

So the poem still awaits the eye that sees the mountain in the engine; the ore of the mountain in the cylinders and pistons; the oil-fields of continents distilled in the tanks; the magnetism of the whole earth itself leaping in fire across the plug points; while the engineer, with half-unconscious ear, apprehends the final harmony so justly that let there be introduced a 'new noise' beyond the power of poet's ear to distinguish, and down dodges the head and at a touch the sphere-music is re-established.

Even more than that, as this particular engine demonstrated; for the engineer, with the great artist's economy, begins eliminating forces, such as magnetism, and starts his engine by compressing the air we breathe. An astral conjuror, at the touch of whose fingers the *Rena* comes alongside so nicely that you can step ashore without throwing a rope.

And it showed us some mountains, too, when it was at it. I thought I had seen Ben Cruachan plain, for it dominates Taynuilt, and from the Quiet Bay we had nightly observed its great peak take the dying sunlight. But we never saw it in full majesty until we had gone beyond Bonawe Narrows and looked back. For Ben Cruachan is rightly a mountain closely attended by six others, each of them over 3,000 feet, and the majesty is for him who gazes back on the group rising from the sea.

From Bonawe up to the head of Loch Etive is some twelve miles, and as a display of near mountainous scenery, the region is impressive. The day was full of sunshine, and though it brought a haze to distant peaks, where the Crew craved definition in outline for her camera, it was perfect for a traveller adventuring for the first time into this high rock-glittering land, with soft green of lower slopes and narrow wooded glens. An occasional shooting lodge or shepherd's house emphasised the stillness and remoteness. Once the small boat we towed went ashore with letters for a sheep farmer, and once we stopped to deliver a package for workmen renovating a lodge some miles inland; for this country is all deer forest and full of landlords and clegs (though you can kill the clegs).

Glen Noe, Glen Liver (with a good bay), and Glen Kinglas to starboard; to port, Cadderlie River with its bay and Dail—with the antiquary's theory. 'Thereabouts', said the engineer, 'is the site of Deirdre's garden; and do you see that rocky place with the three trees (at high water it's an island)? Well, that's supposed to be the spot where Deirdre's treasure lies buried.'

'The garden', said the Crew, with an expert's eye, 'would be where that man is cutting hay. I wonder if she went in for rock plants.'

'Of course, no one can be sure about anything,' said the engineer with a smile. 'There was a man here last year hunting for the treasure—'

But I missed the story because at that moment a cleg landed on the rubicund cheek of a clergyman, who was listening to us, and who hated the brutes as much as I did. 'Cleg!' I shouted. He held up his cheek, which in my enthusiasm I smacked so loudly that other passengers turned round.

'Thanks,' he said gratefully. 'Thanks so much. They specially rejoice in me.'

Farewell to Deirdre's Garden

All the passengers were like children on a holiday, delightful folk, and the *Rena* and her crew let no one down. Not even over the golden eagle of the handbill, for presently the second-in-command was pointing to a mountain-top, where, sure enough, the great bird was slowly circling on extended wings.

'Pretty good,' I said to the engineer.

'We try to do our stuff,' he answered modestly, and asked us where we had been. He knew every corner, had re-timed a Kelvin in a storm, and spoke of the wanderings of Alan Breck from the wreck on Erraid Island to the spot where Colin Campbell was murdered, 'over beyond the eagle there. It makes a difference', he added, 'when you know the country.'

We spoke a trifle diffidently about these literary matters; still, they had their place.

'I had hoped', I said, 'to go down Jura way and through the Gulf of Coirebhreacain, but the weather has been against us.'

'Terrible currents down there,' he said. 'I was talking to a skipper once who told me that in a calm they had got drawn slowly into the current entering Coirebhreacain and couldn't pull out of it. A sailing vessel. So they battened her down and abandoned her, getting to shore themselves in the small boat. She was carried away and got into the whirlpool, and went round and round and down until at last they could see nothing but the tops of her masts. But the pool threw her up again and they dodged alongshore in the eddies and picked her up none the worse. I believe that is quite true.'

The glory of it put gloom over my day, until the talk got going on landlords (for our little adventure had been noised abroad). That we had not lifted anchor when ordered to was all in our favour. There were folk who would have had us there yet, for oddly enough landlords as a general body are not beloved. I was told stories of petty tyrannies that I dare not repeat, in the interests of those concerned. Here is a typical one, which may pass. Those who run the *Rena* also own her, and one day at high tide they beached her at a certain spot in order to get her bottom scraped. In due course an emissary from the landlord appeared demanding the sum of two shillings as dues for beaching on his land—i.e., on an open beach below high-water mark.

'Did you pay?' I asked.

'No,' he said. 'But I wish I had—and got a receipt.'

But the hardest case I encountered was that of a sheep-farmer, who after many lean years (lambs had been selling in Oban the previous year at as low as a shilling each) had been warned out of his farm, just when prices were looking up and losses might be recouped, as the ground was required for sport.

Damning landlords of sporting estates is a warming and friendly business and doesn't do anyone any harm, least of all the landlords.

The head of the loch is a wonderland of mountains. In front of us the two Shepherds of Etive lifted their heads into the haze. To our right Ben Starav, with Stob an Duine Ruaidh before it and many peaks behind. To our left mountain after mountain until, faint as a pencil line against the sky, we recognised Bidean na mBian, the highest ridge in Argyll.

The wooden pier, at whose front we drew alongside, is privately owned, as was soon made clear to us by a shout from a motor launch, which had been fishing at mid loch. The *Rena* had immediately to stop disembarking us, and the crew hauled on their ropes until they had her clear away from the pier altogether. The launch drew up to the side of the pier (not the front), landed its fishers, and then proceeded to its anchorage. We hauled on the *Rena*'s ropes and got her back into position. Some of the fishers watched the operation without word of apology or greeting or farewell. The clergyman killed a cleg or two with real spirit.

It was with regret that we waved our farewells from the dilapidated jetty at Bonawe, with a special wave for the engineer. The *Rena* runs from Achnacloich, and our return ticket from Bonawe had cost us only three shillings each. We had had tea and tomato sandwiches on board and two hours ashore at the head of the loch. A song to the *Rena*, like *Speed Bonnie Boat*, would have real point to it. And you can rely on the engine.

Over we went to the railway station, and presently the Mate bore down upon us, under full canvas. It was the open sea now. So that night the weather broke down.

XIX

'I dislike being long at a time'

By catching the last of the ebb down the Falls of Lora, we should have the flood with us up the Lynn of Lorn.

The engine had not been touched for ten days, yet she fired at the first priming—on two cylinders and backfired two flames the size of saucers over the flooded carburettor. Not very promising, so we changed a plug and proceeded to get the anchor up. It was bedded to the hilt. A splendid anchorage, which every yachtsman in that region, anxious for good holding ground, would be well advised to use. It started raining.

We opened out a residence and saw a comfortable bay in front of it, with a jetty, and what looked like boathouses, but no yacht. Behind us, Ben Cruachan was shrouded. The day was heavy and sombre. The mists came over the water. It was a glen of weeping. Why it was different from the day on which we had entered I cannot explain. But it was.

To starboard was the Ardchattan country, well wooded, with hay cocks at precision in the fields. There was good land right on to the point, and we could see how in such a mountainous country this part was of value in early times.

Leaving the north shore, we soon had the second upright of Connel Bridge ahead. The submarine ledge still had some water tumbling over it, and as we cleared the bridge we got caught in tide rips that swung us about in summary fashion, while I worked the tiller from side to side, meeting shock after shock, but never quite losing control. It was exhilarating while it lasted.

Now to get hold of Dunstaffnage, which we had missed on the way in. Out of curiosity we decided to try the inside passage round the island. And at last we did descry the upper parts of a turret and gable, pointed like the tall trees amid which they stood, and agreed that anyone might be forgiven for not picking up the building, as a sailing direction, even close at hand.

The Mate was now getting the benefit, in snatches, of our inflated knowledge of legendary times.

'Did you know that the Stone of Destiny was once Jacob's pillow?' inquired the Crew.

'No.'

'Did you know that it went to Ireland, via Egypt, and from Ireland came over here to the Dun of the sons of Uisneach—even to this very Dunstaffnage?'

'And from there to Scone. No.'

'No. From here to Iona where it was Columba's pillow?'

'Iona! Columba! Really? Now you're talking. *His* pillow! And to think that the part that occasionally rests on it now is no longer the head. O tempora! O Moses!'

I had to talk to them pretty sharply for the mists were thickening and all I could see was the northern point of Lochnell Bay. Sometimes I thought Lismore loomed vaguely ahead. The rain was coming straight down on a windless slow-heaving oily sea; and our intention of spending the day on Lismore got swallowed in the gloom. A gigantic and fathomless gloom. We kept well clear of the north point, which is very foul, and presently picked up some small islands to port, one looking as if it carried a ruined fortress, but astern they bore an astonishing resemblance to four great ships riding at anchor in a row.

'I dislike being long at a time'

'Sad that I should have learned the limitations of a camera,' sighed the Crew. 'When you start a thing, you think there's no end to it.'

'And you end by being unable even to land on Lismore,' said the Mate.

'Columba landed there. A horrid story,' said the Crew.

'Never about Columba!'

'Yes. It's about churches, so you'd better ask him. He's getting good on churches.'

'Lismore', I said, 'was an important ecclesiastical centre in ancient times. St. Moluag was the founder. He was a contemporary of Columba, and there is a legend to the effect that Moluag and Columcille were racing for the shore, each anxious to land first and so claim the island. Columcille would have won, of course, but Moluag, seeing this, cut off his finger and threw it on the shore and in a loud voice claimed possession by his flesh and blood and blessed the island in the name of God.'

'There were no clegs on him,' murmured the Mate, regretfully.

'Obviously a Lismore man's story. But the tone of the conversation that followed is more interesting. "May you have the alder for your firewood," said Columcille. "The Lord," replied Moluag, "will make the alder burn pleasantly." "May you have the jagged ridges for your pathway." Moluag smiled sweetly: "The Lord will smooth them to the feet." '

'They had a suavity!' admitted the Mate. 'Not like Dr. Johnson at Lochbuy. I have been looking up Boswell. Lochbuy was told that Johnson did not hear well so he went up and bawled in his ear: "Are you of the Johnstons of Glencro or of Ardnamurchan?" And then Boswell's superb comment: "Dr. Johnson gave him a significant look but said nothing." Do you think that Boswell sometimes, by himself, roared with laughter?'

'I am afraid he has given himself whole.'

'I wonder. For it is the very consistency of his character that raises doubt. It looks too like a character made by a novelist. He dramatised this character for a specific purpose. And succeeded beyond the cunning of any novelist. For we do know that Boswell's detachment was absolute.'

'You are getting on to dangerous ground. For you are almost implying that if the English stopped seeing him as a glorified batman to one of their great men they might wake up and get a shock. Too diabolic.'

'It must be the weather,' said the Crew. 'Is that Lismore?'

'It is. And talking of writers, once a Dean lived on it who compiled a book. It is a collection of odd stuff in phonetic Gaelic, made about the beginning of the sixteenth century. The Dean of Lismore's Book it is called, and very marvellous it is. Deirdre's Farewell to Albyn is in it and many other curious pieces. The Crew copied one or two typical passages in Taynuilt. What about the dislikes?'

> ' " *I dislike to journey for a year;*
> *I dislike the table where a woman sits;*
> *I dislike sorrow and sadness;*
> *I dislike a great house without joy;*
> *I dislike seeing a good man with a bad wife;*
> *I dislike weak drink at a high price;*
> *I dislike being long at a time;*
> *I dislike the men who grudge me food;*
> *I dislike the widow who is not cheerful;*
> *I dislike the man of melancholy mind;*
> *I cannot tell to any man*
> *All the things that I dislike.*
> *I dislike.*"

'I dislike being long at a time'

'I've missed out a few of the dislikes.'

'You wouldn't notice it,' said the Mate. 'But tell me—are there no holy passages? I thought they would be all—'

'Yes. There's the talk between Ossian and St. Patrick:

> *"For thy love's sake, Patrick, forsake not the heroes,*
> *Unknown to Heaven's King, bring thou in the Feinn."*
>
> *"Though little room you'd take, not one of your race,*
> *Unknown to Heaven's King, shall get beneath his roof."*
>
> *"How different MacCumhail, the Feinn's noble King:*
> *All men uninvited, might enter his great house."*

And Ossian's final comment:

> *"Better the fierce conflict of Finn and his Feinn,*
> *Than thy holy master and thyself together." '*

'Is the shore clean along Lismore?' asked the Mate. 'I'd like to have a look at it.'

It was, so we went over and presently were able to distinguish that green island fairly clearly. Sheep were plentiful and the cottages looked very trim. Here and there the rock showed the unmistakable pallor of limestone and possibly this explains the greenness of the grass and the name Lismore—'the big garden'. An Irishman once told me that Ireland breeds the finest horses in the world on a limestone foundation.

Eilean Dubh is an islet in the middle of the Lynn of Lorn, and has a nasty and slightly deceptive reef running well out on its west side. It is advisable to give it a wide berth. We were now getting anxious again about our navigation, as in our small chart the cluster of rocks and shoals to the north of Lismore looked very confusing, even under a magnifying glass. And just at that moment, two things happened: a

314

squall of sou'easterly wind struck us, with lashing rain, and the engine began to miss and labour. It looked as if a valve was sticking or a drop of water interfering with the jet, if it wasn't a faulty plug or two, so I could do nothing except try to keep her going. We were a long way from the presiding genius of Iona now!

As we came abreast of Port Appin, its sheltered anchorage looked very inviting. Even in the rain, its white walls and cultivated fields seemed to indicate a smiling land of plenty. Every now and then we struck such fertile spots on the West, and the rain did no more than bring out their colour.

I put it to the whole crew whether we should go into Port Appin rather than risk Loch Linnhe, with the weather and the engine as they were. But a sort of legend had grown up on this boat that having said we would go to a certain place, go we must; and some way back we had settled on Kintallen. So the crew voted onward and we began picking up our islets and shoals. We luckily made no mistake, though the island of Shuna did loom on us so near at hand (for it was thick here) that we wondered what it was. We kept on its farmhouse for a little and then bore away for the open firth, the engine reduced to three cylinders, the rain remorseless, and a cold wind out of the sou'east that whitened the Crew's fingers.

Presently she called our attention to the land of Morven. 'The mountains look twenty thousand feet high.'

We had opened out Loch Corrie and the hills behind were certainly of a fabulous magnitude. It is the sort of moment when Ossianic legend becomes real. We had never seen these gloomy formations on so gigantic a scale. They overwhelmed human discontent and lifted the mind to a strange and wondering happiness.

And on the strength of it the Mate addressed the Crew

elaborately: 'The milk and the sandwiches, though doubtless nourishing in themselves, are debarred from attaining their proper effect from lack of warmth. Now if he had anything good in his heart, such as a thimbleful of the ancient Scottish spirit—'

At which final word, as though Ossian himself had been waiting for it—and this at least is no legend—our rare old vintage of an engine uncorked her fourth cylinder with a roar. There were panic glances for a moment, before we understood. It was a command I could hardly refuse, though the precious store was indeed very low.

After which, the Mate of course had to set his sail, and when it drew the wind he looked upon us with benevolence.

'It can snow now,' said the Crew.

So we went up through that fabulous world, seeing no ship, passing from Benderloch to Upper Lorn, from the Lynn of Morven to Loch Linnhe; and it was as if all the legends and all the ancient histories were run into one, caught in the long syllable of Lorn, in the two-winged cry of Morven.

Eilean Baile Ghabhain came to meet us, but Ru-more, its finger on the sea, beckoned us on. So we brought it abeam and stood along a clean shore, until the land fell back in invitation and at last we saw a pier and knew we were entering Kintallen. Beinn Bheithir, behind, was all dark-driving storm cloud and we wondered whether Kintallen Bay, like Loch Corrie in Morven, might not be subject to those fierce mountain squalls that can make an anchorage a terror. 'Anchor well in-shore, just before the point jutting out from the W. side of the bay.' But we did not like the look of this point, with its steep rock and all the firth in front, and held on round it, opening a small inner bay where there was a red

316

buoy, a boathouse, and a yacht half out of the water. We cast envious glances at the buoy, but obviously we were now in some landlord's 'private anchorage', so I throttled down all I dared while the Crew started sounding. When she couldn't get bottom, I went into reverse and then into neutral, quite calmly. We were by this time inshore from the buoy. Nine fathoms. Too close in. A shout from the boat-house and a hand pointing to the buoy. So I put her ahead, swung round, shut off and glided slowly up with an ease that must have looked the real thing from the shore. The Mate picked up the buoy's float and in a few minutes we were all fast. I subdued any outward signs of pride, but expected at least some complimentary remarks on my handling of the engine. The Crew, however, was looking about her as if she had lost something.

'Anything wrong?' I inquired.

'No. Only—it was all so tame. There was no excitement.'

There is a small red-headed boy in Kintallen who manages a very large boat and shoots his own net. He was obviously attracted by our arrival and came and examined us all round critically. In no time he and the Mate were in deep conversation as to the lie of the fishing grounds.

'You might get a rock cod there,' the red-head summed up, with a waif of a smile, 'if you're lucky not to get a dog-fish.'

'Do you ever get much in your net?'

'Yes. We often get trout.'

'Not sea trout?'

'Yes.'

'Hm,' said the Crew, unnaturally.

'A boat should never put to sea without a net,' said the Mate sententiously.

317

'I dislike being long at a time'

'You're telling me,' I replied bitterly.

But first of all we had to go ashore to get milk and eggs. We walked up a deep green glen, past a splendid herd of cattle, and came to a farm house. The rain had taken off and the freshness of the nether world was very vivid. I suggested we should walk on and down the glen to Duror. 'The map shows "Church and Inn" together, and it's interesting historically.'

'The only thing I'm frightened of is that it might rain,' said the Mate dubiously.

So I smiled and returned with him to the fishing. He had brought a tin of mussels from Loch Etive, and to the Crew's 'Good luck!' he replied, 'It's not that I mind having to pay for your old fish.' She laughed and said, 'I dislike being long at a time.'

So we spent an evening on Loch Linnhe in our dinghy, until the gloom of the day passed into the gulf-deep gloom of night and the light from the red beacon that divides Loch Leven from Loch Aber shone warningly upon us.

I knew that country well, and as we sat there fishing into the rain-pitted sea, memories of odd and adventurous days came back. The Moor of Rannoch towards a summer midnight, where I had gone with a Glencoe crofter to inspect the village herd (which included three beasts of his own). The one-armed Irishman who looked after the herd, and his lonely hut in the waste of the moor, with bog-pine candles leaning against its wall. The collie—the twining lean tawny collie—that couldn't believe the miracle of a digestive biscuit. The bog-pine fire that flared at the touch of a match; and the tea. There were one or two miracles in that place. Passing west of Kingshouse in the dead of the summer night and two hulking tramps stopping us to inquire—the time! But we had coolly faced up to them and they had gone on. Then down Glencoe of the massacre with the dawn breaking in bright silver and the birds singing. A riot of loveliness and singing over the graves of the murdered.

Or coming along the road here towards Kintallen with Captain MacDougall, the harbourmaster from Kinlochleven, to meet a foreigner and pilot her up the narrows. (One good man's name will give a halo to a clan.) Capital fellows these Norwegian skippers, with their white-jacketed stewards and generous saloons. I used sometimes to take the wheel and respond, 'Steady it is, sir,' for I got to know the seaway to Kinlochleven almost as well as the pilot himself. What friendly outings, what rich laughter often!

All that caught into time—the murders, the riot, and the singing, and the steadiness in the heart of the pilot like the beacon light.

'Everything in the sea is drowned,' said the Mate; 'even the dogfish.'

So he wound in his lines and we rowed back to where a light was shining from the open door of our boat.

XX

Homeward Bound

We left Kintallen in time to catch the first of the tide up the Corran Narrows. It was a day of tall cloud and sun and fragrance after the rain. The transformation that makes life on the West so dramatic; from glooms and drowning deeps to the sky-shepherd driving his white flocks down the blue fields of paradise (as the ancients saw it).

Even the Mate vowed he would catch fish, and told us that the red-headed boy had caught nothing in his short net last night, and that all his father had got in his long net after rowing many miles to set it were five dogfish. But the Crew, for once, did not respond and we wondered what was wrong.

'I don't know,' she said. But we could see she did, and at last she owned up frankly. 'I am sorry we are going back.'

Shades of the fear and excitement that had stuck her lips! We laughed; but all the same there was something in her remark that affected us, and we too were suddenly sorry to think that this was the last salt-water trip of the cruise.

The Morven hills were alive with light and shadow but no longer fabulously high; Glencoe opened out its dark passage to the sun; Ballachulish slate quarries; the bright homesteads of Ardgour; the brilliant white of the Corran lighthouse; and here we were rounding last night's red buoy with its 'staff and globe and white light every six secs.' It marked the end of Culchenna Spit, and over against it on the Corran side was a red and white ringed beacon, with ball on top, marking the end of Salachan Spit. We sailed between, picking up two black buoys on our port side and so straight for the Narrows where the flood tide makes six knots. We saw a passenger steamer coming from Fort William and judged that we should meet right in the Narrows. Which we did. But the *Thistle* has her moments, and merely heaved her stern once or twice at the retreating *Lochfyne*. The engine paid little attention to us to-day. Couldn't be bothered, and once eased off her throttle as if she, too, were a bit sick at going home.

There is an anchorage round the lighthouse in Camus Asaig, and, passing in front of the hotel, we went and had a look at it; but somehow we felt that to anchor here would be unreal, a malingering, a mere stop-gap, so we put about and headed for Fort William, not even altering course to look at Inverscadle Bay, two miles farther on, though it was inviting, with a glen behind.

Soon we saw Fort William in the distance and presently came on a road with hurrying cars, and enclosures by houses with tents and caravans. The sight quite depressed the Crew, and even the Mate, lying on his back on top of the house in the sun, wondered lazily what all the haste was about (though he has a lot of motoring to do himself). This hurry, and grouping of folk in enclosures, and congested social activity generally, did seem a bit of a mistake that afternoon.

'The cars sound from here like buzzing bees,' said the Mate.

'That never find any honey,' said the Crew.

A large pier ahead confused us, until we discovered two piers on our starboard side—the anchorage being anywhere inshore for half-a-mile south of them. This is an exposed place, for the prevailing summer winds are sou'westerly and quite a sea can beat up here in an hour. We dropped anchor in about four fathoms just south of the first pier and went ashore for stores.

In the sunshine, Fort William was alive with cars and visitors. As the core of extensive aluminium works, it is a busy place. In the summer time it is a natural tourist centre: for motorists doing the Big Glen, for steamer tourist traffic, and for climbers and hikers. Wild Glen Nevis behind it has a youth hostel half-way up. For those who are anxious to keep the Highlands insulated from taint of industry lest, *inter alia*, it affect the tourist industry, Fort William provides an answer, for the increase in tourism since the establishment of the aluminium works has been enormous. It is not implied that the tunnelling and pipe lines and factory buildings attract visitors (though they may, for we are drawn to behold the more striking works of our fellows), yet it does seem clear that the presence of these things has not kept visitors away. If our trip brought home to us one thing more than another it is that from the independence of crofting and sea-fishing or other natural industry to the dependence on tourism and sport is a regrettable descent in the history of any people, if it is not indeed the end of their history.

The Mate bought two haddock in Fort William and paid one shilling and eightpence for them, so the Crew brightened up a bit. (Some weeks later I went to sea with a seine-net boat, and the fishermen realised just about this sum net—for each box containing six stones of haddock.) Meantime the wind had risen and we were nearly beaten in rowing the two hundred yards to our boat. So up came the anchor and we rolled across to Camus na Gall on the other side, looked at it, went round the point into Loch Eil, looked at that, successfully circumnavigated the deceitful Corpach Islands, and came back to rest in Camus na Gall, which was sheltered, if with slow currents going everyway.

Homeward Bound

And we were glad we came back, for Ben Nevis that evening was a fine sight, with yellow sunlight on its massive shoulders and pure white cloud in its ravines. When the darkness descended, the town strung itself along the shore in points of light that went deep into the water, wavering like electric eels, while four bright eyes, penstock-high, looked out from the mountain's dark face. Below, the factory was very bright, and further north the new town of Inverlochy was a faint wash of light.

Inverlochy! That marvellous march of Montrose and his men over the passes, and the surprise and bloody defeat of the Campbells!

And across the water from us, the last stones of the Fort to which Glencoe of the Macdonalds had come to hand in his people's submission—too late for their enemies and those who remembered battlefields like Inverlochy.

How great the change since then! Though hardly yet a suggestion of what will be when the Highlands develop their natural industries through water power and recognise they have fish and trout and salmon, mutton and game and meat, heather honey and milk and berries, roots and vegetables and whisky, that cannot be excelled, if they can be equalled, for quality and flavour anywhere in the world. The end is not yet. To realise that this is no vague prophecy— consider the envious eyes of industrial combines. These combines will beat the landlords and the scenic sentimentalists. And if it does not go well with the workers after that, the workers will fight. There will never again be a repetition of the defeatism of the Clearances. The folk will come into their own. God hurry the merry day!

We spent a forenoon round about Corpach, talking to the lock-keepers, buying an official chart of the Caledonian

Canal (one shilling), and arranging to begin the through passage to Inverness at three o'clock (£3). We discussed the prospect, for we had never passed through locks and wondered about head and stern ropes. We had a good head rope, and tied the two long sheets of the foresail for a stern rope. At one o'clock a canal official called and asked us if we could arrange to enter at two-thirty, as two fishing boats were going through at that time. We of course said we could; but we were a bit disappointed, for I had a good idea of what packing three boats into one lock would mean in the way of care. A drifter can hit an iron stanchion a fair side-wallop without damage; but if she closed in on us in a back wash, it would be like crushing an egg. Not but that we might look after ourselves, if we could rely on the engine. Moreover, it takes over two hours to clear the locks here, for after the two entering locks you come to what the guidebooks poetically call 'Neptune's Staircase'—a series of eight locks.

When we got under way it was with more misgiving than we had faced rocks and seas. If we had thought all excitement over, the first two days in the Caledonian Canal made us think again.

We got round sharp on two-thirty to find the drifter *Invernairne* (Hopeman) and the seine-netter *The Gleaners* (Lossiemouth) already in the open lock. The Mate had to stand forward, ready with rope and fender, so I had to watch where we were going, disappear to the engine, reappear, and bespeak the Crew at the helm. I was more anxious to make a decent entrance before these fishermen than I would have been before any yachtsmen, but if I kept going too long and then could not get out of gear—well, that must not happen. I judged my distance—but not the flow of water from the lock against me; I went forward again and again came short, for there was nothing less than a spate flowing; my bobbing up and down may have amused the onlookers, but I kept that engine going and finally drew alongside the *Invernairne* with the flywheel still revolving. For which I was more relieved than any steam engineer might guess!

How friendly were the crews! In no time we were fast to the *Invernairne* and when I explained my difficulties the engineer and his mate came aboard to have a look at the engine, while the skipper, a dark obliging man, full of humour and fun, explained what he thought was wrong. The cones of the clutch were sticking because they were dirty and were not getting enough oil. This, too, was the engineer's opinion, and he advised a cupful of oil in the gearcase before each long run. Otherwise the engine looked a good one, he said. I had long been certain that all that was necessary was a proper overhaul. However, she would get the cupful of oil—even if she had got it before!

Meantime the sluice gates were opening and in the boil of the waters the large vessels swung in a way that kept us busy. But soon we were moving forward into the next lock, towed by the *Invernairne*, having to drop astern to avoid the gates, before again hauling up to her starboard quarter. Then we discovered our dangerous moment, for when the *Invernairne* gave a few kicks astern, we were caught in the backwash and our own stern swung out to the lock wall. I dived with the fender, but the Mate checked the movement with our stern rope; instantly we surged ahead, and before I could get back to our bow we had scored a heavy hit on the stern of *The Gleaners*. This was bad. But now we were getting the hang of the business, and when we began the ascent of the eight locks at Banavie, I was ready for the *Invernairne's* kick astern, while the skipper of *The Gleaners* had fendered his own stern to help us. The surge came, we strained ahead, I dropped the fender over our stem; but three inches from taking the impact, we stopped, and glancing up at the steering house I saw the skipper's face hanging out the window, smiling at me.

I laughed back at the sheer neatness of the operation. After that we never bumped, for the skipper, spinning his wheel like a top, gave us the maximum of room while he took the gates as a Parisian cabman takes a kerb. What perfect control he had over his vessel, and how sympathetic the response of the engineer! We got great pleasure from watching this, and in the hours it took to ascend old Neptune's Staircase, we had many a friendly talk.

What astonished us most in this talk was the good humour and human friendliness that prevailed amongst men who had been fishing for three months in the western seas and had barely cleared their working expenses. At thirty pounds a week, these expenses had beaten them in the end, and they were now returning for a month to get ready for Yarmouth and the hope of better luck.

During the three months, they had missed only one night at sea. That very morning at three o'clock they had hauled their drift of over seventy nets eighteen miles south-east of Castlebay, and here they were, regretting that the two hours' hold-up at Corpach on account of low tide, would prevent their getting through the Caledonian Canal the same night!

'You didn't get any herring this morning, then?'

'If we had, we wouldn't be here now! No, we only got a few mackerel. Would you like some?'

And before we could properly protest, the skipper had his knife out and his young son had three fat mackerel on the gunwale. Then—a small thing this, but somehow typical—the skipper's pocket knife was so sharp that it cut right through the hard head of the mackerel and along the bone as if it were slicing butter. Inside a couple of minutes he presented us with the three fish split and cleaned. At once he wanted them back, for the galley was in good trim and would fry them for us in no time. But we refused to give them back.

Later on when we were presented with three fresh herring out of a dozen or so which they were obviously keeping in a small box for their own use, we protested strongly.

'Nonsense!' he said. 'If it wasn't you it would be somebody else.'

We were strangers to them and still do not know their names, as they do not know ours (if they have remembered us at all).

And while this was going on, the rain was coming down in buckets. I hadn't put on my oilskin trousers and my knee-boots were full. The Mate was wet to the skin. Ben Nevis—the most spectacular view is from Banavie—rolled massive rain clouds over its summit and down into its glens. I heard a click! behind me. The rain streaming off her sou'wester, the Crew had tried for a photograph!

They could not give any reason for the failure of the herring fishing on the West, though the mate, a quiet reasonable man, blamed the presence of large numbers of squids. In a long talk with him, wherein old sailing days were contrasted with the present steam age, I found him inclined to think that the courses of nature were nowadays being interfered with. The herring shoals were getting broken up before in the ordinary way they would have come inshore. Ring-netting also tended to destroy immature herring. There must be a limit even to nature's bounty. You cannot go on bagging the golden egg without giving the goose a chance. The same thing could be seen happening to-day in many of the small ports of the Moray Firth. In the old days, with line fishing, you always got white fish and the best white fish.

Along comes the seine-net. For a time there is great profit. Then the drags get less profitable and less profitable, until at last the men are working harder than they did with the lines and not getting so sure a result.

'And not getting the fish to eat themselves, for the best must always go to the market. And the country folk around —they can no longer buy them,' said a member of the crew.

Meantime the sea bottom is being cleaned. Great hauls of immature fish are taken aboard and shovelled back—to help to feed the gulls. 'I have done it myself,' said the mate. A slower process with the herring, no doubt. There are immense shoals in the sea and they move about mysteriously. But the drifters are getting into debt.

'And the Scottish boats, owned on the old family basis, won't stand up in the long run against the English boats, based on shore syndicates or capitalism?'

'Well—I don't know. English capitalism is feeling the draught. Make no mistake about that. And the trawlers, from poaching inshore here, right to the Arctic—they're no longer paying, not as a body. The best of the trawler companies was down thousands last year.'

With line fishing and drift nets, a reasonable balance in nature was kept. Beyond that, some sort of order seemed necessary. A man can take great crops off virgin soil, but not indefinitely. We manure our land and breed our stock. The fishing industry was still pretty much in the early hunter stage. We have been treating the sea as a jungle.

A vast and fascinating subject, with skill and luck and courage and constant danger behind it.

When we were up the eight locks, the skipper of the *Invernairne* hung on to our bow rope. 'Save you bothering with your engine,' he cried cheerfully.

Homeward Bound

Just before then, the Mate heard him entertaining some of the crew of *The Gleaners*. In the midst of the process, his face had disappeared and reappeared with a mask on, a grotesque 'false face', that had increased the merriment. *The Gleaners* had been seine-netting from Ayr and, unlike their neighbour, had done fairly well. But they were all the brethren of adventure, good luck or bad.

For the seven or eight miles up to Gairlochy we got an exciting tow, countering the swing of the bends with strong pressure on our tiller, the tow rope taut as a fiddle string. The dinghy was heavy with rain water and in the narrow passage through a swing bridge yawed a couple of inches short of smashing herself against the stone work.

The banks were wooded and very green in the rain. Distant prospects were half-veiled—in the way a figure in a photograph, thrown very slightly out of focus, may have depth added to its beauty. We wondered if any canal in the world was so beautiful as this one in the same moment as we wondered what might happen to us should the *Invernairne* slacken speed too suddenly on entering the lock for which she was now blowing. The Mate suggested we might get them to cast us off, but I was banking on the skipper—and not without reason, for he reduced speed so smoothly that our rope never even sagged as we pulled to his quarter inside the lock. Then off again, and soon we were in Loch Lochy, with the mate of the drifter standing by to let go. When I gave him the signal, he cast us off, and we waved our farewells.

'Not only the salt of the sea, but the salt of the earth,' said our Mate.

Let me confess (with some difficulty) that we were impulsively moved by all this kindness and friendliness. Whitman seems the poet to quote, though an Indian visionary has achieved the word disinterestedness. And not consciously on the part of these fishermen as a decent or moral thing to do, but naturally as one might tell a joke or pass the time of day. Should they ever read these words, they will smile.

Yet the point has to be made. If any men had reason to curse their luck, to rail against fate, surely these men had, who for months had worked day and night in those wild seas for less than their keep—nay, for years, and would work for years more, while markets were rigged against them and men in safe shore jobs made money out of them. To think of the sure salary I myself had got for mere Revenue accountancy was enough to make me blush.

The more I see of life the more I am convinced there is a primordial goodness in man, a natural generosity. Out of consciousness of this grows the idealism that inspires all political extremism, for it realises, with a sort of wild and maddened anguish, how acquisitiveness and greed and colossal egoism born of power have contorted or crushed the goodness and the generosity.

And of all elements for quickening the free primordial spirit of man, what can surpass the sea, with its thrill of life over the near presence of death?

XXI

Liberty and Property

There is a good anchorage in Loch Lochy round the first point to port just after entering. The Canal chart would not have suffered if the important detail had been made more striking, and even if some extra detail, not strictly useful for navigation, had been added. One hesitates to suggest that it might have said the fishing is free on Loch Lochy but privately preserved on Loch Oich, though if it had, honest folk might be saved unnecessary thought or precaution. Of course, a good angler should row with quiet oars at any time. But in Loch Lochy the stillness of the heron and the cunning of the eel would have had little effect in luring the large trout from their lairs. We heard afterwards that the bottom feeding is exceptionally good here. And we can at least assert that the quality of the half-pound brown trout is high—and pink. But the loch itself is very deep, running to well over seventy fathoms opposite Invergloy. There seemed to be a fair stretch of fishing water from where we rounded the point along towards Achnacarry, and I mention this because it happens to coincide with shelter from the winds which blow up the Great Glen at this season.

It may seem absurd to suggest that a yacht could be storm-bound in Loch Lochy, a fresh-water loch no more than ten miles long, but as we fished along the shore and saw the white-caps racing up mid loch, we decided that stranger things could happen. The downpour had now got broken up into squall showers, and if the trout had been biting in the water like the midges on shore, we might have been there a long time. The ground feeding here must be very good for midges, for they were unusually large in size and fastidious in palate. They are very fond of eyelids, and, like perverts generally, are relentless in pursuit. If you vulgarly swipe them, they will, of course, bite common parts like the wrists and the neck and the inside of the nostrils, but it's the eyelids they are after.

So we viewed Achnacarry and the Dark Mile and the region of Prince Charlie's cave from the safety of the water. This is where yachting has a splendid ease over hiking or the pause that follows the mere rush of motoring. All the marvels of heaven and earth may be contemplated objectively or in deep abstraction without a single bite. 'They're following you,' cries the Crew. So we take a turn across to the edge of the squall and come back unattended.

The following morning the rain had stopped but the wind was still strong, so as the glass was rising we were in no hurry to depart and decided that we would wait until the afternoon and then proceed in an enchanted calm. The glass kept rising slowly but surely, but about five o'clock the weather was very bad and the rain coming down again. So we lifted anchor.

Had the same strength of wind been against us, we certainly could never have faced it. We were astonished at the seas that were running and had to keep a sharp eye on the dinghy. Before getting the full force of the wind, the Mate had hoisted his precious sail. Fortunately, jibbing in the first blast, it flattened most of its wet area against the mast. We were going at a great pace, and in fact we covered the ten miles in about one hour, by far the highest speed of the trip.

It was quite an impressive sight looking back on the wind-blackened water alive with seething crests, and we chuckled at this inland effort to emulate the real sea. The only spot where we were anxious for a few minutes was just after passing the Achnacarry glen, where some deflection of the wind adds to the fury. Later we heard that two sizable yachts had that day decided not to face it in Loch Ness.

Driving along at this speed, we began to wonder with some concern about our approach to the end of the loch with its swing bridge and two locks, but fortunately the loch narrows just before the end and then opens out again into a small but sheltered bay, and with relief and offering much encouragement we watched the Crew get the horn ready. It was the first time it had ever been required. Tilting it up in the best style, she blew a prolonged and splendid blast. We gave her a great cheer. Even the lock-keepers heard it.

I was not now going to make the Corpach mistake of stopping too soon, but the wind being with us and the flow from the locks negligible, we went so far that, before the gates could be opened, we had to tie up against the stone wall, whose base, for no doubt some interesting reason, curved outward immediately below the water. After that, when approaching locks or bridges, we stood well off, until we could enter or pass properly; and that undoubtedly is the right way.

But once inside the lock, we had no difficulty at all; none of the watching and fending of our experiences with the fishing boats. We were tucked into a corner where nothing came at us, and when the next gate was open the obliging lock-keepers hauled us through. It was child's play, and the Crew departed to get fresh milk from a farm and some provisions from a small store close by.

What held most interest for us so far in our journey up the Canal was not clan feuds or hunted princes or battles long ago, but the sight of new forests growing along its banks. It is difficult to describe the curious impersonal pleasure this gave us. Perhaps it is that at the back of his mind the Highlander is tired of his 'romantic' past, particularly when contrasted with his unromantic present. Tired, too, of talking of the failure of his fishings and his crofts, of deer forests and sportsmen, of the decay of his native tongue, Gaelic; even tired of the chronic habit of grousing against the Government, and not a little ashamed of the recent fungus growth of State aid in direct cash or other payments, free potatoes or assisted settlements.

An impartial factual history of the Highlands in modern times by one also able to deal with the psychological factors involved would make an amazing story. To find a parallel to some of the treacheries and cruelties to the inhabitants, one would have to go to Armenia and the Turks. I am not now referring to the wholesale evictions, or even to solitary efforts by chiefs to try to sell some of their clansmen into slavery, but to the open acts of responsible British governments. Here, for example, is part of a letter from a man, taken prisoner a few weeks after Culloden (1746) and sent to the hulks on the Thames: '. . . In the latter end of June we was put on board of a transport of 450 tons called the "Liberty and Property," in which we continued the rest of the eight months upon twelve ounces of oat shilling [a day] as it came from the mill. There was 32 prisoners more put aboard of the said "Liberty and Property", which makes 157, and when we came ashore we was but 49 in life. . . . They would take us from the hold in a rope, and hoist us to the yard-arm and let us fall in the sea in order for ducking of us, and tie us to the mast and whip us. This was done to us when we was not able to stand. . . . We had neither bed nor bed-clothes, nor clothes to keep us warm in the day-time. The ship's ballast was black earth and small stones, in which we was obliged to dig holes to lie into for to keep us warm. . . .' (Though he was lucky in this last respect, as in another transport the prisoners had to lie on horse manure.) Having survived those pleasantries, he was transported to the Bar-badoes. Many of the prisoners had surrendered on a promise having been given that no action would be taken against them.

But it is not pleasant to write about. Even thinking over it gives one a grue. The Highlander has forgotten it; as he has forgotten to wear his kilt; cares little whether his lan-guage dies or not; and is not moved much by Bonnie Prince Charlies or even the lesser orders of Sutherlands or Lochiels or the Lords of the Isles.

What he wants now—where the spirit has been left in him to want anything constructive—is hope for the future, and these new forests along the banks of the Canal and on both sides of Loch Lochy were somehow like a symbol of a new order. The trees were full of sap, of young life, green and eager, larches and other pines, pointed in aspiration, and with an air about them not of privilege but of freedom. They had been planted by the Forestry Commission. They were therefore State forests; the forests of the folk themselves.

It was a heartening sight, with something of gaiety and invitation about it. That the fishing on Loch Lochy should in consequence be free seemed natural. Myriad points of vivid green light in the rain.

'What thousands of Christmas trees!' said the Crew.

335

Liberty and Property

This is no veiled plea for State ownership. I may be presumed to know the inner workings of bureaucracy. Writing simply from observation, I have merely to record that the only two efforts at reconstruction which impressed us in our travels were both sponsored by public bodies: the settlement at Portnalong by the Department of Agriculture, to which I have already referred, and this afforestation by the Forestry Commission. One could hope for less individual mistrust in the Highlander, or, if one likes, the Scot, and so envisage a wide emergence of co-operative effort. One can dream all sorts of dreams. But here at last were two positive beginnings in construction, carried out quietly and unostentatiously. And we have seen no notices—so far—warning trespassers in the new forests that they will be prosecuted. One notice only—a warning against the common enemy fire.

The highway crosses the Canal just before the entrance to Loch Oich, and here we watched the Crew trying to waken the dead with her horn. It was a stupendous performance. The dead appeared.

'It makes you think,' said the Mate, looking far away. She blew one in his ear, but I caught him as he was going over.

Loch Oich is a small but lovely loch, with bends and shallows and wooded islands. The passage is clearly indicated by beacons and buoys—red to port going north and black to starboard. We passed an ivied ruin on our left which the Mate said was the old castle of the Macdonells, the rock it stood on being the gathering place of the clan ('the rock of the raven'—their war-cry). It had direct connection with the Well of the Seven Heads near by—a ghastly story. But we were concerned about an anchorage, for none is shown on the official chart. There is a sheltered one, however, just off the wooden pier at Port Macdonell. Going

rather far in, we lay abreast of the pier, and on taking soundings from the dinghy discovered a soft-bottomed bank inshore within range of our anchor chain, but as it had four to
five feet of water over it, we did not move out. The gear
lever had stuck in the old-fashioned way coming in, despite
the cupful of oil, so we all felt friendly about it.

It was now after eight o'clock and the Mate and I decided
that if we hurried we might get some business done ashore.
Once safely clear of the *Thistle*, we called to the Crew that
we should be expecting a good supper. She came and looked
at us and, words failing her, blew a blast that made the trees
shiver.

It was over a mile and a half to Invergarry Hotel, and
when we arrived there we could not find the entrance marked
Bar. But I knew this peculiarity of Highland hotels, and
searching round the back premises we came on a door that
led through a dark passage down which we stumbled until
we pushed suddenly into a bare room where the working
men of that district were having their pint. (In Fort Augustus
we failed to find the Bar altogether, but then we had left ourselves only a quarter of an hour to look for it, though we
were assured in the luxurious lounge that there was one.)

As we had never overcome a reluctance to drink the water
straight out of the tank, we found the draught beer excellent; and the company was friendly, with talk of fishing and
bees and crops. One small oldish man had taken a drop too
much, but they bore with him good naturedly and with an
attentive politeness. Even when the talk had the utmost
cordiality and warmth, there was always this reserve of good
manners: a sort of instinct against exhibiting oneself and
against intrusion. It produced a pleasant atmosphere wherein
sober talk and laughter jostled each other naturally. The
Mate was moved by it to remember the Crew, and the dear

old lady who served us answered him hopefully in a low and confidential voice. We had to wait by the back door so long that we were giving up hope, when at last she appeared from the high and inner sanctum with apologies for delay.

In this contrast between back door and front, there is no institution more typical of the Highland social scene than the Highland hotel.

As remarkable a contrast as between the fresh water and the salt, which it took us some time to get used to. There was no concern now over filling the tank. One dropped a bucket overboard. But we could not remember the absence of a tide and frequently surprised ourselves strenuously hauling up the dinghy.

We stayed the week-end, and on Sunday set off to explore the tale of the ivied castle. The country is heavily wooded and the undergrowth lush. Wild raspberries weighted their bushes with a dark red ripeness. The rain had gone and we wandered down by the old bridge where there is a simple and effective war memorial and some obviously sound salmon pools. But the water of the Garry was too dark to spot a fin or a tail.

No one, however, can stop the traveller looking, though in these keepered regions the fish take on something of the untouchable quality of the holy water beasts of ancient Egypt.

And in time we came to Tobar nan Ceann, the Well of the Heads. This memorial to a bloody deed is a pillar of four sides, each of which tells the same tale in a different language: Gaelic, English, French, and Latin. The four sides are brought to a point surmounted by seven stone heads, cut off at the throat, with a hand grasping a dirk laid vengefully on top of them.

Liberty and Property

The story is of two sons of Keppoch (a branch of the Mac-donells) being educated in France, and, in their absence, of seven male cousins at home enjoying the family power. On their return the two were murdered by the seven, and at last the bard of the family managed to avenge the deed by slaughtering the seven. Thereupon (as the memorial puts it): 'The Heads of the Seven Murderers were presented at the foot of the Noble Chief, in Glengarry Castle, after having been washed in this Spring: and ever since that event, which took place early in the Sixteenth Century, it has been known by the name of "Tobar-nan-ceann," *the Well of the Heads.*' It was erected in 1812, by the reigning chief, 'As a Memorial of the ample and summary Vengeance, which, in the swift course of Feudal Justice . . .'

Looking around this grim record, you may think the well is gone, but if you go down off the road, on the loch side, you come on a low archway extending right under the road. As we entered, past some tramp's litter, the darkness of the vault after the bright day made us blink and grope carefully. I must have gone between twenty and thirty feet, doubled up, when my hand, feeling before me, went to the wrist in the bloody well.

As we came out, I looked at my hand. It was quite clean. But the cold water had in an instant obliterated the centuries more effectively than had the thirty-six lines of sculptured letters in four tongues. In fact, the contact for some time induced an odd sensation, that seemed akin to, if not part of, complicity in the deed itself!

For the power of the well is extremely strong. Of Druidic practices, worship of or at the well is perhaps the only real survival. On the first Sunday in May, great crowds still gather at the Culloden Wishing Well, above Inverness, to drop their coin in and wish their secret wish and make festival, crowds of the folk themselves who would never dream of going the extra mile or two to look at the Culloden battle-field. There, too, they tie their pieces of coloured cloth to the trees, leave their secret hopes to the gods. But the wishing-well hopes are pagan hopes, hopes for love and well-being and laughter on the earth where life is good; not hopes for personal salvation in some shadowy hereafter, made to seem as full of righteous gloom as the insides of their churches.

And as around Loch Lochy, so by the Culloden Wishing Well there is now growing a State forest, and to the top-knot of a young pine I saw, the other year, a girl tie a gay pink strip torn from her clothing. She swayed more lissom than the released pine and her laughter bubbled more deliciously than ever did the old pagan well. Well and forest and young girl, and love among them in a laughing breeze for a few thousand years. Humanity may make something of that, without either feudal memorial or sculptured letters about summary vengeance.

For it is remarkable how all the bloody deeds are remembered, and the happiness, the greatness, and the love forgotten.

XXII

The Last Trump

And so we came to the lifting of our anchor on the last day, and as we stood down the second half of Loch Oich, the weather was moist and windless and the white sail lay sodden along the deck. Our hope had been for sparkling water and a following wind, so that we might have set both sails in a final splendid run up the twenty-four miles of Loch Ness and have come with gratitude, if regret, to our last anchorage. But this was denied us. And, unfortunately, the sad weather did not make the prospect of leaving the sea more appealing. It merely deepened the sadness. An odd sort of perversity this, but there it was.

Yet so valiantly did the Crew 'Whistle for Bridge' at Aberchalder that the adventurous spirit was restored, and we smiled and admired the land and saw the mists dragging their phantom armies up Corrieyairack Pass.

At the first lock I shut off the engine in such good time that we finally moved by slow inches while the lock-keepers, when they could spare their hands from the midges, waved us in with not unnatural impatience. But presently it was explained to them how we had so strange a beast in our keeping that, given its head at the wrong moment, it might charge the locks and break them down and so spread havoc over this sunny land.

So they laughed and helped us through.

'You find the midges bad?' said the Mate to one keeper.

'I do that,' he answered. 'I am not a native and have never got used to them.'

'How long have you been here?'

'Thirty-four years.'

'And the clegs?'

'Aye, there are clegs. See that man over there—when he came first he could not shave for three months with the lumps on him.'

We exchanged sympathies in the moist weather and so off again on our winding wooded ways to Kytra. There is a friendliness in being helped through locks in a small vessel. And here a stranger addressed me by name and asked if we could take two little girls and a boy to Fort Augustus.

I said we should be delighted and helped our shy passengers on board. The *Thistle* was being promoted in the sphere of social service, and we were not untouched by this evidence of trust in her. She responded very properly, making a steady wash behind and waves that ran up the banks in a pretty rhythm. The Mate suggested that if the worst came to the worst, I might seriously contemplate turning her into a passenger vessel—to run hazardous trips, based, say, on Iona.

'Or Arisaig of the perches,' said the Crew.

But I refused to be drawn, for the thought had been vaguely worrying me as to what, in fact, I was going to do with her. Our rule had been to live from day to day. And actually at that moment I did not know where we were going to tie up in the evening—which must be our last, for the reason that we could go no farther, except into the North Sea, and already the corn was turning to gold and the rowan berries were red.

The Last Trump

But here was Fort Augustus and the Crew got ready to sound the last trump.

'Take off your sou'wester,' said the Mate.

She blew and better blew, but no one answered that last impressive summons.

'A poor show for Fort Augustus,' she said, 'and it with a monastery.'

We tied up alongside the wooden landing stage at top of the five locks and I set off to find what was wrong. The lock-keepers were down at the bottom end awaiting the great event of the day, the arrival of the *Gondolier*, with her cargo of tourists from Inverness, and though that paddle steamer was not due for over twenty minutes—and did not appear for half an hour—our small craft must wait until she had come, and climbed, and passed. As we were going nowhere in particular, we did not mind the wait of two hours. For it had stopped raining for the time being and we wandered about this open little town which has arisen around the ancient fort.

There is still some of the old wall left, though in place of the fort there is now a Benedictine Abbey, with a school and green lawns, and we watched a black robe floating out behind a cricket pitch roller. Peace here now.

For Fort William, Fort Augustus and Fort George are no longer required as Hanoverian outposts of civilisation to keep the Gaelic barbarians in check. Which, taking all things by and large, is maybe a pity.

The lock-keepers said they were sorry about the delay and did all they could to make our transit comfortable. Tourists watched our descent. While the last gate was being opened, I got the engine going, for immediately beyond was the bridge of the busy main road already swinging to let us through. Just the sort of moment for the engine to show off her trick of social satire. And for a little we struggled together, for she

343

obviously wanted to spite the waiting motor-cars; but at last she thought better of it and we sailed away.

As Loch Ness opened before us the rain started again, and soon it was coming down straight and pitiless. The Crew was putting a new spool in the camera, for there was talk of the Monster. 'I should like more than one photograph of him,' she explained. But soon she and the Mate went inside to cook some food.

There was no life in the water underneath. On the calmest day at sea there is always some movement, a faint swell, a restlessness. Here the engine went plugging solidly on, and the way seemed long; though I knew this stretch could be stormier than Loch Lochy. I also knew that it was deeper here than anywhere in those western seas we had travelled or seen, for one has got to go far into the Atlantic to get the depth of some 130 fathoms recorded off Urquhart Castle, the favourite haunt of the Monster. I had once tried to illustrate this depth by saying that if the earth were raised or the waters dried until the North Sea vanished and one could go to St. Kilda on foot, there would still be deep water in Loch Ness; but the illustration was considered complicated.

Now as we headed up the loch, I got a fresh view of this land, which had been my home for so many years. Out of the mist, headland behind headland plunged down into the deeps. In the tortured rock fissures far below, there was room for any sort of life. I knew of one diver who had gone down some distance, come back to the surface and refused to go down again, though he would not say why.

Even in the translucent waters of the sea, long before one reaches the 900 feet of Loch Ness, red, orange, yellow, green, and violet have in turn disappeared, leaving only a blackish blueness. In the deeper parts of the opaque waters of Loch Ness, there must be perpetual night.

The Last Trump

But when Professor Beebe the other year went down in his bathysphere to a depth of 3,000 feet he still found life, although a life of which we had hitherto not even dreamed. Schools of luminous fish in the absolute darkness; strange monsters lit up as a ship is seen lit up through its portholes.

We know little of the living marvels of the deep, and when we have rigged up a bathysphere (a steel ball with a small window), complete with telephone and electric beam after the Beebe model, to take us to the bottom of Loch Ness, we may be able at least to provide a new thrill for our tourists, some sort of alternative to the Well of the Heads. Always assuming we could first overcome the more difficult matter of arranging landlord rights by getting royalties per peep fixed at a reasonable figure.

And now through the haze arose the ruins of Urquhart Castle. Edward First, that old hammer of the Scots, had actually laid siege to it. He probably had had the luck to get good weather. And in any case would have ravaged all he could for his comfort. When Edward got hold of Scots he did the only completely satisfying thing with this bad brood: he killed them. Wallace saw the perfect logic in this, and so when there were Englishmen within his reach, he slew them to a man. And if Edward got as far as Urquhart Castle, Wallace got as far as St. Albans. But Wallace hadn't the real royal logic in him through and through. The old Celtic stock of the Cuchulains and the King Arthurs (from whom he had the misfortune to be descended) had that drooling pathetic regard, yclept chivalry, for women and children, and even for priests, that is about as remote from high statesmanship as Beebe's bathysphere. So Edward stuck Wallace's head on top of his Traitor's Gate and distributed his limbs throughout his kingdom for all to see. When chivalry is carried beyond the ladies' coloured ribbons of the jousts (whence our school ties), it does no more than provide some ditchside old poet with a theme, as he scratches the thigh of a verminous poverty.

Yet they continued to have great wallops at each other, the English and the Scots, and are inclined to have a sly one still when the chance offers, though it looks at last as though the English have got the Scots where and how they want them, helped nowadays by the proletarian dream, as personified in the Clydeside communist, which happily lifts us far above consideration of paltry national issues. We are all Englishmen now.

Urquhart Castle was once the stronghold of the Grants, but the Grants were even simpler than Wallace. A few of them out of Glenmoriston agreed, after Culloden, to surrender to Cumberland's written offer of free pardon. But once Cumberland had got hold of them he forgot his offer, and had them promptly tied up and sent to the hulks on the Thames. One can imagine Cumberland's expression and even his possible words: 'You thought to save yourselves, did you?' It is difficult to forgive the Grants for such credulity in face of such an enemy.

Perhaps my thoughts were a bit gloomy, like the landscape. Though in a moment one saw there was no mere gloom in the landscape; rather some quality of fantasy, near and remote; and one could readily imagine a traveller from a flat country being so deeply impressed that he would have searched for elements of mysticism in the inhabitants (the 'Celtic twilight' is hardly a native product).

But there is little mysticism in sailing home a boat and suddenly it came to me that I should take her to Bona at the north end of Loch Ness, where a yachtsman lives in a wooden house by the water. He had been very helpful when I was fitting out, and in his spare hours from his town business, he deals in boats; which is about the next best thing to sailing them on new seas.

The Crew and the Mate appeared with some hot food, which the gentle rain cooled.

'This is very dull,' said the Crew.

'What?'

'This calm water.'

'The rain is taking off,' said the Mate.

So I told them my plan.

It was voted sound. The Crew had promptly an irrational affection for the boat, but, as I pointed out, the important thing for us was the discovery that living on a boat was cheaper than living in a house.

'For one thing you don't eat so much,' said the Mate, when he had made sure where the horn was. But the Crew merely went in to begin packing up.

Castle Urquhart was now behind and in front the smoke of a vessel which turned out to be a drifter going west, so I moved towards him a little to get his wash. The skipper leant out of his wheelhouse and we saluted each other. I must have been wishing him good luck or envying him, for I forgot to warn the Crew. As we pitched, she grabbed the nearest support in astonishment.

'The Monster!' we cried. But she was not deceived.

We came abreast of Tor Point and went slowly towards Bona and the white house of the ferry, where we dropped our anchor in less than a fathom of water on the Dores side. As we looked around the sun came out, warm and brilliant. We sat in it until my friend appeared from Inverness, and, after a proper seaman's welcome, dispelled all doubts and difficulties over the laying up of the *Thistle*.

The Last Trump

Hurtling through space at nearly thirty miles an hour, we mutinied, and the Mate at the wheel eased off a bit, and gave us time to realise that we had acquired some elementary knowledge of navigating a small boat in unknown waters. With a bigger boat we might adventure farther—say, to Norroway over the foam, to the west of Ireland, to the Orkneys, the Shetlands, the Hebrides, even in some nostalgia for the sun to the Mediterranean and so open out for ourselves the fabulous mountains of Africa.

So the peace of Iona and its light came back upon the mind, the tumultuous seas of the Torranan Rocks, the spacious bays of Oban and Tobermory, the granite walls of the Bull Hole, the lobster fishers, the seaweeds, the calling of night birds, that day—already bordering the realm of the unreal—when we had rounded Waternish and Dunvegan and seen the fixed dream of the Outer Isles over the fins of basking sharks. Portnalong and Eigg, the Cuillin and Rum. Loch Etive of legend and sun. Should we ever find anything more memorable? One may perhaps hazard the enigmatic smile the Crew directed upon us when she saw the cloud of light over Iona. All the same, it would be fine to make sure. And with a land like this behind us, how naturally generous should be our appreciation of the marvels and beauty of a strange land. For all lands have one common bond—the sea.